ELLERY QUEEN'S MAZE OF MYSTERIES

edited by Ellery Queen

Here is a rare treat for mystery fans – a novel, a novelet and 14 short stories by the best crime writers in print. In the novel, *The Will-o'-the-Wisp Mystery* by Edward D. Hoch, a semi-official supersleuth pits his skill against six criminals who escaped on the way to prison. The novelet, *The Sark Lane Mission*, is by Michael Gilbert and is another adventure of Sergeant Petrella, this time trying to break up an international drug ring. The stories are by such favorites as Ruth Rendell, E. X. Ferrars, Thomas Walsh and Lawrence Block.

Ellery Queen's Maze Of Mysteries

Edited by Ellery Queen

John Curley & Associates, Inc.
South Yarmouth, Ma.

Library of Congress Cataloging in Publication Data

Main entry under title:

Ellery Queen's maze of mysteries.

1. Detective and mystery stories, American.
2. Detective and mystery stories, English.   3. Large type books.
I. Queen, Ellery.   II. Title: Maze of mysteries.

[PS648.D4E386   1984]   813'.0876'08   83–15439
ISBN 0–89340–661–9

Published in Large Print by arrangement with Davis Publications, Inc.

Distributed in the U.K. and Commonwealth by Magna Print Books.

COPYRIGHT NOTICES AND ACKNOWLEDGMENTS
Grateful acknowledgment is hereby made for permission to reprint the following:

The Strong and the Weak by Ruth Rendell; © 1976 by Ruth Rendell; reprinted by permission of Georges Borchardt, Inc.

Printed in Great Britain

The Dead Past by Thomas Walsh; © 1977 by Thomas Walsh; reprinted by permission of the author.

Don't Cry, Sally Shy by Barbara Callahan; © by Barbara Callahan; reprinted by permission of the author.

The Second Reason by William Brittain; © 1976 by William Brittain; reprinted by permission of the author.

The Sark Lane Mission by Michael Gilbert; copyright © 1958 by Michael Gilbert; reprinted by permission of John Cushman Associates, Inc.

Attention to Detail by Robert Edward Eckels; © 1976 by Robert Edward Eckels; reprinted by permission of the author.

The K-Bar-D Murders by Gerald Tomlinson; © 1976 by Gerald Tomlinson; reprinted by permission of the author.

The Final Twist by William Bankier; © 1976 by William Bankier; reprinted by permission of Curtis Brown, Ltd.

A More-or-Less Crime by Edgar Wallace; copyright 1975 by Penelope Wallace; reprinted by permission of Curtis Brown, Ltd.

A Kind of Madness by David Bradt; © 1976 by David Bradt; reprinted by permission of the author.

Beauty Is As Beauty Does by Jack Ritchie; © 1977 by Jack Ritchie; reprinted by permission of Larry Sternig Literary Agency.

The Long Glass Man by Rosalind Ashe; © 1976 by Rosalind Ashe; reprinted by permission of Curtis Brown, Ltd.

The Death of the Bag Man by Stephen Wasylyk; © 1977 by Stephen Wasylyk; reprinted by permission of the author.

The Rose Murders by E. X. Ferrars; © 1977 by E. X. Ferrars; reprinted by permission of Harold Ober Associates, Inc.

Gentleman's Agreement by Lawrence Block; © 1977 by Lawrence Block; reprinted by permission of the author.

The Will-o'-the-Wisp Mystery by Edward D. Hoch; © 1971 by Edward D. Hoch; reprinted by permission of the author.

Contents

NOVEL
Edward D. Hoch   *The Will-o'-the-Wisp Mystery*   299

NOVELET
Michael Gilbert   *The Sark Lane Mission*   81

SHORT STORIES
Ruth Rendell   *The Strong and the Weak*   3
Thomas Walsh   *The Dead Past*   21
Barbara Callahan   *Don't Cry, Sally Shy*   51
William Brittain   *The Second Reason*   67
Robert Edward Eckels   *Attention to Detail*   128
Gerald Tomlinson   *The K-Bar-D Murders*   145
William Bankier   *The Final Twist*   167
Edgar Wallace   *A More-or-Less Crime*   181
David Bradt   *A Kind of Madness*   199
Jack Ritchie   *Beauty Is As Beauty Does*   214

Rosalind Ashe   *The Long Glass Man* 229
Stephen Wasylyk   *The Death of the Bag Man* 256
E. X. Ferrars   *The Rose Murders* 287
Lawrence Block   *Gentlemen's Agreement* 478

Ellery Queen's
Maze of Mysteries

Introduction

Dear Reader:

Part of the dictionary definition of "maze" reads:

maze. n. A state of bewilderment. or amazement. A confusing and baffling network, as of paths or passages; a labyrinth.
v.t. To perplex greatly; to make intricate.

State of bewilderment or amazement. Surely you experience either or both of these emotions when you read convoluted mysteries, especially complicated detective stories; and surely tangled mysteries and tantalizing detective stories are "a confusing and baffling network" – until the denouement when the maze of darkness disappears and the blaze of light appears. And, of course, every well constructed plot in our genre is a tortuous labyrinth.

The selections in this anthology illustrate the "maze" of the title – "to perplex greatly; to bewilder." This volume is, to quote Alexander Pope, "A mighty maze!

1

but not without a plan." The contributors, agreeing with Pope, have planned their stories just that way – with menace aforethought. They have taken infinite pains "to make intricate" their knotty puzzles for your reading excitement and enjoyment.

So we now invite you, with this book in hand, to enter the Ellery Queen maze. Take the thorny path, avoiding dead ends, skirting blind alleys, eschewing red herrings. Aim for the bull's-eye of each mystery. Every maze has only one correct route to the end – you can find it, with a tremble of fear and a twinge of alarm, if you follow the 'tec trails from page 2 through page 477.

Revelations ahead!

ELLERY QUEEN

RUTH RENDELL

The Strong and the Weak

A tale of two sisters named May and June because they were born in those months – a tale of hate and love, of misery and happiness, of despair and hope . . . Ruth Rendell is masterly at this kind of story – she feels the heartbeats of her characters, and she can make you feel them too. Reading one of her stories is like having your finger on someone's pulse . . .

Their parents named them May and June because their birthdays occurred in those months. A third sister, an April child, had been christened Avril but she had died. May was like the time of year in which she had been born, changeable, chilly and warm by turns, sullen and yet to know and show a loveliness which could not last.

In the 1930s, when May was in her twenties, it was still important to get one's daughters well married, and though Mrs. Thrace had no anxieties on that score for sunny June, she was less sanguine about May. Her older daughter was neither pretty

3

nor graceful nor clever, and no man had ever looked at her twice. June, of course, had a string of admirers.

Then May met a young lawyer at a *thé dansant*. His name was Walter Cheney, he was extremely good-looking, his father was wealthy and made him a generous allowance, and there was no doubt he belonged in a higher social class than that of the Thraces. May fell passionately in love with him, but no one was more surprised than she when he asked her to marry him.

The intensity of May's passion frightened Mrs. Thrace. It wasn't quite "nice." The expression on May's face while she awaited the coming of her fiancé, her ardor when she greeted him, the hunger in her eyes – that sort of thing was all very well in the cinema, but unsuitable for a customs officer's daughter in a genteel suburb.

For a brief period she had become almost beautiful. "I'm going to marry him," she said when cautioned. "He wants me to love him, doesn't he? He loves me. Why shouldn't I show my love?"

June, who was clever as well as pretty, was away at college, training to be a schoolteacher. It had been considered wiser, long before Walter Cheney had appeared, to keep May at home. She had no particular aptitude for anything, and she was useful to her mother about the house. Now, of course, it turned out that she had an aptitude for catching a rich, handsome, and successful husband. Then, a month before the wedding, June came home for the summer holidays.

It was all very unfortunate, Mrs. Thrace said over and over again. If Walter Cheney had jilted May for some other girl, they would have been bitterly indignant, enraged even, and Mr. Thrace would have felt old-fashioned longings to apply a horsewhip. But what could anyone say or do when Walter transferred his affections from the older daughter to the younger?

May screamed and sobbed and tried to attack June with a knife. "We're all terribly sorry for you, my darling," said Mrs. Thrace, "but what can we do? You wouldn't marry a man who doesn't love you, would you?"

"He does love me, he does! It's just because she's pretty. She's cast a spell on him. I wish she was dead and then he'd love me again."

"You mustn't say that, May. It's all very cruel to you, but you have to face the fact

5

that he's changed his mind. Isn't it better to find out now than later?"

"I would have had him," insisted May.

Mrs. Thrace blushed. She was shocked to the core.

"I shall never marry now," said May. "She's ruined my life and I shall never have anything ever again."

Walter and June were married, and Walter's father bought them a house in Surrey. May stayed at home, being useful to her mother. The war came. Walter went straight into the army, became a captain, then a major, finally a colonel. May also went into the army, where she remained a private for five years, working in some catering department. After that there was nothing for her to do except to go home to her parents once more . . .

May never forgave her sister.

"She stole my husband," she would remind her mother.

"He wasn't your husband, May."

"As good as. You wouldn't forgive a thief who came into your house and stole the most precious thing you had or were likely to have."

"We're told to forgive those who trespass

6

against us, as we hope to be forgiven."

"I'm not religious," said May, and on those occasions when the Cheneys came to the Thrace home she took care to be absent. But she knew all about them – all, that is, except one thing.

Mr. and Mrs. Thrace were most careful never to speak of June in May's presence, so May listened outside the door, and she secretly read all June's letters to her mother. Whenever Walter's name was mentioned in a letter, or spoken, she winced and shivered with the pain of it. She knew that they had moved to a larger house, that they were building up a collection of fine furniture and valuable paintings. She knew where they went for their holidays and what friends they entertained. But what she was never able to discover was how Walter felt about June.

Had he ever really loved her? Had he repented of his choice? May thought that perhaps, after the first flush of infatuation was over, he had come to long for May as much as she longed for him. Since she never saw them, she could never know, for, however he might feel, Walter couldn't leave June. When you have done what he had done – what June had made him do –

7

you can't change again. You have to stick it out till death.

It comforted May – it was perhaps the only thing that kept her going – to convince herself that Walter regretted his bargain. If there had been children – what the Victorians called pledges of love... Sometimes, after a letter had come from June, May would see her mother looking particularly pleased and satisfied. And then, shaking with dread, May would read that letter, terrified to learn that June was pregnant. But Mrs. Thrace's pleasure and satisfaction must have come from some other source, from some account of Walter's latest *coup* in court or June's latest party, for no children came and now June was past 40.

Trained for nothing, May worked as a canteen supervisor in a women's hostel. She continued to live at home until her parents died. Their deaths took place within six months, Mrs. Thrace dying in March and her widower in August. And that was how it happened that May saw Walter again.

At the time of her mother's cremation, May was ill in bed with a virus infection and unable to attend. But she had no way of avoiding her father's funeral. When she saw Walter come into the church, a faintness seized her and she pushed against the pew rail, trembling. She covered her face with her hands to make it seem as if she were praying, and when at last she took them away Walter was beside her.

He took her hand and looked into her face. May's eyes met his, which were as blue and compelling as ever, and she saw with anguish that he had lost none of his good looks, but had become only more distinguished-looking. She would have liked to die then, holding his hand and gazing into his face.

"Won't you come and speak to your sister, May?" said Walter in the rich deep voice which charmed juries, struck terror into the hearts of witnesses, and won women. "Shall we let bygones be bygones on this very sad day?"

May shivered. She withdrew her hand and marched to the back of the church. She placed herself as far away from June as she could, but not too far to observe that it was June who took Walter's arm as they left and not Walter who took June's; that it was June who looked up at Walter for comfort while his face remained grave and still; that

9

it was June who clung to him while he merely permitted the clinging. It couldn't be that he was behaving like that because she, May, was there. He must hate and despise June, as May, with all her heart, still hated and despised her sister.

But it was at a funeral that they were reconciled.

May learned of Walter's death by reading an announcement of it in a newspaper. And the pain of it was as great as the one she had suffered when her mother had told her he wanted to marry June. She sent flowers, an enormous wreath of snow-white roses that cost her half a week's wages. And of course she would go to the funeral, whether June wanted her there or not.

Apparently June did want her. Perhaps she thought the roses were for the living bereaved and not for the dead. She came up to May and put her arms round her, laying her head against her sister's shoulder in misery and despair.

May broke their long silence. "Now you know what it's like to lose him."

"Oh, May, May, don't be cruel to me now! Don't hold that against me now. Be

10

kind to me now, I've nothing left."

So May sat beside June, and after the funeral she went back to the house where June had lived with Walter. In saying she had nothing left, June had presumably been referring to emotional rather than material things. Apart from certain stately homes she had visited on tours, May had never seen anything like the interior of that house.

"I'm going to retire next month," May remarked, "and then I'll be living in what they call a flatlet – one room and a kitchen."

Two days later a letter came from June:

"Dearest May: Don't be angry with me for calling you that. You have always been one of my dearest, in spite of what I did and in spite of your hatred of me. I can't be sorry for what I did because so much happiness came of it for me, but I am truly, deeply sorry that you were the one who suffered. And now, dear May, I want to try to make up to you for what I did, though I know I can never really do that, not now, not after so long.

"You said you were going to retire and wouldn't be living very comfortably. Will you come and live with me? You can have as many rooms in this house as you want

11

– you are welcome to share everything with me. You will know what I mean when I say I feel that would be just. Please make me happy by saying you forgive me and will come. Always your loving sister, June."

What did the trick was June saying it would be just. Yes, it would be justice if May could now have some of those good things which were hers by right and which June had stolen from her along with her man. She waited a week and then she wrote:

"Dear June: What you suggest seems a good idea. I have thought about it and I will make my home with you. I have very little personal property, so moving will not be a great bother. Let me know when you want me to come. It is raining again here and very cold. Yours, May."

There was nothing, however, in the letter about forgiveness.

And yet May, sharing June's house, was almost prepared to forgive. For she was learning at last what June's married life had been.

"You can talk about him if you want to," May had said hungrily on their first evening together. "If it's going to relieve your feelings, I don't mind."

12

"What is there to say except that we were married for forty years and now he's dead?"

"You could show me some of the things he gave you." May picked up ornament after ornament, gazed at paintings. "Did he give you that? What about this?"

"They weren't presents. I bought them or he did."

May couldn't help getting excited. "I wonder you're not afraid of burglars. This is a proper Aladdin's Cave. Have you got lots of jewelry too?"

"Not much," said June uncomfortably.

May's eyes were on June's engagement ring, a poor thing of diamond chips in nine-carat gold, far less expensive than the ring Walter had given his first love. Of course she had kept hers, and Walter, though well off even then, hadn't been rich enough to buy a second magnificent ring within six months of the first – not with all the expenses of furnishing a new home. But later, surely . . .?

"I should have thought you'd have an eternity ring."

"Marriage doesn't last for eternity," said June.

May could tell June didn't like talking about it. June even avoided mentioning

13

Walter's name, and soon she put away the photographs of him which had stood on the piano and on the drawing-room mantelpiece. May wondered if Walter had ever written any letters to his wife. They had seldom been parted, of course, but it would be strange if June hadn't received a single letter from him in 40 years.

So the first time June went out alone, May tried to open her desk. It was locked. The drawers of June's dressing table disclosed a couple of birthday cards with *Love from Walter* scrawled hastily on them, and the only other written message from her husband June had considered worth keeping May found tucked into a cookbook in the kitchen. It was a note written on the back of a bill, and it read: *Baker called. I ordered a large white bread for Saturday.*

That night May reread the two letters she had received from Walter during their engagement. Each began "Dearest May." She hadn't looked at them for 40 years – she hadn't dared – but now she read them with calm satisfaction.

"Dearest May: This is the first love letter I have ever written. If it isn't much good you must put it down to lack of practise. I miss you a lot and rather wish I hadn't told

14

my parents I would visit them on this holiday . . ."

And "Dearest May: Thanks for both your letters. Sorry I've taken so long to reply, but I feel a bit nervous that my letters don't match up to yours. Still, with luck, we soon shan't have to write to each other because we shan't be separated. I wish you were here with me . . ."

Poor Walter had been reticent and shy, unable to express his feelings on paper or by word of mouth. But at least he had written love letters to *her* and not notes about loaves of bread. May decided to start wearing her engagement ring again – on her little finger, of course, because she could no longer get it over the knuckle of her ring finger. If June noticed, she didn't comment on it.

"Was it you or Walter who didn't want children?" May asked one day.

"Children just didn't come."

"Walter *must* have wanted them. When he was engaged to me we talked of having three."

June looked upset, but May could have talked of Walter all day long. "He was only sixty-five," she said. "That's young to die

15

these days. You never told me what he died of."

"He needed an operation," said June, "and never regained consciousness."

"Just like mother," said May. Suppose June had had an incurable disease and had died – what would have happened then? Remembering Walter's tender look and strong handclasp at her father's funeral, May thought he would have married her. She twisted the the ring on her little finger. "You were almost like a second wife, weren't you? It must have been a difficult position."

"I'd much rather not talk about it," said June, and with her handkerchief to her eyes, she left the room.

May was happy. For the first time in 40 years she was happy. She busied herself about the house, caring for June's things, dusting and polishing, pausing to look at a painting and reflecting that Walter must have often paused to look at it too. Sometimes she imagined him sitting in this chair or standing by that window, his heart full of regret for what he might have had with May. And she thought how, while he had been longing for her, she, far away, had been crying for him. She never cried now, though June did, often.

"I'm an old fool. I can't help giving way," June sobbed. "You're strong, May, but I'm weak and I miss him so."

"Didn't I miss him?"

"He was always fond of you. It upset him a lot to think you were unhappy. He often talked about you." June looked **at her** piteously. "You *have* forgiven me, haven't you, May?"

"As a matter of fact, I have," said May. She was a little surprised at herself. But, yes, she had forgiven June. "I think you've been punished for what you did." A loveless marriage, a husband who talked constantly of another woman . . .

"I've been punished," said June, and she put her arms round May's neck.

The strong and the weak. May recalled that when a movement downstairs woke her in the middle of one night. She heard footsteps and a wrenching sound as of a door being forced. It was the burglar she had always feared and had warned June about, but June would be cowering in her room now, terrified, incapable of taking any action.

May put on her dressing gown and went

17

down the passage to June's room. The bed was empty. She looked out of the window, and the moonlight showed her a car parked on the gravel driveway that led to the lane. A yellower, stronger light streamed from the drawing-room window. A shiver of fear went through her, but she knew she must be strong.

Before she reached the head of the stairs she heard a violent crash as of something heavy yet brittle hurled against a wall. There was a cry from below, then footsteps running. May got to the stairs in time to see a slight figure rush across the hall and slam the front door behind him. The car started up.

In his wake he had left a thin trail of blood. May followed the blood trail into the drawing room. June stood by her desk which had been torn open and all its contents scattered **onto the** table. She was trembling, tearful, and laughing with shaky hysteria, pointing to the shards of cut glass that lay everywhere.

"I threw the decanter at him. I hit him and cut his head and he ran."

May went up to her. "Are you all right?"

"He didn't touch me. He pointed that gun at me when I came in, but I didn't care.

18

I couldn't bear to see him searching my desk, getting at all my private things. Wasn't I brave? He didn't get away with anything but a few pieces of silver. I hit him and then he heard you coming and he panicked. Wasn't I brave, May?"

But May wasn't listening. She was reading the letter which lay open and exposed on top of the papers that the burglar had pulled out of the desk. Walter's handwriting leaped at her, weakened though it was, enfeebled by his last illness. "My darling love: It is only a minute since you walked out of the hospital room, nevertheless I must write to you. I can't resist an impulse to write now and tell you how happy you have made me in all the beautiful years we have been together. If the worst comes to the worst, my darling, and I don't survive the operation, I want you to know you are the only woman I ever loved ..."

"I wouldn't have thought I'd have had the courage," said June, "but perhaps the gun wasn't loaded. He was only a boy. Would you call the police, please, May?"

"Yes," said May. She picked up the gun.

The police arrived within 15 minutes.

They brought a doctor with them, but June was already dead, shot through the heart at close range.

"We'll get him, Miss Thrace, don't you worry," said the Inspector. "It was a pity you touched the gun, though. Did it without thinking, I suppose?"

"It was the shock," said May. "I've never had a shock like that, not in the last forty years."

THOMAS WALSH

The Dead Past

Thomas Walsh is at his best when he views crime as a human equation. He understands the people involved – the guilty, the innocent, and those caught in the mesh of circumstances. Young Ned McKestin was caught in such a web – a web he had helped spin himself. But now others were caught with him. Now there were Kate and the baby for Ned to worry about . . .

But never once was it a dead past, not even years later, for Ned McKestin. After it happened he told Kate and Uncle Gerry the whole story, being that honest with them, but no one else. He had done it, after all. Therefore it was right that he, and he alone, should bear the burden of it. And so he did. He bore it silently, never once able to completely force it out of his mind, not even after three or four years had gone by, and then, five and then six.

He carried it by himself all that time, and

21

his sole comfort was a feeling that he now understood the big secret of human life. To be a straight decent man one simply established straight decent habits. There it was, as simple as that. Then why did he go on worrying and worrying about it?

Yet he did. Occasionally at night, when he found himself tossing restlessly hour after hour; now and again during work hours at the store with Uncle Gerry; but here and there, every so often, he would sense that the dead past was beginning to darken and close in around him, biding its time. Very stupid. How long were the odds now that he would ever see Preston Ruby or Dandy Jack O'Hara again? Yet still . . .

Still. "What's the matter?" Kate sometimes would demand of him. "You seem awfully quiet tonight, Ned. What's wrong?"

"No, no," Ned would insist, managing to slip a reassuring arm around her shoulders. "Nothing at all, Kate. I'm just the original quiet man, maybe. I feel fine."

Because his shadow was not her problem. It was Ned's, and Ned deserved it, and could only do the best he could to live with it. Why was it impossible, however, to feel that the dead past was over

22

and done with for him? Why did he have to have the silly idea that somehow, somewhere, even now, it still waited for him? At 24 he knew at last what really mattered to him, and what did not. The important thing was to concentrate on his new life.

And in the year 1975 the new life became more wonderful than ever. Uncle Gerry retired to the Florida Keys with Aunt Mamie and his fishing tackle and left Ned in complete charge at G. G. McKestin & Company, as a third partner.

"I've got enough," Uncle Gerry said to him that night, "and you've earned what I'm giving you, Ned. You've done better than I ever expected up here. You've settled down, thank God, and there won't be a worry in the world for me with you running things. I'm depending on you. You're the best man I ever had in the store."

And Ned was. He had great manual ability at driving a car, and as a handyman at odd jobs around the house, and at fixing almost anything in the electrical line. So by the time Uncle Gerry retired, the firm of G. G. McKestin, TV Sales and Service, 36 Main Street, was one of the biggest and best of its kind in the whole North Country. For 30 years Uncle Gerry had worked day and night to give it the most trustworthy reputation possible, and in the spring of 1975 Ned's one-third interest meant all clear sailing ahead. He and Kate had it made.

"Oh, golly," Kate said, after hugging Uncle Gerry halfbreathless. "I never had any desire to be rich, Ned. All I ever wanted was to have you and maybe three or four kids. There's only one thing I'd like. Do you suppose we could have our own house now?"

Because Kate had always been a great one for their own house. Until then they had lived in a small apartment over the store, where Ned had often caught her sighing wistfully at night at pictures in home magazines of the newest and most modern in kitchen equipment, or the latest fashion in bathroom fixtures. So that year they got their own house, building it in the woods out of town near the lower lake, with a spectacular view of Whiteface Mountain in back, and he and Kate had never been so happy.

They had a wonderful summer – almost every week there were cookouts or picnics with friends, or swimming and boating off their own dock – and after Christmas, Kate discovered radiantly that she was pregnant. But there were a few complications about a blood factor, and in the end, on the local doctor's advice, Ned took her down to Albany Medical Center when her time came. A few days later she had a fine healthy boy, no problems at all, and driving home to Martinsville that night, 150 miles north, Ned felt wonderfully exuberant.

He got back about ten o'clock and, still too excited to sleep, mixed a mild Scotch for himself in the kitchen. Just as he was taking his first sip the front doorbell rang. That time, when it turned out to be the dead past in brute fact, there was no premonition of any kind. A neighbor, Ned thought, wanting to hear how Kate had made out down in Albany; and with the drink in his hand and a huge happy grin on his lips, Ned walked out to the front door.

But it was not a neighbor who had seen his kitchen light on and had stopped off to hear the good news. Instead, dapper as ever, it was Dandy Jack O'Hara.

Ned stood frozen, his grin dead on his lips, and Dandy Jack allowed himself a moment of maliciously covert triumph.

"Well, what do you know?" Dandy Jack drawled, studying with his foxily wizened face and cunningly observant gray eyes the front hall behind Ned. "Sure enough. Nobody but the kid himself. Long time no see, kid. How you been?"

And he did not wait for Ned to ask him inside. He came in, at once establishing the authority between them, removed a dark green Borsalino hat with a negligent sweep of his right arm and tossed it onto the hall table.

"And you know something else?" he went on, glancing at the antique wall mirror with the gold eagle on it, at the soft green carpeting, and at the beautifully waxed old drum table with the big porcelain bowl of fresh flowers. "What a great layout you got, kid. Everything you'd ever want, eh? Guess you did all right for yourself. But how long has it been anyway? Five or six years, ain't it?"

Ned closed the front door. He closed it numbly, one breathless catch of the heart in him, and with his ears ringing. But Dandy Jack, elegant gold sweater with a knitted white scarf at the throat, red-and-brown houndstooth slacks, and highly polished English brogues, paid no

26

attention at all to the lack of welcome for him.

"Funny how things happen," he remarked, slipping a cigarette out of his monogrammed gold case. "Like tonight. I'm in a taproom downtown just to kill a little time, and a guy on the next stool asks the bartender if he heard how Ned McKestin's wife was getting along down in Albany. Now that's kind of an exceptional name, kid – Ned McKestin. But you know me. I start asking a question here and there to see if you're the same guy I once knew. And what do you know? You turn out to be the same Ned McKestin, all right. The kid himself. You know Preston and me often wondered what the hell ever happened to you."

Ned had to clear his throat. It felt dry as desert sand.

"Nothing much," he got out. "I did what you and Ruby did, that's all. I got out as fast and far as I could, Dandy. I bummed rides up here to an uncle I have."

"Yeah, who wouldn't?" Dandy Jack said, still studying Ned with his mockingly observant gray eyes. "Matter of fact, Preston and me got to hell and gone all the way out to the coast. No sense hanging

27

around for trouble, the way we saw it. Got another drink in the house?"

"In the kitchen," Ned told him. "This way, Dandy."

But he was still numb, although with a slight pressing pain making itself felt at the back of his skull. Yet maybe there was nothing at all to worry about, he tried to convince himself. Why should there be? A couple of old friends meeting unexpectedly and exchanging the news with each other. No need to push the panic button. Best that he take this meeting between them just as casually as Dandy Jack was taking it.

"But it looks," Dandy Jack said, noting with approval the glistening new stove and refrigerator in the kitchen, and the alcove near the back door with the new washer and dryer, "you've done a lot better for yourself than me and Preston. We've had to scamper. I mean, a layout like this, and you married and settled down and all. What's wrong with your wife, kid?"

Ned told him, pouring out his drink.

"Well, well, well,' Dandy Jack murmured. "How sweet it is. A real family man, eh? Great. But how about showing me around the house now? Like to see how you did for yourself. Come on, kid. Give me the grant tour."

So Ned showed him the whole place, upstairs and down – the basement clubroom, the basement garage with the automatic electric door. But the very odd feeling he had while doing so was that it was not Ned and Kate McKestin's new house any more. Something had happened. Something had moved in. It seemed that it was Dandy Jack's house now, and Preston Ruby's.

Back in the kitchen again, Dandy Jack settled himself comfortably and began talking about old times. It was half an hour later before he got up and reached for the Borsalino hat.

"Seem kind of nervous," he remarked casually, "but don't be. Way out in the woods here, who the hell ever saw me come in? See what I mean, kid? Mum's the word. I'm just up here for a couple of days on a little scouting trip, as you might call it. Leaving first thing tomorrow morning."

Ned followed him out to the hall, the pressure noticeably tightening around the back of his skull. He attempted to make his next question very casual.

"Oh? A little scouting trip, Dandy?"

"Well, yeah," Dandy Jack said, daintily wiping off his fingers with an immaculate linen handkerchief. "Only looking around, that's all. Just in case. But of course there's no telling when lightning could strike. You keeping clean?"

"Ever since," Ned told him tightly, to get everything clearly understood between them. "The straight and narrow, Dandy. My first and last experience. Never again."

"Atta boy," Dandy told him, with another slyly covert grin on his lips. "Nothing like it, they tell me. Still, though – we were all damned lucky to get out of it that time, weren't we? Or all of us but Rod Connihan. He's the one bought it, eh?"

Ned had opened the door, but without putting on the porch light. It was a clear frosty night with a lot of stars, but very dark off in the woods. And suddenly, against the dark, like a confused movie montage, Ned could see himself six years ago at the steering wheel of a big Buick, with Preston Ruby and Dandy Jack darting out to him from the bank entrance. Behind them, crawling and scrambling horribly, was Rod Connihan, blood all over one leg of his gray trousers.

Then more shots had rung out in the

blazing stillness that seemed to have frozen all around Ned, and Connihan had sprawled full length on the pavement, at the same time dropping the bag in his hands. "Don't," Ned could hear again, and in the most breathless and anguished tones he had ever heard, "Wait a minute. Give me a hand, fellow! Don't leave me!"

But there was one more shot from inside the bank door, with Connihan jerking forward at it, and then lying rigidly still. It was only Ned who attempted to get out of the car to him, but Preston Ruby had knocked him back with a savage thrust of his right arm. "Get out of here!" Dandy Jack had begun yelling. "They got him, you damned fool. Start driving the car!"

Six years ago – and Ned was only 18.

But now Dandy Jack, out on the porch steps, turned for one more moment.

"Well, all the best," he said. "Sincere good wishes, kid – like all the postcards have it. I'll only tell Preston I saw you, but that's all. And you know what? I kind of got an idea he's going to be pretty damned glad to hear."

Alone then in the front hall, Ned leaned back against it with his eyes closed and his hands behind him. He remembered

31

himself at 18, all alone on the city streets after his parents had died, and how that Ned had thought Connihan and Dandy Jack were just about the greatest guys in the world. They fed him, gave him a few dollars now and again, took him around – and in return he had fixed up cars for them, a lot of cars that he never inquired about, and had run their errands.

"Might have a driving job for you tomorrow," Connihan had told him one night. "You're some jockey, kid. Just love the way you can cut around a corner slick as a whistle at seventy or seventy-five. How about it?"

"Well, sure," young Ned had replied earnestly. "Of course, Rod. Where are we going to go?"

"Let you know," Rod had told him, winking brightly. "Couple of things to arrange first. Just bring the car around here right after breakfast, that's all. I got the idea it's going to go easy as pie for us."

But it had not gone easy as pie, or not for dead Rod. And alone in the hall now, still with the ugly nausea in him, Ned once more had that bad feeling in him. Somehow not his own house any more; and most likely, if he could be useful in any way to

32

Preston Ruby, not even his own life any more.

Later on, sitting on the edge of his bed and staring off into the dark woods, Ned kept thinking about the last remark that Dandy Jack had made to him. "Pretty damned glad to hear," Ned remembered. "I'll tell Preston. I'll tell Preston, kid. I'll tell Preston."

Two days later Ned went down to Albany again, to see Kate and the baby, who were just fine although the doctor wanted her to stay on a few more days for another couple of tests. Ned did not tell her anything about Dandy Jack, however; his problem. Instead he was very cheerful with her, forcing himself; but he went out of her room finally a bit paler than usual, and with his heart heavy in him.

The thing would happen, Ned felt, just as he had always known it would happen. He had too much now, and had got it too easily. He would have to pay. When? How? Those were the only questions. For six years he had not known in what way it would happen, but he had known it would. The dead past was closing in. Preston Ruby had found him.

And that conviction was perfectly

33

correct. It happened that night. It happened in the slight drizzle down in the parking lot, when he saw two men waiting by the car for him. The one in the trench coat and the dapperly slanted Borsalino was Dandy Jack. The one beside him was Preston Ruby.

"Thought we might run into you here," Dandy Jack began affably. "Even waited around till ten o'clock last night, Ned. Look. Preston and I thought you might like to give us a ride with you back to Martinsville. Seems like we got a little unfinished business up there. How about it?"

Ruby said nothing. He did not even bother to say hello. But then he always stuck to the bare essentials in conversation, as Ned knew. Dark hat and overcoat; dark glasses; undersized, very quick body, quick as light when required; calm and narrow white face.

"Well, I don't know," Ned began painfully. "The car's not running too hot. I'd hate it if –"

It was time for the essentials, apparently. Ruby reached over for the car door, opened it and gestured.

"Not asking you," Ruby said. "Telling you. Get in."

And Ned got in. Nothing else for it. Dandy Jack sat in front with him, and Ruby behind. When he spoke again, Ned's voice was a lot weaker and jumpier than he wanted it to be.

"What do you want to go back to Martinsville for?" he asked them. "What's the business?"

"Wait'll you hear," Dandy Jack said, in the same cheerfully persuasive manner of Rod Connihan six years ago. "Easiest thing in the world, kid. Just like old times for all three of us. Preston and I decided that maybe we'd like to board with you for a few days. Little company, see – you being alone in the house and all. Feed us real good and we might even throw you a couple of grand when it's all over. Fair enough?"

Ned took the Northway turn without answering, but it seemed to be time for essentials there too. Ruby stirred.

"Keep it right at fifty," he ordered. "We don't want no trouble with the cops."

"Yeah," Dandy Jack agreed. "We wouldn't like to get stopped by one of them troopers, kid. Your interests, understand? This way nobody's going to know we're in the car with you, just as nobody's going to know when you get us back to Martinsville tonight, either. So there ain't a thing for you to worry about, not a thing. You're all covered. All anyone knows but you, me and Preston could be up on the moon."

"Covered on what?" Ned asked grimly, discovering that his hands had become clammy. There was not only Ned McKestin to think about now. There were Kate and the baby. It was necessary to get hold of himself. The thing had happened.

"On the favour we want you to do for us," Dandy Jack said. "It's this way, see? I hear tell a lot of prominent people live in those big camps off in the woods in your neighborhood, all around the upper lake. Saw some of them the other day when I took a ride. Biggest and best one you can't even see from the road – too private. Forest Ridge, it's called. Mrs. James Devereux Murchison."

Ruby said nothing at all in the back seat – not time yet.

"And that old biddy," Dandy Jack murmured almost reverently, "has just about everything there is, the way I get it. Place in Palm Beach, in New York, in Paris, France, in Washington, and the swellest

36

summer camp in the whole country just about a mile and a half from where you live. Paced it off the other afternoon, just to be sure. She invites people and they get flied in there on her private plane. Land on the lake, then go up the mountain on her own private elevator. Built right into it – saw it myself that afternoon, the whole thing. And three chefs, Preston, did I tell you? Meat chef, salad chef, pastry chef. Maybe thirty or thirty-five in help, but only one watchman. Only one watchman, kid. Kind of careless, huh?"

Fifty miles steady on the speedometer, Ned saw; just as ordered. A bad sign? He struggled to rouse himself.

"Yes, I've heard about it," he said. "Never saw it, though. Quite a place, eh?"

"Just lemme tell you," Dandy Jack said, pressing the most companionable of hands on Ned's right knee and squeezing in gently. "You wouldn't believe, kid. A big main house where they all go for their meals, the old biddy and her friends, and then a lot of little guest cottages all over the grounds, so everybody can be in his own place when he wants to be. Met a fellow down in New York who worked there a couple of years ago, and what he says is that the old lady herself lives in one of them guest cottages, of course the nicest one, when she's in residence, which I found out she is now. You can see her cottage right at the edge of the mountain overlooking the lake. Wonderful view from there. That's where she sleeps. Nobody else in her cottage, either. Not even a maid.

"So this guy brings her breakfast in bed one morning when her personal maid is sick, and just as he walks in with the tray she's opening a big wall safe back of some hangings. Holy smoke, he says. Like a damn jewelry store. Rings and necklaces and brooches, and whatever the hell else you can think of. Dough, even – nice fresh packets of it right from the bank.

"I see this guy around for three or four days maybe, treating him like he's the greatest guy in the world, and little by little coaxing the whole story out of him, and then I come up here to check it out for myself. Of course I never tell him my right name and after the three or four days he never sees me again. So don't worry about that part – no connection at all the way I foxed that dumb jerk. You following all this?"

Ned said nothing. Ruby said nothing.

Dandy Jack inched forward and tightened his affectionate pressure on Ned's knee.

"So there it is, understand? Why keep all that dough in one pocketbook, kid? Why not spread it around? Who the hell is she to have a setup like that all to herself? Only one thing – how to get away afterwards. Damned easy to block off all the roads up in this part of the state, and to check every car that tries to get in or out for the next week. That was what Preston and me really had to figure out. But of course when I met you, and saw the kind of setup you had established for us –"

"Perfect," Ruby cut in, his dark glasses dangling wearily from his right hand, as if he had become just a little impatient with all this talk. "We don't have to try to get away afterwards. You put us up. When we get back tonight, you drive into your cellar garage before we even get out of the car, so who sees anything? Who can even guess we're inside with you? After the caper we make sure we've got a clean hour or so to get back to your place, to that basement clubroom of yours Jack told me about. We're quiet as mice in there, we pull down the shades, you don't invite anybody out to your house – and nobody ever knows a damned thing about it. How can they? So what's your complaint, McKestin?"

"Oh, he's in with us," Dandy Jack said. "He ain't a damned dummy, Preston. The kid's all right. When they stop watching the roads, which he can find out easy for us, he drives his pickup truck down to Albany on business, with a couple of big busted television sets in back – just the cabinets, though, and you and I squeezed inside them all the way down. It's like a dream, I tell you. It's all there right in our hands, kid. Don't you see?"

"G. G. McKestin and Company," Ruby murmured, swinging the dark glasses in his hand – almost happily for Preston Ruby. "Thirty-six Main Street, Sales and Service. I think it's all there, Jack. What else could we want?"

Ned took one hand off the steering wheel and wiped his mouth.

"But maybe she won't tell you how to open the safe," was all he could think of saying. "And you couldn't blow it, not with thirty or forty servants around. If you even tried –"

"Kid, kid," Dandy Jack said, with the foxy little smile on his lips. "She'll tell Preston. In about ten seconds she'll be

40

damned glad to tell him. I give you my word."

Yes, very probably, Ned had to admit. Mrs. James Devereux Murchison, who looked like a nice ordinary old lady, absolutely no side to her. Once or twice he had seen her on the Martinsville streets, and once she had bought three television sets for the servants from G. G. McKestin. She had a nasal but rather pleasant New England twang, and had looked just like an old farmwife to Ned.

But what would she look like in that isolated cottage of hers, when Ruby and Dandy Jack got through? Ned found himself wincing, not wanting even to think of it. Suppose she tried to scream or to make a fight of it? He felt the whole top of his scalp crawling.

"No," he heard himself get out breathlessly. "I don't care how easy it is. I won't do it for you! I was only a kid with Rod Connihan that time, and he didn't even explain first what you were going to do. I told Dandy the other night. I'm through with that business. I've got a wife and a child now. I won't do it!"

In the back seat Ruby whistled *Night and*

41

Day very softly to himself. Dandy Jack chuckled.

"Look," he said. "Look, kid, with what we know about you, you figure you got any kind of a choice? Then figure again. Use your head. We're including you in."

And that night, trying uselessly to think of a way out, with Ruby and Dandy Jack quiet as quiet down in the basement clubroom, Ned realized he was in beyond question. It was not necessary for Preston Ruby even to threaten him. Why waste words? Ned was intelligent enough to see for himself. He had a wife and a child now and a new life – so he had a lot to protect. And Ruby was not a man to be moved by any consideration if you got in his way or spoiled his plans. That attempted bank robbery down in New York City might be still unsolved, but of course the police had the case still open. And just one anonymous phone call identifying the man who had driven the get-away car that day...

No, they had him. And he did not have them. He had been foolish enough, not knowing until too late what he was in for, to leave his fingerprints all over the steering wheel of that abandoned Buick; but they

42

had not left a print. He could still be identified through the fingerprints, identified beyond question. But they could not. And the testimony of an accomplice in crime, Ned had read somewhere, would not be accepted in court without corroborating evidence.

No, Ruby had thought out that part too. There was not a hole anywhere, and Ned had no choice. He would do exactly as they ordered or Ruby and Dandy Jack would turn him in. And then what? Five or ten years in jail probably; G. G. McKestin & Company, after all Uncle Gerry had done for him, would never be trusted or patronized again; and Kate and the baby would be left to fend for themselves. The dead past . . .

He heard, smoking silently, two o'clock chime out from the Town Hall belfry; three o'clock; four. It was no use – nothing came to him, nothing at all. The dead past was back again, blacker and more ominous than ever. He had to accept it. Ned McKestin was caught.

Next morning he was making early coffee for himself in the kitchen when the basement door opened and dark glasses and a narrow calm face – Ruby had always been troubled with bad eyes – looked out at him.

"Think it all out yet?" Ruby inquired softly. "Made up your mind, McKestin?"

Ned, his jaws clamped, kept his two hands on the coffee pot. That was advisable. He wanted to use them at this moment more than he ever had in his life.

"Not yet," he muttered. "Not decided yet, Ruby."

"No?" Ruby said, a faint chilly smile on his lips, so obviously knowing better; just pushing the pin. "Then take your time. Go to the store today, do what you always do, and watch your step. Now bring down some coffee for Jack and me, and don't forget to lock everything up here tight as a drum when you leave. We wouldn't like any visitors, McKestin. We want things just as they are."

All that day Ned sat numbly in his small cubbyhole of an office at G. G. McKestin's, but late in the afternoon, again with set jaws, he took Uncle Gerry's big old .38 revolver out of his desk. There was even more than Ned McKestin and his family to worry about. There was the safety of that one watchman out at Forest Ridge and the physical well-being of a nice old lady named Mrs. James Devereux Murchison. Nobody knew who was in the house with Ned now, in view of the care with which Preston had thought out the whole business. Good.

There was a spade in the basement and a lot of dark empty woods back of the house. Ned McKestin did not want to do anything like that. But if Ruby and Dandy Jack forced him to the last step . . .

But could he actually bring himself to do it? To shoot down two men, even men like Ruby and Dandy Jack, shoot them like caged rats? No, that would mean the dark past would be with him forever. Impossible. What else then? How to manage it?

Nothing came to him until he was closing the store and saw old Charlie Burger walking past on the other side of the street. Ned stopped off at the supermarket for a carton of cigarettes, then made one brief call in the pay-phone booth. It was not even necessary to disguise his voice. It seemed to him that he would never have recognized it himself. "But who's this?" Charlie Burger demanded. "And how do I know that you're not just –"

Ned hung up. He wiped his mouth

45

shakily, the .38 still heavy in his coat pocket, and drove home. But it was a silent meal down in the basement clubroom that night, just bread and butter, hot dogs and baked beans. Then, with television on, Ruby sat there. Ned sat there. Dandy Jack sat there. Yet undoubtedly there built up a certain tension in the air: zero hour. Which meant tonight, Ned told himself, and probably late tonight, without even the least warning to him. Much better that way, Ruby would have decided. Then early tomorrow they would confront him with the *fait accompli*. And what could Ned McKestin do about it? Nothing at all. Just go back to the dead past.

About ten o'clock he went up to bed, making a bit of noise in the bathroom, then slamming the bedroom door to let them hear; but after that, very quietly in stockinged feet, he tiptoed down. He was still sitting motionless in his dark kitchen, the .38 out in plain view on his knee, when the basement door opened noiselessly and Ruby and Dandy Jack came out. It was three o'clock then, and Ned deliberately raised the .38 so that they could see it. Preston Ruby stopped dead, and behind him Dandy Jack gawked.

46

"Now I'm going to tell you what to do," Ned gritted. "Tell you exactly. You're going to take my car and drive down to Albany tonight without a care in the world. I've got something to say. You're not going on with this thing. You can't. Because I've–"

"Now, kid," Dandy Jack said, wetting his lips. "Don't start to act up, will you? Preston and I might be willing to cut you in for a full third, say. Could be a hundred grand right in your pocket. What the hell's the matter with you? Why can't you see the thing?"

Ruby said nothing at all; thinking it out, Ned understood, in the Ruby manner. What Ned forgot momentarily, however, was how quick Ruby could be when he once decided to act. Now his head jerked around and he jumped back, as if in blind panic, for the basement door.

"Who's that?" Ruby cried out. "What are you trying to do here, McKestin? Who's out in your back porch?"

And Ned turned to look. It was altogether instinctive, and of course altogether stupid. Behind him there came the impression that something whizzed in the air, whizzed fast and venomously, and he turned back just in time to get the kitchen hammer, the one Kate always hung up on the basement door, across the top of his head. When he fell under it, Ruby was quick as light once more, and Dandy Jack moved in savagely from the other side.

"No, wait," Ned wanted to say. "You don't understand, Ruby. I'm trying to warn you! I called the town police chief this afternoon and he's waiting for you out at Forest Ridge right now. If you show up there, his men will shoot you down like a couple of mad dogs. Listen to me!"

But it came out in a confused shout, and Ruby, getting hold of the .38, slashed down calmly but grimly with it. The last thing Ned remembered was Ruby's face over him and the .38 smashing . . .

When he came to, he was lying face down on the coolness of the linoleum floor, and the illuminated kitchen clock showed him that a half hour had passed. For some reason, Ned understood, it was a very important half hour. But why?

He lay dazedly, trying to think. At last he managed to push himself up, shaking his head, then realized that half an hour was long enough to cut through the empty woods and run over the little bridge on

Conklin Creek to the Murchison place. Dandy Jack and Preston Ruby could be out there by now. They might already have knocked out the night watchman, or killed him. But wait – wait a minute! If Chief of Police Burger had paid attention to Ned's anonymous phone call this afternoon –

Distantly, in the direction of Forest Ridge, there was a flurry of gunshots. The last few sounded deliberate, final. Ned whispered a few low words, rested against Kate's kitchen stove, and closed his eyes.

There were no more shots. But presently, from the direction of Forest Ridge once more, he could dimly hear men shouting . . .

"But I guess they never counted on somebody like Old Charlie," little Jack Holleran exulted shrilly the next morning. He was the stock boy at G. G. McKestin's, and now he danced around Ned excitedly. "Two guys, Ned. Seems like they kept shooting and shooting when he tried to warn them, and the one little guy, quick as a cat, winged Harry Johansson in the right shoulder. But Old Charlie had his rifle out and they say he can knock the spots off a playing card at a hundred yards. You hear anything yet?"

Ned, a strange pale smile on his lips, nodded. All night he had been waiting motionless in the shadows of his dark kitchen for Old Charlie to ring his front doorbell. He had not known what the delay meant. He could not imagine.

"So he caught them, Jack? Where are they now?"

"Walter Engstrom's funeral parlor," Jack crowed. "I just stole a peek at them in the back room. After they shot Harry, they both got it smack through the head, the damned fools. Dead as doornails, both of 'em!"

Ned went into his cubbyhole and sat down numbly. He had thought that when he told them about Chief Burger they would have no other recourse but to do as he said – to get out of town right away. He had tried to warn them, but they had not let him. So now . . .

He covered his eyes with both hands. But after a few moments, steady as rock now, he took three deep breaths, reached out for his desk telephone, and called Kate. At long last the past was dead.

BARBARA CALLAHAN

Don't Cry, Sally Shy

The influence of Sigmund Freud on modern literature has been colossal – its immensity cannot be measured. Today hardly a story is written, short or long, that doesn't have somewhere in its innards – in the invisible part of the iceberg, the invisible words between the lines, the words left unwritten – the subtle manifestations of the superego, ego, and libido that Freud discovered, named, and revealed in all human beings. Freud has made us see more clearly what has always been true – that writers create characters in our own image . . .

The puppets have been misbehaving lately. They refuse to speak their lines correctly. They miss cues. They sing their songs too loudly. And I've lost my best accompanist because of them.

I tried to explain to him that it was the puppets' fault, not mine. His face grew redder when I told him that. His words still sting whenever I think of them.

"If the puppets are out of control, Miss Jenkins, it is because you, the puppeteer, are out of control. You have crossed the border into fantasyland, Miss Jenkins. You attribute life and will to puppets which have neither. You had better see a doctor, and quickly."

As if to convince him that the puppets reacted on their own, the puppet Bobby Bold who had been lying limply in my hand suddenly became rigid and parroted his words: "You had better see a doctor, and quickly." As I tried to shush the naughty puppet, Bobby added, "*You* see a doctor quickly, you broken-down pulverizer of piano keys."

The accompanist's voice trembled as he told me never to call him again for a performance. He rushed toward the exit of the hall without giving me the opportunity to apologize for Bobby's brazenness. He covered his ears as I shouted that I had nothing to do with Bobby's outburst.

Bobby laughed as I shoved him into the suitcase that houses him and his companions – Grandmother Good, Sally Shy, and Fox Trot. I knew that Grandmother Good would soundly scold him after I closed the suitcase. She never tells me what happens inside their home but I can guess. Sally Shy would cry – Bobby's brashness always frightens her. Fox Trot, that sly old pet, would grin when Grandmother chastised Bobby – Fox Trot enjoys Bobby's transgressions. I believe that tricky fox encourages Bobby in his mischief.

The puppets, even Bobby, used to be quite docile, but since the automobile accident they have been maliciously asserting themselves. I know the accident disturbed them. Although they were safely cushioned in their suitcase, they were informed of all the details by Grandmother Good. I had taken Grandmother into the hospital with me when the police officer drove me there for x-rays.

I needed the sweet consolation that Grandmother Good always provided. That's why I insisted on holding her in my hand throughout the ordeal. The hospital personnel thought the puppet's presence was an indication that I had suffered a concussion when my head bumped against the windshield. It was too difficult to explain to them how soothing Grandmother is, so I didn't try.

After the x-rays I fell asleep on the gurney. When I awoke, Grandmother repeated to me the words I thought I had dreamed: "The little boy, Jack, is dead. He was killed instantly by the impact of your car."

The boy's parents visited me at my apartment. In their grief they told me they held nothing against me. They knew their son Jack, only five years old, frequently dashed across the street without looking out for cars. I brought Grandmother Good out of the suitcase and permitted her to tell the parents how I would re-dedicate my talents as a puppeteer to bringing joy to the lives of children. I sent all the fees from my next three performances to the boy's parents.

It was during the fourth performance after the accident that Bobby began interrupting the nursery rhymes that Sally Shy was reciting. It was so mean of Bobby to disturb her. My audiences always love it when Sally finally speaks. For most of every performance she hides behind Grandmother's skirt. When she grows weary of the taunts of Bobby and Fox Trot, she triumphs by shaming them with her superb memory and diction. The children cheer when Sally recites. So many of the children must identify with her shyness.

She had begun with the rhyme "Jack, be nimble, Jack, be quick" when Bobby pushed her aside and chanted, "Jack can't be nimble, Jack can't be quick, Jack's a broken candlestick." The children, thinking Bobby's rudeness was part of the act, laughed and laughed. Sally cried onstage because she knew that Jack was the dead boy's name.

Fox Trot saved the day by doing the special dance in which he prances around the stage while whisking away Bobby's ball and Grandmother's mixing spoon with his bushy tail. I can always depend on Fox Trot to improvise when it's necessary.

When those awful telephone calls came in the middle of the night, I slipped Fox Trot on my hand to let him answer. I was sure he'd know how to thwart the caller. He is so shrewd that he had only to listen to four of the calls before he knew who was making them. He determined that those terrible words, "If you had stopped sooner, the boy would still be alive," came from a rival puppeteer who desperately wanted all the engagements I was receiving.

"I'll call the cops on you, Mary Reedy,"

he shouted. "I know it's you making these calls. It's the kind of lowdown trick a fox like me can spot right away."

Mary Reedy was so startled that she dropped the phone on a table before hanging up. She never called again.

"She's just trying to ruin your nerves, kiddo, so she can get your jobs. But amateurs can't shake up real pros like us, can they, kiddo?" Fox Trot cackled.

"No, they can't shake us up, dear pet," I told him. To prove it, I spent the rest of the evening sewing new outfits for the entire puppet family. Sally loved her dress, Grandmother was pleased with her apron, and Fox Trot strutted happily in his new feathered hat. But Bobby, vicious Bobby Bold, how he loves to torment me! He deliberately ruined the sweatshirt I had so painstakingly made for him. I had lettered the number 3 on it. When I inspected my handiwork the next morning, I saw what he had done. He had put the number 5 next to the 3. His shirt read 35. When I saw that number, I collapsed on a chair. The last time I had seen 35 was on the blood-stained sweatshirt worn by Jack, the little boy I had hit.

His cruel prank upset me so much that

I could not fulfill the engagement I had at the Hill School. I could only sit sobbing in a chair. Grandmother Good clamored to be let out of the suitcase. She wanted so much to comfort me. I could hear Sally Shy crying and Fox Trot yelling, "Don't let him get you down, kiddo," but I could not move from the chair.

When the doorbell rang, I forced myself to answer it. The detective who had been so kind to me on the day of the accident was standing in the hall. I hated for him to see me looking so forlorn, so I ran into my bedroom and shut the door. I heard him walk into the kitchen. In a few minutes he knocked on my door.

When I didn't open it, he entered the room carrying a cup of tea. "My mother always told me that tea is an excellent remedy for whatever ails a person," he said.

I took the cup from him and we went into the living room. He didn't seem to hear all the noises coming from the suitcase.

"I had some time off this morning," he said, "and I thought I'd like to see you perform. I knew you were going to be at the Hill School, so I went to the auditorium. The children were very disappointed when you didn't come. I thought perhaps you

57

were sick, so I decided to drop by."

"I'm glad you came," I told him after a few sips of tea.

When I had finished it, he handed me my coat.

"Let's go," he said.

The puppets abruptly stopped arguing in the suitcase to listen to him. I heard nothing but my heart beating.

"Go where?" I asked.

"To a restaurant."

"Restaurant?"

"Yes, I know a fine place. You need some lunch."

As I put on my coat, I heard Fox Trot whispering advice. "Charm him, kiddo, charm him. It's good to have a cop for a friend."

I picked up the suitcase and headed for the door.

"Why are you taking that?" the detective asked.

"The puppets are in it. I take them everywhere. They'll be upset if I leave them here."

He laughed, but didn't attempt to dissuade me. He carried the suitcase to his car.

As we drove to the restaurant, I tried so

often to ask him something, but I was too embarrassed. I had to bring out Sally Shy to ask him for me.

"Your name, nice man, is Clark?" she asked.

"No, it's Mark," he said. "Mark Evans. And your name is?"

"Sally Shy," I answered.

Sally cringed when he reached over and lifted her off my hand.

"She's cute," he said, "but I like *you* better, Miss Jenkins."

"You may call me Alice," I told him softly.

I gently tucked Sally into the suitcase. Grandmother Good would take care of her.

It wasn't until dessert that Mark discussed the accident. He said I might be suffering from a delayed reaction to the shock. He told me the best cure would be to keep busy. "Above all," he advised, "don't cancel performances the way you did today."

I nodded in agreement. I was touched by his concern and wanted to tell him that. But I couldn't until we had a glass of wine after lunch. And before I knew it I was telling him all my troubles about the puppets misbehaving.

59

He didn't laugh as I expected, nor did he become angry with me as the accompanist had. He simply said, "You'll have to be more firm with the puppets. Remember, you're in the driver's seat."

I must have blanched at the expression "driver's seat" because he patted my hand. He asked me to forgive him for his poor choice of words.

We took a long walk after lunch, the first of many walks we took in the course of our dating. It would have been awkward to carry the suitcase with the puppets during the walks, so I just put Grandmother Good into my pocketbook. Whenever I felt nervous, I would slide my hand into Grandmother's arms and she would give me a reassuring squeeze.

Although I am 30, I had never dated anyone more than twice. Somehow I could never feel relaxed in a dating situation. Mark seemed to sense this. He never forced himself on me. He was patient, oh, so patient. For the three weeks we saw each other every day, I had never been happier.

Aside from Grandmother Good, the puppets hated to see me so contented. They performed well but they resented not going out with Mark and me. One night after we

60

had come home from a marvelous concert, Mark sat very close to me on the sofa. I was delighted and rested my head on his shoulder.

Suddenly I heard the muffled voice of Bobby Bold coming from the suitcase. He sounded so distressed that I had to release him. Mark seemed annoyed when I jumped up from the sofa to get the vicious puppet. I apologized and told him that Bobby would have to have his say or he would give me no peace.

I asked Bobby what was bothering him. He turned to Mark and yelled, "If you're thinking of marrying sweet little Alice Jenkins, flatfoot, come see me. I could tell you some things about her that would curl your hair."

I heard Grandmother Good gasp and Sally begin to cry and Fox Trot cackle. Bobby had gone so far out of bounds that there was only one thing to do. I slapped him. I slapped him so hard that he flew off my hand. I went to pick him up to hit him again, but Mark restrained me.

"He's a monster," I sobbed, "a vicious monster."

Mark made me tea and sat with me until I fell asleep. When I awoke, I felt cold and numb. I opened the suitcase and saw Bobby sleeping peacefully, not at all affected by what he had said. I reached for Grandmother, but Fox Trot climbed onto my hand.

"Pull yourself together, kiddo. Don't let the little brat get you down. Play your cards right. Be foxy and you'll have that guy eating out of your hand."

"But how?" I asked. "After Bobby's outburst Mark will never want to see me again."

"Fret not. Call him up at the office and tell him how unnerved you've been. Tell him you haven't been able to sleep at night since the accident."

"But I do sleep, Fox Trot."

"Yeah, we know that. You sleep like the dead."

"Don't say 'dead,' you horrible beast."

"Okay, okay, but you do go out like a light."

"Shut up, shut up, I tell you."

"All right, kiddo. But just do what I told you. Call that guy and cry a lot on the phone. He's a pushover for the dependent type. I know. Tell him you need him and he'll be back in a flash. And be sure to cry a lot."

"I can't pretend to cry," I told him.

"Then get Sally Sob to cry for you. It's what she does best."

I gave Fox Trot a big kiss. I knew he liked it. He acts hardboiled, but underneath his sly exterior he's as soft as kitten fur.

The next morning, after I had dialed the phone, I put Sally on my hand. I started the conversation but let Sally talk after I detected a coldness in Mark's voice.

Sally was superb. She never cried better.

She was so good that Mark promised to take me for a drive right after work.

I spent the afternoon soaking in a bubble bath, doing my nails, and setting my hair in a long flowing style. The red dress that I had thought too provocative after I'd bought it seemed to be the perfect selection for my afternoon date.

Mark whistled appreciatively when he saw me. He took my yellow coat from the living-room closet, but I didn't think it blended well with my dress, so I went into the bedroom to get my fur jacket. When I returned, Mark handed me the puppets' suitcase.

"Aren't you going to bring your friends?" he asked.

63

"No, Mark, I don't need them any more."

"Great," he smiled.

We had a beautiful ride, through the River Drive, out into the country, and back toward town for dinner at our favorite restaurant. I slid close to Mark in his car and rested my head on his shoulder. I was so happy and relaxed that I closed my eyes to visualize him pouring the wine out of the little carafe at the restaurant.

I was jolted out of my reverie by the sudden slamming of brakes. I opened my eyes and screamed.

"It's nothing," Mark said. "A cat crossed in front of me."

I quickly looked toward the pavement. I didn't see a cat, but I did see Jack's house. We had stopped at the exact spot where I had hit the little boy. The house was not on the way to the restaurant.

"Why are we here, Mark?" I cried.

"Somebody wants to talk to me," he answered.

"The boy's parents?"

"No," he said, "a young lady."

He reached into his pocket. When he showed me what he held, I started to tremble. He had Sally Shy in his hand. He must have taken her out of the suitcase when I went in the bedroom to get my jacket. He slipped Sally onto my hand. Each time I pulled Sally off, he pushed her back on.

"She has nothing to tell you," I said.

"I think she does," he said quietly.

"I do, I do," sobbed Sally.

"Don't say anything," I begged her.

But the poor distraught puppet didn't listen to me. She blurted out those terrible words.

"She was drunk," Sally choked. "Drunk. She had been drinking just the way she always does before a performance. When the little boy ran out into the street, she didn't even see him."

Then Sally cried as I had never heard her cry before. Mark leaned over and removed her from my hand.

"Don't cry, Sally Shy," he told me. "I'm sorry I had to do this, but I hate sloppy work. The procedure in an accident such as yours wasn't followed through. You didn't have a blood test at the hospital, so the thought occurred to me that you could have been drunk when you hit that boy. I had to find out."

On the way to the police station I tried

to explain to Mark that I had wanted to tell the truth as soon as it happened, but Fox Trot wouldn't let me. The sly fox told me, "Act like you bumped your head on the windshield. They'll have to take x-rays of you at a hospital. When the x-rays are finished, they'll let you lie down and rest. If they don't, carry on, act hysterical. They'll give you a needle to make you sleep and then forget to give you a blood test. Fake them out, kiddo, fake them out."

Mark drove the rest of the way in silence. I needed someone to talk to me. So I listened very hard and soon I heard Grandmother Good calling to me from my apartment. She told me that everything would be all right. Bobby Bold said that I got what I deserved, so I ignored him. As usual Fox Trot voiced what was in my mind.

"That Mark's a sly one," he said. "I'll tell you something, kiddo, not all foxes are puppets."

WILLIAM BRITTAIN

The Second Reason

Mr. Fat, Mr. Tall, and Mr. Short, three mystery men, ordered the construction of a wall in the middle of the desert. The wall was ten feet long, eight feet high, and two cinder blocks thick. Of what earthly use was such a wall in such a place? Keach, who built the wall, just couldn't figure it out. And neither could we . . .

Keach flicked a blob of wet cement onto the base of the cinder block, slathered it with his trowel, then hoisted the block laboriously into place. As he snugged the block home with taps from the handle of his trowel, a bead of sweat dribbled from his chin to the ground. It disappeared almost at once, half evaporating into the dry desert air and half soaking into the baked, hard-packed earth.

Damn it all, it was hot! But then, he hadn't expected a picnic. Not at $200 for a single day's work at a time when nearly everybody in the building trades was screaming for something – anything – in the way of jobs.

Keach wiped sweat from his forehead with the back of his hand and looked about at the landscape. Flat, except for the hills away off to the north. A *playa*, the bed of a lake long since dried up in the blasting heat of the desert sun. Little cracks in the flatness where the parched earth, bullet-hard, had shrunk in on itself. Hell must be something like this, Keach figured – hell or the far side of the moon.

Oh, there were some things to break the monotony of the land. His flatbed truck with the piles of cinder blocks and the drums of water. The three men taking their ease in folding chairs under the shade of a canvas fly, with their fancy new car parked nearby. And off to his left there was even a mound of rock that looked for all the world like a deck of cards with one card in the middle sticking out a little way. I bet it's an ace, thought, Keach, and the dealer's about to hand it to himself.

He shook his head angrily, calling himself all kinds of a fool for seeing a card game in a hunk of rock. But the emptiness was getting to him. The truck and the car. The men sitting there with their iced drinks. Himself. That was all there was.

Except for the wall.

Ten feet long and eight feet high, except for the one corner he hadn't finished yet. It ran almost due north and south with its flat eastern face on a line between holes, each about three inches in diameter, that had been drilled into the earth twelve feet apart. The holes were at least a foot deep – Keach had struck the handle of his trowel into one without reaching bottom.

Oh, the wall was a good one, all right. One of the best walls Keach had ever built. Two cinder blocks thick, and dead plumb from top to bottom. Why, that wall would stop a charging rhinoceros dead in its tracks, or even a bull elephant. There wasn't anything that could bring down the wall. Except –

Except what was it for?

Walls were supposed to keep things out, or in. Or sometimes they were made to enclose an area, but that required corners or curves. They could even provide beauty, as in a garden or around a public building.

But this wall just didn't qualify for anything Keach could think of. There it stood in the middle of the dry lake like some monument erected by a prehistoric tribe. A man could walk clear around it in a few seconds, and the dreary view on one side was exactly like that on the other. Keach remembered a movie he'd seen in which beings from outer space had erected a monolith in the middle of a tribe of apes. The thing had resembled an enormous slab of black marble, its shape not unlike his own wall.

Could the thing he was building be some kind of landmark or signal for creatures from another planet? The dry lake would be an ideal place for a flying saucer to land – remote, perfectly flat. Besides, when the three men had come to ask about his services and give their specifications, they'd been especially interested in how much he watched TV. When he said he didn't own one and only watched at a friend's house once a month or so, they'd obviously been happy, and the deal was closed on the spot.

Things from outer space. In his mind's eye Keach imagined monstrous beings with leathery green skin and reptilian eyes plodding across the lake bed toward the distant hills. He turned around suddenly, half expecting the shapes of the men behind him to waver and begin to change.

But they hadn't changed. The fat one sat with his belly almost out to his knees, drinking deeply from a glass beaded with moisture. The tall thin one was next to him, leaning forward and conversing in a low hum of words. And the shortest one was lounging in a folding deck chair, probably asleep, with his hat over his eyes.

Mr. Fat, Mr. Tall, and Mr. Short. The names were as good as any since Keach didn't know their real ones. They'd just walked in off the street, asked a few questions, and bang! – Keach had a $200 deal just for a long night's drive, followed by a single day's work building the wall. What did he care whether they came from California as their license plate indicated, or from the moon? And it wasn't as if he was doing something wrong. There was no law against building a wall in the desert, was there?

But what's it for, Keach? his brain demanded.

Annoyed with himself, he stomped off toward his truck. First he took a canteen from the shade behind one wheel and drank deeply. He'd had more than a gallon, and here it was just shy of noon. That desert sun did suck the moisture out

71

of a man. Then from under the flat bed he drew out a metal trough, dented and layered with scales of hardened cement.

"Got to mix up a new batch," he said to Mr. Fat, who waved in reply. He dug cement from an open bag with a shovel and followed that with sand from a pile on a tarp near the cab. As he scooped out his first bucket of water from the one drum which hadn't been emptied, he realized that the low hum of speech from the shade under the canvas fly was coming to him clearly through the dry desert air.

"Are you sure this is going to work?" Mr. Tall was asking Mr. Fat. "Isn't he going to notice –"

"Notice what?" Fat answered. "You don't think our big hero will all of a sudden get ambitious and come out here ahead of time, do you? Hell, he always leaves the scut work to us. And when he finally is ready, the light won't exactly be in his favor. Say, you aren't having any second thoughts about this, are you?"

"No, of course not," Mr. Tall pouted. "First time we get to do something where there's a decent amount of money involved, he decides to get rid of us and bring in his own crew. It isn't fair."

"Right. And his yapping about how he's going to tell the chief just because we called him a damn no-good – It's not going to be easy for us to get work after that."

Keach caught himself holding the mixing hoe motionless and staring at the men. With a start he began stirring the slithery liquid concrete which was gray ooze around the blade of the hoe as it sloshed in the trough.

Mr. Short had joined the other two men by this time. Mr. Fat held him by the shoulder with one hand, while with the other he pointed to a spot some 20 yards from the wall.

"I'll be right there, grinding away," he said. "You two will be up in the chopper, same as always. Everything nice and natural."

"Bu-bu-bu-but won't they know it wa-wa-was us?" stuttered Mr. Short.

"How're they going to know?" asked Mr. Fat. "So long as we keep our stories straight, that is. We just say we figured it was something special that some other crew rigged up without telling us. How were we to know it wasn't a phoney?"

"Y-yeah, I suppose," said Mr. Short dubiously.

"C'mon, it can't miss." Mr. Fat gestured toward the wall. "There it is. It's real, and everything's going to happen just the way we planned. And nobody's going to catch on ahead of time because we're the only three who are dumb enough to come out here."

"And him?" Mr. Short nodded in Keach's direction.

"He's not only dumber than us," said Mr. Fat. "He's yellow too. I'll put the fear in his bones, don't you worry."

Mr. Tall gave a harsh dry laugh. "Big hero came through the first reason and picked up more loot than we see in a year. So now that he's making it big, he tries to drop us after all the things we showed him about the business. But I think he's going to have some rough sledding with the second reason."

"Gentlemen," said Mr. Fat, raising his glass, "I give you – the second reason."

"Y-yeah, man!" giggled Mr. Short. "The se-se-second reason. BaLOOM!"

The little area where the men sat was swept by a wave of laughter. And the laughing was cut short as Mr. Fat raised his hand. His gaze locked ominously with that of Keach.

74

"Just finish the wall, Mr. Keach," said Mr. Fat in a low growl.

Less than an hour later the wall was complete. As Mr. Fat doled out the $200 in tens and twenties into Keach's gritty palm, he spoke in a patronizing manner, as if addressing a small child.

"Your work, Mr. Keach, is A-one. And now that you're finished you should keep in mind that we know a lot about you – where you live and work and all – while you don't know anything about us. So maybe you'd just better forget about what you did here today and look on the two hundred as found money."

"Forget? But –"

"Forget, Mr. Keach." The voice was cold, without emotion. "Too good a memory can be a dangerous thing." Mr. Fat's eyes were as grim and menacing as the dry flatness of the desert.

With the money wadded into a ball in his pocket, Keach climbed into the cab of the truck, slammed it into gear, and roared off across the lake bed. The air streaming through the truck's open windows was hot and acrid, but he felt goosebumps rise on his shoulders, and a cold shiver ran up his spine.

Late that night back in town, with the truck put away and his body cleansed by a hot shower, Keach decided to use a part of his $200 to get drunk. He'd earned every nickel of the money, and now he needed the soothing effect of whiskey.

The bar was dark, quiet, with only a few midweek customers. On a stool at one end of the mahogany strip, Keach downed a pair of shots – one, two, just like that. He knew this was going to be a bad drunk. During the good drunks – when a big construction project was in the offing or a new labor contract had been negotiated – he sipped his whiskey slow and easy. But when times were bad, when he was angry or scared or worried, he gulped.

He looked at his image in the mirror and seemed to see Mr. Fat's eyes boring into his.

Why in hell would anyone build a wall out in the middle of the desert?

The aproned bartender switched on the TV at the other end of the narrow room.

"...and now for some scenes from next week's adventure of Barney Kalso, Private Eye."

Two men, pummeling each other. Then a
76

close-up of a hand holding a pistol. The pistol roared twice, and there was a high-pitched scream from off camera. Finally a car plunging in flames from a bridge.

"Too damn much violence," said a boozy voice from a booth. "See if you can find the boxing, huh, Vic?"

"Leave it there," said a powerfully built kid wearing a leather jacket and motorcycle boots. "I wanna see the movie coming up. It's got Cesar Romero and Betty Grable."

The bartender shrugged and moved away from the set as the show's final credits rolled. Prefacing the station break, a filmed commercial began on the screen.

"The Cheetah!" The announcer might have been broadcasting the end of the world, his voice was so deep and serious and compelling. "America's newest small car."

No music. Complete silence as the camera made a half circle about some dimly lit place. Then the camera lifted and there was a bright yellow semicircle on the screen. A blare of trumpets on the sound track.

"Sunrise," the announcer went on. "Time to get up and go – with Cheetah!"

A small dark spot appeared directly in front of the rising sun. Gradually it grew bigger and became an automobile.

77

"The Cheetah. America's move to economy. Tested at thirty-two miles per gallon on the open road..."

The car was nearer now, cruising along a shaft of sunlight, a tiny green insect getting larger every second.

"...and twenty-four miles per gallon in city driving."

The cameraman had switched to a wide-angle lens, and the objects in the foreground of the picture jumped into sharp focus at the same time.

Keach shook his head. It was amazing what those TV cameramen could do.

And then he froze.

The drink in his hand sloshed onto the bar. No. Yes, there it was. Off to the side of the screen.

That rock – the one that looked like a deck of cards. He'd spent the whole day right at the spot where the film of the car had been taken.

An overhead view of the Cheetah, now traveling along the ray of light across the cracked surface of the lake bed.

"Fuel economy. Your first reason to buy the exciting new Cheetah!"

A huge sheet of paper stretched between upright posts occupied the whole TV screen.

78

Splashed across the paper in large red letters:
Reason # 1
Fuel Economy
Buy CHEETAH

And then the car, doing at least 70, tore through the sign with a growl of power, tearing the paper to shreds. The driver skidded to a halt a hundred yards beyond.

Keach's mind screamed with things remembered.

The deck-of-cards rock.

The three-inch-wide holes.

The wall, with its solid cinder-block surface facing due east – toward the rising sun.

The announcer continued: "You've seen our film of Reason Number One for buying the new Cheetah. Next week on this same channel we will show you Reason Number Two. Be sure to watch."

Keach visualized the driver – whose name he didn't even know – smashing unsuspectingly into the paper sign, expecting thin air behind it.

But he, Keach, had built a wall – a solid wall in the middle of the desert.

And if he said anything? If he could warn the unknown driver before the second reason was filmed? What would Mr. Fat do then?

As Keach leaned across the bar, he could feel the raw whiskey churning in his stomach and burning his throat. His groan of outrage, shame, fear, became a high keening in the small barroom.

And from the TV came the announcer's voice in a final message:

"Buy Cheetah. It's a hit!"

MICHAEL GILBERT
The Sark Lane Mission

In which Detective Sergeant Petrella is offered a most serious narcotics investigation – a case involving "an international crowd who are calculating their profits in the millions," and even more frightening, "who must be responsible, directly or indirectly, for hundreds of deaths a year," and to whom – a fact that Petrella must weigh carefully – "a single life is not of great importance"... a superlative example of Mr. Gilbert's police-procedural novelets...

Detective: SERGEANT PETRELLA

"You're wanted down at Central," said Gwilliam. "They want to have a little chat with you about your pension."

"My pension?" said Detective Sergeant Petrella. Being nearer 20 than 30, pensions were not a thing which entered much into his thoughts. "You're sure it's not my holiday? I've been promised a holiday for eighteen months."

"Last time I saw the pensions officer," said Gwilliam, "he said to me, 'Sergeant Gwilliam, it's a dangerous job you're doing.' It was the time I was after that Catford dog-track shower and I said, 'You're right, there, my boy.' 'Do you realize, Sergeant,' he said to me, 'that every year for the past ten years one hundred and ninety policemen have left the force with collapsed arches? And this year we may pass the two hundred mark. We shall have to raise your insurance contributions.'"

Petrella went most of the way down to Westminster by bus. It was a beautiful morning, with spring breaking through all round. Having some time in hand he got off the bus at Piccadilly, walked down St. James's, and cut across the corner of the park.

It was a spring which was overdue. They had had a dismal winter. In the three years he had been in Q Division, up at Highside, he could not remember anything like it. The devil seemed to have got among the pleasant people of North London.

First, an outbreak of really nasty holliganism, led, as he suspected, by two boys of good family; but he hadn't been able to pin it on them. Then the silly business of the schoolgirl shoplifting gang. Then the far-from-silly, the dangerous and tragic matter of Cora Gwynne.

Gwynne was the oldest by several years of the Highside detectives. He was a quiet but well-liked man, and he had one daughter, Cora, who was 17. Six months before, Cora had gone. She had not disappeared; she had departed, leaving a note behind her saying that she wanted to live her own life. "Whatever that means," Gwynne had said to Haxtell.

"Let her run," Haxtell had replied. "She'll come back."

He was right. She came back at the end of the fifth month, in time to die. She was full of cocaine, and pregnant.

Petrella shook his head angrily as he thought about it. He stopped to look at the crocuses which were thick in the grass. A starved-looking sparrow was trying to bolt a piece of bread almost as large as itself. A pigeon sailed smoothly down and removed it.

Petrella walked on, up the steps into King Charles Street, across Whitehall, and under the arch into New Scotland Yard.

He was directed to the office that dealt with pensions, allotted a wooden chair, and told to wait. At eleven o'clock a messenger brought in a filing tray with six cups of tea on it, and disappeared through a swing door in the partition. Since the tray was empty when he returned, Petrella deduced that there must be at least six people devoting attention to the pensions of the Metropolitan Police and he hoped one of them would soon devote some attention to him.

He became aware that the messenger had halted opposite him.

"You Sergeant Pirelli?" he said.

"That's right," said Petrella. He had long ago given up correcting people about his name.

"C.I.D., Q Division?"

"Ten out of ten."

"Whassat?"

"I said you're quite right."

"I'll tell 'em you're here," said the messenger.

Five minutes later a cheerful-looking girl arrived and said, "Sergeant Petrella? Would you come with me, please?"

His opinion of the Pensions Section became a good deal more favorable. Any department that employed a girl with legs like that must have some good in it.

So engrossed was he in this speculation that it did not, at first, occur to him to ask where they were going. When they reached and pushed through a certain swing door on the first floor, he stopped her.

"You've got it wrong," he said. "This is where the top brass works. If we don't look out we shall be busting in on the Assistant Commissioner."

"That's right," said the girl.

She knocked on one of the doors on the south side of the corridor, then opened it without waiting for an answer, and said, "I have Sergeant Petrella here for you."

He advanced dazedly into the room. He had been there once before, and he knew that the gray-haired man behind the desk was Assistant Commissioner Romer, of the C.I.D., a man who, unlike some of his predecessors, had not come to his office through the soft byways of the legal department, but had risen from the bottom-most rung of the ladder, making enemies at every step, until finally he had found himself at the top; and when, there being no one left to fight, he proved himself a departmental head of exceptional ability.

In a chair beside the window he noted Superintendent Costorphine, who specialized in all matters connected with narcotics. He had worked for him on two previous occasions and had admired him, although he could not love him.

Romer said in a very friendly voice. "Sit down, will you, Sergeant. This is going to take some time. You know Costorphine, don't you? I'm sorry about this cloak-and-dagger stuff, but you'll understand better when I explain what it's about, and what we're going to ask you to do. And when I say 'ask' I mean just that. Nothing at all that's said this morning is anything approaching an order. It's a suggestion. If you turn it down, no one's going to think any the worse of you. In fact, Costorphine and myself will be the only people who will even know about it."

Assuming a cheerfulness which he was far from feeling, Petrella said, "You tell me what you want me to do, sir, then I can tell you if I want to run away."

Romer nodded at Costorphine, who said in his schoolmasterly voice, "Almost a year ago we noted a new source of entry of cocaine into this country. Small packets of it were taken from distributors *inside* the country. It was never found in large quantities, and we never found how it got in.

"Analysis showed it to be Egyptian in origin. It also showed quite appreciable deposits of copper. It is obviously not there as the result of any part of the process of manufacture, and it is reasonable to suppose that it came there during some stage in shipment or entry.

"Once the source had been identified, we analyzed every sample we laid hands on, and it became clear" – Costorphine paused fractionally, not for effect; he was a man who had no use for effects, but because he wished to get certain figures clear in his own head – "that rather over half of the total intake of illicit cocaine coming into this country was coming under this head. And that the supply was increasing."

"And along with it," said Romer, "were increasing, at a rate of geometrical progression, most of the unpleasant elements of criminal activity with which we have to deal. Particularly among juveniles. I've had some figures from America which made my hair stand on end. We're not quite as bad yet, but we're learning."

Petrella could have said, "There's no

need to tell me. I knew Cora Gwynne when she was a nice friendly schoolgirl of fourteen, and I saw her just before she died." But he kept quiet.

Romer went on, "I suppose if youth thinks it may be blown to smithereens inside five or ten years by some impersonal force pressing a button, its predisposed to experiment. I don't know. Anyway, you'll understand why we thought it worth bringing down a busy Detective Sergeant from Q. Division.

"Now, I'm going to give you some facts. We'll start, as our investigators started about nine months ago, with a gentleman named Batson. Mr. Batson is on the board of the Consort Line, a company which owns and runs three small cargo steamers: the *Albert Consort*, the *William Consort*, and the *Edward Consort* – steamers which run between various Mediterranean ports, Bordeaux, and London."

When Romer said, "Bordeaux," Petrella looked up at Costorphine, who nodded.

"Bordeaux, but not the racket you're thinking of," he said "We've checked that."

"Batson," went on Romer, "is not only

on the board of the Consort Line. It has been suggested that he *is* the board. But one thing about him is quite certain. Whatever his connection with this matter he, personally, takes no active part. He neither carries the stuff nor has any direct contact with the distributors. But I think that, at the end of the day, the profit goes to him.

"That being so, we looked carefully at his friends, and the one who caught our eye was Captain Cree. Ex-captain now, since he has retired from the services of the Consort Line, he lives in considerable affluence in a house at Greenwich. He maintains a financial interest in the *Consorts* through his friend, Mr. Batson, and acts as chandler and shore agent for them – finds them crews and cargoes, and buys their stores.

"All of which might add up, in cash, to a nice house at Greenwich, but wouldn't really account for" – Romer ticked them off on his fingers – "two personal motor cars, with a chauffeur bodyguard to look after the same, a diesel-engined tender called *Clarissa* based on Wapping, with a whole-time crew of three and, in addition to all these, a large number of charitable and philanthropic enterprises, chiefly among seamen and boys in the dockside area."

"He sounds perfectly terrible," said Petrella.

"Such a statement, made outside these four walls," said Romer, "would involve you in very heavy damages for defamation. Captain Cree is a respectable, and a respected, citizen. One of his fondest interests is the Sark Lane Mission."

"The Sark Lane –"

"The name is familiar to you? It should be. The Mission was one of the first in Dockland, and it was founded by your old school."

"Of course. I remember now. We used to have a voluntary subscription of five shillings taken off us on the first day of every term. I don't think anyone took any further interest in it."

"I should imagine that one of the troubles of the Sark Lane Mission is that people have not taken enough interest in it. The Missioner for the last twenty-five years has been a Mr. Jacobson. A very good man in his way and, in his early years, energetic and successful. He retired last month, at the age of seventy-five.

"I should imagine that for the last ten

years his appearances at the Mission have been perfunctory. The place has really been kept going by an old ex-naval man named Batchelor – and by the regular munificence of Captain Cree."

"I see," said Petrella. But he felt that there must be something more to it than that.

"The appointment of the Missioner lies with the School Governors, but they act on the recommendation of the Bishop of London. Sometimes the post is filled by a clergyman. Sometimes not. On this occasion the recommended candidate was the Reverend Freebone."

"Philip Freebone!"

"The present incumbent of the Church of St. Peter and St. Paul, Highside. You know him, I believe?"

"Very well indeed. He started up at Highside as curate, and when the incumbent died he was left in charge. I can't imagine anyone who would do the job better."

"I can," said Romer.

When he had got over the shock, Petrella did not pretend not to understand him.

"I don't think I could get away with it, sir," he said. "Not for any length of time.

91

There'd be a hundred things I'd do wrong."

"I'm not suggesting that you should pose as a clergyman. You could go as *Mr.* Freebone. You've had some experience with youth clubs, I believe."

"For a few months before I joined the police, yes. I wasn't very successful."

"It may have been the wrong sort of club. I have a feeling you're going to be very successful in this one."

"Has Freebone been told?"

"He knows that he's got the job. He hasn't been told of the intended – er – rearrangement."

"I think you may have some difficulty there. Phil's one of the most obstinate people I know."

"I will have a word with his Bishop."

"I am afraid clergymen do not always do what their Bishops tell them these days," remarked Costorphine.

"This isn't a job on which we can afford to make a second mistake," continued Romer.

Petrella looked up.

"We got a man into the Consort Line about six months ago. It took some doing but we managed it without, as far as we

92

know, arousing any suspicions. He was engaged as an ordinary seaman, under the name of Mills. He made voyages on all three of the ships, and gave us very full but absolutely negative reports. He was on his way home a fortnight ago in the *Albert Consort,* and was reported as having deserted ship at Marseilles."

"And hasn't been seen since?"

"He's been seen," said Romer. "The French police found him in the foothills behind Marseilles two days ago. What was left of him. He'd been tortured before he was killed."

"I see," said Petrella.

"I'm telling you this so that, if you go in at all, you go in with your eyes wide open. This is an international crowd, who are calculating their profits in the millions. And who must be responsible, directly and indirectly, for hundreds of deaths a year. A single life is not of great importance."

"No," said Petrella. "I can quite see that ..."

A fortnight later the new Missioner came to the Sark Lane Mission. This was a rambling, two-story, yellow brick building in the style associated, through the East

End, with temperance and good works.

The street doors opened into a small lobby in which a notice said, in startling black letters, WIPE YOUR FEET. Someone had crossed out FEET and hopefully substituted a different part of the body. On the left of the lobby was a reception office, which was empty.

Beyond, you went straight into the main Mission room, which rose the full two-story height of the building and looked like a drill hall half-heartedly decorated for a dance. Dispirited red and white streamers hung from the iron cross-bars which spanned the roof. A poster on the far wall bore the message, in cotton wool letters, *"How will you spend Eternity?"*

At the far end of the hall three boys were throwing darts into a board. Superficially they all looked alike, with their white town faces, their thick dark hair, and their general air of having been alive a lot longer than anyone else.

When, later, Mr. Freebone got to know them, he realized that there were differences. The smallest and fattest was a lazy but competent boy called Ben. The next in height and age was Colin, a dull boy of 15, who came to life only on the football

94

field; but for football he had a remarkable talent, a talent which was already attracting the scouts from the big clubs, and was one day to put his name in the headlines.

The oldest and tallest of the boys was called Humphrey, and he had a long solemn face with a nose which started straight and turned to the right at the last moment, and a mouth like a crocodile's. It was not difficult to see that he was the leader of the three.

None of them took the slightest notice of Mr. Freebone as he padded across the scarred plank flooring to watch them.

In the end he said, "You're making an awful mess of that, aren't you?" He addressed this remark to the fat boy. "If you want fifteen and end on a double it's a waste of time going for one."

The boy gaped at him. Mr. Freebone took the darts from him and threw them. First a single three, then, at the second attempt, a double six.

"There you are, Ben," said the tall boy. "I told you to go for three." He transferred his gaze to Mr. Freebone. "You want Batchy?" he said.

"Batchy?" said Mr. Freebone. "Now who, or what, would that be?"

95

"Batchy's Batchelor."

This was even more difficult, but in the end he made it out. "You mean the caretaker. Is his name Batchelor?"

"'Sright. You want him, you'll find him in his room." He jerked his head toward the door at the far end of the building.

"Making himself a nice cupper," said Ben. "I once counted up how many cuppers Batchy drinks in a day. Guess how many? Seventeen."

"I'll be having a word with him soon, I expect," said Mr. Freebone. "Just for the moment I'm more interested in you. I'd better introduce myself. My name's Freebone. I'm the new Missioner."

"What's happened to old Jake?" said Ben. "I thought we hadden seen him round for a bit. He dead?"

"Now that's not nice, Ben," said the tall boy. "You don't say, 'Is he dead?' Not when you're talking to a clergyman. You say, 'Has he gone before?'"

"Clergyman or not," said Mr. Freebone, "I shouldn't use a ghastly expression like that. If I meant dead, I'd say dead. And Mr. Jacobson's not dead, anyway. He's retired. And I've got his job. Now I've told

96

you all about me, let's hear about you. First, what are your names?''

The boys regarded him warily. The man-to-man approach was not new to them. In their brief lives they had already met plenty of hearty young men who had expressed a desire to lead them onward and upward to better things.

In the end it was Humphrey who spoke. "I'm Humphrey," he said. "The thin one's Colin. The fat one's Ben. You like to partner Ben we'll play 301 up, double in, double out, for a bob a side."

"Middle for diddle," said Mr. Freebone.

At the end of the third game, at which point Mr. Freebone and Ben were each richer by three shillings. Humphrey announced without rancor that he was skinned and would have to go home and get some more money. The others decided to pack it up, too.

"I hope we'll see you here this evening," said the new Missioner genially, and went in search of the resident caretaker, Batchelor, whom he found, as predicted, brewing tea in his den at the back of the hall.

He greeted the new Missioner amiably enough.

"You got lodgings?" he said. "Mr. Jacobson lived up at Greenwich and came down every day. Most days, that is."

"I'm going to do better than that," said Mr. Freebone. "I'm going to live here."

"*Live* here? *Here?*"

"Why not? I'm told there are two rooms up there."

"Well, there *are* two rooms at the back. Gotter nice view of the factory. It's a long time since anyone lived in 'em."

"Here's someone going to start," said Mr. Freebone.

"There's a piler junk in 'em."

"If you'll lend me a hand, we'll move all the junk into one of the rooms for a start. I've got a camp bed with my luggage."

Batchelor gaped at him.

"You going to sleep here *tonight?*"

"I'm going to sleep here tonight and every night," said Mr. Freebone happily. "I'm going to sleep here and eat here and live here, just as long as they'll have me."

The next week was a busy one.

As soon as Batchelor saw that the new Missioner was set in his intention and immovable in his madness, he made the best of it, and turned to and lent a hand.

Mr. Freebone scrubbed and Batchelor scrubbed. Windows were opened which had not been opened in living memory. Paint arrived by the gallon.

Almost everyone fancies himself as a decorator, and as soon as the boys grasped that an ambitious program of interior decoration was on foot, they threw themselves into it with zeal. One purchased a pot of yellow paint, and painted, before he could be stopped, the entire outside of the porch.

Another borrowed a machine from his employer without his employer's knowledge and buffed up the planks of the main room so hard there was soon very little floor left. Another fell off the roof and broke his leg.

Thus was inaugurated Mr. Freebone's Mission at Sark Lane, a Mission which in retrospect grew into one of the oral traditions of the East End, until almost anything would be believed if it was prefaced with the words, "When ol' Freebone was at Sark Lane."

It was not, as his charges were quick to remark, that he was a particularly pious man, although the East End is one of the few places where saintliness is estimated at its true worth. Nor that he interested himself, as other excellent missioners had done, in the home life and commercial prospects of the boys in his care. It was simply that he lived in, with, and for the Mission. That, and a certain light-hearted ingenuity, allied to a curious thoroughness in the carrying out of his wilder plans.

The story will someday be told more fully of his Easter Scout Camp, a camp joined, on the first night, by three strange boys whose names had certainly not been on the original roll, and who turned out to be runaways from a Borstal institution – to whose comforts they hastily returned after experiencing, for a night and a day, the vigorous hospitality of the Sark Lane Scout Troop.

Nor would anyone who took part in it lightly forget the Great Scavenger Hunt which culminated in the simultaneous arrival at the Mission of a well-known receiver of stolen goods and the Flying Squad; or the Summer Endurance Test in the course of which a group of contestants set out to swim the Thames in full clothes and ended up in a debutante's Steamer Party. In which connection Humphrey claimed to be one of the few people who has danced, dripping wet, with a Royal personage.

Captain Cree turned up about a month after Mr. Freebone's arrival. The first intimation that he had a visitor was a hearty burst of bass laughter from the clubroom. Poking his head round the door he saw a big heavy figure, the upper half encased in a double-breasted blue jacket with brass buttons, the lower half in chalk-striped flannel trousers. The face that slewed round as he approached had been tanned by the weather to a deep russet and then transformed to a deeper red by some more cultivated alchemy.

"Mussen shock the parson," said Captain Cree genially. "Just showing the boys some pictures the Captain of the *William* picked up at Port Said on his last trip. You're Freebone, arnchew? I'm pleased to meet you."

He pushed out a big hand, grasped Mr. Freebone's, and shook it heartily.

"I've heard a lot about you," said Mr. Freebone.

"Nothing to my credit, I bet," said Captain Cree, with a wink at the boys.

"I know that you're a very generous donor to the Mission," said Mr. Freebone,

101

"and you're very welcome to come and go here as you like."

Captain Cree looked surprised. It had perhaps not occurred to him that he needed anyone's permission to come and go as he liked. He said, "Well, I call that handsome. I got a bit of stuff for you outside. The *William* picked it up for me in Alex. I've got it outside in the station wagon. You two nip out and give my monkeys a hail and we'll get it stowed."

Humphrey and Ben departed, and returned escorting two sailors, dressed in blue jerseys, with the word *Clarissa* in red stitching straggling across the front.

"Dump 'em in there, David," said Captain Cree to the young black-haired sailor. "There's a half gross of plimsolls, some running vests, a couple of footballs, and two pairs of foils. You put them down, Humphrey. I'm giving 'em to the Mission, not to you. Where'd you like 'em stowed?"

"In the back room, for the moment, I think," said Mr. Freebone. "Hey – Batchelor."

"Old Batchy still alive?" said Captain Cree. "I thought he'd have drunk himself to death long ago. How are you, Batchy?"

"Fine, Captain Cree, fine, thank you,"

said the old man, executing a sketchy naval salute.

"If you've finished stewing up tea for yourself, you might give a hand to get these things under hatches. You leave 'em out here a moment longer, they'll be gone. I know these boys."

When the Captain had left, Mr. Freebone had a word with Humphrey and Ben, who were now his first and second lieutenants in most club activities.

"He's given us a crate of stuff," said Humphrey.

"Crates and crates," agreed Ben. "Footballs, jerseys, dart boards. Once he brought us a couple of what's-its – those bamboo things – you know, with steel tips. You throw 'em."

"Javelins?"

"That's right. *They* didn't last long. Old Jake took 'em away after Colin threw one at young Arthur Whaley."

"Who were the sailors?"

"The big one, he's Ron Blanden. He used to be a boy round here. The other one's David," Ben explained. "He'd be off one of the ships. Old Cree gets boys for his ships from round here, and when they've done a trip or two, maybe he gives 'em a job on the *Clarissa*. That's his own boat."

"I see," said Mr. Freebone.

"He offered to take me on, soon as I'm old enough," said Humphrey.

"Are you going to say yes?"

Humphrey's long face creased into a grin. "Not me," he said. "I'm keeping my feet dry. Besides, he's a crook."

"He's a what?"

"A crook."

"He can't just be *a* crook," said Mr. Freebone patiently. "He must be some sort of crook. What does he do?"

"I dunno," said Humphrey. "But it sticks out he's a crook, or he wouldn't have so much money. Eh, Ben?"

Ben agreed this was correct. He usually agreed with Humphrey.

Later that night Mr. Freebone and Batchelor sorted out the new gifts. The foils were really nice pairs, complete with masks and gauntlets. Mr. Freebone, who was himself something of a swordsman, took them up to his own room to examine them at leisure. The gym shoes were a good brand, with thick rubber soles. They should be very useful. Boys in these parts wore gym shoes almost all day.

"We usually wash out the vests and things," said Batchelor. "You know what foreigners are like."

Mr. Freebone approved the precaution. He said he knew what foreigners were like. Batchelor said he would wash them through next time he had a boil-up in his copper . . .

A fortnight later – in the last week of May – the officer on the monitored telephone in the basement at New Scotland Yard received a call. The call came at six o'clock in the evening, and the caller announced himself as Magnus.

The officer said, "Count five slowly, please. Then start talking." He put out his hand and pressed down the switch. The tape recorder whirred softly as the man at the other end spoke. Later that evening Romer came down to the Yard and listened to the playback. The voice came, thin and resonant, but clear.

"Magnus here. This is my first report. I've settled into my new job. I feel little real doubt that what we suspect is correct but it's difficult to see just how the trick is pulled.

"The *Clarissa* meets all incoming *Consorts*. She takes out miscellaneous

105

stores and usually fetches back a load of gear for the Mission. It must be the best equipped outfit in London. The customs experts give the stuff the magic-eye treatment before it's put on the *Clarissa*, and I've managed to look through most of it myself. Once it's in the Mission it's handed straight over to the boys, so it's a bit difficult to see how it could be used as a hiding place.

"Cocaine's not bulky, I know; but I gather the quantities we're looking for are quite considerable. I have a feeling this line in sports goods might be a big red herring. Something to take our eye off the real job.

"Carter, the mate of the *Clarissa*, is, I think, an ex-convict. His real name is Coster, and he's been down a number of times for larceny and aggravated assault. He carries a gun. Nothing known about the crew.

"Captain Cree" – here the tape gave a rasping scratch – "Sorry. That was me clearing my throat. As I was saying, Captain Cree's a smart operator. I should think he makes a good bit on the side out of his chandlering, but not nearly enough to account for the style he lives in. You'd imagine a man like him would keep a little woman tucked away somewhere, wouldn't you? But I never heard any whisper about the fair sex. A pity. We might get a woman to talk. That's all for now."

The weather was hot and dry that summer, and through July and August increasing supplies of illicit cocaine continued to dribble into London as water through a rotten sluice gate; and the casualty figures and the crime graphs climbed, hand in hand with the mercury in the thermometer. Superintendent Costorphine's face grew so long and so bleak that Romer took to avoiding him. For all the comfort he could give him was that things would probably get worse before they got better.

At Sark Lane, Mr. Freebone was working an eighteen-hour day. Added to his other preoccupations was an outbreak of skin disease. The boys could not be prevented from bathing in the filthy reaches and inlets of the Thames below Tower Bridge.

When he could spare a minute from his routine work he seemed to cultivate the company of the crew of the *Clarissa*. Carter was surly and unapproachable, but the boys were pleasant enough. Ron Blanden was a burly fair-haired young man of 20. He had ideas beyond the river and talked of leaving the *Clarissa* and joining the Merchant Navy.

David, the young black-haired one, seemed to be a natural idler, with few ideas beyond taking life easy, picking up as much money as he could, and dressing in his smartest clothes on his evenings off. He once told Mr. Freebone that he came from Scotland, but his eyes and hair suggested something more Mediterranean in origin. There was a theory that he had been in bad trouble once, in his early youth, and was now living it down.

Mr. Freebone had no difficulty, in time, in extracting the whole of the candid Ron Blanden's life story, but David, though friendly, kept his distance. All he would say – and this was a matter of record – was that he had made one trip on the *Albert Consort* that April, and had then been offered a job by Captain Cree which he had accepted.

"I don't like that David," said Batchelor one evening.

"Oh? Why?" said Mr. Freebone.

"He's a bad sort of boy," said Batchelor. "I've caught him snooping round this place

108

once or twice lately. Fiddling round with the sports kit. I soon sent him packing."

"Hm," said Mr. Freebone. He changed the subject somewhat abruptly. "By the way, Batchelor, there's something I've been meaning to ask you. How much do we pay you?"

"Four pounds a week, and keep."

"And what does Captain Cree add to that?"

The old man stirred in his chair and blinked. "Who said he added anything?"

"I heard it."

"He pays me a pound or two, now and then. Nothing regular. I do jobs for him. Anything wrong with that?"

Magnus had fallen into the routine of reporting at the appointed hour on every second Wednesday. Toward the end of September his message was brief and contained a request. "Could you check up on the old boy who acts as caretaker at the Mission? He calls himself Batchelor and claims to be ex-R.N. I don't believe that's his real name and I don't believe he was ever in the Navy. Let me know through the usual channels and urgently."

Costorphine said to Romer, "Something's brewing down there. My contracts all tell me the same story. The suppliers are expecting a big autumn run."

Romer made a small helpless gesture. "And are we going to be able to stop it?" he asked.

"We can always hope," said Costorphine. "I'll find out about that man Batchelor. Jacobson will know something about him. He took him on, I believe."

It was a week later that Humphrey said to Mr. Freebone, apropos of nothing that had gone before, "He's a character, that David, all right."

"What's he up to now?" said Mr. Freebone, between gasps, for he was busy blowing up a batch of new footballs.

"Wanted to cut me in one a snide racket."

Mr. Freebone stopped what he was doing, put the football down, and said, "Come on. Let's have it."

"David told me he can get hold of plenty of fivers. Good-looking jobs, he said. The *Clarissa* picks 'em up from the Dutch and German boats. He had some story they were a lot the Gestapo had printed during the war. Is that right?"

"I believe they did. But they'd be the old white sort."

"That's right. That's why he wanted help passing 'em. If he turned up with a lot of 'em, it'd look suspicious. But if some of us boys helped him –"

In a rage Mr. Freebone sought out Captain Cree, who listened to him with surprising patience.

"Half those lads are crooks," he said, when the Missioner had finished. "You can't stop it."

"I'm not going to have your crew corrupting my boys," said Mr. Freebone. "And I look to you to help me stop it."

"What do you want me to do? Sack David?"

Mr. Freebone said, "I don't know that that would do a lot of good. But he's not to come near the Mission."

"I'll sort him out," said the Captain. He added, "You know, what you want's a holiday. You've had a basinful of us since you came, and you haven't had a day off in six months that I can see."

"As a matter of fact," said Mr. Freebone, "I was thinking of taking a long weekend soon."

"You do that," said the Captain. "Tell

me when you're going and I'll keep an eye on the place for you myself."

He sounded almost paternal.

"This is report number thirteen," said the tape-recorded voice of Magnus. "I hope that doesn't make it unlucky. I had a narrow escape the other day, but managed to ride the Captain off. I'm bound to say that, in my view, things are coming to a head. Just how it's going to break I don't know, but some sort of job is being planned for next weekend. Cree and Carter have been thick as thieves about it.

"Talking about thieves, I was glad to hear that my hunch about Batchelor was correct, and that he had been inside. There's something about an old lag that never washes off. It was interesting, too, that he worked at one time in a chemist's shop and had done a bit of dispensing in his youth. All he dispenses openly now are cups of vile tea. That's all for now. I hope to be on the air again in a fortnight's time with some real news for you."

Costorphine said, "That ties in with what I'd heard. A big consignment, quite soon."

"We'd better put the cover plan into

operation," said Romer.

"You've got two police boats on call. Whistle them up now."

"A police launch would be a bit outgunned by the *Clarissa*. I've arranged a tie-up with the Navy. There's a launch standing by at Greenwich. We can have her up when we want her. Only we can't keep her hanging about for long – she's too conspicuous.

"I've got an uneasy feeling about this," said Romer. "They're not fools, the people we're dealing with. They wouldn't walk into anything obvious."

"Do you think Petrella –?"

"You've got to admit he's been lucky," said Romer. "It was luck that the job was going, and luck that we managed to get it for him. And he's done very well, too. But luck can't last forever. It only needs one person to recognize him – one criminal he's ever had to deal with, and he must have had hundreds through his hands in the last few years."

"He'll be all right," said Costorphine. "He's a smart lad."

"I'm superstitious," said Romer. "I don't mean about things like black cats and ladders. I mean about making bargains with fortune. You remember when we were talking about this thing in here, way back in March, I said something about a single life not being important. It might be true; but I wish I hadn't said it, all the same."

Costorphine confided to his wife that night, "It's the first time I've ever seen the old man jumpy. Things must be bad. Perhaps the politicians are after him."

That Saturday night there were about two dozen boys in the clubroom of the Mission, and it says a lot for the enthusiasm engendered by Mr. Freebone that there was anyone there at all, for if ever there was a night for fireside and television this was it. The wind had started to get up with the dusk and was now blowing in great angry gusts, driving the rain in front of it.

At half-past four Captain Cree, faithful to his promise, had come up to keep an eye on things in the Missioner's absence. There had been nothing much for him to do, and he had departed for the dock where the *Clarissa* lay. Now, through the dark and the rain, he drove his big station wagon carefully back, once more, through the empty streets, and maneuvered it into the unlighted cul-de-sac beside the Mission Hall.

Carter, a big unlovely lump of a man, was sitting beside him, smoking one of an endless chain of cigarettes. This time Captain Cree did not trouble with the front entrance. There was a small side door, which gave onto a dark lobby. Out of the lobby bare wooden stairs ran up to Mr. Freebone's bedroom; on the far side a door opened through to Batchelor's sanctum.

Captain Cree stood in the dark empty lobby, his head bent. He was listening. Anyone glimpsing his good-natured red face at that particular moment might have been shocked by the expression on it.

At the end of a full minute he relaxed, went back to the street door, and signaled to Carter. The back of the station wagon was opened and the first of four big bales was lifted out and humped indoors. The bolt of the outer door was shot.

Batchelor was waiting for them. Everything about him showed that he, too, knew that some crisis was impending.

"You locked the door?" said Captain Cree. He jerked his head at the door which led into the Mission Hall.

"Of course I locked it," said Batchelor. "We don't want a crowd of boys in here. How many have you got?"

"Four," said Carter. He was the coolest of the three.

"We'll do 'em all now," said Captain Cree. "It'll take a bit of time, but we won't get a better chance than this. When's *he* coming back?" An upward jerk of his head indicated that he was talking about the occupant of the back attic.

"Sunday midday, he said. Unless he changed his mind."

"He'd better not change it," said Carter.

He helped Batchelor to strip the thick brown-paper wrapping from one of the bales. As the covering came away the contents could be seen to be woolens, half a gross of thick woolen vests. In the second there was half a gross of long pants. Gray socks in the third. Gloves and balaclava helmets and scarves in the fourth.

Carter waddled across to the enormous gas-operated copper in the corner and lifted the lid. A fire had been lit under it earlier in the afternoon and was now glowing red; the copper was full of clean hot water.

What followed would have interested Superintendent Costorphine intensely. He would have realized how it is possible to bring cocaine into the country under the noses of the smartest customs officials, and he would have appreciated just why those samples might contain minute traces of copper.

The three men worked as a team, with the skill born of long practise. Carter dumped the woolens by handfuls in the copper. Captain Cree took them out and wrung each one carefully into a curious contraption which Batchelor had pulled from a closet. Basically this was a funnel, with a drip tray underneath. But between funnel and tray was a fine linen gauze filter. And as the moisture was wrung from each garment a grayish sediment formed on the filter.

When the filter was so full that it was in danger of becoming clogged the Captain called a halt. From a suitcase he extracted an outsize thermos bottle, and into it, with the greatest possible care, he deposited the gray sediment.

It took them over an hour to go through the first three packages. During this time the water in the copper had itself been emptied and filtered, and the copper refilled. Twice during this time a boy had rattled on the door that led into the hall and

Batchelor had shouted back that he was busy.

"Tip the last lot in," said the Captain, "and be quick about it." They were all three sweating. "We don't want anyone busting in on us now."

He had never handled such a large quantity before. The third bottle was in use. Two were already full. He had his back to the door leading to the lobby and none of them heard or saw it open.

"What on earth are you all up to?" said Mr. Freebone.

The three men swung round in one ugly savage movement. The plastic cap of the bottle fell from Captain Cree's hand and rolled across the floor.

"What is it – washing day?"

There was a silence of paralysis as Mr. Freebone walked across the room and peered down into the bottle. "And what's this stuff?"

"What – where have you come from?" said Captain Cree hoarsely.

"I've been up in my room, writing," said Mr. Freebone. "I changed my mind and came back. Do I have to ask your permission?" He extended one finger, touched the gray powder in the bottle, and carried his finger to his lips.

Then Carter hit him. It was a savage blow, delivered from behind, with a leather-covered sap, a blow which Mr. Freebone neither saw nor heard.

They stared at him.

"You killed him?" said Batchelor.

"Don't be a damned fool," said Carter. He looked at Captain Cree. The same thought was in both their minds.

"We shall want some rope," he said. "Have you got any?"

"I don't know –"

"Go on. Get it."

It took five minutes to truss up Mr. Freebone. He was showing no signs of life, even while they manhandled him out and dumped him in the back of the station wagon.

Captain Cree seemed to have recovered his composure.

"You stay here and watch him," he said to Carter.

"Are we going to gag him?"

"I think that would be a mistake," said the Captain. "Leave too many traces." They looked at each other again. The thought was as clear now as if it had been spoken. "If he opens his mouth hit him again."

Carter nodded, and the Captain disappeared into the building. In half an hour the job was finished and he came out carrying a suitcase.

"Not a blink," said Carter.

The Captain placed the suitcase carefully in the back of the car, where it rested on the crumpled body of Mr. Freebone. Then he climbed into the driving seat, backed the car out, and started on the half-mile drive to Pagett's Wharf, where the *Clarissa* lay.

The wind, risen almost to gale force, was flogging the empty streets with its lash, part rain, part hail, as the big car nosed its way slowly across the cobbles of the wharf.

Captain Cree turned off the lights and climbed out, followed by Carter. Twenty yards away, in the howling wilderness of darkness, a single riding light showed where the *Clarissa* bumped at her moorings. At there feet the river slid past, cold and black.

The Captain said into Carter's ear. "We'll take the rope off him first. I put 'em on over his clothes so they won't have left much mark. If he's found, what's to show he didn't slip and knock his head going in?"

"*If* he's found," said Carter.

Back at the mission, Batchelor was facing a mutiny.

"What've you been up to, locked in here all evening?" said Humphrey. "That was the Captain's car in the alley, wasn't it?"

"That's right," said Ben.

"And what've you done with Mr. Freebone?"

"He ent here," said Batchelor. "And you can get out of my room too, all of you."

"Where is he?"

"He went away for the weekend. He'll be back tomorrow."

As soon as he had said this, Batchelor realized his mistake.

"Don't be soft," said Humphrey. "He came back after tea. We saw him. Pop upstairs, Ben, and see if he's in his room."

"You've got no right –" said Batchelor. But they were past taking any notice of what he said.

"And what were you doing with all those clothes?" He pointed at the sodden pile in the corner. "Is this washing night or something?"

Batchelor was saved answering by the reappearance of Ben. "He's been there," he said. "The light's on. And there's a letter on the table he was finishing writing. *And* his raincoat's there."

"He wouldn't go out without a coat," said Humphrey. "Not on a night like this. He's been took."

Here Batchelor made his second mistake. He broke for the door. Several pairs of hands caught him and threw him back ungently into the chair. For the moment, after the scuffle, there was silence and stillness.

Then Humphrey said, "I guess they were up to something. And I guess Mr. Freebone came back when he wasn't expected. And I guess the Captain and Carter and that lot have picked him up."

"So that's all you can do, guess," said Batchelor viciously. But the fear in his voice could be felt.

"All right," said Humphrey calmly. "Maybe I'm wrong. You tell us." Batchelor stared at him. Humphrey said, "Is that water hot, Ben?"

Ben dipped the tip of his finger in and took it out again quickly.

Humphrey said, "Either you talk or we hold you head-down in that."

It took six of them to get him halfway

122

across the floor. Batchelor stopped cursing and started to scream. When his nose was six inches away from the water he talked.

"Pagett's Wharf," said Humphrey. "All right. We'll lock him up in here. If he's lying to us, we'll come back and finish him off afterwards."

"How do we get there?" said one of the boys.

"Night like this," said Humphrey, "the quickest way to get anywhere's to run."

The pack streamed out into the howling darkness.

In the big foredeck cabin of the *Clarissa,* Captain Cree was giving some final instructions to Carter when he heard the shout. Carter jumped across to the cabin door and pulled it open.

"Who's out there?" said the Captain.

"Ron's on deck," said Carter. "David's ashore somewhere."

"Who was that shouted?"

"It sounded like Ron," said Carter.

This was as far as he got. The next moment a wave of boys seemed to rise out of the darkness. Carter had time to shout before something hit him, and he went down.

The attack passed into the cabin. Captain

Cree got his hand to a gun, but he had no time to fire it. Humphrey, swinging an iron bar which he had picked up on deck, broke Cree's arm with a vicious side swipe. The gun dropped from his fingers.

"Pull him in," said Humphrey. "Both of them."

Captain Cree, his right arm swinging loosely in front of him, his red face mottled with white, held himself up with his sound hand on the table.

Carter lay on the floor at his feet, and Ben kicked him, as hard and as thoughtlessly as you might kick a football. The boys had tasted violence and victory that night, and it had made them drunker than any strong drink.

"There's one thing can keep you alive," said Humphrey. "And that's Mr. Freebone. Where is he?"

For a count of ten there was silence. The Captain's mouth worked, but no sound came out of it.

Almost gently Humphrey said, "So you dropped him in the river. He's going to have three for company. Right?"

That was right. That was the way things were done in the land of violence and hot blood. Humphrey swung his iron bar delicately.

"You can't," said the Captain. "You can't do it. I'll tell you everything. I'll do what you like. There's ten thousand pounds' worth of cocaine in that suitcase. It's yours for the taking."

"We'll pour it in after you," said Humphrey. "It'll be useful where you're going."

"You can't do it –"

"Who's stopping us?"

"I am," said a voice from behind them. The third member of the *Clarissa*s crew, David, stepped through the door into the cabin.

He was drenched with rain and out of breath from running; but there was something about him which held all their eyes.

"How –"

"It'll save a lot of time and trouble," said David, "if I tell you that I'm a police officer. My name, not that it matters, is Petrella. I'm a Sergeant in the plainclothes branch, and I'm taking these three men into custody."

"But," said Humphrey, "they've killed Mr. Freebone."

"They meant to kill him," said Petrella. "No doubt of it. But there've been two police launches lying off this wharf ever since dusk, and one of them picked him up. He's at Leman Street Police Station, and from what he's told me we've got more than enough to send both these men away for life. So don't let's spoil a good thing now."

There was a bump at the side of the boat as the River Police tender hitched on alongside. The first man into the cabin was Superintendent Costorphine, looking like a bedraggled crow. He pounced on the suitcase.

"Three months' supply for London," said Petrella. "It'll need a bit more drying out, but it's all there . . ."

Later Petrella found Philip Freebone propped up on pillows in St. George's Hospital, where he had been taken under protest and deposited for the night.

"There's nothing wrong with me," he said. "I'd just as soon be back in my bed at the Mission. There's a lot to do. I shall have to find a replacement for Batchelor."

"Are you going on with that job?"

Freebone looked surprised. "Of course I am," he said. "I've enjoyed it. I knew I would. That's why I wouldn't let you do it."

"The trouble is," said Petrella, "that you've set yourself too high a standard. The boys will never have another night like tonight as long as they live. Do you realize that if I hadn't turned up, they really were going to knock Captain Cree off and put him and Carter over the side?"

"Yes, I expect they would." Freebone thought about it and added, "It's rather a compliment, really, isn't it? What are you going to do now, Patrick?"

"Take a holiday," said Detective Sergeant Petrella. "A good long holiday."

ROBERT EDWARD ECKELS

Attention to Detail

A now-it-can-be-told story – how in 1942 a single enemy agent invaded the United States on the most important mission of the war . . .

The U-boat lay low in the water, its decks almost awash, and shrouded by night fog so thick that from the conning tower even the outline of the forward gun was hazy and indistinct. But only fools lingered on the surface so close to danger, and by the time Steiner came up on deck the crew had already got the rubber raft inflated and over the side.

Steiner found himself shivering – and not from the damp. From excitement. Because less than a hundred yards beyond the fog bank lay the enemy coast – Long Island – and no one in the six months that the U.S. had been in the war had got closer. Not yet anyway.

Arrogantly he looked up toward the conning tower where Prien and the captain were stationed and smiled sardonically. Prien was all right – a good party man. But the captain – Still smiling, Steiner saluted them both, knowing it would infuriate the captain but that he would respond punctiliously anyway.

Beside him, one of the sailors said, "All ready."

The "sir" was omitted deliberately, Steiner knew, but he didn't say anything. The two sailors who would row him were already in the raft. Steiner cast one last glance at the occupants of the conning tower, then let himself be lowered into the bobbing boat. As it began to make way, one of the sailors still on deck knelt to pay out the line that would haul it and its crew back through the surf after Steiner had been safely put ashore.

Steiner sat stiffly in the rear of the raft. He was no boatman and now, as the fog closed in, the confidence he had felt back on deck ebbed fast. He was frightened by the pitching and tossing, and, worse, he knew, showing it.

Then, almost before he was aware of what was happening, a wave larger than the rest shot them forward dizzyingly. Steiner opened his mouth to shout, but no sound came. Then suddenly the water was foaming back away from them and somehow, miraculously, they were ashore. In almost blind panic he scrambled out of the boat and up above the wave line.

The two sailors watched him impassively, waiting until he had got control of himself again. One of them tossed him the waterproof bag with his American clothes, then both sailors dragged the boat back into the surf.

Steiner made no move to help them. They could drown for all he cared. The clods. His was the important mission, and only he could accomplish it. The Commandant himself had said as much back at the training camp.

"The reports are uniformly excellent," Reinboldt had said. "Which in a way, of course, is only to be expected since you were well screened before you were selected. But even so, your progress in response to the training has been much faster than any of us anticipated."

"Thank you," Steiner said quietly. He sat at ease across from the Commandant's desk, behavior unthinkable under any other circumstances, but insisted on here as an

130

essential part of his "Americanization."

"As a result," Reinboldt went on as if uninterrupted, "the Fuhrer has decided to move your mission forward. You will leave for the United States next week. Your targets remain unchanged, of course. First Roosevelt, then Marshall." Reinboldt paused to light a cigarette. "I don't have to tell you the consequences of success," he said. "Or of failure."

Steiner smiled faintly. "I won't fail," he said.

"No," Reinboldt said, "you won't." He took an envelope from his desk and passed it across to the other man. "Your cover has been well prepared. These are the documents you will need to start: driver's license, draft registration – deferred status, of course – Social Security number and all the other paraphernalia Americans seem to find indispensable."

Steiner looked at the papers approvingly. All had a slightly worn look as if they'd been carried about in a man's wallet for some time, and included among them was a certified copy of a birth certificate indicating he had been born in Milwaukee, Wisconsin, on October 14, 1918. It was, he reflected, his real birthday.

"Your name," Reinboldt went on, "was chosen with equal care – Frederick William Johnson. Frederick William because it's close to your own and thus, like the birth date, easy to remember. Johnson because it's one of the most common American names but yet not suspect like Smith or Jones. You should practise writing it until your signature flows naturally."

"I will," Steiner said.

"We have also arranged for you to be given $10,000 in various denominations of American currency. Used carefully it should be more than enough. One word of caution, though. For security reasons it was necessary to obtain the bills from sources solely within the Reich and the larger denominations are from a single shipment received by the Berliner Kreditanstalt in 1932. Ten years is a long time, but the serial numbers are consecutive, and it would be less than wise to assume that no record exists by which they could be traced. For safety's sake spend or exchange them in different places and where you are not known or likely to return."

Steiner smiled wryly. "You don't overlook anything, do you?"

Reinboldt didn't return the smile. "The

secret of success," he said, "is attention to detail. Remember it. It pays."

It did, indeed, Steiner thought, shivering purely from the cold now as he stripped to change from his submariner's uniform to his American clothes. It was a pity, though, that all that careful planning hadn't taken the American climate into account and provided some sort of heating arrangement.

Or perhaps it had been considered. Steiner smiled to himself as he pulled his trousers on. It would be just like Reinboldt to have thought of it and then discarded the idea on the theory that the cold would drive his man to work faster. And in any case Steiner did finish quickly, stuffing the discarded uniform into the bag and then carrying it down to bury it below the wave line where the lapping water would erase the last traces of digging. The small shovel – a child's toy really, he simply discarded several yards farther down the beach where it would appear just another piece of holiday litter.

Now all he had to do was head inland away from the water. Here the fog – great gray billows that reduced visibility to a matter of yards at most – was a complicating factor. But he had his compass and even if he did drift slightly off course, sooner or later he was bound to hit the rail line that ran parallel to the coast for miles in both directions. Then it was just a matter of following the tracks to the next town and picking up the first train out in the morning.

All the more then was his surprise when he stumbled onto the dog halfway across the beach.

It was a shepherd dog, not yet fully grown, running free but trailing a leash. It stopped, hackles rising, when it saw Steiner and for a moment man and animal eyed each other warily. Then Steiner began to edge around it, careful to keep the distance constant and his eyes steady on the dog's. The dog continued to bristle but didn't move. Steiner began to breathe easier.

Then he heard the voice calling out of the fog, "Rex! Rex! Where are you, boy?"

The dog hesitated, distracted momentarily by its master's voice; then as Steiner reached too quickly for his gun the dog launched itself straight at him.

Steiner forgot the gun and ducked down instead to grab the leaping animal's extended forepaws and jerk them violently apart.

The dog died instantly. Steiner let it fall, then crouched beside its dead form, his hand tight on the gun again. The voice was more urgent now and coming closer.

"Rex! Rex!"

Go back, you fool, Steiner thought. Go back!

But he came on, first the glow of his light visible through the murk, then the man himself. He was young – in his early twenties, and wearing a blue sailor's uniform but with military leggings and web belting. As far as Steiner could see, though, he wasn't armed, and Steiner rose slowly to face him.

"What's going on here?" the sailor said. His flashlight picked up the dog's limp body. "Rex?" He bent over the dog. "My God, what happened?"

Steiner struck swiftly, smashing the gun into the base of the sailor's skull. The man dropped like a stone. Steiner hit him twice more to make sure, then felt for the carotid pulse. There was none.

Steiner knelt beside the dead sailor. He felt no remorse or regret, only annoyance that this might complicate his mission. The bodies were bound to be discovered and that would bring questions about who and why that Steiner didn't want raised. Or maybe not. Maybe he could confuse the issue at least long enough to let him get clear, and that was all he really needed.

The trigger guard on the gun had bent slightly under the force of his blow and there was a smear of blood along the underside of the barrel. Steiner wiped it clean on the sailor's blouse before tucking the gun back under his jacket. Then catching hold of the man's body under the arms he dragged it down into the surf, soaking himself in the process and losing his sense of direction so that he wasted ten precious minutes searching for the dog.

But luck was still with him, and finally he found it. The dog wasn't a heavy animal and there was no blood. He picked it up in his arms and carried it into the woods beyond the beach, hiding the animal's body under a pile of rotting underbrush. The leash and collar he took with him to throw into a field on the other side of the railroad tracks.

By then his clothes had begun to dry and he felt more himself again. It helped too when he found a town sooner than he had expected. The train station was closed for the night, but there was a convenient patch of woods across from it. Steiner found himself a spot near the middle where he was sure he couldn't be seen, put his back up against a tree, and closed his eyes . . .

He awoke to find it full light, the sun already high enough to have burned off the last traces of the night's fog. That confused him, because even exhausted as he'd been, the noise and clatter of trains arriving and leaving should have awakened him. Even more confusing, though, was the station itself. It should have been crowded with commuters headed for the city, but in fact it looked as deserted now as it had the night before.

Steiner watched the station quietly for several more minutes, then got up cautiously and went over to investigate. It was deserted. The door was locked and the ticket window shuttered, but there tacked up on the wall beside it was the schedule: 5:18, 5:45, 6:14, 6:40, and so on up to 8:13, then every hour thereafter.

Steiner looked at his watch: 8:05. And that was the right local time – he'd set it himself on the U-boat from a New York radio station they had monitored. But 8:05 became 8:30 and then 8:35 and still no train appeared.

Steiner began to sweat. What had gone wrong? A breakdown on the line? Or something worse? Something that had to do with a body on the beach – and with him?

He was still trying to make up his mind when he heard someone approaching up the path from the town, whistling as he came. Steiner hesitated, then stepped back carefully against the wall in case the whistling wasn't as innocent as it sounded.

Moments later a tall thin-shouldered man with a bony young-old face came around the corner of the building. The man stopped whistling when he saw Steiner but otherwise went on about his business, pulling out a large key and unlocking the door.

Steiner tried to follow him in, but the man shook his head. "Station's closed. Buy your ticket on the train."

It hadn't been covered in his training, but Steiner reacted the way he thought an American would. "What the hell happened to the 8:13?" he demanded.

The stationmaster looked at him

138

impassively, then tapped the tacked-up schedule. "Memorial Day, mister," he said. "Same schedule as Sundays." He went on inside, closing the door after him.

Steiner almost laughed with relief. There was nothing wrong after all. It was just a holiday. It would be a good joke to share with Reinboldt when it was all over – assuming Reinboldt was ever in a joking mood. In any case, his good humor restored, he turned back to the schedule, this time noting the smaller one at the bottom, the one for Sundays and holidays.

The train was at 10:23 – less than two hours. Too long just to hang around the station, though, and to kill the time he strolled casually down into the town itself.

It was a pleasant little place, especially in the quiet of a holiday morning, and Steiner decided he might like to come back sometime – on vacation after the war perhaps – when he would have the leisure to really enjoy it. Now, however, he was content to stroll about, until the sight of an open restaurant reminded him he hadn't eaten since the day before. Suddenly ravenous, he went in.

It wasn't crowded and he had no difficulty picking a booth near the rear where he could watch the entrance without being seen himself. The varied bill of fare astounded him, and he ordered heavily: hot cakes, eggs, sausages, and coffee – real coffee. It was almost as if there were no war. They'd learn differently quickly enough, but for the moment, Steiner reflected, the plentiful food was there to enjoy, and he ate with gusto, remembering, at the last minute to cut with his right hand and then transfer the fork to eat. That, strangely enough, pleased him more than anything else.

The good feeling died quickly, though, when a policeman came in and headed toward him. He was a big man in his mid-fifties with a lined weatherbeaten face and a heavy gun worn butt forward on his right hip. Automatically Steiner's own hand slid under the table to close over the gun beneath his jacket. But then the other man pulled out a chair and sat down at a table across the aisle, refusing the menu the waitress proffered.

"Just coffee, Sal."

Steiner took his hand off his gun.

"I guess that was some excitement down at the beach this morning," the waitress said.

The policeman looked up at her wryly.

"Well, now, word sure does get around fast, doesn't it?" he said.

The waitress shrugged. "Well, you know," she said, "small town and all that. One of the Coast Guard boys, wasn't it?"

Steiner stiffened. So the tide hadn't taken the body out after all. He cursed himself for a fool for having wasted the night. If he'd kept on, even hiking, he'd have been well clear by now instead of sitting here possibly trapped and, being obviously a stranger, suspect.

"Got himself killed, didn't he?" the waitress said.

"Something like that," the policeman said. "You can read all about it in the paper tonight. Now, how about that coffee?"

"Sure," the waitress said. She wasn't the least offended and poured the coffee nonchalantly. "While I think about it, Charley's looking for you. He picked up some Indianheads he wants you to look at."

"I'll stop by on my way out," the policeman said. He picked up his cup, then, leaning back in his chair, looked around casually, stopping as his eye caught Steiner's. "New around here, aren't you?" he said.

Steiner's hand started to glide back toward the gun.

"Come up for the fishing?" the policeman said.

Steiner's hand stopped. "Yes," he said, picking up the cue easily. "Yes, of course."

The policeman nodded slowly. "Seems half of New York comes out these days," he said. "Don't know where they get the gas. Still, you've got a nice day for it."

"Yes," Steiner said. "A very nice day." He turned back to his food. Half of New York! An exaggeration, of course. But still it meant a crowd of strangers among whom he could safely lose himself.

Deliberately he finished the last of his breakfast, then signaled the waitress for his check. The policeman, Steiner noted with satisfaction, had lost all interest in him – had in fact taken his coffee forward and was chatting earnestly with the cashier, presumably about those Indianheads.

American fashion, the waitress left his check face down on the table. It came to $1.70, and feeling generous Steiner tossed two of Reinboldt's one-dollar bills on the table to cover the amount plus tip, then sauntered out.

He was halfway down the street when

he heard someone calling after him.

"You! Hey, you!"

He paused and looked back. The policeman had followed him out and was striding toward him now, holding something in his hand.

Fear rose like a hot flood in Steiner's throat. Because even at this distance he could recognize what it was – the two bills he'd left. Without really thinking what he was doing he began to run.

He heard the shout behind him, full of surprise, then the pounding footsteps, and ran faster. Then as suddenly as he had begun he stopped and swung around, pulling the gun out smoothly and dropping down onto one knee to steady his aim.

Caught off guard, the policeman threw himself desperately to one side, clawing – much too late – for his own gun. Steiner tracked him expertly. His finger tightened on the trigger.

It moved a fraction of an inch, then jammed, and the last thing Steiner remembered before the policeman's bullet smashed all thought in him forever was the bent trigger guard and Reinboldt saying. "Attention to detail . . ."

"Who was he actually?" the reporter said.

"No way to tell for sure," the policeman said. It was much later, and they sat together over coffee in that same small restaurant. "The address on his driver's license was a phony, and none of his other papers checked out either. The Coast Guard thinks he might have come in off a U-boat because of that murdered beach-pounder, but there's no way to prove it."

The policeman's weatherbeaten face looked even more leathery than usual. "Funny thing, though, all I really wanted to do was ask him about the money. Money's my hobby, you know."

"Mine too," the reporter said, grinning.

"No, I mean seriously. Old coins, old bills – that sort of thing. And here was somebody paying a restaurant check with two practically mint-condition greenbacks. Of course," he added ruefully, "anybody would have spotted it. Hell, those old big bills have been out of circulation for close to eight or nine years now – ever since Roosevelt took us off the Gold Standard in '33."

GERALD TOMLINSON

The K - Bar - D Murders

Meet Robert Ollinger, "one of the most powerful journalists in Washington," and his junior assistant, Mort Bell, in one of the most bizarre cases of multiple murder on record – bizarre, yet not bizarre in "the formlessness and chaos of modern life," in a world whose newspaper headlines and columns report daily on scandals and scoundrels, madmen and murderers...

Robert Ollinger, the syndicated columnist, swept into the reception area of his K Street office like a dreadnought under full steam. A hulking, combative man of 54, one of the most powerful journalists in Washington, his column *Capitol Hot Line* ran in 112 newspapers from Maine to California. Ollinger dredged up news, molded news, insinuated news, and made news.

In 25 years of investigative reporting he had left a host of enemies in his wake. "The terrible price of telling the truth," he explained to David Suskind on late-night television. "I'm America's witness at large, David. The Diogenes of the Potomac." After his 1959 exposé of TV's soap-opera scandals, a wave of angry mail had nearly swamped his office, but Ollinger survived the deluge. His twelve staff members called their K Street office "The House of Storm."

Over the years a dozen foes had thrown punches at him. A critic from San Francisco had tried to run him through with a sword. An unidentified woman from Albuquerque had mailed him a plastic bomb. A slight, soft-spoken hairdresser from Indianapolis had sprayed 25-caliber bullets in his direction. Each time he had escaped without serious injury.

But his enemies were everywhere. So were his paid informants and his electronic bugs. "An investigative reporter," *Time* quoted him as saying, "needs the eyes of Argus, the ears of Panasonic, and the cold playback capability of Memorex." He had many secret sources of information. "More secret sources than the Nile," his fourth wife Cleo was fond of burbling at Georgetown dinner parties.

Ollinger had just returned from a

meeting in the basement of an abandoned warehouse in Bethesda, Maryland, where he had talked secretly with Vice-Presidential press secretary Wayne Davidson. Ollinger had given Davidson the code name of "Batman." A brash, spiteful fellow with narrow shoulders and bulging eyes, Davidson was trying to link Steven M. Arcato, the wealthy Hyattsville attorney, to a local Satanism ring, after having failed to wring Arcato dry in an extortion squeeze.

The phone in Ollinger's reception area jangled. Sally Pickerel, his secretary, reached for it, but the columnist grabbed it from under her darting fingers.

"Ollinger here."

An operator answered. "I have a collect call for Mr. Robert Ollinger from" – she paused for an instant, then finished the sentence flatly, with no change in her voice – "from Mr. Napoleon Bonaparte in Honotassa, New Mexico. Will you accept the charges?"

Ollinger had no source with the code name "Napoleon Bonaparte" and no regular contacts in Honotassa. His nearest secret source was "Chief Thundercloud" in Santa Fe. But he did have a policy of taking unexpected phone calls. He took them because one such call early in his career had led him to a small but newsworthy scandal in the Department of Health, Education, and Welfare.

"Put the man on."

Ollinger nodded curtly to his secretary, retired to his soundproof inner office, and lifted the receiver.

The man from Honotassa spoke in a pleasant Western drawl. *"Merci, monsieur. Bonjour."*

"Talk English," Ollinger snapped. "My French is terrible."

"Mine too," the man said. "I never could get the accent right. Corsica, you know. Douglas County. Cold, cold, cold up there, especially this time of year. A hundred and sixty miles from Pierre as the crow flies."

"What's on your mind, Emperor?"

A sigh. "Field Marshal Kutuzov. Moscow winters."

"That does it, Bony. So long." Ollinger started to hang up.

"No, wait." Napoleon's voice rose imploringly from the earpiece. "Listen to me, Mr. Ollinger. Your life is in danger."

Ollinger grunted. "So what else is new?"

"I mean it. I'm not kidding. This

148

Poindexter is bad news. I mean he's *really* bad news."

"Poindexter? – got that, Sally? Poindexter. Yes?"

"He's already killed Baker and Grant –"

"Spell it out, Corporal. No riddles. Baker. Grant. Who?"

"– Beckwith, Hindman. He shot Baker down right here in New Mexico. Over in Roswell. It was terrible. When I say bad news, Mr. Ollinger, I mean *bad* news."

"Come again?"

"The K-Bar-D murders. The big ones. The branding-iron jobs. Don't you read the newspapers?"

"I've got two assistants to do that."

"You're kidding."

"I'm not kidding. I never kid. Okay, I've heard of the K-Bar-D murders. Vaguely. But fill me in."

"Four murders in two months. Frank Baker over in Roswell. He was a plumber, I think. Joseph Grant in St. Louis. Robert Beckwith – where? I forget. George Hindman out East. Pittsburgh. Bad news, eh?"

"I'll check it out."

"Check it out? There's no need to check it out. It's in all the papers. And I'm telling

149

you, the kid's going to kill you too. He's going to kill Robert Ollinger somewhere, sometime."

"Why?"

"Why? You get to be a big-shot Washington columnist and that's all you know? You're *Robert Ollinger*. You're not Dick Brewer or J. H. Tunstal. Do you think I'm a pal of the Duke of Wellington? Do you think John Dillinger still likes the Lady in Red? You see what I mean?"

"No."

"Poindexter shot Hindman a week ago in Pittsburgh. Hindman. Pittsburgh. Get it? It means he's moving east. Toward you. And you're so well-known I just can't see him going through a dozen phone books to find some *other* Robert Ollinger. Can you?"

"This Poindexter – what's his first name?"

"I don't know. But be careful, Mr. Ollinger. I'm giving you fair warning. Don't take chances. Remember Waterloo. That was a bad day in *my* life. I'll tell you. If only Marshal Grouchy –"

"I'll check it out, Bonaparte. Thanks for calling."

Ollinger lowered the receiver to its

150

cradle, leaned back in his swivel chair, and studied the Mondrian canvases on his far wall. Their pure geometry, he thought, contrasted nicely with the formlessness and chaos of modern life. Madmen. Murderers. Scandals. Scoundrels. A soft-spoken Napoleon Bonaparte out in Honotassa, New Mexico, worried that Bob Ollinger, hard-nosed Washington columnist, might be gunned down by a kid named Poindexter. Crazy? Sure. Almost as crazy as some of the happenings on the Hill.

He leaned forward and punched a button on his desk. "Sally, ask our high-rise cage king to come in here. That means Bell."

Mort Bell, a former college basketball star, six-feet-four-inches, with sleepy brown eyes and a black handlebar mustache, had joined the Ollinger investigative team three months before, hired on the rebound from routine reporting. A motorcycle enthusiast, he craved excitement, the open road, the whiff of diesel oil. His work had offered nothing of the sort. For a couple of months after college he had idled away his time on the police beat of a Baltimore daily, a job he found as dreary as the drunk tank and as boring as the police blotter.

One rainy morning in November Bell had shouted, "I quit!" at precisely the instant his managing editor had screamed, "You're fired!" They sealed it with a fight in which Bell lost his Sigma Delta Chi key and two front teeth. Nothing daunted, he jumped on his Yamaha and barreled through the Harbor Tunnel, bound for glory.

"Mort," said Ollinger as Bell strolled into his office, "grab a seat. What's on the front burner?"

Bell dropped into a chrome-and-cowhide sofa and scowled. "Payoffs in the Jersey legislature," he said. Glory was still around the corner.

"Give it to Armstrong. Jersey's his bag – graft and corruption in Trenton – he's handled it for years. I've got a new job for you. A hot one. I want you to dig up everything you can on the K-Bar-D murders."

Bell looked startled. An embarrassed grin widened beneath the handlebars.

"As a matter of fact, Chief," he said, "I've been writing a five-thousand-word article on the K-Bar-D case for *Smashing True Detective*. As a free-lance."

Ollinger stared hard at him, his cold eyes pitiless as a time clock.

"In my spare time," Bell added lamely.

"In your spare time," Ollinger echoed, lighting a perfecto and exhaling a cloud of smoke. "Sure. Well, at least you're in the right ballpark for once." He leaned forward. "What about these K-Bar-D murders?"

Mort Bell crossed his long legs and took a sip of coffee from the styrofoam cup he had brought in with him.

"It's short and simple, Chief. The killer, whoever he is, is as crazy as the Mad Hatter. A trigger-happy psychopath. He shoots his victims with an old-fashioned .41-caliber revolver, usually in their living rooms. Then he brands their foreheads –"

"Hold on, Mort. He does *what?*"

"So help me, he brands their foreheads with a branding iron. From the K-Bar-D Ranch. Just like out West, only he uses a hibachi to heat the branding iron. When he's finished, he leaves the hibachi and takes the branding iron with him."

Ollinger whistled. "Not exactly the man next door. Not your usual domestic squabble: a hasty wedding, bang-bang. Where's the K-Bar-D Ranch?"

"There isn't one. There never has been. It's his own private brand."

"Who are the victims? What are their names?"

"Let me think. They all have common names. Grant is one, I think – yes, Joseph Grant, a stockbroker. Let's see. There's a Beckwith. A Baker."

"Okay, Mort. That's the Mad Hatter I'm after. What's the link between the victims? What's the pattern? What's the motive? Why the K-Bar-D brand?"

"It's a four-star mystery, Chief. There's no motive. No robbery. No violence except the bullet hole and the brand. No sex angle. One man's been murdered in New Mexico, one in Missouri, one in Indiana, the latest one in Pennsylvania. Four altogether. And the victims don't have a thing in common. Nothing. They didn't all serve on the same jury, or fight in the same platoon in World War Two, or take the same plane from Dulles to O'Hare, or receive the same coded message from Hong Kong. It's as if the guy is killing names, not people."

"But why those particular names?"

"Nobody knows. Or nobody's talking. If the police have come up with any link
154

between them, they haven't said so. And I couldn't find any."

"Do they expect the killer to try again?"

"Sure."

"Why?"

"I told you, he's nuts."

Ollinger adjusted his steel-rimmed aviator glasses, ran his fingers through a dark and expensive hairpiece. "The killer's name is Poindexter, Mort. And I think we'd better find him pronto. In time to prevent another man's murder. Maybe mine."

Bell studied his boss through sleepy eyes. "We're reporters, Chief. We're not private eyes. This is a job for the police, isn't it? Or the F.B.I.?"

"This is a job for you," Ollinger said evenly, pointing his finger for emphasis. "It's your assignment as of this minute. I want you to work on it night and day. No more moonlighting. I want you to run scared this time, Mort. I want you to find the K-Bar-D killer or else find yourself another job."

"You're kidding."

Ollinger never kidded. He made his ultimatums, carried them out, and ignored whatever human debris he created. "I never look back," he once informed Mike Wallace in a TV retrospective on his career.

Mort Bell accepted the assignment, aware that gumshoeing netted more than unemployment insurance. No man missing could be a greater menace than Robert Ollinger threatening. Bell headed for the privacy of his cubicle and the dubious solace of his telephone.

Concentrating once again on his Mondrians, Ollinger began putting together the next *Hot Line* column in his head. It concerned a prominent politician's wife suffocated in her Miami hospital bed by a nurse with anarchist leanings. "While the patient slept, death stole softly into Room 18 –" the column began. Ollinger intended to make it poignant. "Tears that smear the newsprint," he often advised his staff, "grow cabbage that pays the rent."

Before the final line of *Capitol Hot Line* was fixed in his mind, Mort Bell burst back into Ollinger's office, bypassing Sally Pickerel like a Harley on a shunpike.

"How about that, Chief? An hour and ten minutes on the case and I've found out what K-Bar-D means."

"Let's have it." Ollinger punched a button on his tape recorder.

Bell's voice hummed with excitement. "Well, a few days ago the police in St. Louis – that's where Grant was killed – turned up a cocktail waitress named – you're not going to believe this, Chief – Kay Bardee. Perfect, no? It must take a kook to catch a kook. Who would think of going through the local phone book to find a person named Kay Bardee? Sergeant Vickers of the St. Louis P.D., that's who. He did, and there she was. Kay Bardee, 317 Hunting's End Road. Sergeant Vickers' triumph."

"I doubt it."

"You're right. But the police checked into Miss Bardee like the Warren Commission checking into Lee Harvey Oswald. They learned so much about her private life that they've booked her on charges of petty larceny, loitering, possession of a controlled dangerous substance, and impairing the morals of a minor."

"But not on the K-Bar-D murders."

"No. She's innocent of those. She had no connection with the murders. She was loitering with her boy friend in Jefferson City at the time Grant was being killed in St. Louis."

Ollinger waved his hand in irritation.

"So all you've really found out is that K-Bar-D doesn't mean Kay Bardee."

"No, there's more. During the Kay Bardee publicity a professor of American History at Dahlgren University wrote a letter to the St. Louis *Chronicle,* telling them that the cattle brand they'd been showing on the front page wasn't a K-Bar-D brand at all."

"What do you mean?"

"The bar in the K-Bar-D brand was a Roswell police lieutenant's mistake. Everybody else followed his lead. What was being called a bar is actually, in the heraldry of the range – that's what the professor called it – a sideways *I*. A 'Lazy *I*.' So the brand is K-Lazy I-D. K-I-D. Get it?"

"I'm beginning to. Back to work, Mort. Hunt with the hounds."

Bell left for his cubicle, and Ollinger, after handing Sally Pickerel the tape for transcription, began putting in a series of phone calls, picking up a brief liberal education in Western Americana. His first two calls went to the Library of Congress and the Smithsonian Institution. His last call went to the Melora Valley Sanitorium, near Honotassa, New Mexico. After some insistence on his honored status in

158

American journalism he got through to an assistant director, Dr. Mervyn Keller. "Dr. Keller," Ollinger said, "do you have a Napoleon Bonaparte there?"

The doctor chuckled. "You're in luck, Mr. Ollinger. We have two Napoleons. One is from Arizona, the other from South Dakota. They're splendid fellows, sharp as tacks. Most of the time they're as rational as we are. But they do have their one little delusion. And how they fight about that delusion – about who's the real Napoleon and who's the fake."

Dr. Keller cleared his throat as if to annul his chuckle and his commentary. In a businesslike voice he concluded, "We also have a Winston Churchill, a Madame Curie, and a Joan of Arc."

"Do you have a Billy the Kid?"

There was a telltale silence. "I'd rather not talk about the patients who have left us, Mr. Ollinger. I prefer to speak no evil of the departed. You realize that we are a private institution. Many of our patients have, or their families have, a great deal of money – enough money to hire psychiatrists, nurses, guards, companions, and the like. Sometimes we release patients who are still quite disturbed, knowing these patients will receive excellent care at home."

"In other words, you once had a Billy the Kid. You set him loose while he was still trying to figure out where you'd hidden his six-guns."

A sigh. "At various times in the past," the psychiatrist said, "we have had Jesse James, Annie Oakley, Billy the Kid, John Dillinger, and Judas Iscariot. Jesse James, I might add, is now a prominent dentist in Albuquerque. John Dillinger is an estate planner in Kansas City. There's no predicting how these things will turn out."

"Thank you, Doctor."

So that was the answer, the crux of the case. Bill the Kid, resurrected in the addled brain of a man named Poindexter, was roaming the countryside, reliving a legendary past, killing innocent plumbers, stockbrokers, and others who happened to have the same names as Billy the Kid's old victims. The branding iron was a bizarre touch, but one that gave the crimes a cachet.

Napoleon Bonaparte, the informant of the Honotassa Bonapartes, had been right. Poindexter was big news, bad news.

Ollinger dialed the number of Mort Bell's cubicle. No answer. He slammed

160

down the receiver. If that lazy jock had left for the day . . .

At six o'clock, as dusk was settling over the city, Ollinger, according to custom, was switching from black coffee to straight Scotch, partly to unwind from the day, partly to escape the night.

He tried Bell's extension again. Still no answer.

He stalked across the room and threw open the door. Sally Pickerel, who worked the same exhausting hours as her boss, thrust a paperback book hastily into a top drawer. "What's up?"

"Where's Bell?"

"I don't know. He left the office about five hours ago. I asked him where he was going, but all he would tell me was that he was bound for glory."

"He's bound for the unemployment line," Ollinger grated, heading for Bell's cubicle.

The light had been dimmed for the night in the large room that held twelve pea-green cubicles topped by frosted glass. No one was there. To Ollinger the silence was offensive and oppressive. Offensive because he felt that at least one of his assistants should work through the night;

161

Ollinger had provided a metal cot for the purpose, but it stood unused at the far end of the room. Oppressive because he knew his life really was in danger.

He walked toward Bell's cubicle near the cot. As he did so, he heard a slight sound behind him. Not usually a nervous man, he whirled at the noise and yelled, "Who's there?"

In the dim light he saw a tall figure approaching, a cowboy hat pulled low over his brow. The man wore a plaid shirt and blue levis. A gun glinted in his hand.

The figure approached without speaking, as Ollinger backed up to the cot, stood there, his legs trembling, his mind racing. He often carried a tear-gas pencil on the street, but he never did in the office.

As the figure swaggered closer, Ollinger caught sight of a handlebar mustache and – a grin.

"Hi, Chief," Mort Bell said. "In the immortal words of Wilt Chamberlain, 'Relax.'"

Bell turned without replying and sauntered past Sally into the inner office. He flopped down on the cowhide sofa, lit a perfecto, pointed his finger at Ollinger, and said, "Chief, you're safe. Billy the Kid is in the hands of the F.B.I."

"You're kidding."

"I never kid. You gave me an assignment, I carried it out. I took Poindexter into custody myself."

"How did you find him?"

"It took some time. About four hours on the phone, as a matter of fact. I started with the name you gave me: Poindexter. I also tried William Bonney, which was the Kid's real name. Four hours later, bingo. The jackpot. Alvin Poindexter, an eighteen-year-old kid with an Adam's apple the size of his big delusion, was in the Washington area, registered under the name of William Bonney."

"Registered where?"

"At the El Rancho Rio Motel in Arlington. I tried thirty or forty hotels and motels, asking for either Poindexter or Bonney, before I found him. He still had seven thousand dollars in his wallet when I picked him up. The Poindexters of Corsica, South Dakota, are very rich, you know."

"I didn't know. Did Poindexter have a gun?"

"A .41-caliber Double Action Colt with enough ammo to fight the Lincoln County

War. Also a branding iron, five hibachis, and a spiral notebook with a list of names."

"My name was on the list?"

"It sure was, Chief. Right at the top. It seems you were once a deputy marshal in southern New Mexico. The Kid killed you back in April, 1881.

"How did you capture him?"

"By craft and low cunning."

Ollinger looked respectful. "That's the way to do it. Did you go to his motel?"

"About an hour ago. I'm about the right height and weight for the role." He paused.

"The role?"

Bell winked. "The role I had to play. Mort Bell, lawman. I've got a black handlebar mustache. But I had to change into these blue levis and a plaid shirt. Then I went out and bought a ten-gallon hat –"

"I get it!"

"– borrowed an antique .44 revolver from a friend of mine, and took off for the motel. I knocked on Bonney-Poindexter's door. When he opened it, I ambled in, leveled the .44 at him, and told him I was –"

"Sheriff Pat Garrett!"

"Right."

"Great Scott! And it worked?"

164

Bell puffed his perfecto coolly. "It worked. The kid was scared to death. He knew, he just *knew* I was going to gun him down. After all, I'd killed him once, back in 1881. He cried, He begged and pleaded. He offered me his money and his hibachis."

"Son of a gun," Ollinger muttered.

"Right on. I won his confidence by telling him we'd call him 'a youthful blue-eyed killer' in the column. Finally I talked him into coming with me. About ten minutes ago I dropped him off at the J. Edgar Hoover Building."

Ollinger slammed a congratulatory fist on his rosewood desk. "Good work, Mort. And to think I figured you for the office clinker. Using that Pat Garrett trick was an inspiration. Worthy of Bob Ollinger himself in his younger days."

Mort Bell grinned. "I'm glad I used somebody's else's name, though. Two of the other men on Poindexter's list were William Morton of Syracuse and James Bell of Boston. I don't know whether I would have survived with my own name."

"You'd have survived, Mort. You've got class. You're still wet behind the ears, you've got no top-level sources, but you've got potential. Let's talk bonus."

Before they could settle on an amount, Sally Pickerel poked her head inside the office. She smiled at the sheriff and spoke briskly to the columnist. "There's a 'Captain Hook' on the line, Mr. Ollinger. Would you like to take the call?"

"I'll take it," Ollinger snapped. "But I already know what it's about." He pointed a triumphant finger at his junior assistant. "The Captain is my secret source in the F.B.I., Mort. He'll want to tell me they've solved the K-Bar-D murders."

WILLIAM BANKIER

The Final Twist

It was a small advertising agency – the boss, an art director, a copy writer, and a production manager. The boss was despised and hated by his three underlings – for good and sufficient reasons. So the three employees concocted an imaginative murder scheme – as only the Creative Department of an ad agency could dream one up. "The premise was preposterous, but we kept the monster alive . . . and it put on weight and developed a sort of zany credibility" . . .

There are three things that need to be said about the killing of Murphy Stevenson. First, he deserved to die. Second, he died quickly where some might have said he deserved to suffer. Third, he *did* experience at the end a few seconds of exquisite mental anguish because of a simple action performed by Eloise Knott. She could not resist giving him the final twist, the final cruel shock. I don't think I would have thought of it, but then Eloise is a woman.

167

And Murphy had made her furious.

I remember how she sounded off to me after Stevenson had played his dirty trick on her. "That man has stepped on my toes," she said, sounding like a heavy in a spaghetti Western. Eloise is "one of the boys" and sometimes speaks with very little lip movement. She rolls her own cigarettes, yet she is female all the same. "I don't like it," she emphasized, "when they step on my toes."

"Hell hath no fury," I ventured, "like a woman's corns."

She let it pass and we got on with planning Murphy Stevenson's leap to death which was to be witnessed by the man in the top-floor office of the high-rise building across the alley. We made sure that he saw Stevenson alone on the roof, saw him position himself on the parapet and take his final dive. That's what made the coroner's verdict a clear case of suicide. That is how we got away with murder.

Let me emphasize right here that I, Brendan Tilford, am not in favor of people committing murder and getting off scot-free. On the other hand, I believe that extermination is a legitimate activity and should be pursued with efficiency whether the object is a nest of cockroaches under a kitchen floor or the sadistic head of a small advertising agency.

It would be hard to imagine an ad agency more compact than Murphy Stevenson Associates or a man more cruelly sadistic than our president, good old Murph. A couple of examples from his long and nasty record should establish our case against him.

Take the Christmas Bonus Deception which was perpetrated last year. We were accustomed to receiving a bonus of two weeks' salary on December 15th. We depended on it to buy our presents and our holiday booze. But it had been a bad year in the business community; the economy was on the rocks, profits were down the drain, and most firms had let it be known there would be no melon to slice this time around.

So we went to see the boss one afternoon late in November, Eloise and myself and Farley Dixon who make up the entire staff, and we put the question to him. If there was to be no money, we wanted to know now.

Stevenson hung that big face in front of us, gnarled and russety like the last apple

169

in the barrel. "You get your bonuses, that I promise you." He raised his arm and we could see a salty circle in the armpit of his pin-stripe jacket. "Have I ever lied to you?"

We went about our business then, I writing copy, Eloise designing the layouts, and Farley Dixon looking after everything else – typesetting, engravings, shipping of material to publications. When December 15th came and went and we received only our regular paychecks, a tremor of angst ran through the office. But Stevenson strode about with a smug grin one side of his face, humming *Santa Claus Is Coming to Town*. So we waited.

Then on the afternoon before Christmas Day he came round to our offices, delivered sealed envelopes, and said in his loudest client voice, "Glad tidings of comfort and joy!" – and stepped into a descending express elevator. We opened our envelopes and each of us found a $5 bill wrapped in a typewritten note which said:

"As you know, it has been a bad year for this and every other agency. But Stevenson maintains his unbroken record of always awarding a bonus, even though this time it has to be only a token payment. The spirit is there, if not the substance.

    Merry Christmas,

      Murphy K. Stevenson."

We drank up our bonuses quickly in the bar downstairs and I think the plot to get rid of Mr. Stevenson was hatched then, and there. Not the details but the idea – the wish to see it done. Never underestimate the power of such a wish. Because of a determination no more sincere than ours, today there are man's footprints on the moon.

You may be wondering why we did not simply hand in our resignations while telling Murphy K. Stevenson to stick his five-dollar bills into his checking account. Well, to begin with, the economy was indeed slow. Jobs in advertising agencies were scarce as subway seats at rush hour, and when you had one, you sat on it.

Besides, we were a picturesque group of misfits not ideally suited to job interviews. I am a former high-school English teacher with a drinking problem. It shows in my nose. Eloise is a good designer but she is also a hysteric and a compulsive talker. I have seen people crawl out of her meetings, stunned like blast victims. As for Farley Dixon, he had suffered from some sort of obscure illness when he was a teen-ager. He still has a full deck to play with, but his eyes don't focus too well and his speech contains a lot of air and bubbles.

So we slave on for wages, putting up with Stevenson because he puts up with us. Why, then, make plans to eliminate the man? Would that not be, so to speak, killing the lizard that lays the golden eggs?

Not at all. If Stevenson cashed in his chips, the firm would go on. Our clients would still need their ad campaigns and we three were the team who wrote, designed, and produced them. Without old Murph, the client contact, we would simply do our jobs while arrangements were made for new leadership. Most likely some larger agency would absorb us into their operation.

Perhaps the crucial example of Stevenson's inhumanity was his treatment of Eloise Knott. This happened shortly before I joined the company and was told to me by Farley Dixon over beer in the bar. It seems my copywriting predecessor was a youth named Skippy Schiff. He was handsome, a competent writer, and because he was young and single and simple, Stevenson was able to pay him peanuts.

Anyway, Eloise and Skippy began having lunch together and one day they realized they were in love. Since this was a new experience in Skippy's young life and a rare phenomenon in Eloise's older one, they made no secret of it. They had got it, so they flaunted it. Naturally Murphy Stevenson became aware of what was going on.

Then he did three things. He began courting Eloise Knott with great energy, wining and dining her every night, whipping her away for weekends in Vermont, walking her significantly past windows where diamond rings were on display. When she succumbed to the seriousness of his approach and told Skippy it was finished between them, Stevenson fired the copywriter, gave him two weeks' pay, and sent him packing. Then he let one more week go by before ending his courtship of Eloise Knott. He never took her out again.

A shaken Eloise went looking for Skippy, but the boy had climbed aboard a boat for South America. Gone on the tide.

"Why do you suppose the boss did a rotten thing like that?" I asked Farley.

"He looks on all of us as his property,"

Farley said. "He resented the boy coming in and taking over his art director."

"Crafty guy," I said. "If he'd just fired Skippy straight away, she'd have quit and followed him. Right?"

"Right." Farley's eyes looked two different ways, his mouth ajar with beaded bubbles winking at the brim. "She almost left anyway, but I asked her what would happen to me, so she stayed on."

This loyalty of Eloise Knott's turned out to be Stevenson's tough luck. Because the plan to do him in originated with her – the "hell hath no fury" thing. I remember sitting in her office one afternoon as she doodled on her pad and started the idea rolling. The premise was preposterous, but we kept the monster alive for a couple of days and it put on weight and developed a sort of zany credibility. If you have ever worked in advertising, you'd realize this sort of thing can happen.

So we talked and dreamed and drank in the evenings and made lists of what props we'd need. We went up on the roof which was just two floors above us and looked down 23 stories to the alley below. From the roof Eloise noted the line of sight into the office of the man in the next building who always worked late and would become our eyewitness. We observed that he could see the rooftop but that a ledge blocked his view of the alley below. Perfect. Then we got down to the details.

I was sent to the hardware store to buy a gallon of flat white exterior paint and a brush. Farley organized a slide projector and a tape recorder and I helped him dub the required sounds on tape. Eloise herself went round to the publicity department of the Municipal Fire Department and borrowed the required photograph which she converted into a color slide.

Then it only remained to choose our evening and set the plan in motion. We were under no pressure; if something went wrong, we could abort at any stage and postpone our retribution to a more suitable night.

But nothing went wrong.

On the afternoon of the appointed day I went into the alley and painted a large area of the pavement flat white. There was no vehicular traffic in this narrow lane; the most the surface might acquire would be a few dusty footprints.

Farley Dixon then tested the slide projector. He took it into the washroom near his office and extended it through the window on the wooden frame he had built, aiming it down at my white patch on the alley and switching it on. The image was pale, but after dark it would be fine.

Then, at a quarter to five, Eloise set up Murphy Stevenson. She went into his office and said, "Mr. Stevenson, we are having a little drink in the Creative Department."

Our peerless leader glanced glanced at his watch. "Not for another fifteen minutes, I hope."

"Of course not. And we'd like you to come and join us."

"Why me?" he probed.

"Why not?" she countered.

So in he came, pausing in the doorway, observing the gin, ice, mixer, and polished glasses, his shifty eyes darting here and there. Back in the days when he was a despised schoolboy, good old Murph must have been the butt of many a practical joke and he could sense the setup here. But he could not put his finger on it. He sniffed his empty glass before I poured the gin, he let us drink first, then he sipped tentatively. And immediately his own physical condition betrayed him. He became drunk quickly, and from then on it was easy.

We let him do most of the talking, arrogant and abusive and then incoherent, while I kept on pouring and Eloise raised her glass occasionally to the man in the office across the alley. Then, as darkness fell over the city, we moved our plan ahead. First, Farley Dixon excused himself and I knew he was organizing his slide projector and his tape recorder. When he came back, Eloise went out and set the fire. She did a good job. Within minutes of her return the smell of smoke reached us from the hall.

"Hey," I said, "the place is on fire!"

"What do we do?" Eloise asked.

"Stay away from elevators and stairwells. They're death traps in these tall buildings."

"What, then?"

"The only safe place is the roof." I took Stevenson's arm and dragged him into the hall. Farley and Eloise followed, closing my office door to keep the smoke, which was thick out here, from becoming visible to the man across the way.

Stevenson's eyes got big when he saw the smoke. He was moving erratically under his load of booze and I had to guide him up the two flights of stairs to the roof. There I snapped on the tape recorder Farley had planted behind a ventilator. Below us I knew Eloise was using soda water to extinguish the fires in the wastebaskets before the smoke alarmed the building staff.

I went to the parapet overlooking the main street and looked down. At the same moment Farley's tape-recorded fire sirens began to sound through a mix of traffic noises, the sirens distant at first, then drawing nearer.

"Do you see the fire engine?" Stevenson was hanging back from the edge.

"They're heading around to the alley side. Traffic is too thick over here."

My boss confronted me, his dazed eyes full of panic. "Listen, they don't have ladders this tall. How do we get off?"

"They have safety nets," I said. "Just like jumping into a feather bed."

The sirens stopped. It was not in the plan for me to be seen on the roof, so I said, "Take a look over the alley side. See if the net is up."

Stevenson went and looked over. "That was fast," he said. "There's a ring of firemen down there holding a net." He rubbed his gin-dimmed, smoke-bleared eyes.

"Don't think about it then, Murph. The longer you hesitate, the harder it will be. Just jump."

And he did.

I was surprised, really, that he went for it. I was also surprised that as soon as he disappeared over the edge, he screamed all the way down. Men jumping into safety nets don't scream; they probably hold their breath.

I asked Eloise and Farley about that when we had tidied up the premises and the police ambulance had come and gone, taking away Murphy Stevenson's body. Their report was terse and I noticed a wary tension between the two of them.

"The slide looked beautiful on the white paint," Farley said. "Just like on a screen. The firemen looking up and the big net held between them – very realistic."

"As soon as you were on the roof," Eloise said. "I telephoned the man across the way. I said my boss had run out of the place and we were worried. Could he see him on the roof? That got him to the window looking up."

"Fine," I said. "There's our eyewitness if needed. Stevenson was alone, he jumped, therefore suicide." Then I asked the

179

question that was on my mind. "I wonder why he screamed like that on the way down? As far as he knew, he was jumping into a safety net."

Farley Dixon threw as much of a critical glance at Eloise as he could manage. "It was her," he said, and I could hear disapproval in his halting voice. "As soon as Murph stepped over the edge of the roof, she turned off the projector."

EDGAR WALLACE

A More - or - Less Crime

April 1, 1975 marked the 100th anniversary of Edgar Wallace's birth. To celebrate the centenary there were BBC TV programs on Wallace's life, considerable radio and press coverage, and reissues of some of his books – according to Penelope Wallace, his daughter, about 50 Edgar Wallace titles are still in print and selling well. And to commemorate the Edgar Wallace centenary, though belatedly, Ellery Queen's Mystery Magazine brought you an Edgar Wallace story never before published in the States – a tale told by the "Sooper" involving "a real bit of detective work." As always in Mr. Wallace's stories, you will find his smooth, easy style and his quietly persuasive economy of characterization...

Detective: SUPERINTENDENT MINTER

"It's a strange thing," said Superintendent Minter, "that when I explain to outsiders the method and system of criminal investigation as practiced by the well-known academy of arts at Scotland Yard, they always seem a bit disappointed.

"I've shown a lot of people over the building, and they all want to see the room where the scientific detectives are looking at mud stains through microscopes, or putting cigar ash in test tubes, or deducting or deducing – I don't know which is the right word – from a bit of glue found in the keyhole that the burglar was a tall dark man who drove a gray touring car and had been crossed in love.

"I believe there are detectives like that. I've read about 'em. When you walk into their room or bureau or boudoir, as the case may be, they give you a sharp penetrating look from their cold gray eyes and they say, 'You came up Oxford Street in a motorbus; I can smell it. You had an argument with your wife this morning; I can see the place where the plate hit you. You're going on a long journey across water; beware of a blue-eyed waitress – she bites.'

"I believe that the best way to detect a man who's committed a crime is to see him do it. It isn't necessary even to see him do it. In nine cases out of ten the right man will come along sooner or later and tell you he did it, and what he did it with.

"Most criminals catch themselves. And I'll tell you why. Not nine out of ten, but ninety-nine out of every hundred of these birds of paradise don't know where to stop, and as they don't know where to stop they stop halfway. I've never met a crook who was a whole hogger and could carry any job he started to a clean and tidy finish. There never was a burglar who didn't leave something valuable behind, but that's understandable, for burglars are the most nervous criminals in the world. They lose heart halfway through and there's a lot of people like 'em. As Mr. Rudyard Kipling, the well-known poet, says: 'All along of doing things/Rather more or less.'

"The most interesting more-or-less crime I ever saw was the Bidderley Hall affair. Bidderley Hall is a country house in the Metropolitan Police area – right on the edge of T Division near Staines. It was an old Queen Anne house – it's been pulled down lately – standing in a ten-acre park, and it was owned by a gentleman named Costino – Mr. Charles Costino. He was a rich man, having inherited about half a

183

million from his brother Peter.

"In the beginning Peter was rich and Charles was poor. Peter boozed but Charles never got happy on anything stronger than barley water. Charles was artistic and knew a lot about the Old Masters; he never bought any but he knew about 'em. His brother Peter knew nothing except that two pints made a quart and two quarts made you so that you weren't responsible for your actions.

"As a matter of fact, he was a bit of a bad egg, Peter was – gave funny parties at his home in Eastbourne and was pinched once or twice for being tight when in charge of a motorcar.

"One morning the coast guard found Peter's car at the foot of a two-hundred-foot cliff, smashed to blazes. They never found Peter. The tide was pretty high when his car went over – about three in the morning, according to a revenue boat that saw the lights; and after a time Charles got leave to presume Peter's death and took over all that Peter had left of a million.

"I saw Peter once. He was one of those blue-faced soakers who keep insurance companies awake at night.

"It was a grand bit of luck for Charles, who had this old house on his hands and found it a bit difficult to pay the taxes.

"When he came into money, Charles didn't live much better than when he was poor. The only time he broke out was when he took in a man-of-all-work, who was butler, footman, valet, and fed the chickens. In a way it was not a good break, as I could have told him if I had only known him at the time.

"Mr. Costino, it seems, had had an old lady looking after him – I forget her name, but anyway it doesn't matter. She'd been in the family for four generations, and she either left to better herself or died. Whatever she did she bettered herself.

"Anyway, Mr. Charles Costino was without a servant. He only lived in four rooms of the house since he came into the money and there wasn't much cleaning to be done, but he did have a bit of silver to clean, and there were the chickens to look after. The silver used to be locked in a cupboard in the dining room and was pretty valuable, as I happen to know.

"Now, the new man he employed was named Simon. He's no relation to anybody you know, and I very much doubt whether that was his real name at all. He was a graduate of the University of Dartmoor where he had spent three happy years at the taxpayers' expense. I knew him as well as the back of my right hand.

"One day, by accident, I was passing through the Minories and I saw Simon come out of a shop that buys a bit of other people's silver now and again, so I pulled him up. According to his story, he had been to this pawnbroker's shop to buy a ring for his young lady, but they didn't have one to fit. I know most of the young ladies Simon has promised to marry – they've all been through my hands at one time or another – but I've never met one that he bought anything for, except a bit of sticking plaster. So I took him back to the shop, and the fence blew it and showed me the silver Mr. Simon had parted with.

"It was not in my division at all and perhaps I had no right to interfere. To tell you the truth, the Divisional Inspector was a bit nasty about it afterwards, but what made it all right for me was when Simon said it was a cop and volunteered to come back with me to Staines.

"He didn't want any trouble and he told me he was tired of working for Mr. Costino

186

and would be glad to get back amongst the boys at the dear old college. He said he had sold four pieces and had six hidden in the house ready to bring away.

"'Costino wouldn't notice them going,' he said. 'He's soused half the time and the other half he's in delirium tremens.'

"It was news to me, because I didn't know that Costino drank.

"We drove from the station to the house in a cab and on the way there Simon told me how slick he'd had to be to get the stuff out of the house at all. Apparently he slept in a room over a stable, some distance from the house but on the grounds. Nobody slept in the house but Charles Costino.

"We drove up to the Hall – and a miserable-looking building it was. I think I told you it was a Queen Anne house. Queen Anne is dead and this house was ready to pop off at any minute. None of the windows was clean, except a couple on the ground floor. It took us a quarter of an hour to wake up Costino and even then he only opened the door on the chain and wouldn't have let us in, but he recognized me.

"I have never seen such a change in a man. The last time I saw him he was a quiet sober feller and his idea of a happy evening was to drink lemonade and listen to the radio. Now he was the color of a bad lobster. He stared at Simon, and when I told him what the man had told me, Charles sat down in a chair and turned gray – well, it wasn't gray, but a sort of putty color.

"After a bit he said, 'I'd like to speak to this man. I think I can persuade him to tell me the truth.'

"I don't like people coming between me and my lawful prey, but I humored him, and he took Simon into the other corner of the room and talked to him for a long time in an undertone.

"When he finished he said, 'I think this man has made a mistake. There are only four pieces of silver stolen, and those are the four pieces he has sold. I can tell you in a minute.'

"With that he unlocked the door of a high cupboard. It was so crowded with silver that it was impossible for any man to count the stuff that was in it. But he only looked at it for a minute and then he said, 'Quite right. Only four pieces are missing.'

"So far as I was concerned it didn't matter to me whether it was four or ten, so long as he gave me enough for a conviction. It was not my business to argue the point.

I took Simon down to the cooler and I could tell something had happened, because he was not his normal bright and cheery self. Usually when you take an old con to the station he is either telling you what he's going to do when he comes out to your heart, lungs and important blood vessels, or else he's all friendly and jolly. But Simon said nothing and sort of looked dazed and surprised. He was hardly recovered the next morning when I met him at the police court and got my remand.

"It was a very simple case. It came at the Sessions, and Mr. Costino went into the box and said Simon was one of the best servants that had ever blown into a country house. You expect perjury at the Assizes but not that kind of perjury. But that was his business.

"Anyway, Costino made such a scene about what a grand fellow Simon was, how he fed the chickens so regular that they followed him down the street, that Simon got off with six months, and that, so far as I was concerned, was the end of it till it came my turn to take him in again.

"About seven months after this I was on duty on the Great West Road, watching for a stolen motorcar. It was one of those

189

typical English summer days you read about – raining cats and dogs, with a cold north wind blowing – and I was getting a bit fed up with waiting when I saw a car coming along following a course that a yachtsman takes when he is tacking into the breeze.

"The last tack was against an iron lamp standard, which smashed the radiator and most of the glass, but it didn't apparently kill the driver, for he opened the door and staggered out. I had only to look at him to see that he had about twenty-five over the eight.

"My first inclination was to hand him over to my sergeant on a charge of being drunk while driving. It would mean a lot of bother, because if he had plenty of money he'd produce three Harley Street doctors and fourteen independent witnesses to prove that the only thing he'd drunk since yesterday morning was a small glass of cider diluted with tonic water.

"I was deciding whether or not to pinch him when I recognized him. It was Simon.

" 'Hello!' I said. 'How long is it since *you* came out of the home for dirty dogs?'

"He didn't know me at first, and I oughtn't to have known him at all, because

190

he was beautifully dressed, with a green tie and a brown hat, and a bunch of forget-me-nots in his buttonhole, not that anybody who had ever put their lamps on this dial would ever forget him. I asked him if it was his car, and he admitted it was.

"While I was talking to him one of my men came up and told me that they had stopped the stolen car about a hundred yards down the road, so I was able to devote myself to my little friend.

"We helped him along and got him into the substation round the corner. He was, so to speak, flush with wine. He got over his shock and began to talk big, flash his money about, and gradually, as he recognized the old familiar surroundings – the sergeant's desk and the notice on the wall telling people not to spit on the floor – he saw he was in the presence of law and order and it gradually dawned on him that I was me.

" 'What bank have you been robbing?' says I.

"He laughed in my face. 'Costino gave it all to me for saying that I only pinched four bits of silver.'

"He started to laugh again and stopped. I have an idea that in the thing he called his mind he realized he had said too much. Anyway, he couldn't say any more. We took his money away from him, counted it, and put him in a nice clean cell.

"Now I am not a man who is easily puzzled. Things in life are too straightforward for anybody to have anything to puzzle about, but this certainly got me thinking. Costino must have given him the best part of a thousand pounds to admit that he had stolen only four pieces of silver. Now why did he do that?

"I thought it out. At about eleven o'clock that night I said to my sergeant, 'Let's go and do a real bit of detective work.'

"I drove him down in my car to the road in front of Bidderley Hall. We parked the car in the drive, just inside the old gates, and walked up to the house. The rain was pelting down. I don't remember a worse night. The wind howled through the trees and gave me one of those bogey feelings I haven't had since I was a boy.

"When we got up to the house, we made a sort of reconnaissance. All the windows were dark; there was no sign of life; if there had been any sound we couldn't have heard it anyway. We went all round trying to find a way in, and just as got back to the front of the house one of the worst thunderstorms I can remember started up without any warning.

"My sergeant was all for knocking up Mr. Costino and putting the matter to him plump and plain, but I saw all sorts of difficulties and my scheme was to pretend that we found a window open and being good policemen and not being able to make Costino hear, we had got in through the window and had a look round. There was only one place possible, we decided, and that was a window on a small balcony at the back of the house.

"We searched round and found a ladder, and put it against the balcony. I went up first and I had just put my leg over the parapet and was facing the window when there came a blinding flash of lightning that made my head spin. It was one of those flashes of lightning that seem to last two or three seconds, and in the light of it, as plain as day, I saw right in front of me, staring through the window, a horribly white face with a long untidy beard.

"I was so startled I nearly dropped back. I called my sergeant up the ladder. I wasn't afraid, but I wanted somebody with me. I don't know whether you have ever had that feeling. Two can be frightened to death better than one.

"I told him just what I had seen, and then I got my pocket lamp and flashed it into the room. As far as I could see through the dirty window the room was empty. Between the window and the room was a set of iron bars. They weren't very thick; they looked like the kind put up in West End houses so that children can't escape from a nursery when the room catches fire.

"We got the window open. The sergeant and I not only bent the bars, but we bent the whole frame. It was not very securely fastened – a bit of carpentry work done by a plumber.

"There was no furniture in the room. It was thick with dust. On the wall was a picture hanging cockeyed. The door was open and we went on and found a landing and a narrow flight of stairs leading down. But the curious thing about those stairs was that they didn't stop on the ground floor. In fact, there was no door opening until we got to the basement. There had been a door on the ground floor, but it had been bricked up.

"We were going down the last flight of steps when we heard a door bang and the sound of a bolt being shot. When we got to the basement level we found a door. It was shut, and we couldn't move it. I could find nothing on the stairs in the light of my lamp except evidence that somebody was in the habit of going up and down.

"When I went back up to the room with the balcony and examined the bars we had bent, I made rather an interesting discovery. Three of the screws on the lower left-hand corner had been taken out, and they had been taken out with a jagged top of a sardine tin. We found the 'opener' lying on the floor. It must have taken a long time to loosen those screws, for one of the screwholes was quite dark, and must have been exposed for months.

"There were two courses left to us: one was to come the next day with an official search warrant, which no magistrate would grant on the information we had; and the other was to go round and wake up Costino and ask him to let us go through the house. But there was a good reason for not doing that.

"I took off my shoes and went down the stairs in my stockinged feet, with my sergeant behind me. We crept up to the door and listened. For a little time I heard nothing, partly because the thunder was still turning the house into a drum, and partly because we could not quite tune in. But after a while I heard a man breathing very quickly, like somebody who had been running.

"We waited for a quarter of an hour and then another quarter of an hour. It seemed like a week. And then we heard the bolt being very gently pushed back. A man on the other side of the door opened it an inch. In another second I was through. He ran like the wind along the cellar and was just reaching another door when I grabbed him. He fought like six men, but we got him down.

"And then he said, 'Don't kill me, Charles. I'll give you half of the money.'

"And that was all I wanted to know.

"We pulled him up and sat him on an old box, and I explained that we were just innocent police officers, that we very seldom kill anybody except under the greatest provocation, and after a while we got Mr. Peter Costino calm, and he told us how his brother had come down to Eastbourne to see him and borrow some money, and how Charles got him drunk and intended driving him and the car over the cliff.

"Peter wouldn't have known this but his brother told him afterwards. Charles had lost heart and let the car go over by itself, then brought Peter back to Bidderley Hall, and shut him up in the cellar. Peter didn't know very much about it till he woke up the next morning and found himself a prisoner, and after two years of this kind of life he got more or less reconciled, expecially as he was allowed to go up to the room with the balcony. It was the only bit of the world he was allowed to see, and then only at nights.

"That's the trouble with criminals – they never go the whole hog. Charles didn't have the nerve to kill his brother. He just locked him up. He got the house and half a million pounds, but he got about two million worries. Those two years made Peter a sober man and turned Charles into a drunkard. Peter might have eventually died in this cellar if Mr. Charles Costino hadn't given Simon a thousand quid to keep his mouth shut about the silver he had stolen and hidden in the house. Charles was in mortal terror that we would search the house for the missing silver, and if we had searched the house we'd have found Peter.

"Charles is in Dartmoor now. So is Simon. He got a lagging for a big smash-and-grab raid, and drew five years. From what I've heard, he and Charles are quite good friends. The last I heard of Charles he was painting angels in the prison chapel. As I say, he was always a bit artistic."

DAVID BRADT

A Kind of Madness

This was the 451st "first story" published by Ellery Queen's Mystery Magazine...

The author, David Bradt, is now thirty. He was born and raised in southern California, but for the past eight years he and his wife Janice have been living in the state of Washington. He has a degree in journalism from California State U. in Fullerton. His first job after graduation was as "a shipping clerk for a gasoline and oil storage tank manufacturing firm" during the "gas shortage" when "the big oil companies were buying 10,000-gallon tanks as if the Alaska Pipeline had just been completed and there was nowhere to put the incoming oil. Makes one wonder." After that he worked as a warehouseman – until he was laid off.

His outdoor interests include skiing, camping, fishing, and backpacking. Otherwise he "keeps busy reading and shooting pool on a funky $50 used table with rolls that would befuddle Willie Mosconi."

With this background you might guess the

type of crime story that Mr. Bradt would write. Easy to guess, isn't it? Would you expect a story of loneliness and love and the long arm of the law? ...

Maybe it wasn't right, her Jim dead and buried only a year and all, to sit here by his grave in the clearing back of the house and fret over the Sheriff arresting Wayne Chandler today. But the glade was quiet and peaceful when the still summer days retreated before the warm dark nights, and Sarah seemed to always end up here when something was troubling her mind.

Just a couple months before she'd been leaning against this same sturdy little pine, letting her loneliness and her fears melt into the June night, when she'd first heard Wayne call. He'd ventured up the road, tired and looking for a bed and maybe a bite to eat, insisting he'd pay her husband or help with the morning chores for his night's keep.

When Sarah told him her Jim had passed on, Wayne flushed and wrung his hands together for no reason and said he'd be off now and was sorry to have bothered her. But the hired man hadn't shown for two days and she'd heard he was drinking his paycheck again, so she told Wayne she surely could use some honest work around the place as the chores were piling up faster than she could get to them.

She'd fed him supper that night, she remembered as she sat in the clearing watching the moon rise just above the treetops. And after supper she'd boiled up a pot of coffee and they got to conversing until before she knew it dawn spilled over the hills and the rooster was crowing. When she laughed at his jokes or near cried when he described some of the pretty places he'd seen, the lonely ache inside her disappeared for the first time in a year.

Recollecting the first evening with Wayne made her cry for what seemed the hundredth time today. She got to her feet and tried to think of the crops and the harvest coming up soon. But when she shut her eyes she saw Wayne just as plainly as if he were standing in front of her. She knew she couldn't visualize Jim so clearly any more without pulling out one of the photographs she'd hidden away in the bureau drawer shortly after Wayne had moved in. But she supposed what with time passing and a new man on her mind this was natural.

Then this morning, when Wayne was working out in the barn and she was scrubbing the last of the breakfast dishes, everything had gone bad again. Sheriff Tucker and his deputy, Charlie Weber, they'd come and taken him away.

Sarah opened her eyes. The moon was big and round and she wondered if Wayne could see it from the jailhouse. And she wondered crazy things, like if they'd fed him a proper supper and if he was thinking about her as much as she was thinking about him. Seemed this was a worse fit of loneliness than when Jim went and got killed in the fields.

The noise of a car bouncing up the rut-filled road broke the solemn tranquility of the moment. Sarah sprinted from the clearing. Could be the Sheriff was bringing Wayne back. It was all a mistake and now they'd forget it ever happened and return to things just as they were.

She raced around the corner of the house and saw the Sheriff's black and white jeep approaching. And it did seem that two people were riding in the front seat. Straining her eyes, wishing she could turn up the moon's brightness like a lamp, she waited nervously on the porch.

Her heart plummeted like a bird shot on the wing. It was Charlie Weber who rode next to the Sheriff. A flash of disgust went through her. She suspected Charlie was just as happy to see Wayne Chandler in jail as she knew he'd been when her Jim had died.

"Evening, Sarah," Sheriff Tucker called too loudly, braking to a halt in front of the porch. She watched the two men closely but did not acknowledge the greeting. Charlie Weber jumped out the far door and strode around the car. He looked at her the way he always did, real calculating and cold, like he was sizing her up in a way she didn't appreciate.

"Evening, Sarah," he said slowly, a strange half smile cracking his face.

She dropped her gaze for an instant and when she raised her head again it was the Sheriff she watched.

"What do you want, Sheriff?"

"We got a few facts about Wayne Chandler I think you ought to know. I figured I best tell you right away and maybe it would ease your mind some." He glanced over at Charlie Weber before continuing. "This information came over the wire today. Just like we thought,

Chandler's a wanted man. We've got enough on him to send him up for a right long stretch, it appears to me. It's all on paper, Sarah." He pulled a folded piece of paper from his shirt pocket, stepped onto the porch, and handed it to her.

"It's all right there on the paper," Charlie Weber said from below. He struck a match and lit a cigarette. The acrid smell of the sulphur and the thick smoke he blew her way nearly turned Sarah's stomach. She snatched the paper from the Sheriff and tossed it onto the wooden planks of the porch.

"I don't need to read those lies. I know my Wayne."

The Sheriff shrugged and bent down to pick up the paper. "I'm just trying to make it easier for you."

Sure he was, she thought. Ever since her Jim died folks had tried their darnedest to make it easier for poor Sarah. Trouble was, their sympathy seemed to come not from their hearts, but from some sense of obligation, as if it was a duty they had to perform. Sarah knew the womenfolk didn't like her because she was young and pretty, and when she watched them as they brought their baskets of food and listened to their idle chatter, she thought she sensed in them a secret relish for the tragedy of others.

If the women weren't bad enough themselves, they sent subdued young men around after a proper mourning period, who sat quietly watching her and not sure how to act. Worse yet were the heartless fellows like Charlie Weber, who barely concealed their intentions when they came calling and saying they could make her forget all about her Jim.

Jim had been a good man, more decent than any of the folks who gathered in the clearing the day he was buried, standing uncomfortably under the hot sun in their dark suits and heavy dresses. Never had she regretted marrying him. And when he died there was an emptiness that all the visitors could no more fill than could the few farm animals she had kept.

Then Wayne had burst into her life and swept away her sorrow even that first night when they'd talked until dawn, opening to her an enchanting and joyous way of life she'd never experienced before.

Theirs was a love she never had dreamed possible. While her relationship with Jim had developed slowly, maturing only after marriage, steady and sure as the seasons, with Wayne it was as if a winter storm had exploded or spring rains were falling or the fall winds were blowing so hard you could hardly walk against them. A kind of madness she had never before felt. It was as if they were made of the same dreams and desires, sorrows and sadnesses. When he held her that night she had to be the happiest woman on earth.

"Let me tell you somethin', Sarah," Charlie Weber drawled. "If that boy were free to go he'd hightail it to the stateline so fast a fellow wouldn't even see him go by. No way that joker'd come back to you after we've exposed him for what he is."

"He would too. I know Wayne. He don't have anything to be ashamed of."

Exasperated, the Sheriff shook his head. He peered down the road into the darkness and then spun quickly around toward Sarah. Too bad she'd gotten mixed up with Chandler. He felt sorry for her. She was a sweet good-looking woman, and if he could convince her of what a lowdown character Chandler was she'd be making one of the local boys a fine wife in no time. He approached her and placed his hands firmly on her shoulders.

"Listen, Sarah. Men like Wayne

Chandler just prey on women like you. They have ways of finding out you collected that big policy when Jim died. They know you're gonna be lonely. Chandler would talk you out of every cent you own and the farm too, give him half a chance. Now why in the devil can't you understand that?"

Her arms shot up from her sides and slapped Sheriff Tucker's hands off her shoulders. "Then why didn't he try?" she said, wheeling around and stalking to the far end of the porch. From this side of the house you could see around the corner just enough to view where Jim was buried. She stood with her arms crossed and her back to the men, and tried to catch the peaceful feeling a quiet night in the clearing brought her. She felt the rough boards under her bare feet. A wisp of warm wind, sluggish as the river in late summer, blew through her dress.

The Sheriff eyed her apprehensively, then sighed loudly and walked down the steps to the jeep. "Just thought you ought to know, Sarah," he said. "Sorry you had to find out this way. Let's go, Charlie."

She heard the car start and the engine rumble when the Sheriff gunned it a couple

207

times, and then the crackle of the gravel crunching under the tires as the jeep pulled away. Suddenly, desperately, she bolted down the steps, ran across the sharp gravel, and dashed down the dusty road.

"Wait!" she cried.

The jeep halted, but she ran until she reached Sheriff Tucker's open window.

"What is it, Sarah?"

"Can you take me to see him? Right now?"

"What for?"

"I've got to tell him I'll wait. He needs me now. I know it."

"Needs a good lawyer, is what he needs," Charlie Weber laughed from the far side of the jeep.

"Charlie's right," Sheriff Tucker said. "And dammit, girl, I spelled it out for you plain as day. Wayne Chandler was after your money. I can't make it any clearer than that."

Sarah didn't answer, but stared at the Sheriff so intently that he turned his head and studied the dashboard, as if some wisdom were lurking in its gauges. "Tomorrow morning," he said finally. "Come down tomorrow morning. By then we'll probably have a rap sheet on this guy long enough to paper your bedroom walls with."

"You gonna tell her what he said?" Charlie Weber asked the Sheriff.

The Sheriff's head snapped to the side as if it had been slapped. "You tell her since you had to go and bring it up," he snarled.

Charlie leaned low so he could see Sarah through the window. "You want to hear somethin' kind of humorous considering all we've told you, Sarah? That boy wanted us to let you know that he loves you. Imagine him saying he loves you." He laughed harshly and sat up straight as soon as he saw the pain in her eyes. "Let's get goin', Sheriff."

Sheriff Tucker shifted into first gear and the jeep lurched down the road. Standing still as a tree on a near-windless night, Sarah watched until the red taillights vanished in the distance. The moon wrapped her in its somber light and made her tears glisten faintly.

Early the next morning Sarah awoke from an uneasy sleep. She grabbed the cotton dress off the foot of the bed and stepped through the waning darkness to the bathroom, where she switched on the lamp. Every movement she made, it seemed, she'd rehearsed during the restless night. She bathed and pulled her dress on and brushed her hair until it sparkled like rich golden grain when the sun washes over it at dawn. Each stroke with her brush seemed to add more luster.

Looking serious in the mirror, she combed her bangs just the way Wayne liked them, pulled to one side and drooping close over her eye. What a joy it would be to see him. If she could just hold him for a minute, hear his whisper in her ear, then everything would be fine again.

Already the day was warm, the air heavy, she noticed as she hurried down the eroded driveway to the dirt county road, and then, after a mile or so, onto the paved highway to town. She was regretting that she hadn't listened to Jim and learned to drive the truck, when she heard an approaching car behind her. She twirled around and waved. An old pickup loaded with produce for the town market skidded to a halt on the dusty shoulder.

She climbed in unhesitatingly and listened as well as her concentration allowed while the driver complained of the dry weather and how it was going to ruin his season unless a bit of rain fell soon. He was still carrying on when he let her off at the jailhouse, and never did inquire as to what business she had there.

She ran up the concrete walkway and flew expectantly through the door, as if she thought Wayne would be standing there all set to go free.

The Sheriff and Charlie Weber, though, were alone in the office, and she was disappointed to discover that the cells weren't visible except through a small window on a massive gray door. The Sheriff mumbled a greeting and turned away. Charlie, sitting with his feet propped on his desk, smiled, but didn't rise.

"Can I see him now?" she asked breathlessly.

The Sheriff spoke, and she could barely hear him. "That's not possible."

"But you said I could," she pleaded. "I have to!"

He didn't answer right away, and when he started to speak no words followed the first few.

"Sheriff seems a bit tongue-tied," Charlie Weber said. "Don't know why. Every jail has to deal with an escapee now and then."

Sheriff Tucker glanced forlornly at his

deputy, breathed deeply, then walked up to Sarah. She'd gone pale and her hands were trembling. "Wayne Chandler escaped last night, Sarah," he said rapidly. "Don't know how, but a trustee or somebody got hold of the office key. We usually keep it pretty well hidden. We finally caught up with him and when we called and he didn't stop we had to fire."

Sarah stood still as the words settled into her mind, looking into his face but not really seeing it. Suddenly she sprang toward Charlie Weber. "You killed him!" she screamed. "*You* killed him!"

Charlie fended off her small fists and the Sheriff, grabbed her shoulders and twisted her around. "I did," he whispered, eyes inches from her own. "I had to."

Her body went limp and the Sheriff tightened his grip on her, fearing she would fall if he let go. Then she slowly stiffened, as if coming back to life. Without looking at either man she walked to the door. "I'm sorry," the Sheriff said.

She opened the door and stepped outside. "What surprised me," she heard Charlie Weber say purposefully loud enough for her to hear before she shut the door, "was where we caught up to him.

Hell, I would've sworn he'd go for the stateline. But you had to shoot him, Sheriff. He didn't give you a choice. No tellin' what he had in mind for poor Sarah if he'd actually made it to her place, like he was tryin'."

But the Sheriff was thinking about the key. There was no sure way of knowing who got it to Chandler. He looked at Charlie sitting with his feet on the desk and smiling like he hadn't really seen a man die last night. There was no sure way of knowing.

Sarah closed the door. The street glared brightly in the morning sun. But it was still too early for people to be up and about much, and the only sound she heard was the whisper of a loneliness like she had never known before.

JACK RITCHIE

Beauty Is As Beauty Does

Being one of the judges, especially the senior judge, of the Fifty States Beauty Contest wasn't as easy and pleasant a task as it seemed. In fact, it was downright perilous.

Jack Ritchie is one of the most prolific and most admired short-story writers in the mystery field. He has written and published more than 450 short stories, and is going stronger than ever . . .

When I noticed the lavender envelope protruding from under the door of my suite, I picked it up. Inside I found a single typewritten sheet of paper.

Dear Mr. Walker: If I am not selected Miss Fifty States in the finals tomorrow, I promise that I will kill you. I mean this quite seriously. My entire life would be ruined and so I might just as well murder you. I think I would even enjoy it.

I showed the note to Stubbins and McGee.

214

McGee rubbed his jaw. "Now that's peculiar."

I regarded him coldly. "That is clearly the understatement of the year. It is a threat to murder me."

"I mean that the note isn't *signed*. How are you supposed to know which girl to vote for?"

I read the note again. "Hmm. You are quite right, McGee. I didn't notice it at first. Then what the hell is the point of sending me the note in the first place?"

McGee gave it thought. "Possibly she just forgot to sign her name."

McGee, Stubbins, and I are the three judges of the Miss Fifty States Beauty Contest. However, since I am the senior judge and McGee and Stubbins were likely to defer to any decision I might make, I was obviously the person to influence if someone wanted to win the contest.

"You *do* want to find out who wrote that note, don't you?" Stubbins asked.

"Of course. But there are *ten* finalists."

Stubbins quickly paged through the files of the contestants, apparently searching for one item in particular. He put three folders aside. "There we are."

I had been looking over his shoulder. "There we are what?"

"You will notice that the note is typed," Stubbins said. "There is not a single typing error and the entire message is nicely centered on the sheet of paper. In other words, the typist is obviously not a novice at the machine." He indicated the folders. "These three girls are the only finalists who can type – Miss Wisconsin, Miss New York, and Miss South Carolina."

I frowned. "I still can't figure out that lack of a signature. Could she actually have forgotten?"

McGee brightened. "Maybe she first wanted to see how you would *react* to a threat, even if it was anonymous. If you are frightened and intimidated, she will press home the advantage and make herself known."

"She will be disappointed," I said. "I am neither frightened nor intimidated."

"Ah, yes," McGee said. "But suppose you *pretend* that you are?"

I saw his point. "Very well, summon the three girls here."

McGee and Stubbins accomplished the errand and brought back the girls and their chaperones. I had the latter remain in an

216

ante-room while we spoke to the girls and showed them the note.

Gretchen – Miss Wisconsin – handed it back to me and smiled sweetly. "Why isn't it signed?"

"I don't know. Perhaps the writer forgot?" I gazed at the three of them and got innocent silence.

Olivia – Miss New York – could smile sweetly too. "Why pick on us three? There are *ten* finalists."

Stubbins beamed his information. "You three are the only ones who can type."

I allowed my hands to tremble slightly as I folded the note and returned it to my pocket. "I don't see why anybody wants to kill me just because of this contest. I have been nice to all of you, haven't I?"

"Of course, Mr. Walker," Melissa – Miss South Carolina – said. "You've been a dear, sweet, intelligent man."

I nodded. "It's quite a difficult job to judge a beauty contest. All I'm trying to do is be fair." I used my handkerchief to wipe my forehead. "Now I want whoever wrote this note to think it over carefully. You wouldn't *really* want to kill me, now would you?"

Behind them, McGee lifted a book a foot

above the table top and raised a questioning eyebrow.

I read his message and nodded almost imperceptibly.

He dropped the book and it made a loud bang.

I leaped wildly. "What was that?"

McGee apologized. "I'm sorry, Mr. Walker. The book just slipped."

I laughed nervously. "That sounded rather like a pistol shot." I wiped my face again. "Now, girls, I just want you to remember that I am your friend. Honestly and truly your friend. I'm here to help you in any way I can. If there is anything troubling you, I would be only too happy – yes, *eager* – to do whatever I can."

It was nearly nine o'clock that evening and I was alone when there came a knock on my door.

I found a huge young man with a look of determination in his eyes. "Are you Mr. Walker? One of the judges of the Miss Fifty States Beauty Contest?"

I nodded cautiously.

"This has got to stop," he announced firmly.

"What has got to stop?"

"I am not going to let you crown Gretchen Miss Fifty States."

"And why not?"

"Because I intend to marry her."

I sighed. "Come in and sit down."

He found a chair. "I just can't have her gawked at."

"She has been gawked at from Sheboygan to Milwaukee."

"I know. But this time it will be on nation-wide television. Can't you just imagine what all those millions of men will be *thinking* when they see her in that skimpy bikini?" He brushed sandy-colored hair from his forehead. "Gretchen and I grew up together. We went to the same grade school, the same high school. We took Biology together."

"You were that close?"

He breathed heavily. "I shouldn't have let it go on and on. First it was the Montmorency Cherry Queen, then the Sebago Potato Princess, and on to the McIntosh Apple Darling. I thought that would finally satisfy her, but it all just went to her head."

He seemed quite desperate. "Do you realize what will happen to her if she wins this contest? She'll be famous and meet all kinds of rich men and celebrities and get married a half a dozen times before she's through. And she'll be dieting all the time and that isn't healthy. When she weighed a hundred and forty she was always cheerful and light-hearted. Have you come to a decision yet about who's going to be Miss Fifty States?"

"I am still giving it thought."

He rose and hovered over me. "Mr. Walker, if you pick Gretchen, I swear I'll kill you. I won't have any reason for going on anyway." He paused at the door. "The last time I went trap-shooting, I got ninety-nine out of one hundred."

I took optimistic comfort in that he had missed at least one.

When he was gone, I decided I needed a drink. I was making it when there was another knock on the door.

It was Olivia.

I glanced past her. "Where's your chaperone?"

She shrugged. "I got some sleeping pills from the hotel doctor and accidentally spiked her milk." She closed the door behind her and a moment later I was a bit astonished to find that we were sitting side by side on the sofa. Her raven-black hair seemed to exude an aggressive fragrance.

She showed the whitest of teeth. "Mr. Walker, I can see that a man of your educated type likes a woman with brains and a lot of culture. How did you like my painting?"

As her contribution to the talent segment of our contest, Olivia had entered one of her paintings of what was very possibly a bridge in the moonlight entitled *Spanscape*.

She leaned closer. "You've been so nice to all of us, and I, for one, am very appreciative."

I cleared my throat. "Appreciative is an adjective."

Her fingers crawled about the back of my neck. "I could be ever so grateful for any little favor you might do for me tomorrow, Mr. Walker. So very grateful." Her eyes were close. Her lips were close. As a matter of fact, all of her was close.

The memory of my Puritan ancestors pulled me to my feet. "Young woman," I said sternly, "that won't do you a bit of good."

She studied me for a few seconds and then shrugged. "All right, then I'll play it straight. I was the one who wrote you that note and I meant every word of it."

I moved to the phone. "I am going to call the police."

She smiled. "Go ahead if you want to. But I'll just deny that I said anything at all. It will be your word against mine." She put a gleam into her eyes. "You're as good as dead if I'm not Miss Fifty States by this time tomorrow."

She swept out of the door.

Fifteen minutes later I had finished my drink and was working on the second when I had to answer the door again.

It was Melissa.

She carried what appeared to be a liquor bottle gift-wrapped. "Just a token for all the nice things you've done for little old helpless me. It's really good bourbon."

"Where is your chaperone?" I asked routinely.

"The dear thing's fast asleep. Just drank her milk and conked out." She put the bottle on the table. "We won't drink any of this now. I know the rules and I wouldn't want to be accused of trying to influence you in any way. So we'll just save the bottle for a *private* victory celebration tomorrow in case I somehow *happen* to become Miss Fifty States."

Her green eyes looked into mine. "You

know, you look so distinguished and educated and all that you remind me of my Uncle David who writes poetry and has it published in the *Tuskachee Clarion*. Right on the editorial page."

Her fingertips began a Braille exploration of my lapels.

"Young woman," I said stiffly, and perhaps a little tardily, "I will not be swayed by any blandishments, present or promised. My judging integrity remains unshaken."

There were some seconds of silence. Then she smiled coldly. "I didn't think there was any harm in trying sugar first. All right then, buster, have it your way. I'm the one who wrote that note. And killing runs in my family because my great Aunt Phoebe once shot a Yankee captain who had the gall to walk into her drawing room wearing spurs."

She went to the door, turned, and decided to restore some of the warmth to her smile. "Keep the bottle and think it over. We could get to be such *good* friends tomorrow night."

She was gone less than ten minutes when I was called to the door again. Frankly, I expected to find Gretchen, but it was a tall young man with untamed red hair.

"Ha," I said, "I suppose you want to kill me too?"

He blinked. "I wouldn't kill anybody. I'm a pacifist. Except in time of war, of course."

"You are refreshing. What can I do for you?"

"If you could get my painting back, I'd be very appreciative."

"What painting are you talking about?"

"*Spanscape.*"

"You own the picture?"

"I also painted it. Then I left it to Olivia, but that was before I knew that it was worth anything."

"Let me get this straight. Olivia did *not* paint the picture?"

"No, I did. And I just got a five hundred dollar offer from somebody who saw it in my studio last week and you simply can't pass up something like that. But Olivia says that she's going to keep it for a year while she's Miss Fifty States and after that she doesn't give a damn who knows or doesn't know that she didn't paint the picture."

"Does she know that you came to me?"

"No. She said she'd kill me if I did, but five hundred bucks is five hundred bucks."

He looked a bit worried though. "You don't suppose she actually would kill me?"

"Cross your fingers," I said. "I'll see what can be done."

When he left I locked the door and I had no intention of answering it again that night, even if Gretchen didn't miss her turn.

The next evening at eight, Stubbins, McGee, and I were seated at the judges' table on the stage of the arena as the finals of the Miss Fifty States Beauty Contest began.

As I watched the ten girls, it seemed to me that Gretchen, Olivia, and Melissa were clearly a notch above the seven others. Perhaps that was just coincidence, perhaps it had something to do with learning how to type, or perhaps it was just because I'd seen more of them than I had the other girls.

I sighed. Two of the girls had threatened to kill me, but which one of them was actually responsible for the note?

Olivia?

She had verbally threatened to kill me, but had she written the note too or was she just taking advantage of a trend?

And there was the matter of *Spanscape*.

225

She had not painted the entry herself and that automatically disqualified her from consideration in the contest.

Yes, Olivia was definitely out.

That left Gretchen and Melissa.

Gretchen had not come to visit me last night, but was that because she was not the letter writer, or was it because she could not get her chaperone to drink spiked milk?

And Melissa?

Had her Aunt Phoebe pleaded self-defense and been freed by a sympathetic jury or had she been sent to prison?

It was nearly ten o'clock when Stubbins, McGee, and I went into a huddle to make our decision and found that our choice was unanimous.

I stepped to the microphone and announced to the waiting world that the new Miss Fifty States was none other than Melissa – Miss South Carolina.

The usual pandemonium, of course, ensued.

Melissa broke into tears of joy. Gretchen and Olivia instantly followed suit. Gretchen hugged Melissa and *sincerely* congratulated her. Olivia hugged Melissa and said that she knew all along that

Melissa really *deserved* to win the contest. And finally Olivia and Gretchen hugged each other and wept over their sheer happiness at Melissa's good fortune.

It was past eleven before I managed to get back to my suite.

There was a knock on my door.

Damn, I said, but I opened it.

Melissa stood in the doorway and she appeared to be somewhat breathless.

I blinked. Had she really meant it last night when she said that we would have a cozy little celebration?

My eyes went to the gift-wrapped bottle still on the table. I felt a bit warm. Melissa's offer hadn't influenced my decision in the slightest, but now that the contest was over –

I smiled.

"You've been *so* considerate," she said. "But I'm afraid that I really won't have time for our little old victory celebration tonight. A Miss Fifty States is *so* busy, you know. You *do* understand, don't you?"

I sighed at the vanish of a dream. "Never mind. I'll drink the whole bottle myself."

Her lashes fluttered over innocent blue eyes. "That's just it and I'm *so* glad I got here in time. If I were you I wouldn't touch one teensy-weensy drop of that bourbon. Because if you do, you'll get an awful, awful tummy ache. If you know what I mean?"

When she was gone, I emptied the bourbon bottle down the drain and poured myself a full tumbler of my own safe brandy.

ROSALIND ASHE

The Long Glass Man

Edgar Allan Poe, the most famous of all mystery writers, died on October 7, 1849 – 133 years ago. In memory of that sorrowful date, and in memory of other mystery writers who were interested in spiritualism and the supernatural, particularly A. Conan Doyle and Agatha Christie, we offer you an unusual ghost story – about a ghost who haunted a staircase at Oxford University and who was summoned – materialized – with terrifying and tragic results. Are you afraid of the dark? No? Then meet the long glass man – more accurately, "a gray man – gray and shiny like dirty glass"...

"I take it we all agree on the fact of A Supernatural, and that so-called ghosts that most of us accept as the supernatural take form only for a select few. But the idea of a *harmful* ghost is to me simply ridiculous."

We had finished dessert and adjourned to the smaller common room at the top of the staircase, a move that tended to sort the men from the boys. Only the hard-drinking, hard-talking brigade usually made the final assault up the spiral staircase, headed by the bachelors, natural climbers with nothing to lose, closely followed by the long-married – those who knew that, by this late hour, their North Oxford home fires would be banked down with tea leaves for the night, and the only voice in the house would be a note of instructions on the kitchen table concerning cats and dustbins.

Here the firelight glowed through one's malt whiskey, and the deep leather chairs were difficult to get out of. But Littlemount did not sit; he was in good voice and needed props and space to make his points: three strides to the sideboard and back, tap out pipe, eat a Chocolate Oliver from the silver biscuit box especially stocked for him – and never once a pause in his flow. He was summing up an argument that had started at his end of the long table. I had asked someone quite casually, "Are you afraid of the dark?" and it had all stemmed from that.

"So we must conclude," said Littlemount, "that the only harm a ghost can do is to drive us into self-inflicted harm, mental or physical: we can die of fright; or flee, and fall downstairs and break our necks; or allow our shaking candle to set the bed curtains alight; but we cannot be stabbed or strangled by an immaterial being. How could it hold a knife? Or press insubstantial thumbs on our windpipe? They would pass right through, would they not, and meet ineffectually on the other side. Admit, sir, ghosts do not have the molecular structure to commit murder."

The target of his punch line was a stranger, presumably someone's guest. He too was on his feet; he stood very tall and saturnine, observing Littlemount's restless terrier-like scuttling. Only his eyes moved, bright under heavy brows. "In that case, we must take care not to alter that molecular structure," he said.

"Oh, come now, Littlemount –" Stacey, one of the younger dons, was busy with bottles at the sideboard and seemed not to notice the hush of confrontation, all eyes on the tall guest. "Surely ghosts must have *some* sort of structure or, according to your theory, they would simply sink through the floor."

It was the stranger who answered him.

"It seems that apparitions run along well-defined tracks, the grooves carved out by the horrific circumstances of their own peculiar tragedy. Extreme suffering or guilt, or both, appear to be the commonest causes. The happy ghost that haunts its favorite spot is as surely a cosy Victorian invention. The strongest motive for a ghost to return is that of completion – something unfinished, something still to do, whether it's revenge or the expiation of guilt. Hidden treasure? Aye, sir, but usually come by foul play. True love? But unrequited, unsatisfied: 'I will hang my heart on the weeping willow tree –'

" 'So that the nun who wrings her hands –'

" 'And the horseman who rides over the cobbles and up to the door –'

" 'The baby in the guest wing that crouches by the grate –'

Yes, they are all endlessly replaying their tragic moment, fixed in their groove. And that, gentlemen, is some people's idea of hell."

"Certainly, certainly –" Littlemount clearly felt it was time to gather up the reins again. "We are not disputing that ghosts are attached to one place; no well-documented apparition *follows* folk to haunt them, or materializes anywhere but in its proper lair. But that is not to say that a ghost, even an armed ghost, like Hamlet's father, could inflict an injury –"

"You mean if, even briefly, it could have assumed some sort of corporeal solidity."

"Ah, by possession of a living person – that is an altogether different matter, my good fellow, if you will forgive the pun."

"Very well, we shall agree to keep Possession out of this, or we will get bogged down in Demonism and have to resort to the Power of the Church. There is an example of materialization in its full sense of which I could tell you, if you have the patience to hear. It is a disturbing documentary but sufficiently rare to amount to a curiosity rather than a threat to your peace of mind."

Littlemount himself recharged the stranger's glass and installed him in what was habitually the Master's chair. Another log was thrown on the fire, and someone even suggested turning down the lights.

"No," said our storyteller, "they will do very well. Let us approach this in the spirit of the well-illuminated scientific inquiry – for that is just the way it started.

"It was nearly thirty years ago, just after

the war, in this university; the college we can ignore, and for the individuals we shall invent names. Many undergraduates were older then, coming back from the front. Black, let us call him, had served in Burma and returned to finish his degree, changing from mathematics to philosophy.

"Now, Black was psychic – abnormally so. Early in his country childhood he had shown what is commonly called 'second sight,' in everything from party games to the revelation of distant disasters. His adolescence had been troubled by poltergeists; in the army he learned to conceal his powers both from his commanding officers – it does morale no good to have a clairvoyant in the lines – and from his fellows, for whom he confined it to light betting; he was never short of cigarettes.

"In Burma he made contact with the mystic sect of a religious order who accepted him as a gifted seer, and opened their sacred books to him. So, equipped with a full appreciation of his powers, and the discipline to disguise them, he returned to Oxford. His purpose was research, but not quite on the lines laid down by his tutors.

"Our other protagonist is an American, a Fulbright scholar who amply merited the hopeful title. White, we shall call him, was a child prodigy, a so-called 'Whiz kid,' who had been 'discovered' early and overexposed on wireless and television in the United States. His had been a childhood of tutors and business managers, of hotels, taxis, the bright lights. He had a nervous breakdown in his teens, after being accused of cheating – a resounding scandal in that deeply puritan nation, and the occasion for extended editorial heartsearching. He took the only other way out; he cut loose from his family, changed his name, and buried himself in a small midwestern college. There he covered himself with honors, *summa cum laude*, and won a scholarship to Oxford, England.

"White knew he was psychic, but had never fully exploited his powers; he was afraid of them. Now, like a reformed alcoholic, he refused even to touch the charmed bottle – he did not know what sort of djinn he might release. But, like the reformed alcoholic, he grew confident, and halfway through his first term he decided to test himself. He saw an ESP Meeting advertised on the Junior Common Room notice board, and dared to attend.

"He found it disappointing. It seemed chiefly concerned with the phenomenon of coincidence. In the darkened church hall fuzzy slides of drawings that approximated each other, produced by subjects in isolated cubicles, were flashed onto a screen; lists of numerals were analyzed and hummed over. All so much Wincarnis to the alcoholic. He left early, and was followed and joined by a fellow deserter. They walked back toward College together.

"Now, Black had already marked down the young American as a fellow psychic; seeing him at the ESP gathering had simply determined him to make a move. White was flattered by the attentiveness, indeed the concentration, with which his cautious observations were treated by his senior. He had found his fellow freshmen generally hearty and callow, straight from school, unlike the war heroes now in their second and third years. They, he felt, had lived; he, who had already been through so much, longed to be accepted by them – and especially by Black, the loner in his army greatcoat, for whom he sensed a peculiar affinity.

"So the acquaintanceship flourished;

they visited each other's rooms, went to concerts together, walked on Otmore, and at the end of term Black invited the American home for Christmas. Before they left, they made arrangements for White to move to his friend's staircase; the freshman who had the small attic room there was only too glad to agree to the exchange, though at the time White did not understand the reason for this eagerness.

"Up to this point the two young men had discussed the supernatural only because they had discussed everything. White had told his new friend of his prodigious childhood and the traumatic denouement that ended it. Black had spoken of the monks and their teachings, but both had avoided the subject of the extrasensory powers of which they were increasingly aware.

"In White this was fear; in Black, the patient taming of that fear. Full revelation Black left to the vacation, and to his possessive mother – a simple woman who had been cheated of her maternal rights by Black's violent independence. As he foresaw, she took the young American under her wing and used him at once as a second son and confidant. To him, late one

237

evening, she unburdened her worries about her dark lamb – so clever, but so unstable; and the mess the poltergeists used to make; and how he had known when a favorite cousin in Inverness was killed rock climbing.

"The American spent the night in heartsearching; but he knew he could not deny this supernatural gift now summoned by one of even greater strength. The reformed alcoholic reached for the bottle.

"I have dwelt on this relationship to show how emphatically young Black was the prime mover; it also helps to explain the load of guilt he carried ever after.

"But at the time it felt more the shedding of a load. It was Christmas morning; they celebrated their new partnership with juvenile high spirits; on the way to Church they predicted the hymn numbers. Both hit on the same numerals, in the same order, and the board beside the pulpit simply confirmed the result. Without a word they abandoned the family and service, turned their backs – symbolically? – on the Church, and walked and talked on the moors till dark and dinnertime.

"Now for the first time in his life Black

opened his whole mind to another individual. From their original encounter they had found themselves anticipating each other's thoughts, answering unspoken questions, meeting without arranging time or place. Now, in a few hours, the older told the younger all he knew, all the monks had taught him, all he planned to do. For his great experiment was with the supernatural, his goal to effect a true materialization, and he needed a more powerful 'current' than he alone could supply. He explained his deliberate choice of rooms in college: they were said to be haunted.

"Back at Oxford, term had not yet started, and they had the staircase to themselves. It was in the corner of the inner quadrangle; White's was only a small fusty garret, but he spent most of his time in his friend's rooms below. Even here the large study was dark, set in the angle of the two high walls, but there was always a bright fire in the opulently carved fireplace, for Black had a well-trained and devoted scout. Bunce had been with the college all his life and was held to be the authority on the staircase ghost; he could remember it all being told when he was a lad and considered too young to listen to such things.

"It seems that Black's rooms had been the scene of a Victorian scandal, when the rooms were occupied by an aging and eccentric theologian in holy orders, as most dons still were. It was said that he had been the cause of driving a pupil mad, to the point of suicide. Soon after, the don himself had died of causes unknown – had been discovered lying by that same ornate chimney-piece; and it was he who apparently haunted the staircase – footsteps on the creaking treads, sometimes the frantic rustling of pages. Once he had been seen, a tall gaunt figure standing motionless with his hands on the mantel shelf.

"Fifty years later these were still the hardest rooms in college to fill; none of the Fellows wanted them – too dark, they said. So when Black volunteered, on condition he could have the whole suite to himself, the Bursar had agreed. In this way Black acquired an inner sanctum, the dressing room, which he kept locked, even to his cleaner. There his precious books were safe from curious eyes, and he could meditate without interruption.

"Moreover, he covered the window with blackout material and developed photographs in the basin. He told White how for many nights he had set up a camera with its shutter open, focused to take in the whole of the fireplace, in an attempt to capture an impression of the ghostly theologian. One of the prints was quite interesting.

"In it there appeared to be two things hanging from the mantel shelf, barely discernible among the carved swags and curlicues – they might have been a pair of socks put there to dry. He let White pore over it, then produced his masterpiece, a blowup of one of the 'socks'; now one could guess that it was not furry, or gauzy, as it had seemed at first sight, but that it had moved. And the upper edge, pale against the back wall, was corrugated, bumpy, like a row of knuckles.

" 'I believe that is where it stands,' said Black. 'Why only its hands appear I don't yet know. But I propose to stand in just that place – hence the importance of this photograph – and concentrate on putting out as much current as I can summon. If I feel anything, well, that is where you come in. For then we will need to boost the output. According to my theory, my batteries would be drained before our aim is achieved – a theory that explains many of the disastrous attempts at materialization in the past. But between us we may have enough psychic 'juice' to bring this thing about. And if one of us should suffer, or worse, there is a helper at hand, someone to give first aid, and – more important in my eyes – to be a witness.'

"Out of term college retires early. By eleven only a few dim squares of light showed where the midnight oil burned, and by twelve our psychic investigators decided there was no further fear of interruption. They locked the door, built up the fire, and turned out all except one small reading lamp. Then, while White stood where the camera had been and directed him from the photograph, Black positioned himself with his hands on the mantelpiece.

"At first Black gazed down at the fire, but it distracted him. He closed his eyes and summoned up all his concentration into a single fierce imperative: 'Come.' Fifteen minutes passed by White's watch, and still his friend hung, his head fallen forward, crucified against the high carved fireplace.

"Suddenly he gave a low moan. 'It's *cold*,' he whispered, and turned his head towards his left hand. White could see nothing. 'My hand is so cold.' As they watched, a mistiness appeared over the fist that clung to the shelf. Slowly a line of light emerged along the translucent blur, defining its upper edge: a long delicate bony hand apparently fashioned out of cloudy glass – for the whiteness of the knuckles was still visible through it.

"Then with a sharp cry Black twisted his head the other way, his eyes staring. 'Quick, help me! It's got both my hands –' His friend was beside him. 'Take over its left hand with your right,' Black whispered, 'palm to palm, remember. I will concentrate on this one – oh, the cold is creeping through me –'

"White moved warily round him; whatever might be standing there, he had no wish to pass through it. He stood close to the two left hands, felt the chill radiating from them, and saw the horrible perfection of the 'glass' one, engraved with the outline of nails and a fine mesh of wrinkles. It was only the desperate, voiceless appeal in his friend's face as he twisted round for a moment that gave White the strength to put his right hand forward. He slid it, palm upward, under the transparent hand, as Black gently removed his.

243

"The penetrating cold struck into White; it seemed to paralyze everything but the memory of Black's reiterated command: 'When it comes, do not flinch. Think, this is what we have worked toward; it is in our grasp. And give it all your strength.'

"Concentrating on that, White slowly raised his frozen hand; the glass one rose with it, and he could feel the answering pressure, as of something living, through the clinging tackiness of something dead.

"Black flexed his free hand, held it briefly to the fire's warmth, then placed it, palm up, under the icy mist that was gathering over his right. He reached out to White, and their grip completed the circuit. Now they stood with their backs to the fire, and grateful for it, pressing against a force they could not see, passing their vital strength to it, willing it with all their combined psychic powers to take form. There appeared before them a cloudy shape; next, the glassy outline, high and narrow. They felt their strength fading as it grew more solid, like a sketch being colored in, obscuring the room behind it, and even casting a flickering shadow across the carpet.

"It was a villainous old man, tall and

stooping, in a crumpled dog collar and a long rusty academic gown. It nodded sharply and withdrew its hands from theirs. 'Thank you, dear boys – that will suffice.' The voice was a harsh whisper carried on foul carrion breath. It grinned wolfishly. 'Your part is over for the present. It will be interesting to see, will it not, how long your little experiment holds shape.' It stalked to the door. 'I will be back again when I have need of you.'

"White took a step forward and crumpled up in a dead faint. Black had fallen to his knees, his senses weak and whirling. He tried to crawl forward, and caught at the creature's gown, but he heard the key turn, the door slam, and it was gone. His fading thought was: Lord, what have we done?

"The scout found them still unconscious beside the dead fire. The room was icy cold. He called the cleaner from the next staircase, and she covered them with blankets while he brewed coffee and built up a roaring blaze in the grate.

" 'Such goings on all in one night!' Black heard them from a great distance, clucking together as they set the room to rights – and was suddenly wide-awake.

He kept his eyes closed and listened.

"'I don't surmise, Mrs. Hart, that the two happenings could be in any way connected. I observe no signs of violence here – overindulgence, perhaps – but nothing like the state of the Lodge. Poor Mr. Cartwright – porter for twenty-two years – and then to be bludgeoned to his death like a dog by some interloper!'

"'So you don't think it can have been anyone from College, Mr. Bunce?"

"No, Mrs. Hart. Mr. Cartwright was, I imagine, persuaded to open the night door to this stranger, tried to ring the police when he was attacked – and there's the switchboard mangled, the door left open –'

"Black groaned and sat up. 'Ah, you're better, sir. What happened to you and Mr. White? Nothing odd was it, sir? Can you remember?'

"Black felt extraordinarily weak, and needed time to disentangle the events of the night. He pleaded a hangover, and dismissed the raised eyebrows and pursed lips with a boyish appeal for lots of ham and eggs. 'It must have been some gin one of the medical students pressed on us to try,' he said; 'tasted more like methylated

246

spirits – ' Murmuring indulgently, they went off to the kitchen.

"Then Black tried to wake his friend who still lay, breathing stertorously, wrapped in a blanket on the floor. He carried him to his own bed, tried to rouse him with brandy, and placed wet towels on his forehead, but without success. He closed the door on him when his scout carried up the breakfast, and was forced to hear out, and react suitably to the awful tale of the murdered porter.

" 'I'll bring you up the *Mail* when it arrives, sir. Terrible thing. The police will want to question everyone who was in College last night, I understand, sir.' And at any moment White might stagger through the door saying, 'Where did it go? What has it done?'

"At last Black was alone again. He put his friend's breakfast on a trivet by the fire and went into the bedroom. White was lying with his eyes open, dazed and feeble; he let himself be helped into the study, and sat hunched, sipping his coffee, while he heard about the disastrous results of their experiment. Neither of them was in any doubt that the spirit they had summoned

247

and given corporeal being was the porter's killer.

"'It will not get far,' Black said over and over again; 'not enough current. No, it will just disappear, and revert to its proper place. And that is where we shall leave it.'

"'But a *double* tragedy! To have indirectly caused a murder, and worse still – for the interests of science – to have succeeded so triumphantly and have no proof. For now we are forced to remain silent, and we cannot, we must not, call it back.'

"Bunce arrived with the newspaper, from which he read aloud the full account of the Lodge murder and the findings so far. The murder weapon was identified as a heavy shovel that was kept in the Lodge in winter for clearing snow from the doors; and a policeman on his beat in the High Street had seen a tall bent man in a cloak or gown hurrying towards Magdalen. He followed, but found only a drunk drowsing on one of the benches along the bridge, babbling of a 'long glass man.' 'Must have seen a deal too many long glasses already that evening, I don't doubt,' commented Bunce. 'And please, sirs, to come down to the Bursary. The police want fingerprints of everyone in College.'

"Black and White answered the few questions put to them by the detective inspector. They knew that the glass man must have disappeared, and that their story was too incredible to put forward; so they felt their implication in the affair was best forgotten. Let it be another unsolved murder – for now there was no murderer.

"No, they said, they had heard nothing, seen nothing; they had drunk too much and slept heavily and late. Their fingerprints were taken – and, abruptly, the whole situation changed. When the sets of imprints were compared with those the police had found, it became clear that those of Black's left hand and White's right hand *were the same as those on the shaft of the shovel;* and again, among others, on the handle of the night door and its key.

"Every whorl and twist was there, crisply reproduced, totally incriminating, even down to the cut on the cushion of Black's thumb from testing the keenness of the Christmas carving knife two weeks before. The law gathered round, holding the glass slides of ink imprints up to the light, and comparing them with the photographs taken of the marks on the handle of the shovel. It was an open-and-shut case.

"The accused men were white and dumfounded. 'But we didn't do it!' stammered Black. 'I mean, how could we *both* have held the shovel –'

" 'Perhaps you will tell me,' said the inspector; 'but you both seem to be in pretty bad shape. I suggest that it was simply a matter of neither of you being strong enough the manage the wretched business alone.'

" 'Please, sir –' It was the young policeman who had been on the beat. "There's something funny about these here prints. We've been holding them the wrong way round.'

" 'Nonsense, Constable. See here – exact!'

" 'Yes, sir, but the ink is on the other side of the glass. Look, sir, they're the right imprints but the wrong way round – mirror images like, sir –'

"White leaped to his feet and was pressed down by heavy hands.

" 'But that's what happened!' 'Don't you *see?*' He turned to Black. 'We gave it *our* fingerprints. It had no form: its hands took shape aginst ours – like ectoplasm, like putty –'

" 'Yes, and during the time it was drawing on our strength its hands were against ours, your right, my left. The rest of it grew solid in its own form – but it kept the mark of its first contact, the prints we passed on to it.'

"Then there was nothing for it but to tell the law all that had happened – all about their precious, closely guarded experiments, their extrasensory powers, the materialization. The police took it all down, as they were bound to do. But the did not believe a word of it.

"But don't you see? *There is no murderer!*'

" 'Just because he has not been found? How can you prove your story? I suggest rather that you have worked yourselves – through this tampering with the so-called occult – into a sort of irresponsible, indeed vicious, stupor – drugs may have been involved. And in attempting to leave College after midnight you encountered opposition from the porter and, together, killed him. You may plead temporary insanity – but *only your prints* are on that shovel.'

" 'But *reversed!*' How were they reversed? Give us a chance to show you

251

what happened –' Black pleaded.

" 'Oh, no!' said White. 'Not that way –'

" 'It's all we can do, you fool! Let them be at hand and arrest It if they can, fingerprint I, put It behind bars. And I wish them joy of It.'

"The mystery of the mirror-image fingerprints would not, as they well knew, stand up in court; so the police agreed to give them one night to prove their case. They were kept under strict surveillance in Black's rooms, and at midnight the detective inspector and the constable went out and waited on the landing.

"The two policemen were weary and skeptical, and as the hour they had granted crawled by, only the cold and their hard upright chairs kept them awake. Beyond the door all seemed quiet; once they tried it and found it had been locked on the inside. For a moment they suspected an attempted escape, but then were reassured by the low murmuring of two voices.

"At a quarter to two there was a terrible moan, a piercing cry, a crash. They hurled themselves against the stout oak door but barely shook it. All at once they heard the sound of the key turning, and stood back. A hinge creaked, and in the doorway was a tall gaunt figure in a gown, outlined by the firelight beyond. The two men tackled it but it shook them off with a terrible strength, and rushed past them and down the staircase like some monstrous evil-smelling bat.

"The stalwart band of policemen in the quadrangle overpowered and handcuffed the wild creature, and locked it, still fighting and howling obscure obscenities, in the back of the Black Maria.

"On the floor of the study by the fireplace lay two huddled figures. First aid was brought, a doctor was called, but adrenalin injections did not rouse them. White died without coming out of coma: it was as if his soul had been sucked out of him. Black's faint pulse continued, and soon after dawn he opened his eyes. 'It was too soon. No time to recharge,' was all he said.

"And inside the police van? The commotion ceased suddenly on the way to the station. The constable in the passenger seat looked through the grille and saw what he described afterwards as a 'gray man' slumped on the bench – 'gray and shiny like dirty glass, sir. We pulled in to the side of the road and opened up the back, and all there was were the handcuffs. They were still locked, sir.' "

In the common room there was a general letting go of breath.

"Excellent," said Littlemount, rising and stretching. "It illustrates your tenets very well – and I promise solemnly not to tamper with the molecular structure of ghosts, should I ever get the opportunity to do so."

Nervous laughter and movement and the drawing back of curtains on the pale first light. Thank-yous and goodbyes were said, and soon the common room was empty – except for myself and the teller of tales. "And you are Black," I said.

"Yes. I guessed you knew. I have come to revisit my old rooms. The College has very kindly agreed to my writing up the materialization theory for *Mind*. Needless to say, I changed my name long ago; they have no idea I was involved in the case, which was hushed up, of course."

"Are you really going to try to bring White back?"

"Yes, indeed. It is the least I can do in an attempt to expiate my guilt – and the only way I can ask his forgiveness."

254

"And you know he will be there – 'something unfinished,' I think you said, 'something still to do.' "

"Yes, he will be there. It is for him I shall call, and hope it is he who comes. Of course, I may achieve nothing alone, in spite of the years between I have spent in developing my 'current' –"

I heard myself offering assistance. "My gift is not much," I said, "but at least I can help bear the strain, help complete the circuit."

He was accepted, although reluctantly. We shall attempt the materialization tonight. I hope we succeed in raising poor young White, and not the old Victorian bat. I set this down more to kill the hours of waiting than as any form of testament. Now it seems a little melodramatic; it will no doubt be an embarrassment to me when I reread it tomorrow morning.

The whole idea is mad, and so is "Black" himself; and I shall seal this lest anyone read it in my absence; I would never hear the last of it! But I am superstitious enough to write: *To be opened in the event of my demise.* I believe one calls it hedging one's bets.

STEPHEN WASYLYK

The Death of the Bag Man

*There is something appealing about two
septuagenarian snoops who still have all their
wits about them – well, nearly all. Mr.
Morley and Mr. Bakov, 75-year-old
residents of the Golden Age Retirement
Center, Inc., prove that the name of the
Center is a contradiction. True, the senior-
citizen sleuths are in their Golden Age, but
where the detection of crime is concerned, they
are far from retirement. As we said to begin
with, there is something appealing about two
old timer 'tecs . . .*

Detectives: MR. MORLEY
and MR. BAKOV

In spite of the cheery rays of the rising sun
slanting through the windows, a pall
seemed to hang over the first-to-breakfast
residents in the dining room of the Golden
Age Retirement Center, Inc., destroying
their appetites and causing them to pick at
their food despondently.

Even Morley and Bakov were affected. Morley's newspaper lay untouched alongside his plate, his eggs and toast growing cold as Morley sipped at his coffee unhappily; and Bakov spooned up his oatmeal slowly, without his usual complaint about his diet.

Bakov put down his spoon with a sigh. "It is a terrible thing, Morley," he said. "What are we to do?"

"I do not know, Bakov," said Morley, his face sober. "When they raised the rates last time, we captured the bank robber and the bank gave us a reward, but I do not think we can go out and capture a criminal this time, even though the city has many criminals who should be captured. We must think, Bakov. Surely there must be a way for each of us to earn the few dollars that are necessary. Although we are seventy-five, we must be good for something."

Bakov passed a chubby hand over his bald head carefully, as if not to disarrange the hair that was no longer there. "That is true. We are not senile or stupid. But I do not see how poor Miss McIlhenny will manage. She stayed awake in the recreation room all night watching the old movies on the TV as usual because she is afraid to go to sleep because she thinks she will die, but this time she cried and she is still crying. Where can she go and what can she do? She is eighty-two and not well."

Morley rose, his gaily patterned Hawaiian shirt hanging loosely from his bony shoulders, his bushy gray hair haloed by the slanting rays of the morning sun. "There are others also, Bakov, but it is as the Director says. The Center must pay the bills or it will go bankrupt and then there will be no Center at all for anyone. But what the Director does not understand is why no one will give him the money. He has been everywhere and seen everyone. They will not help, even though it is really not a large amount."

Morley tucked his newspaper under his arm. "But . . ." He shrugged. "We have yet a week, Bakov. We will sit in our deck chairs and think as we watch the men destroying the apartment building across the street. Perhaps I will get a brilliant idea. I am good at getting brilliant ideas."

For more than a week workmen had been gutting the gracious old building across the street, sending debris down long wooden

258

chutes to waiting dump trucks. Now that phase was over. A shell of marble and brick was all that remained, and rows of black rectangles that had once been windows stared at Morley and Bakov like vacant eyes that presaged death.

"It is a terrible thing to destroy such a fine building," said Bakov.

"Nothing lasts forever," said Morley pompously.

"Some things," said Bakov. "Just the other night on the television I saw the things in the Egypt that they call the Pyramids. They have lasted for a long time."

"It is simple, Bakov. In Egypt there is not enough progress because there are not yet many cars. Some day the Egypts will all own cars like people in America and they will tear down the Pyramids to make a shopping center with a big parking lot."

The demolition crew had erected a plywood wall well out from the base of the building, closing off the sidewalk and part of the street to protect passersby, leaving only an opening at each end so that the trucks could pull in and out. Now one of the men appeared in the near opening, shouting and waving his hard hat, and the other men ran toward him, all disappearing inside.

"Aha," said Morley. "Something is wrong."

One of the men reappeared in the opening and ran into the street, looking one way and then another. He spotted a police car that had parked to one side, either because the two officers had been assigned to the demolition or they were as interested as everyone else in seeing the building come crashing down. The man darted toward the police car, spoke to the driver, and in a few minutes all three ran into the building.

Morley leaped to his feet, his hair bristling, his shirt flapping. "Something has happened, Bakov. Let us go see."

"No," said Bakov. "Always when you go see, we get into trouble."

"What trouble can there be in an empty building?"

"Wherever the police go, there is trouble."

"Then stay, Bakov. I will go alone." Morley started down the broad lawn toward the gate in the wrought-iron fence.

Bakov watched, sighed, then heaved his bulk from his deck chair and followed, muttering to himself, "If I do not go, he will get into trouble. If I go, he will still get into trouble, and I also. So why do I go?" He lumbered across the lawn after Morley, both of them moving rapidly in spite of their age, and they crossed the street together.

They stopped at the opening in the plywood wall, peered inside, and saw nothing except a debris-littered sidewalk.

"Come on," said Morley.

Bakov nervously peered upward. "A brick will fall on my poor head."

Morley cocked his head, listening to the approach of police sirens, blue eyes sparkling with excitement. "Listen," he said. "More police are coming."

"Then I am going," said Bakov.

Morley took his arm and pulled him with him as he crossed the sidewalk. "They can only tell us to leave," he said. "By that time we will have seen what is wrong."

They went through the doorless opening that once had been the main entrance. The lobby was now a gloomy cavity illuminated only by daylight filtering through the entrance. The demolition men were gathered around the two policemen, one of whom was taking notes. Beyond the

261

group lay what appeared to be a large bundle of rags.

Morley identified it first, clutching Bakov's arm fiercely. "It is a man, Bakov!" he whispered.

He sidled forward almost to the body when one of the policemen yelled, "Hey! Get away from there!"

Morley stepped back, his eyes still on the body, his brow furrowed.

Bakov moved aside quickly as several men came through the door, led by a heavyset man with close-cropped hair who stopped when he saw Morley, lifted an arm with index finger pointing at the doorway, and said, "Get out!"

Morley drew himself up, his shoulders squared. "Do not speak so to a private citizen who has committed no crime."

Arm still extended, finger pointed, the man repeated, *"Out!"*

"You will be sorry," said Morley. He motioned to Bakov. "Come," he said. "When Lietuenant Hook cannot find the murderer, as usual, perhaps he will speak to us nicely and then we will decide to help."

An internal pressure seemed to make Hook swell a little. *"OUT!"* he said.

Morley moved toward the door, stopping the moment Hook's attention left him.

"All right," said Hook to the policeman. "Let's have it."

"One of the demolition men was giving the building a final check," said the policeman. "He found the body and called us. No one has been near it except me. I could see someone shot the man in the chest and he was dead, so I kept everyone away."

Hook motioned to one of his men.

The detective went through the dead man's pockets. "No identification," he said, rising to his feet. "The last time that coat was pressed was during the Lyndon Johnson administration. The shirt and pants are two sizes too big and came out of a ragbag somewhere. He doesn't have any socks and I don't know what holds the shoes together."

"How old?" asked Hook.

"Hard to say. Late fifties, early sixties."

"Some old bum or wino, I guess," said Hook.

The detective shook his head. "I think not. Looks more like an old guy down on his luck."

Hook raised his voice. "Does anyone know this man?"

Morley stepped out of the shadows. "He is the Bag Man," he said.

Morley whirled. "I thought I told you to get out."

Morley's eyebrows arched. "And if I had gone, who would answer your question? I tell you, he is the Bag Man."

"The what?"

Morley spoke as if Hook were a child. "The Bag Man. He walks the streets with a big brown cloth bag over his shoulder and sometimes he asks the people who pass if they will give him a quarter. Bakov and I watched him many times and we were curious, so one day we crossed the street and talked to him because no one else paid attention. They just pushed him aside and we felt sorry for him. I asked him what he was doing and he smiled and said he was looking for help and did I have a quarter. I explained I did not have a quarter and neither did Bakov, but if he was hungry he could come into the Center and be our guest at the mid-morning tea time, which he did."

"He was not hungry," said Bakov. "He gave me his little sandwiches."

"You took a bum into the Center?" asked Hook.

"What bum? He was a poor old man asking for quarters, so we gave him tea instead."

"What did he carry in the bag?" asked Hook.

"I do not pry," said Morley loftily.

"I do not think it was money," said Bakov, "or it would not be necessary for him to ask for quarters."

Hook looked from one to the other. "Tell me," he said carefully, "did it occur to either of you to ask his name?"

"Of course," said Morley. "Were we to call him Mr. Bag Man? He said his name was Chaucer Galinsoga."

Hook blinked. "He must have made it up. No one could be named Chaucer Galinsoga."

"It is indeed a strange name," said Bakov, "but a policeman once told me your name is Ironhead Hook, which is also a strange name although not as strange as Chaucer Galinsoga."

Hook glared at him. "Did he tell you where he lived?"

"No," said Morley. "He said only that the Center was a fine place and we were lucky, which we already knew."

"What else did he say?"

"He did not say much," said Bakov. "He was too busy writing in his little book."

Hook almost yelled. "What little book?"

"The little book he kept in his coat pocket," said Morley.

Hook turned to the detective who had gone through the dead man's pockets. The detective shrugged. "No book," he said.

Hook folded his arms. "Tell me something," he said to Morley and Bakov. "You take an old bum in off the street because you feel sorry for him, you give him tea and sandwiches which he doesn't eat because he isn't hungry although he is asking people for quarters, he asks you questions and he writes the answers in a little notebook while he tells you very little of himself. Did it occur to either of you that this was a little unusual?"

"Of course," said Morley. "Because we are old, we are not stupid. He said he was writing a book."

Hook's voice rose. "An old bum with no socks was writing a book?"

"I am not a writer but I know one does not require socks to write a book," said Morley patiently. "Perhaps he did not like

266

to wear socks, but that is not important. I have told you that he carried a brown cloth bag always, but there is no bag here." His eyes scanned the dark recesses of the lobby. "Where can the bag be?"

"The bag won't be here," said Hook. "The man was killed else where and his body brought here." He pointed. "You can see where it was dragged across the floor through the brick and plaster dust."

"It is very clever of you to puzzle that out," said Morley admiringly. He stiffened suddenly, his eyes bright. "The car! It was the car!"

"What car?" asked Hook.

"The car I saw last night," said Morley.

Hook's eyes narrowed. He thought for a moment, then took Morley and Bakov by the arms. "There is too much confusion here," he said. "Let's go across the street and talk about this."

At an outdoor table on the quiet patio Hook produced his notebook and held his pen expectantly. "Now tell me about the car."

Morley cleared his throat. "We were all upset at the Center yesterday. Many found difficulty in sleeping, I among them, so I looked out the window and thought about our problem. From the window it is possible to see the front of the building across the street. Naturally I saw no person because only fools, criminals, and policemen walk on the street at that hour.

"Then a car came. It stopped and the driver made it go backward to the wooden fence the building wreckers put up so that the innocent people would not be hit on the head by a falling brick. Then the headlights went out. I could see nothing more because it is dark there. After a few minutes the car drove away again and I went to sleep because I did not consider the car important."

"What kind of car was it?" asked Hook.

Morley shrugged. "Who can tell? Do they not all look alike these days?"

"Could you at least see the color?" asked Hook. "Was it light or dark?"

"In the dark it was dark and in the light it was light," said Morley testily. "It was no color." He scratched his nose gently and his eyes twinkled as he glanced at Bakov. "It does not matter. I have already solved the crime for you."

Hook leaned back. "Tell me," he said tightly.

"The Bag Man was writing a book," said Morley. "Obviously it was a book about the graft and the corruption in the city of which everyone already knows but can prove nothing, but the Bag Man had the proof in his book that the Mayor does not work for the people but for the greedy gangsters, so it is necessary that the greedy gangsters steal his book and destroy him, for which they hire an evil hit person who shoots the Bag Man and takes his body to the empty building because he thinks they will knock the building down on top of the poor Bag Man and destroy the evidence of the crime. You see? It is necessary only for you to go to the Mayor and demand that he confess and the crime will be solved because the Mayor will tell the names of his greedy friends."

Bakov nodded. "That is true. All the famous detectives on the television have solved this crime many times. The only thing that is different is how the evil hit person pays for his crime. Sometimes the evil hit person's car goes over a big cliff and explodes."

His face solemn, Morley nodded at Hook. "So you see, you have only to go demand that the Mayor tell you who is responsible."

269

Hook's face seemed to have swelled and acquired a tinge of purple.

Morley looked at him closely. "I think perhaps you have the high blood pressure like Bakov."

Hook slammed his notebook closed and put it in his pocket.

Morley's voice held laughter. "Do not be so angry. Bakov and I were only making a joke. We know that such a crime is only for the television." He shook his head. "I do not know who killed the Bag Man."

Hook made an effort to smile. He took a deep breath. "At least I am pleased to hear you will not interfere this time."

"I will not interfere," said Morley. "Bakov and I have other problems and we cannot help you."

Hook's eyes rolled up. He mumbled a few words gratefully and left.

"Come, Bakov," said Morley. "It has occurred to me that I have not yet read my morning newspaper and there are many jobs advertised there for people who would like to work. We will look at them. Perhaps we will find something."

"I do not think anyone would advertise

for two seventy-five-year-old men," said Bakov."

"We will lie about our age," said Morley. "We will tell them we are only sixty."

Across the street the demolition proceedings had been suspended for the day to preserve the scene of the crime and Morley occupied himself in reading each little ad in the Help Wanted section. Finished, he sighed.

"There is nothing, Bakov. Perhaps there will be others tomorrow."

He began turning the pages, scanning the headlines, when he stopped, adjusted his glasses, and bent forward.

"That is strange, Bakov," he said, pointing. "Here on the page that tells of the parties of the rich people, I see the name Mrs. Galinsoga. I wonder if she could be a relation of Chaucer Galinsoga, the Bag Man."

"The Bag Man was poor," said Bakov. "How could he be the relation of someone rich?"

Morley folded the paper slowly. "But he was strange, Bakov. He was writing a book even if he had no socks. Perhaps he was a rich man in disguise."

"Rich men do not write books," said

Bakov. "They are too busy being rich."

"It is a strange coincidence," said Morley. "Perhaps we should go talk to this Mrs. Galinsoga."

"We do not know where she lives," Bakov pointed out.

"The phone book will give us the address," said Morley. He stood up and dropped the paper into the deck chair. "I am interested in this, Bakov. Let us go investigate."

"Let Lieutenant Hook investigate."

"Hook is not too bright a person, Bakov. Already we have found it necessary three times to help him catch a murderer. Let us go."

"I do not wish to go."

"The paper calls her the beautiful Mrs. Galinsoga."

"Rich ladies are always beautiful," said Bakov. "Never once have I seen the newspapers call a rich woman ugly, even though there are just as many ugly rich people as there are poor ones and I have met many beautiful women. What is one more?"

Morley pointed at him. "You are truly getting old, Bakov."

Without a word Bakov stood up, tried

to pull in his bulging stomach, patted his nonexistent hair, and brushed off his sleeves. "For what do you wait, Morley?" he asked.

They located the address and reached it by a combination of free rides for senior citizens on bus routes that took them across the city to the suburbs, where they found the numbers and the name *Galinsoga* on a brass plate fastened to a head-high stone wall pierced by a driveway. They followed the driveway through a stand of trees until they saw the house itself, a handsome combination of dark-brown brick and peaked roofs surrounded by tailored shrubbery.

To one side of the house the driveway flared out into an apron before a garage. Three cars were parked there; a foreign-made light-green station wagon, a two-seater off-white sports car, and a metallic gray Mercedes sedan.

A small thin man, no bigger than Morley, his gray hair cut short and his clothes protected by white coveralls, was industriously running a cloth over the hood of the Mercedes.

"The tradesmen's entrance is in the rear," he said.

"We are not members of a union," said Morley. "We are here to see Mrs. Galinsoga." He peered into the windows of the sedan. "Is this the car of Mrs. Galinsoga?"

The man pointed at the two-seater. "That is Mrs. Galinsoga's. This one belongs to Mr. Galinsoga."

"Her husband?"

"No. Her brother-in-law." The man placed his hands on his hips. "What do you want, anyway?"

"Do not be rude," said Morley, "or I will tell Mr. Galinsoga you have missed a big spot on his car and he might wish to hire a younger man whose eyes are better."

They left the man polishing carefully and went up to the front door where Morley pushed the bell.

A pretty, dark-haired young woman in a black uniform with a white apron opened the door and frowned. "You two can't be selling subscriptions."

"We wish only to speak to Mrs. Galinsoga about Mr. Chaucer Galinsoga," said Morley.

She held the door wide. "Come in."

The room in which the young woman asked them to wait was low-ceilinged, the

274

walls were lined with books, the furniture was leather-covered, soft, and grouped around a huge fireplace.

A tall slim woman about 40, with brown wavy hair framing a delicate, aristocratic face, entered the room, concern in her eyes. The fingers of one hand pulled nervously at the neck of her soft pullover as she looked from one to the other. "I am Mrs. Galinsoga," she said. "You have news of my husband?"

Morley's eyes were puzzled. "Perhaps there are two Chaucer Galinsogas. I speak of the one who does not shave and wears old clothes and shoes but no socks and carried a brown cloth bag, which is hard to believe of a man married to such a beautiful rich woman."

"That is true," said Bakov. "He would at least have socks if he was *your* Mr. Chaucer Galinsoga."

"Then you have seen him," said Mrs. Galinsoga excitedly. "You see, Chaucer is a professor of sociology at the university but he is writing a book on the socio-economic difficulties of our senior citizens, so he dresses in old clothing every few days and goes into the city to experience the problems from a personal

275

viewpoint. He feels it is necessary to study the subject first-hand." She waved at the room. "Obviously, he could get no feeling for the matter here."

"What did she say, Morley?" whispered Bakov.

"I think the Bag Man was writing a book about old people who have no money," said Morley.

"That would indeed be a very thick book," said Bakov.

Morley shifted uncomfortably. "I do not know why the police have not already told you. I am very sorry but Mr. Chaucer Galinsoga of the old clothes and no socks has been murdered."

Mrs. Galinsoga gave a little scream and covered her face with her hands.

A middle-aged man with full-iron-gray hair and a square face came into the room.

Mrs. Galinsoga wailed, "Oh, Jeffrey," and collapsed on his chest, her tears wetting the lapel of his tweed jacket.

The man looked over her head at Morley. "What is this?"

The woman looked up. "They say that Chaucer has been murdered."

"Nonsense," snapped the man. "I just reported him missing to the police. They would have told me."

"The police have many departments," said Morley. "Who are you?"

"Jeffrey Galinsoga. Chaucer is my brother."

"And are you also a professor?"

"We are both professors of sociology. Suppose you tell me what this is all about."

Morley explained.

Mrs. Galinsoga wailed, "I told him it was dangerous to walk around the city like that, but he insisted."

The doorbell rang. Morley heard the door open and then the maid led Hook and a detective into the room. Hook stopped short and glared at Morley and Bakov.

"Why are you so late?" demanded Morley. "It was necessary for me to tell Mrs. Galinsoga and the Bag Man's brother everything. It remains only for you to question them."

Hook pointed at the door. "Get out!"

"We will go," said Morley. He turned to Mrs. Galinsoga. "I am sorry about your poor husband. He was a nice man."

The pretty young maid stood in the entrance hall, obviously eavesdropping. Her chin lifted and she looked at Morley defiantly. "I want to hear what the policeman says."

"Do not worry about the policeman," said Morley. "I will tell you all about the crime. Let us go into the kitchen."

Bakov brightened. "I like kitchens."

"Are you hungry?" asked the young woman.

"He is always hungry because the diet person at the Center will not allow him to eat what he wants to eat," explained Morley. "Your kitchen is for talking, not eating."

They sat at a small table while Morley told the maid what he knew.

"What is your name?" asked Morley.

"Sue Ann," said the young woman.

"You live here?"

"Of course. So does the cook, but she is off today."

Bakov sighed. "That is just my luck."

Sue Ann went to a sideboard and came back with a bowl of fruit. "Take your choice," she said. "It is good for you and will not hurt your diet." She patted Bakov's bald head. "My grandfather has the same problem."

Bakov beamed. "You are a fine young person." He selected three bananas, placing one in each shirt pocket and peeling the third.

"Was last night the first time Mr. Galinsoga did not come home?" asked Morley.

"Oh, he was home," she said. "He came in about eight when Mrs. Galinsoga was upstairs dressing for the party. He went directly to the den. I brought him a sandwich and a cup of coffee. Then his brother came into pick up Mrs. Galinsoga and take her to the party, which he often does because Mr. Galinsoga has been busy with his book for months. The two men talked until Mrs. Galinsoga came down. She and the brother left about nine, shortly before I did." She smiled. "I had a date."

"Was Mr. Chaucer Galinsoga wearing his old clothes?"

She nodded.

Morley frowned. "That is indeed strange. If Mr. Chaucer Galinsoga was working in his den at nine, how then did he end up murdered in the empty apartment building?"

Bakov peeled his second banana. "That is a good question, Morley, but as you told Lieutenant Hook, there was the car."

"That is true," said Morley

thoughtfully. He rose to his feet and paced the kitchen slowly. He stopped. "Aha," he said. He resumed pacing, stopping once again. "Aha," he said. He resumed pacing, stopping once again. "*Aha,*" he said, more loudly this time. He went back to his pacing, coming to a sudden halt with his arm thrust into the air. "*AHA!*" he said.

"What is this *Aha?*" asked Bakov.

"Come, Bakov," said Morley.

"I have not finished my banana," said Bakov.

"Eat while you walk," said Morley.

He led them back to the library where Lieutenant Hook and the detective were still questioning Mrs. Galinsoga and the murdered man's brother, the four of them standing in front of the fireplace.

"I thought I told you to leave," snapped Hook.

Morley held up a hand. "I would like only to ask a few questions, which will not bother anyone."

"Let him ask," said Mrs. Galinsoga. "He was nice enough to come here and tell me about poor Chaucer."

"When you and Mr. Jeffrey Galinsoga came home from the party, was Mr.

Chaucer Galinsoga in his den?" asked Morley.

She shook her head. "The den was dark. I assumed he had gone to bed."

"Would you not know this when you also went to bed?"

"We had separate bedrooms," she said. "Naturally, I would not disturb him and I didn't know he was gone until this morning."

Morley scratched his nose reflectively and then pointed at the couple. "Arrest them!" he said to Hook.

"What for?" asked Hook.

"Together they killed Mr. Chaucer Galinsoga."

"That's ridiculous!" said Mrs. Galinsoga.

"No," said Morley. "I will explain. It is called the love triangle. Mr. Jeffrey Galinsoga and Mrs. Galinsoga were lovers and they wished to get rid of Mr. Chaucer Galinsoga, so they came home from the party and murdered the poor man and took his body to the empty building so the building would fall on top of him and conceal the crime."

Mrs. Galinsoga's eyes were wide. "Jeffrey and I?"

281

"Of course," said Morley. "Did you not go out often with Jeffrey Galinsoga to parties? Did you and your husband not have separate bedrooms? Is it to be believed that Jeffrey Galinsoga could associate with such a beautiful rich woman and not have romantic feelings? Is it to be believed that because your husband was always busy that you would not turn to Jeffrey Galinsoga in your loneliness?"

"You are a ludicrous old man," said Jeffrey Galinsoga. "The wild fantasies emanating from your senile brain are hardly amusing. There is not one single fact to justify your conjecture."

"There is the car," said Morley. "Your car – the metallic gray one. A car of such a color is dark in the dark and light in the light and of no color at all. Lieutenant Hook has only to take it to the building when it gets dark while I look out my window as I did last night and I will identify it as the same car, which means that you took the body of your poor brother to the building."

Jeffrey Galinsoga's face paled. With one quick movement he threw Mrs. Galinsoga into Hook and the detective, all three collapsing, whirled, and sprinted for the front door.

Only Bakov was in the way, his partly consumed banana halfway to his lips. Galinsoga thrust Bakov aside, the banana arching gracefully through the air, and, in one of those freak accidents that can never be duplicated deliberately, the banana landed on the floor a split second before Galinsoga's heel came down on the same spot, and Jeffrey Galinsoga gave an excellent imitation of an overweight Peter Pan before crashing to the floor.

Bakov looked down at him ruefully. "He has ruined my good banana," he said.

Morley and Bakov settled into their deck chairs after dinner for a breath of fresh air before joining the other residents in front of the big color TV in the recreation room.

"I wonder if Lieutenant Hook is still angry," said Bakov.

"I do not understand Lieutenant Hook," said Morley. "Did I not solve the crime as usual and did you not capture the criminal with your banana?"

"He said you almost blew it," said Bakov. "I do not know what that means."

"It means only that I was wrong about the love triangle," said Morley. "Mrs. Galinsoga loved her husband dearly, even

283

if he did not wear socks. Does it matter instead that Jeffrey Galinsoga killed his brother because he said his brother stole his idea of a book about old people with no money? For many months Jeffrey had been making notes but it was his brother who had the idea of pretending to be an old person with no money to see what it was really like, so he became the Bag Man, walking the streets and talking to old people as if he was one of them, and Jeffrey Galinsoga knew that such a book would be better than his.

"Could I know that while Mrs. Galinsoga was upstairs, Jeffrey demanded that his brother stop because the book about old people was really his idea, but his brother refused? Also, could I know that Jeffrey took Mrs. Galinsoga to the party but sneaked out and came back and murdered his brother because he was angry and jealous, and that he then placed the Bag Man in the trunk of his car and went back to the party to bring Mrs. Galinsoga home?"

"It was not very nice of him to drive around with Mrs. Galinsoga while her poor husband's body was in the trunk."

"Jeffrey Galinsoga was not a nice person

284

or he would not have murdered his brother over a book about old people with no money because there are enough old people with no money for everybody. But it was obvious that only he could drive into the city to dispose of the body. I did not see how he could do this without Mrs. Galinsoga's knowing, so I thought she also was guilty. When Jeffrey Galinsoga saw the empty building he thought that would be an excellent place, but he could not know I was looking out the window, and even Lieutenant Hook said that if I had not seen the car it would have been very difficult to prove that Jeffrey Galinsoga was guilty."

He shook his head. "Lieutenant Hook has only a little imagination for a homicide person. He sent his men to check the records of the Social Security and the Welfare to find where Chaucer Galinsoga lived instead of looking in the phone book as any sensible person would do, which was why you and I had to tell Mrs. Galinsoga her husband had been murdered."

"Mrs. Galinsoga is not only rich and beautiful, but a nice person," said Bakov. "She forgave you for saying she killed her husband."

"Her husband told her so many stories

of old people with no money he had met, she feels she must take the pages he had written and his notes and finish his book."

"I do not see how she can do this," said Bakov. "She is not a professor of the sociology with no socks."

"It is simple, Bakov. Did I not say that we were good for something? I explained to her she requires the assistance of two intelligent old people such as us, because who knows better what should be in such a book? So she said we will be her consultants and she will pay generously for our valuable experience. We will then give the money to the Director and no one will have to leave the Center, including Miss McIlhenny." Morley smiled. "The dead Mr. Galinsoga would be very happy to know of this."

Bakov sat upright. "Is this true, Morley?"

"Of course. I would not lie about such a thing."

"I did not hear her say this. Where was I?"

Morley sighed. "In the kitchen with Sue Ann, eating a banana."

286

E. X. FERRARS

The Ross Murders

*"The dangerous rage that had possessed him
only a few times in his life had exploded like
fireworks in his brain"* . . .

It was on the day that Mrs. Holroyd
refused Mr. Pocock's offer of marriage that
he first thought of murdering her.

The rejection, so gently and kindly put
but so utterly unexpected, filled him first
with astonishment, so that he felt as if he
had tripped over something uneven in his
path and fallen flat on his face, and then
with a searing rage.

For a wild moment he wanted to clasp
his hands around her slender neck and
squeeze the life out of her. But after that
flare of hatred came intense fear. He had
made up his mind, after his last murder,
never to kill again.

On that occasion he had escaped arrest
only by the skin of his teeth and he knew
that the police still believed he was guilty,
although they had never had enough

287

evidence to bring a charge against him. That had been largely because of Lucille's passion for cleanliness. She had polished and washed and scrubbed everything in her little flat at least twice a week, so that the police, in their investigation, had not been able to find a single one of Mr. Pocock's fingerprints.

Dear Lucille. He remembered her still with a kind of affection, partly because she had cooperated so beautifully in her own death. Except, of course, for that business of the roses. It was the love she had had for roses and the pleasure it had given him to bring them to her from his own little garden that had almost destroyed him.

There had been no complications like that about his first murder. Almost no drama either. He had nearly forgotten why he had committed it. Alice had been a very dull woman. He could hardly recollect her features. However, it had happened one day that she told him in her flat positive way that she did not believe a word he had told her about his past life, that she was sure he had never been an intelligence officer during the war, that he had never been parachuted into occupied France, that he had never been a prisoner of the Nazis and

survived hideous tortures at their hands –
in all of which she had been perfectly
correct; and really the matter had been of
very little importance, but her refusal to
share his fantasies had seemed to him such
a gross insult that for a few minutes it had
felt impossible to allow her to go on living.

Afterward he had walked quietly out of
the house, and it had turned out that no one
had seen him come or go, and her death had
become one of the unsolved mysteries in
the police files. There had been a certain
flatness about it, almost of disappointment.

But in Lucille's case it had been quite
different. For one thing, he had been rather
fond of her. She had been an easy-going
woman, comfortable to be with, and she
had never expected gifts other than the
flowers he brought her. But one day when
he had happened to say how much he
wished she could see them growing in his
glowing flowerbeds, but that the anxious
eye of his invalid wife, who would suffer
intensely if she even knew of Lucille's
existence, made this impossible, she had
gone into fits of laughter.

She had told him there was no need for
him to tell a yarn like that to her of all
people, and he had realized all of a sudden

that she had never believed in the existence of any frail, lovely, dependent wife to whom he offered up the treasure of his loyalty.

The dangerous rage that had possessed him only a few times in his life had exploded like fireworks in his brain. It had seemed to him that she was mocking him not merely for having told her lies that had never deceived her, but for having tried to convince her that any woman, even a poor invalid, could ever love him enough to marry him. His hands, made strong by his gardening, although they were small and white, had closed on her neck, and when he left her she had been dead.

By chance he had left no fingerprints in her flat that day. But he had been seen arriving by the woman who lived in the flat below Lucille's. Meeting on the stairs on his way up, he and the woman, an elderly person in spectacles, had even exchanged remarks about the weather, and it turned out that she had taken particular notice of the bunch of exquisite Kronenbourgs he had been carrying.

The rich velvety crimson of the blooms and the soft gold of the undersides of the petals and their delicious fragrance had riveted her attention, a fact which at first he had thought would mean disaster for him, but which actually had been extraordinarily fortunate. For afterward she had been able to describe the roses minutely, but had given a most inaccurate description of the man who had been carrying them, and in the lineup in which he had been compelled to take part when the police had been led to him by a telephone number scrawled on a pad in Lucille's flat, the woman had picked out the wrong man.

So the police had had no evidence against him except for the telephone number and the rose bush in his garden. But half a dozen of his neighbors, who had imitated him when they had seen the beauty of that particular variety of rose, had Kronenbourgs in their gardens too, and so Lucille's murder, like Alice's, had remained an unsolved mystery.

Yet not to the police. Mr. Pocock was sure of that and sometimes the thought that he might somehow betray himself to them, even now after two years, that he might drop some word or perform some thoughtless action, though heaven knew what could do him any damage after all this time, made terror stab like a knife into his nerves. He would never kill again, of that he was certain.

But that was before Mrs. Holroyd refused to marry him.

It had taken him a long time to convince himself that marriage to her would be a sound idea, even though he was certain she had been pursuing him ever since she had come to live in the little house next door to his. She was a widow and she believed him to be a widower, and she often spoke to him of her loneliness since her husband's sudden death and sympathized with Mr. Pocock because of his own solitary state.

She admired his garden and took his advice about how to lay out her own, was delighted with the gifts of flowers he brought her, and when he was ill with influenza she did his shopping for him, cooked him tempting meals, and changed his books at the library. And she had let him know, without overstressing it, that her income was ample.

"I'm not a rich woman," she had said, "but thanks to the thoughtfulness of my dear husband, I have no financial worries."

So it seemed clear to Mr. Pocock that Mrs. Holroyd's feelings were not in doubt and that it was only his own which it was necessary for him to consider. Did he want marriage? Would he be able to endure the continual company of another person after all his years of comfortable solitude? Would not the effort of adapting his habits to fit those of someone else be an extreme irritation?

Against all that, he was aging and that bout of influenza had shown him how necessary it was to have someone to look after him. And marrying Mrs. Holroyd might actually be financially advantageous instead of very expensive, as it would be to employ a full-time housekeeper. She was a good-looking woman too, for her age, and an excellent cook. If he wanted a wife, he could hardly do better.

Of course, she had certain little ways which he found hard to tolerate. She liked to sing when she was doing her housework. If he had to listen to it in his own house, instead of softened by distance, it would drive him mad. She chatted to all the neighbors, instead of maintaining a courteous aloofness, as he did. And she had a passion for plastic flowers. Every vase in her house was filled with them, with a total disregard for the seasons, her tulips and daffodils blooming in September and her chrysanthemums in May.

She always thanked him with a charming lighting up of her face for the flowers he brought her, but he was not really convinced she could distinguish the living ones from the lifeless imitations. But no doubt with tact he would be able to correct these small flaws in her. On a bright evening in June he asked her to marry him.

She answered, "Oh, dear Mr. Pocock, how can I possibly tell you what I feel, I am so touched, so very honored! But I could never marry again. It would not be fair to you if I did, for I could never give my heart to anyone but my poor Harold. And our friendship, just as it is, is so very precious to me. I think we are wonderfully fortunate, at our age, to have found such a friendship. To change anything about it might only spoil it. So let us treasure what we have, won't that be wisest? What could we possibly give to each other more than we already do?"

He took it with dignity and accepted a glass of sherry from her. What made the occasion peculiarly excruciating for him was his certainty that she had known he was going to propose marriage and had her little speech already rehearsed. It disgusted him to discover that all her little kindnesses to him had simply been little kindnesses that had come from the warmth of her heart and not from desire to take possession of him.

Looking at her, with her excellent sherry tasting like acid in his mouth, he was suddenly aware of the terrible rage and hatred that he had not felt for so long. However, he managed to pat her on the shoulder, say that of course nothing between them need be altered, and go quietly home.

The most important thing for the moment, it seemed clear to him, was not to let her guess what her refusal had done to him. She must never be allowed to know what power she had to hurt him. Everything must appear to be as it had been in the past. In fact their relationship was poisoned forever, but to save his pride this must be utterly hidden from her. Two days later he appeared on her doorstep, smiling, and with a beautiful bunch of Kronenbourgs for her.

She exclaimed over them with extra-special gladness and there was a tenderness on her face that he had never seen there before. She was so happy, he thought, to have humiliated him at apparently so little cost to herself. Tipping some plastic irises and sprays of forsythia out of one of the vases in her sitting room, she went out to the kitchen to fill the vase with water, brought it back, and began to arrange the roses in it.

Up to that moment he had not really intended to murder her. He would find some way of making her suffer as she was making him suffer, but when his hands went out to grasp her neck and he saw at first the blank astonishment on her face before it changed to terror, he was almost as surprised and terror-stricken as she was. When she fell to the floor at his feet in a limp heap and he fled to the door, he was shaking all over.

But then he remembered something. The Kronenbourgs. Once before they had almost destroyed him. This time he would not forget them, and leave them behind. Turning back into the room, he snatched the roses from the vase, jammed the plastic flowers back into it, and only pausing for a moment at the front door to make sure the street was empty, made for his own house.

Inside, he threw the roses from him as if they carried some horrible contagion and for some time left them lying where they had fallen, unable to make himself touch them. How mad he had been to take them to the woman, how easily fatal to him they could have been.

He drank some whiskey and smoked several cigarettes before he could force himself to pick the roses up and put them in a silver bowl which he placed on a bookcase in his sitting room. They looked quite normal there, not in the least like witnesses against him. It was very important that everything should look normal.

The next morning, when two policemen called on him, he was of course prepared for them and felt sure that his own behavior was quite normal. But he was worried by a feeling that he had met one of them before. The man was an inspector who now told Mr. Pocock that the body of his neighbor had been discovered by her daily woman, then went on to ask him when he had seen the dead woman last and where he had spent the previous evening.

He supposed that such questions were inevitable, but he did not like the way, almost mocking, that the man looked at him. But standing there, looking at the roses in the silver bowl, the inspector remarked admiringly, "Lovely! Kronen-bourgs, aren't they?"

"Yes," Mr. Pocock said, "from my garden."

"I've got some in my own garden," the inspector said. "There's nothing to compare with a nice rose, is there? Now your neighbor doesn't seem to have cared for real flowers. She stuck to the plastic kind. Less trouble, of course. But a funny thing about her, d'you know, she kept some of them in water? Some irises and forsythia, they were in a vase full of water, just as if they were real. That's carrying pretense a bit far, wouldn't you say, Mr. Pocock?

"Unless there'd been some real flowers there first like, say, your roses. You'd a way of giving her flowers, hadn't you, Mr. Pocock? That's something she told the neighbors. But really you ought to have learned better by now than to take them with you when you're going out to do murder."

EDWARD D. HOCH

The Will-o'-the-Wisp Mystery

In this 40,000-word novel, complete in this anthology, Mr. Hoch has set a difficult goal for his detective – a goal as elusive as the will-o'-the-wisp . . .

How would you go about finding six convicted felons who have nothing in common except that they all escaped from a prison van that was transporting them to the state penitentiary. Where would you begin?

Meet David Piper, Director of the Department of Apprehension, but better known in the press as "The Manhunter." A semi-official supersleith, Piper is faced with the most puzzling mystery of his career – the case of the six criminals who gambled against the odds . . .

Detective: DAVID PIPER

Chapter One: The Pawn

The prison van made the run between the Raker County Jail and the state penitentiary about twice a month, on an irregular schedule dictated more by the contingencies of space and the whims of the Sheriff than by any action of the courts in sentencing offenders. Often a convicted felon remained in his cell at the county jail for several weeks before taking the 65-mile ride to his new home.

Thus it was not unusual for five handcuffed men to be led from the side door of the jail one chill Monday morning in early November. The guards glanced at them only casually as the prisoners were motioned inside the back of the van. It was not until the stout matron appeared with her charge that it became clear the trip would be out of the ordinary.

Women prisoners were usually taken to the penitentiary in a special car, since there was the necessity of transporting them with a matron. It was obvious at once that this blonde young woman with the high cheekbones and piercing eyes could not be expected to share the van with five hardened criminals. The driver and the guard discussed the matter and finally decided that the matron and the young woman would ride up front in the cab, while the guard rode in the locked van with the other prisoners. It was not exactly according to regulations, but there seemed to be no other choice.

The arrangement took only a few moments, and a glance at his watch assured the driver that they still had time to reach the penitentiary for the noon meal. On the expressway it was only a 90-minute trip, even counting the frustrations of the downtown traffic.

The young woman did not speak during the early part of the trip, and the driver found himself wondering what her crime had been. He offered her a cigarette, and when she refused, he asked, "What are you in for, Miss?"

She held her head high and did not answer. At her side the matron snorted. "Don't you read the papers? She killed her husband."

"Oh."

"She's a small-time compared to what's in back, though. You've got a real prize today."

The driver started to ask which of the five she meant, but he never had a chance. He was just turning onto the feeder road leading to the expressway when something rammed the van from behind. Then the air was suddenly filled with smoke – dense, heavy, choking smoke.

"Stay with her!" the driver shouted to the matron as he pulled out his pistol and jumped from the cab. For an instant he could see nothing at all as he struggled through the smoke, his eyes smarting. Then a figure in a gas mask, holding a carbine, broke through the haze before him. The driver fired one wild shot at the masked figure, then tried to dodge aside, but a spurt of bullets caught him across the chest.

The man in the gas mask bent over the body and quickly found the driver's keys. In a moment he was unlocking the van's rear door. He stood carefully aside, but there was no reason to worry. The men in the back had known what to do through sheer instinct. They had overpowered the guard a moment after the van had been rammed.

"Take care of the matron," someone ordered. They dragged her screaming from the front seat and one of the masked men hit her with a gun butt.

Then the five male prisoners and the girl were led through the smoke to a station wagon. It would take them to a point where other cars waited for the transfer. By the time the smoke began to clear, there was nothing to be seen but the open van and the bodies on the road beside it.

The entire operation had taken exactly four minutes.

Newspapers and some of the more sensational magazines liked to refer to David Piper as "The Manhunter," a name he disliked. He said it made him sound like little more than a bloodhound – an animal whose sole purpose in life was to hunt down the missing and the wanted. In actuality he had come to his present position following ten years with the state's prison system and another five working with the Probation Department.

When the state legislature became the first in the nation to establish a Department of Apprehension, David Piper had been the logical choice as the Director. He'd chuckled more than once at the ambiguity of the Department's title, but in the end he'd accepted the position. And that was when his troubles really began.

The Department of Apprehension had the assignment of working with established law-enforcement agencies in the capture of escaped convicts, the location of parole

303

violators, and even on occasion the return of runaway teen-agers to their parents. On paper it was a coordinating agency whose aim was to funnel state aid to prisons, parole boards, and local police. That was on paper.

In practice David Piper had come to be considered as something of a semi-official supersleith, available to any prison or community in the state for everything from mediating a convicts' riot to tracking down an escaped killer. The Department of Apprehension had always been understaffed, and when a budget cut further sliced his work force, he'd resigned himself to doing much of the leg work in person. Though he complained to his superiors at every opportunity he privately rather liked the situation – even though it brought with it the distasteful sobriquet of The Manhunter.

David Piper was tall and reasonably good-looking, with a weatherbeaten face that might have come from too many years spent at sea. He was 41 years old, though he looked younger, and married to a career-minded fashion designer whom he seldom saw. She spent most of the year in Manhatten, while he lived a bachelor-like existence in a three-room apartment in the state capital. For better or worse, the job had become his life and lifework.

"Of course you know why we're here," the man facing his desk said. "I'm Inspector Fleming and this is Sheriff Barker, the man in charge of the Raker County Jail."

"Yes," David Piper nodded. "The escape from the prison van."

"Exactly. It's been a week now, and there's not a ghost of a clue. The six of them might as well have been swallowed up in an earthquake. Frankly, Mr. Piper, we need the state's help in this. It's like chasing a will-o'-the-wisp!"

David Piper shifted his eyes from the sincere, professional face of Inspector Fleming to the flushed, nervous features of Sheriff Barker. "Any idea how it happened, Sheriff? Or who was behind it?"

Barker shook his head. "I only know the papers have me pegged as the fall guy. They claim if the guard had been up front where he belonged it wouldn't have happened. They say it's my fault for sending the woman and the matron along. Hell, I didn't tell them where to sit! I sent the Gallery girl along to save the cost of a special trip. I try to save the taxpayers a little money and the papers blame me!"

Inspector Fleming interrupted, trying to soothe him. "The girl's presence had nothing to do with it. The whole operation was carefully planned, with rifles and smoke grenades and getaway cars. Besides, they weren't after the girl."

This last part interested Piper. "Who were they after? Nick Bruno?"

"Of course. Who else?"

If any man in the state deserved the title of King of the Underworld it was Nick Bruno. At 55 his personal wealth was estimated at many millions of dollars, and he was said to personally control most of the drug traffic in the state. Though he was not Sicilian he had close ties to the Mafia, and to organized crime in other states. Oddly enough,, for a man in his position, Nick Bruno's arrest record until now had been limited to a few youthful offenses in the midwest. Since moving east twenty years ago he had led the outward life of a prosperous local businessman, operating a string of first-class restaurants. It was one of these that had caused his downfall. He'd hired two men to burn down one of his own restaurants for the insurance, and the men had bungled the job badly, involving Bruno, who had then been convicted of arson.

"You think Bruno's men sprang him?" Piper asked.

"It had to be. He even boasted at the trial that he'd never spend a single day inside the penitentiary."

Piper frowned and studied the wall. "So he traded it for a life of hiding from the law? He could have been out on parole in two years."

Inspector Fleming shrugged. "Men like Bruno build up such a sense of power that anything is preferable to the loss of esteem that a stretch in the pen might bring."

Piper picked up the list of escapees. "What about Jack Larner? He could have underworld connections. His record indicates he was once a bodyguard for a Miami gangster."

"That was twenty years ago. Larner served time for manslaughter and came out of prison free of the gangs. Besides, most of that Miami crowd is dead now. No, he's been specializing in bank robbery these last few years, all by himself."

"Doesn't bank robbery rate a spell in a Federal prison?"

"The teller couldn't identify him, so we only got a conviction for auto theft and assault. Anyway, he's strictly a loner. It was Bruno they were after."

David Piper looked up smiling as Susan, his secretary, placed the morning mail on his desk. But the smile faded as his hard eyes returned to meet those of his two visitors. "If Nick Bruno's crowd sprang him from that prison van, why did they carefully arrange transportation for the other five as well? And why hasn't at least one of the six turned up by now? There seems to be no connection among them, so it isn't likely they'd stick together. Yet that's what happened."

Fleming spread his gnarled hands in a gesture of defeat. "And that's why we're here. Our investigation is at a dead end."

"And the papers are yelling for my scalp!" Sheriff Barker joined in. "All because I sent that girl along."

David Piper nodded, reaching for his favorite pipe. "I'll see what I can do through the usual sources. But please keep in mind that I'm no bloodhound, whatever the newspapers may say. I use informers and follow standard police techniques. Occasionally I get lucky on my contacts, but otherwise I'm no better equipped for this than you are."

Fleming stood up and shook hands. "We have every confidence in your ability, Mr. Piper. You've already suggested a few questions which we hadn't asked ourselves."

"I'll do what I can," Piper promised.

He saw them to the door and then went back to his desk. After a moment Susan entered with coffee. "They want you to find those six who escaped from the prison van?"

He sipped the strong black coffee and nodded. "Another job for The Manhunter. They're beginning to believe my publicity."

She grinned in her impish way. "Just so long as you don't start believing it yourself."

Shaking his head, he flipped through the pages of his private telephone directory. "I'll have to get in touch with some of Bruno's crowd."

"Do you think they'll talk?"

He smiled up at her. "I think they will – to me."

But the following afternoon David Piper

knew it would not be that easy. He'd talked with Tommy, the one-eyed drifter who was his most reliable informer, and with a couple of men on the fringes of Bruno's multimillion-dollar crime empire. They all told him the same thing – that Bruno's friends had nothing to do with the escape from the prison van, that they were as much in the dark as the police.

Piper picked up the alphabetical list of escapees and read it for the hundredth time:

Nick Bruno – underworld king

Hugh Courtney – impostor and murderer

Kate Gallery – murderess

Charlie Hall – swindler and card cheat

Jack Larner – bank robber and car thief

Joe Reilly – forger

There was nothing to link them, nothing but mere chance having thrown them together in that prison van. Even their crimes were dissimilar. Larner had killed in the past, and Bruno was suspected of having been implicated in a dozen killings, which gave them something in common with Courtney and the girl; but Hall was a small-time swindler and Reilly had probably never carried a weapon in his life.

Six people. Five men and one woman.

Somebody had wanted them free – wanted it badly enough to murder two guards and injure a prison matron. Piper decided he should talk to the matron, the only living witness.

Her name was Mrs. Tidings and she was resting at home after several days in the hospital. Piper found her with a covering of bandages that almost obscured her graying hair.

"It was terrible," the woman told him, holding a hand to her bandaged head and speaking with just a trace of brogue. "Those poor men who were killed!"

"You said there were three in the gang that attacked the van, Mrs. Tidings?"

"Three that I saw. There might have been more in all that smoke. One drove the truck that rammed into us, and another drove the station wagon."

"They all wore gas masks?"

"Yes. There was no chance of identifying them."

"Did they call any of the prisoners by name?"

"I was up front with the woman prisoner. I didn't see the others at all after they were freed."

David Piper nodded. There was nothing

311

to be learned from Mrs. Tidings. "Thank you," he said. "I'm sorry I had to bother you."

"You'll find them. You're The Manhunter, aren't you?"

He smiled. "I'll get them, Mrs. Tidings."

He went out to his car, hoping he could keep the promise. Ahead, over the city, November clouds were drifting in like sooty blankets, covering the sun.

Only because he had to start somewhere, David Piper chose the last name on the alphabetical list. Joe Reilly was the youngest of the five men, though at 31 he was still six years older than Kate Gallery, the convicted murderess. His photograph showed a short slim man with black hair and mustache, an ordinary type who wouldn't have got a second glance on the street.

He was married to a successful Broadway and television actress named Margo Miller, who lived in Raker County between shows. Reilly had been arrested two years before, after forging her name to three checks, but charges had been dropped before the trial. This time he'd forged her name and that

312

of her business manager to a whole series of checks. The judge had given him two to five years.

Margo Miller's home was in the fashionable Brookwood section, secluded behind a row of spirelike poplars. Piper parked his car at the foot of the driveway and walked up, noticing the tented bushes and mulched roses already fortified against winter's blasts. The doorbell was answered by a thin pale young man in overalls who, speaking in Spanish, asked David's name.

"David Piper, from the State," he answered, not knowing if he was understood. "I wish to see Señorita Miller."

The man nodded and went away. Presently he returned to motion Piper through a doorway. Margo Miller was inside waiting for him, standing behind a cluttered oak desk and wearing a beige pants suit that accentuated the deep tan of her skin.

"I'm David Piper," he said.

She put down the letter opener she'd been using on the morning mail and turned on her brightest smile, which wasn't bad at all. He guessed her to be a few years older than her husband, but she moved and

313

smiled and gestured with the supreme confidence of youth. She was an actress – not a great one, but successful nonetheless.

"Please have a seat, Mr. Piper. I'll be with you in a jiffy. And I hope you'll excuse Manuel. I don't usually allow my gardener to answer the front door."

He shrugged and sat down. "I've come about your husband."

"The police have already been here. I understand he's still at large."

"He escaped with five others, Miss Miller. They're all still at large, and we suspect they might still be together." He lit his pipe. "Joe Reilly has made no attempt to phone you?"

"Hardly! He cheated me, forged my name to checks! My business manager, Marc Litzen, got taken even worse. My husband wouldn't dare show his face around here."

"But you dropped the charges the previous time."

"I was foolish and in love then. I thought he deserved another chance." She finished with the mail and tossed down the letter opener. A troubled frown crossed her brow for just an instant, then vanished. "I've learned a lot in two years."

David Piper nodded. In that moment she could have been his wife, the dedicated career woman, scorning husband and public alike. He had a fleeting memory of Jennie, a world away in New York, but he shut it out of his mind.

"Anyway," she continued, "I can't tell you anything about Joe. He can be in prison or in Timbuktu for all I care."

"I'd like to talk with your manager if I may."

"Marc? He can't tell you anything."

"I have to start somewhere."

She leaned across the desk, studying him with cold, hard eyes. At that moment she was neither a beauty nor a career woman, only a female. "I read the papers, Mr. Piper. They call you The Manhunter, and you only go after the big ones. What's so big about a punk forger doing two to five?"

"He was traveling in fast company when he escaped. And two guards were killed, remember? He could be tried as an accessory."

She thought about that, and finally said, "I'll phone Marc and tell him you're coming."

As she spoke on the phone, her face turned away from him, he stepped to the

315

desk and glanced down at the pile of opened mail. He remembered her sudden frown and was wondering what had caused it. A bill from a Beverly Hills hotel, a card from Compass Galleries with the handwritten notation *Again open for business,* a letter from a little-theater group in Ohio.

"All right," she concluded, hanging up the phone. "Marc can see you in an hour. He's in the Globe Building."

"Thank you."

"This time if you find my husband, lock him up and throw away the key."

He nodded, left the house, and walked down the driveway to his car. As he passed the little Spanish gardener he called out, "Goodbye, Manuel." The man glanced up and smiled.

Piper drove downtown to the glass-sided building where Marc Litzen had his office. Margo Miller's manager proved to be a beefy man with thick eyeglasses and a sense of failure hanging over him. He wondered why she stuck with him, when she could have had any of a dozen New York agents.

"Margo said you'd be coming," he told Piper, extending a limp pudgy hand. "But there's really nothing I can tell you about Joe Reilly."

316

"Nothing at all? I understand he forged your name to a number of checks."

"Yes."

"Why did he need the money? I'd have thought life with Margo Miller would have been comfortable enough."

"Does there have to be a reason?"

Piper nodded.

"The most likely ones are gambling debts, another woman, or an expensive drug habit."

Litzen blinked his eyes. "Which one do you favor?"

"Reilly escaped with five other prisoners. One of them, Nick Bruno, is the kingpin in a narcotics empire. Drugs could be the thing connecting the six prisoners."

"Nonsense!" the beefy man snorted.

"Margo Miller has a Spanish gardener who might be taking dope. He acted a bit strange this morning."

"Manuel?"

"Yes, if that's really his name. How long has he worked for her?"

Litzen's eyes widened and his gruff manner relaxed into a broad grin. "You think Manuel might be Joe Reilly, don't you?" That's the funniest thing I've heard all year!"

Piper didn't see the humor of it. "A man can change his appearance quite a lot by shaving off a mustache and darkening his skin. She admitted she loved him once. Maybe she still does. Maybe she's hiding him there and supporting his drug habit."

Litzen laughed some more, then stopped to wipe the tears from his eyes. Without his glasses he was almost handsome. "First of all, Manuel has worked for Margo ever since she bought the house, four years ago. Second, Joe Reilly doesn't take dope. Third, if Manuel does take it, so what? Four or five percent of the population smokes marijuana these days. You struck out, Mr. Piper."

"Then I'll repeat my question. Why did he need the money?"

"The man's a forger. He had to buy supplies."

David Piper didn't understand. "Supplies? Ballpoint pens to sign more checks?"

Litzen sighed. "An *art* forger! He specializes in Gothic paintings imitating some of the lesser-known Thirteenth Century Italian artists. He paints them, ages them cleverly, then sells them to collectors. But it's an expensive hobby, and

318

a dangerous one. Margo wouldn't pay for his supplies or set him up in the fake art business, so he forged the checks to cover his expenses."

Piper remembered the mail on her desk, and the sudden frown. One card had come from Compass Galleries – *Again open for business.* "Thanks, Mr. Litzen. I think you've been a big help."

The gallery was on the ground floor of an apartment house near the river. It was in a fashionable section of the city where one might expect to find a small private art gallery. David Piper walked down a few steps and entered from the street, pausing near the door to study a brightly spotlighted abstract in greens and blues.

A youngish man with blond hair and a ready smile appeared from the back room. "May I help you?"

"I'm looking for the owner," Piper told him.

"The owner resides in New York. I'm Vince McGraw, the manager. Perhaps I can help."

Piper glanced around at the paintings. It was not a large gallery, but there seemed to be a good selection. "I'm looking for an anniversary gift for my wife. She likes the Gothic period. Do you have anything, maybe by one of the Italians?"

"Step this way, please." McGraw led him into the next room, where the contemporary atmosphere gave way to a formalized, heavy-framed grandeur of an earlier age. "Our stock is limited at the moment, but I can show you some fine paintings priced at five thousands dollars."

"That would be about right," Piper agreed, playing for time.

"Here are some fine Spanish examples from the period, all done on wood."

Piper grunted. "All of them are religious subjects, aren't they?"

"The early Church was the major patron of art, especially in the Gothic period. It's only natural that painters chose religious subjects."

Piper was at a loss. The paintings before him could have been priceless relics or clever fakes, and he wouldn't have known the difference. He shifted his gaze to the young man's hairline, seeking evidence of a bleach job. With the mustache gone and the hair bleached, could this be Joe Reilly? Or was he jumping to conclusions as he had with the gardener?

"Do you have anything else from the same period?"

"Gothic?"

"Yes. Thirteenth Century."

The young man hesitated a moment, then motioned toward a workroom in the back. Piper followed him. "Here's one of our very latest acquisitions," he said, sweeping his hand toward a large painting of a nobleman. "I don't even have it framed yet. It's an oil on wood, probably painted around 1306 or earlier by Pietro Lorenzetti or his brother Ambrogio."

Piper studied the portrait. For all its faded colors it was still a work of power. It showed a nobleman standing by his horse, wearing body armor and holding a crossbow, about to join knights already battling each other in the background. The nobleman's free hand was raised toward heaven as if in supplication, and a ray of light from the sky suggested that his prayer would be answered.

"Very nice," Piper commented. "And not *too* religious."

"Notice the fine detail work here. The painter would have known his subject well. The Italians of the period were famed for their skill with the crossbow while on horseback. It was a favorite weapon of the Genoese."

"I know," David Piper agreed. "Weapons are a special hobby of mine." He was studying the painting with care. "What are you asking for this?"

"It's more than six hundred and fifty years old. The price would have to be ten thousand, and you'd be getting a bargain."

Piper whistled. "That's a lot of money."

"This painting formerly occupied a place of honor in a European collection."

"I couldn't pay that much –"

A bell rang from the gallery signaling someone's entrance. David Piper turned and saw Margo Miller standing in the outer room. She caught sight of McGraw and started to speak, but Piper stepped forward to block her line of vision. Her mouth froze as she tried to look from one to the other. Just at that moment, Piper decided, she wasn't much of an actress.

"Hello again," he greeted her, smiling.

"I – what are you doing here?"

"I'm thinking of buying a painting."

She glanced at McGraw. "He's David Piper, from the police. The one the papers call The Manhunter."

McGraw took the whole thing much

better than Margo. His brow knitted into a puzzled frown. "What would the police want here?"

David Piper smiled. "I'm searching for this lady's husband, an escaped convict named Joe Reilly. And I've found him."

The young man looked irritated. "Here? Don't be foolish."

"I don't think I am. The gallery was closed till recently. You sent Margo a notice that you were back in business, and it seemed to disturb her. She hurried down to see you. Litzen told me Reilly is an art forger who specializes in paintings of the Italian Gothic period, and you just tried to sell me a beautiful Gothic fake."

Irritation changed to indignation on the young face. "No art expert in the world could call that Lorenzetti a fake after just a casual glance!"

"I'm not an art expert. I don't know a thing about brush strokes and pigment and aging. But I do know weapons. I know them backward and forward. Crossbows were such a fearsome weapon in the Middle Ages that the Catholic Church – specifically Pope Innocent the Second – forbade their use in 1139, except in hunting or against infidels. The ban had little effect in practice, but that's not the point. The point is that the painting shows combat between knights, and a knight with a crossbow praying before battle. In an era when most painting was subsidized by the Church, no artist would have painted such a picture, and no nobleman would have posed for it. You knew Italians were experts with crossbows, so you put one in the picture. What you didn't know was that their religion forbade the weapon's use."

McGraw let out his breath. "All right," he mumbled. "I'm Reilly."

"Joe, you fool!" Margo screamed. "Why did you come back so soon? Why didn't you tell me what you were doing?" And then, in one sudden burst of love or loyalty, she swung her handbag straight at Piper's face. "Run, Joe! Run!"

Piper batted her arm away and dived for Reilly's legs, bringing him down near the door. He sat on top of the fallen man and brought out his gun. "No more games," he told Margo. Then, to Joe Reilly, he said, "Cheer up, fella. I guess at least she still loves you."

David Piper was reading a copy of Menninger's book, *The Crime of*

Punishment, when Inspector Fleming and Sheriff Barker arrived at his office the following morning.

"Odd sort of book for someone in your business to be reading," Barker commented.

"Not at all," Piper assured them, putting it down. "His ideas are quite interesting, even if I'm not prepared to accept all of them."

Inspector Fleming lit a cigar. "If it'll help you find those other five as quickly as you found Reilly, I'm all for it."

"What did he tell you about the escape?" Piper asked.

"Very little. He didn't know any of the men who freed him. They just drove him into Connecticut and dropped him at a motel. He doesn't know what happened to the other five."

"Interesting."

Sheriff Barker shifted in his chair. "Sorta ruins your theory that the six of them are somehow linked, doesn't it?"

"Perhaps," David Piper answered slowly. "And yet – any successful prison break is really a battle against odds, isn't it? In most mass escapes, one or two of the prisoners are usually recaptured almost at once. Isn't it possible that to beat the odds our fugitives would be willing to sacrifice one of their number? Possibly Joe Reilly was merely a pawn in their game of chess – a pawn to be sacrificed."

"You think of this as a chess game?"

"I don't know," Piper admitted. "I only know that finding Reilly hasn't gotten us any nearer to the other five, or to the people behind the break. I still have the feeling that when we find the rest, we'll find them all together."

"Even the girl?"

"Yes, even the girl."

Susan stuck her head in at the door. "Pardon me, Mr. Piper, but you asked to be informed immediately of any developments on the missing prisoners. There's an important phone call for you."

"I'll take it here," Piper said, punching a button as he picked up the phone. He listened intently, frowning and giving an occasional grunt. When he hung up he faced the two men across the desk.

"I'm afraid the news puts an entirely different aspect on the whole case, gentlemen." He couldn't hide his deep puzzlement. "What I've just learned puts us even further from the solution than we were."

Chapter Two: The Rook

"What is it?" Sheriff Barker asked, leaning forward in his chair.

David Piper was frowning down at his pipe, discarded on the desk top. "That was one of my contacts at police headquarters. A man was found shot to death in a hotel room last night."

Inspector Fleming nodded. "I glanced at the report on the way over here. What about it?"

"He's just been identified as Charlie Hall, one of our missing five."

"What!"

"Are they sure?" Barker asked.

Piper nodded. "With that bald head he's hard to miss. One of the detectives noticed the resemblance when they found the body. They just checked his fingerprints and it's Charlie Hall, all right."

Fleming was on his feet. "We'd better get down there. Want to come along?"

"I'd better." On the way out Piper said

to Susan, "Take my calls. I'll be back after lunch."

It was a gray November morning, which did nothing to lessen the sense of sterile gloom that David Piper always associated with the City Morgue. He followed Barker and Fleming down the long tiled hallway of the old building to the room where the Medical Examiner was waiting for them.

"We'll be doing a full autopsy this afternoon," the man told him, "but I don't think there's much problem as to the cause of death." He swept back the sheet and they stared down at the body.

Charlie Hall had been 52 years old, of medium build and running a bit to a potbelly. He was completely bald, and only the black of his eyelashes stood out against the pallor of his skin in death. The blood had been washed away, but the three head wounds were all clearly visible – two in his right temple and one in his right cheek.

"A small caliber weapon," the Medical Examiner explained. "Probably a .22. Looks as if all three bullets are still in there."

"Powder burns?" Inspector Fleming asked, bending close to the wounds.

"Oh, yes. I'd say the shots were fired

from a distance of not more than one foot. probably while the victim was sleeping. The body was found in bed, and there were no signs of a struggle."

"I'd better get back to headquarters," Fleming grumbled. "I have to get on this right away."

He left them and David Piper strolled out to the parking lot with Barker. The air felt good on his face after the antiseptic odor of the morgue. "Well, that only leaves four to be found," Barker commented.

"True enough."

"Your job's getting easier all the time."

Piper took out his worn tobacco pouch. "What's the background on Charlie Hall?"

"Nothing special. He's been a gambler all his life. If they were still running Mississippi riverboats, that would be the place for him. Cards, mostly. Fast with his fingers."

"Arrest record?"

"Not in this part of the country, but the police knew him. Lately he's been engaged in a more or less legit business – running charter flights to Las Vegas for some professional people around town. Doctors and lawyers, mostly. They fly out with their wives or girl friends for a long weekend.

329

Charlie ran the flights once a month. The suckers got their plane trip and hotel room for $200, but they had to buy $1500 in chips along with it. Charlie got a cut from the Vegas casinos."

"Sounds like quite a business."

Sheriff Barker nodded, sticking a piece of gum in his wide mouth. "It was. Big money."

"What went wrong to get him arrested?"

"That was a funny thing, and we never did get the full story. A few months back he reported a robbery to the police. A suitcase full of money was supposedly stolen from the office where he conducted this charter-flight business. Some reports had it that the suitcase contained over a hundred grand in cash. Anyway, it was never found and Charlie Hall seemed to be on the spot over it. The word around town was that he had to raise money fast. He tried to borrow money using some stolen stock certificates as collateral, and that's what we grabbed him on. I think Inspector Fleming himself made the arrest. The judge gave him five years on several counts of attempted fraud."

"Interesting."

Barker ground his teeth into the chewing

gum. "Hell, let's not worry about Charlie Hall. You just find the other four the way you found Joe Reilly."

"But don't you see, Sheriff, I still need a motive for the mass break. A suitcase full of money could provide that motive."

"You think somebody sprang them all so they could force Hall to talk about the money? Where it is?"

"Stranger things have happened." David Piper suddenly made up his mind. "I'm going to ask a few questions around town. The killing of Charlie Hall, rather than putting us further from a solution, just might be the break we've been looking for."

In the early afternoon at the Winking Moon Tavern the crowd at the bar was likely to be more interested in the free lunch than in the drinks. It was not until evening that the place took on its true character, attracting third-rate grifters anxious to spend their day's earnings on neighborhood women anxious to help them.

David Piper came to the Winking Moon often, but always during the day. He would sit in the last booth on the right, hidden from the bar customers by the tall

331

partitions, and wait for Tommy One-Eye to come in. Sometimes he would have to wait more than an hour, gingerly nursing a single beer; but Tommy always came.

Tommy, who had no last name that anyone had ever heard, was a drifter who had become, over the years, David Piper's most reliable paid informer. Often a single visit to the back booth at the Winking Moon had brought Piper the information he needed to crack a case. Tommy would sit there, his eyelid twitching nervously over his good eye, and tell Piper exactly where a missing man could be found, or where he might turn up the next day. Piper would nod solemnly – because one never joked with Tommy One-Eye – and slide a couple of folded bills across the table. The information, if Tommy gave it, was always accurate.

This day Piper had been seated in the booth for about twenty minutes when the stool pigeon slid in opposite him. He had his glass eye in place, and that made him look at least halfway human. "How's The Manhunter today?" he asked.

"Not so good, Tommy. I'm still trying to pick up the trail of Bruno and the others who escaped."

332

"I just heard on the news that Charlie Hall got it."

Piper nodded. "That's what I want to talk to you about. I had the idea he was strictly a small-time swindler, but I heard this morning he'd moved into the big time. Something about a stolen suitcase."

Tommy scraped at the growth of bristle on his chin. "He might as well have moved into the cemetery. When he pulled that suitcase trick he was a dead man."

"Tell me about it."

"Well, he had an office downtown and he's been running monthly flights to Las Vegas. They were popular around town with some of the wealthy swingers. The gimmick is that you get a cheap trip out as long as you promise to gamble big money. They do it all over the country, I guess. Guys like Hall organize the flights and go along, and the casinos take good care of them. When some of the guests run through all their cash on hand, the Vegas hotel is happy to extend credit. The way this works, when they get back home the swingers have to cough up the money to cover their losses. They pay it to Hall in cash and he brings it to the casinos on the next flight."

Piper was beginning to understand. "The stolen suitcase!"

"Right you are. Hall had collected from all the previous month's big losers and was ready for another trip to Vegas. Then he claimed someone stole the suitcase from his office. Could be, but the word was the Vegas boys weren't buying it. They told him he had to come up with the missing dough, and you can be damned sure he wasn't going to get it again from the suckers who'd paid it once."

"So he pulled the stock swindle."

Tommy nodded, he eyelid twitching. "Hall was too old for anything else. He picked up some stolen stock certificates cheap and tried to use them as collateral to borrow the hundred thousand he needed. That's when the cops grabbed him."

Piper mulled over it. "The fact that he tried to borrow the money would seem to prove that he was desperate, that he didn't fake the theft of the suitcase."

But Tommy was wise to the way of the underworld. He waved a finger like a professor of history making a point about the Hundred Years' War to a class of freshmen. "No, Charlie took the suitcase himself, but he blew the whole hundred grand playing roulette in the Bahamas."

"You know that for a fact?"

"I know it."

"Then any number of people might have wanted Hall dead – the Vegas gambling interests or the people whose losses he'd collected."

"Right – because those poor chumps still have to pay off their Vegas losses."

Piper pondered this new information. "It ruins one of my theories – that Hall was sprung by someone to lead the way to that suitcase. But it still raises the possibility that he was sprung simply to murder him."

Tommy One-Eye shook his head. "No chance, Manhunter. They could have hired a con in prison for fifty bucks to stick him with a rusty icepick. They sure didn't need to spring him to kill him."

"Did he have any Mafia connections?"

Tommy laughed at that. "A guy named Hall? You kiddin'?"

"Bruno has Mafia connections, and the Mafia's strong in Las Vegas. It's the first real tie-in I've had between Bruno and anyone else in that prison van."

"Forget it."

"Let's get back to the missing money.

335

Could you get me a list of the losers Hall collected it from?"

Tommy thought about it. "Sure, I guess so."

"See what you can do. Meanwhile, I'll check a couple of my Vegas contacts."

Piper slipped a folded bill across the table to Tommy, signifying the conversation was at an end. Tommy pocketed the bill with a nod and slid out of the booth. The session was over.

Back at the office of the Department of Apprehension, David Piper hung up his coat and called out to Susan in the next office. "Any messages?"

She came in and stood by the doorway. "The usual things. Plus one unusual."

"Oh?"

"Your wife phoned from New York."

"Oh." He lit his pipe and considered whether to return the call. Jennie was a fashion designer who had her own life, her own career. He seldom saw her any more, and they hadn't lived together in two years. "All right," he decided finally. "Call her back."

Susan made a face and returned to the outer office. She didn't approve of career-minded wives who lived away from their husbands.

Presently the phone on his desk rang and he picked it up. "Jennie?"

"Yes, David. How are you?" The voice was still the same, husky and full of promise. He thought it was her voice he had first fallen in love with.

"Fine, I guess. As well as could be expected. What's new on the winter fashion scene?"

She laughed good-naturedly. "We're already showing the spring fashions."

"In November?"

"Of course. You never did understand the business, David."

He sighed into the phone. Same old Jennie. "What can I do for you today? It must be business for you to phone me."

Her voice suddenly went serious. "David, somebody showed me a newspaper article about this case you're investigating – the six escaped prisoners."

"Yes?"

"There were pictures of the six, and I think I know the girl – Kate Gallery. Do you know her maiden name? Was it Kate Simpson?"

He flipped open the file by his elbow. "That's her."

"I thought so!"

"How do you know her?"

"I used her as a model a few seasons ago, for that bathing suit line I did. She appeared in all the picture layouts. My God, David, what was she doing in prison anyway?"

"It seems she killed her husband."

"No!"

"Blasted him right in the back with a shotgun. Nice friends you have."

"Do you have any idea where she's hiding?"

"Not yet, but I'm working on it. At first I was convinced the six of them were connected somehow, but so far two of them have turned up separately."

"David, let me know what happens with her, will you? It's very important to me."

"Sure, if you want me to."

"Thank you, David. Take care. I have to get back to my drawing board now."

"All right," he said into a dead receiver. She'd always had a habit of ending conversations quickly . . .

The street lights were just going on as he walked into the lobby of the Capital Arms, where Charlie Hall had slept his last sleep. It had been a high-class hotel in its day, but that day was 50 years ago. Now the lobby was littered with dirty ashtrays and yesterday's newspapers, and the faded peach paint was beginning to peel from the ceiling.

"You the night-desk clerk?" Piper asked the man behind the registration book. He was a slim Englishman wearing tweeds and pince-nez, and he seemed quite out of place in the setting.

"Is it night?" he asked, with a trace of British accent.

Piper sighed and showed his gold identification card bearing the Governor's signature.

"I'm looking for Ronald Summerhill, the clerk on duty from five to one. Since it's after five, I assume that's you."

"That's me," he admitted. "But I've already talked to the police."

"I'm not the police. I'm special and you talk to me, too. You found Charlie Hall's body in Room 540 shortly after midnight?"

Summerhill took off his glasses and began polishing them. "That's right. He checked in just after I came on duty. Alone, under the name of Charles Ball."

"Not much of an alias," Piper observed. "Let's see the register." Summerhill swung it around and pointed to a line halfway down the page. Piper compared the signature with Charlie Hall's own as it appeared on his Wanted circular. There was no doubt he'd signed the register himself. "All right. Tell me the rest of it."

"Well, I saw or heard nothing more from him. Just after midnight the party in the next room, 452, phoned the desk and said she had heard shots in 540. It was a Miss Melrose, a schoolteacher who'd been complaining all day about her accommodations. It seemed she'd stayed here years ago when things were better."

As if on cue the doors of the single self-service elevator opened and a stern-faced woman with gray hair stepped out, carrying a small suitcase. "You're checking out, Miss Melrose?" the clerk asked.

"I certainly am! This hotel is bad enough, but I certainly don't intend to spend another night here and be murdered in my bed!"

Piper showed her his identification. "Could I ask you a few questions before you leave, Miss?"

"Please be fast about it – I have a taxi coming."

"Did you see or hear anything of the dead man before the shots? Any noise at all?"

"No, nothing."

"How long after the shots did you phone the desk?"

"Why, immediately. There were three quick shots and then I picked up the phone."

"Mr. Summerhill here answered at once?"

"Of course. And he came right up to investigate."

She started for the door and Piper had to yell "Thank you" at her receding back. Then he turned back to Summerhill. "What did you find in the room?"

"The door was open about an inch. Mr. Hall was in bed, shot three times through the head."

"You were alone? No house detective?"

Summerhill shrugged. "Our security man has a drinking problem. Most nights he doesn't even show up."

"If Hall was asleep, how did the killer enter the room?"

"Those locks aren't worth much.

341

Anyone with a strip of plastic could get in, provided the inside bolt and chain were left off."

Piper nodded pensively. "Let's take a look at the room."

The fifth floor reflected the same shabbiness he'd seen in the lobby. With peeling paint and missing light bulbs all too evident, he could well understand Miss Melrose's complaints. The door to Room 540 was still open, its wooden frame coated with the dustings of fingerprint powder.

"We've closed off this entire floor. Except for 542, the other rooms are empty anyway."

Piper grunted and opened the door wider. The room clerk flipped on the light switch and the Manhunter saw only a drab cubicle with a bed, a dresser, and one narrow window. There was not even the usual television set. Places like the Capital Arms didn't bother with luxuries. The sheets had been pulled back from the bed, but Piper could see patches of blood still on them.

"Did he have any luggage?" Piper asked.

"Not a thing except the clothes on his back. They were hanging in the closet, and the police took them away."

Piper stepped to the door of the tiny bathroom and glanced inside at the neatly folded towels. At least the maid service at the Capital Arms appeared efficient. "How did the killer get up here without passing the desk downstairs?" he asked.

"There's a back door and a service elevator. He probably left the same way."

"Did anyone ask at the desk for Hall's – or Ball's – room number?"

"No."

David Piper bit his lip and frowned. In a mystery story the killer would have been the departed schoolteacher, but things didn't work out that way in real life. "All right," he said finally. "Thanks for your help. I may call on you again."

He left the Capital Arms more puzzled than ever.

Susan was just putting on her coat when he returned to the office. It was almost six o'clock, and the place was empty except for her. "Oh, I'm glad you got back. Tommy has been trying to reach you. He left this number."

"Thanks. You go home now. It's starting to rain."

"See you in the morning."

343

He dialed the unfamiliar number and listened to the phone ring four times. On the fifth ring Tommy answered. "Hello?" Cautiously.

"This is Piper."

"Hi, Manhunter!" His tone relaxed. "I got the list you wanted."

"Is this phone safe for you?"

"Sure. It's my girl's apartment."

"Oh." He'd never thought of Tommy having a girl. "What about the list?"

"These guys are all pretty unhappy with Charlie Hall. For my money any one of them might have killed him."

"If they knew where he was hiding," Piper said. "How many are on the list?"

"Seventeen names in all, Manhunter."

"Give me just the names of the big losers – the ones who had at least ten grand in the missing suitcase."

"That's easy. There are only three big ones. Dr. Gilbert Mendez, $34,000; Samuel Sloane, $28,500; and Marc Litzen, $12,000."

"Who? Give me that last name again!"

"Marc Litzen. Know him?"

"He's Margo Miller's theatrical agent. And she's the wife of Joe Reilly – the first of the six to be recaptured."

"Think there's a connection?"

"Either a connection or it's a damned funny coincidence."

"From what I hear, none of them cared much for Hall. They had him pegged as a rook, a swindler."

"A rook," Piper mused. And he'd already called Joe Reilly a pawn. Perhaps after all it really was a giant chess game.

"Anything else, Manhunter?"

"No, nothing else tonight, Tommy. I'll be in touch. At the usual place."

He sat by the phone for a long time, staring down at the three names.

Marc Litzen was working late at his office and Piper found him there poring over airline schedules that covered his desk. He looked up, surprised, and said, "I didn't expect to see you here again. Haven't you done enough to Margo, sending her husband back to prison?"

Piper studied the beefy man as he took a chair opposite the cluttered desk. "This time it's about you, Mr. Litzen. Are you planning your next flight to Las Vegas?"

The eyes squinted at him from behind thick glasses. "So that's it. Charlie Hall."

Piper nodded. "You didn't tell me you two were acquainted."

"You didn't ask."

"What are the schedules for?"

"If you must know, I'm booking a client of mine on the folk-singing circuit – one-night stands at college campuses. I'm arranging his travel schedule, It doesn't include Las Vegas."

"The word is you dropped a bundle out there."

"Sometimes I win. This time I lost."

"You lost twelve thousand and they gave you credit. Charlie Hall collected it when you got back home."

"Collected it and lost it, the damned crook!"

"Did you tell him that?"

"I would have if I'd had the chance!"

"Would you have killed him if you had the chance?"

"I don't go in for murder."

"Piper scratched his chin, studying the beefy agent. "Where'd you get the money to pay Hall?"

"That's my business."

"From Margo Miller?"

"I told you it was my business."

"Did Hall and Joe Reilly know each other?"

"I doubt it."

"Reilly never took a Vegas flight with you?"

"No."

Piper sighed and stood up. "Keep your nose clean, Mr. Litzen. You are in this thing deeper than anyone else at the moment."

"How do you mean?"

"So far you're the only one I've found who knew at least two of the six who escaped."

Piper left him at his desk and drove across town to the swank apartment house where Samuel Sloane lived. Sloane was a stock-broker, and with the market closing in mid-afternoon it wasn't likely he'd still be at the office after seven. Piper was right. He answered the door on the second ring.

"Yes?" He was big, but well-built – a handsome man in his mid-thirties whose eyes seemed to sparkle when he smiled a greeting.

Piper showed his identification card. "Just a few questions, Mr. Sloane. You probably read in the evening papers of the murder of Charlie Hall."

"That escaped convict? Yes, I read about it."

Piper edged his way in. The place was laid out like a lush movie set, with a thick furry carpet and floor-to-ceiling drapes. He must have had a wife in the decorating business. Or a girl friend.

"I understand you paid Hall a large sum of money to cover gambling losses in Las Vegas."

Sloane towered over him, seeing on the verge of denial. Finally he sighed and motioned to a chair. "Sit down, Mr. Piper."

"The sum I have in mind is something like $28,500."

"Your information is accurate."

"Charlie Hall collected this sum from you, in cash, and was supposed to have taken it to Las Vegas. He didn't, so you still owe the money."

"That's right. He stole it from me. It's as simple as that. But try and tell that Veagas crowd! He attempted to borrow it and got himself arrested. Then he broke out of that prison van and got himself killed."

"Any idea who pulled the trigger, Mr. Sloane?"

"Given the opportunity I might have

348

done it myself. I threatened to, when I heard the money was gone."

"You're a very frank man. Did you kill him?"

"No."

"Did Hall get in touch with you in any way after his escape?"

"No."

"What about the other five? Ever do any business with them?"

"None whatsoever."

It was a blank wall of negatives. David Piper got to his feet. "I appreciate your help. I may call on you again."

Next he drove over to Raker Memorial Hospital, where Dr. Gilbert Mendez was on night duty. This interview, when he finally tracked down Dr. Mendez, was even more unsatisfactory. The doctor was a short dark-featured man with intense eyes and a trace of accent. He looked at Piper and they immediately disliked each other.

"Doctor, it's about this killing of Charlie Hall."

"I don't know the man. If you'll let me pass, I have a patient waiting in Emergency."

"You lost a lot of money in Las Vegas."

"I don't know what you're talking about."

"You deny paying Hall $34,000 in gambling debts?"

"I certainly do deny it. I'd be a fool to do otherwise under the circumstances. Now please let me pass."

That was the extent of their conversation. David Piper went back to his car and brooded. He brooded about Tommy's list and the schoolteacher and Marc Litzen. But most of all he brooded about towels.

At ten o'clock he was back in the lobby of the Capital Arms. It hadn't changed in five hours. The discarded newspapers were still in the same positions by the chairs, and Ronald Summerhill was still behind the desk.

"No business?"

The Englishman shrugged. "It was bad enough before. Now with the murder we'll be lucky if we can stay open."

David Piper leaned on the counter. He asked, almost casually, "You knew Charlie Hall before, didn't you?"

"Me? No, I never laid eyes on him."

"Ronald, Ronald! Am I to believe that a man who had escaped from prison, who was being hunted by every policeman in the state, would calmly walk into a hotel lobby – and at that a lobby littered with old newspapers probably containing his picture – and register under a name almost identical to his own?"

"Well, he did it, didn't he?"

"He did it because he knew you, Ronald. He came here because he knew you. He waited till after five to check in because you'd be on duty."

Summerhill took off his glasses and began polishing them with his handkerchief. "All right, I knew him. We'd had a few business dealings together. He came here and I gave him a room."

"One of your business dealings involved the loss of $8,000 in Las Vegas a few months back, didn't it?"

"Who says so?"

"I have a friend with a list," He should never have asked Tommy not to read the names under $10,000. He hadn't made that mistake the second time he phoned. "You paid Hall the eight grand but he blew it gambling and told you it was stolen from him. So you still owed it to the Vegas people, and $8,000 is a lot of money to someone in your position."

The handkerchief slipped from Summerhill's fingers and he bent to pick it up. "What does that prove?"

"That you murdered him."

Summerhill came up from behind the desk with a long-barreled .22 target pistol in his hand. He was fast, but Piper was ready for him. He knocked the gun aside and brought his fist up in a high arc that just managed to clip the point of the Englishman's jaw."

"You shouldn't have kept the murder weapon around, Ronald," Piper told him, drawing his own gun as he reached for the telephone. "That's what's going to convict you."

Inspector Fleming blinked his eyes and said, "Towels?"

David Piper nodded. "Towels. Among other things. Mostly it was the schoolteacher, though." They were in Piper's office the following morning, relaxing over coffee.

"I thought you said she wasn't involved."

"She wasn't, but she figured very
352

cleverly in Summerhill's scheme. Once I'd established that Hall and Summerhill knew each other because of the Vegas deal. I had to ask myself an even more baffling question than why Charlie Hall picked that particular hotel. I had to ask myself why Summerhill gave him a room directly next to the only other occupied room on the entire fifth floor. It's not the sort of thing you do to a friend who's trying to hide out from the police."

Fleming frowned over his coffee cup. "Why did he do it?"

"Because he needed the schoolteacher to alibi him. She'd complained about everything else, so he knew she'd be on the phone the instant she heard those shots. Before he went up to Room 540 with his gun, he simply plugged 542 into 540 on the switchboard. After killing Hall he picked up the telephone and heard Miss Melrose's voice calling the desk. He answered her, pretending he was at the desk when in reality he was right in the next room. Then he simply waited a few minutes and stepped into the hall, pretending he'd just come up. With a murderer loose he knew Miss Melrose wouldn't come into the hall till he arrived. In fact, he probably told her to stay in her room with the door locked."

"And the towels?"

"When he showed me the room I noticed that the bloody sheets were still there, but the towels were neatly folded in the bathroom. Are we to believe that Hall stayed in his room all evening and then went to bed without using a single towel to so much as wash his hands or face? It's possible, of course, but highly unlikely. More likely is the supposition that the towels were replaced before the police arrived. And that points to Summerhill, the only one who could have replaced them."

"But why?"

"The shots were fired from only a foot away. I assume some blood splattered on Summerhill – at least, on his hands. Or perhaps he washed off some powder burns from the gun. In any event, he dirtied the towels and then had to replace them. He had no choice, remember – he had to appear at Miss Melrose's door spotless, as if he'd just come up from the desk."

"It explains a lot of things – how the killer knew Hall was at the Capital Arms, how he entered the locked room, what he did with the gun."

Piper nodded. "Has Summerhill confessed?"

"His lawyer had indicated that he will. The gun checks out as the murder weapon anyway. Why do you ask?"

"Sheriff Barker sent me a copy of the autopsy report this morning. Have you read it, Inspector?"

"Just glanced at it. Why?"

Piper picked it up from his desk. "The Medical Examiner found evidence that Hall had taken several sleeping pills. Not enough to cause death, but enough to put him in a deep, drugged sleep."

"Summerhill probably gave them to him so he wouldn't wake up before he was shot."

"Then why not enough to kill him and avoid having to use the gun?"

"You think up the damnedest questions! The case is *solved!* You solved it yourself. Don't go creating more will-o'-the-wisps!"

"And why didn't Hall put on the inside bolt and chain before retiring? Everyone always does, in hotel rooms, even if they're not hiding from the police."

"Look, Summerhill killed him. He's

ready to confess. He had a gun in his possession. Ballistics prove it was the murder weapon. What in hell are you trying to say?"

David Piper leaned back in his chair, catching for just an instant a veiled glimpse of some shadowy opponent across an unseen chessboard. The pawn, and now the rook . . .

"What I'm trying to say, Inspector, is that Summerhill killed him all right. But look what Charlie Hall did: he went to a hotel where a man he'd cheated out of $8,000 was employed; he signed the registration book with a simple, transparent alias, then went up to his room; he didn't use the only door locks that might have protected him; he calmly took several sleeping pills; then he went to bed – and waited to be murdered. Does any of that make sense?"

"You think it's tied in somehow with the missing four?"

David Piper nodded. "I think it's all tied in somehow, Inspector. I think we're being maneuvered into making exactly the moves that someone wants us to make. It's all pointing toward something big. Something really big. But what?"

Chapter Three: The Knight

Piper was restless that morning, pacing his office and even emerging on occasion to bark at Susan, something he rarely did. The case was going badly, even though two of the six had now been accounted for. He went out early to lunch, but he didn't eat. Instead, he spent the hour tracking down assorted stool pigeons who frequented the midtown area.

Finally, by one o'clock, he was back in the rear booth at the Winking Moon, waiting for Tommy One-Eye, his most trusted informer. He had to wait longer than usual, and he was almost ready to leave when Tommy slipped casually into the seat opposite him.

"I didn't expect to see you again so soon, Manhunter."

"I'm at a dead end, Tommy. I was hoping you'd heard something more."

"Nothing much – just that it's big."

"It?"

"The reason they were sprung. There's

talk that it might involve a huge robbery, something in the millions."

David Piper came alive with interest. This was the first confirmation he'd heard of his own pet theory. "Why do you say that, Tommy?"

"The three guys who pulled the break – the ones who ambushed that prison van – have been paid off. I hear they got fifty grand each, plus one-way tickets to Brazil."

Piper gave a low whistle. "That's big money for just a few minutes' work."

"Damn right! I hear they were on the plane to Rio within forty-eight hours, too. Somebody wanted them out of the country fast. With an investment like that already made, it has to be a big-money deal."

"Heard anything else?"

Tommy shrugged and scratched at the bristle of his beard. "Just that Bruno is back in operation."

"Back?"

"That's the word I get. He's in hiding, but a couple of the boys have seen him."

Piper felt his heart sink a little at the news. Just when things were beginning to point toward a conspiracy of some sort, here was word that another of the six had broken away and gone on his own. What

358

sort of conspiracy could there be with the remaining three, one of them a girl? "Who's his top lieutenant now?" Piper asked.

"Sammy Sargent, same as always."

"Piper nodded. He knew Sammy slightly – a coldly ruthless operator who wouldn't hesitate to pull a double-cross if enough money was involved. "Think Sammy paid the three guys to spring his boss?"

Tommy chuckled. "You kidding, Manhunter? He was better off with Bruno in jail."

"Could I get to Bruno?"

"He's guarded like Fort Knox. Nobody even knows where he's holed up. The guys I talked to were taken there blindfolded."

"How about Sammy Sargent?"

"Maybe. He turns up around town occasionally."

Piper slipped a folded bill across the table. "See what you can do, Tommy."

The one-eyed man nodded and slid out of the booth. He strolled slowly out the front door of the Winking Moon without looking back. Piper waited five minutes and then he followed the informer out.

The Raker County Jail was a bleak gray structure that was built to resemble a medieval castle. Its turreted battlements were purely decorative, and yet they gave the distinct impression of being capable of withstanding a lengthy siege by the forces of evil. David Piper had always disliked the place. It seemed a symbol of all that was wrong with antiquated prison conditions.

He walked down the whitewashed corridor to Sheriff Barker's office, remembering the first time he'd met the man. It had been a somewhat unpleasant confrontation, following a break three years ago by a single convict. Both Piper and the Department of Apprehension were new then, and he'd been appalled to learn that a jail the size of Raker County's allowed prisoners to roam with a fair amount of freedom inside its walls. This convict, sent back alone to his cell after questioning, had simply climbed through a ventilating duct and escaped.

Practices were tighter and more efficient at the jail now, but he could still understand Barker's concern about being blamed for the prison-van escape. Though it had happened away from the jail, newspapers had been quick to point out the county's past record of lax conditions.

"The Sheriff around?" he asked a deputy in the office.

"He's down in Identification," the man replied without looking up. "End of the hall."

Piper found him with a stack of fingerprint cards, carefully pressing the inked digits of prisoners in the proper spaces. "How are you, Mr. Piper? Be with you in a few minutes."

Piper sat down to watch. "Take your time. Maybe I'll learn something."

Sheriff Barker motioned the next prisoner in line forward and inked his fingers. "Won't learn much here, except how bungling some of my deputies are. Got one damn fool on the night shift can't even take the fingerprints right. I usually have to do it over myself." He rolled the prisoner's thumb and fingers on the card and then reached for the other hand.

"How many sets do you make?" Piper asked.

"Three – one for us, one for the state, and one for Washington. There, that does it." He waved the last of the prisoners away and watched the deputy take them in tow. "Now what can I do for you?"

Piper came right to the point. "There are still four prisoners at large, and I'm stuck with my theory that they're together on some sort of big caper." He didn't bother to add the information about the $50,000 payments to the members of the hijacking gang. "I want to know more about the four – about their backgrounds and any crime specialties they might have."

"Well, the girl's strictly an amateur, of course. Of the four, your best bet for something like that would be Jack Larner."

"The bank robber."

"Right. Here's the card on him. Age forty-seven, stocky build, brown hair and beard when arrested, tattoo of a dancing girl on his left arm."

"If I remember correctly, he's the one who was involved with some Miami gang in his youth."

"Right. But now he's strictly a loner. We got him on a car theft and assault in connection with his last bank job, but we figure he's pulled at least a dozen more in the past year."

Piper nodded and took out his tobacco pouch. "Either you or Fleming mentioned the difficulty of getting a firm identification during the bank job. Why's that?"

"He's used some cute disguises in his time. Dressed up like a girl once. This last time he had the beard, and a bandage round his head. The beard looked fake but it wasn't. The bandage looked real, but it wasn't, either. He's tough to spot."

"You mentioned a tattoo. Does he still like the girls?"

"He likes them. Especially dancers. I asked him about it when I was booking him." The Sheriff chuckled at the memory. "He claimed dancers have the best legs, muscles and all. Right now he's been living with a belly dancer down at the Greek place."

Piper nodded. There was only one Greek place in Raker County that had belly dancers. "The Lifted Veil."

"That's the place. Girl's stage name is Fiona."

"I'll look her up."

"He'd be crazy to go back there. We've had it staked out."

Piper smiled. "I'll look her up anyway. I like dancers' legs, too."

The Lifted Veil was owned by a Greek named Matsoukas who enjoyed drinking ouzo with his customers and even dancing with them in the traditional native manner. David Piper knew him slightly, and recognized his tall frame and mustached face behind the crowded bar.

"Matsoukas, I'm looking for a girl named Fiona."

The Greek nodded his shaggy head. "She's on next, old friend. Have a table and you shall see her."

Piper nodded and chose one of several empty tables up front. This early in the evening, on a weeknight, business at The Lifted Veil was largely confined to the bar. Neighborhood men, mostly, more interested in the ouzo and the companionship of the bar than in the dubious charms of the too-familiar belly dancers up front.

The Greek orchestra switched presently from traditional melodies to the up-tempo beat they used to bring on the next act. An off-stage voice announced the appearance of Fiona, and suddenly she was there, all veils and soft flesh, moving with a grace and speed that seemed to blur the sequined reflection of the spotlights that followed her every move. She was good, Piper admitted reluctantly – much better than the usual run of dancers at the Veil.

He watched her drop the veil that covered her midriff and go down on her knees in the classic position of the belly dancer, throwing back her head and shoulders while she swayed her body in tempo with the music. Then she was up, dancing like a demon, using the veils as Salome must have. She paused at Piper's table, draping one end around his neck, then whisking it away in a burst of twirling.

When she paused by him again, Piper stuffed a dollar bill into the band of her sequined bra and said, "I'll buy you a drink later." She smiled and danced away, seeking more dollars from the men who lined the bar.

Finally she vanished through the stage curtains and the Greek orchestra switched to something slower. Piper sipped his drink and waited. It was ten minutes before she reappeared, dressed now in the regular street clothes that the other dancers wore when not performing. She said a few words to Matsoukas at the bar and then joined Piper at the table.

"You're very good," he said, meaning it.

She shrugged and he was aware for the first time of the handsome straightness of her nose, the inky blackness of her fine Greek eyes. "It's a dying profession," she told him. "I'm the only Greek girl in town still doing it. The rest are retired strippers or topless dancers or just college kids earning a little extra money."

"Your name is Fiona?" He signaled the waiter for drinks.

"That's my name here."

He nodded. After she'd sipped her drink he said, "I'm looking for Jack Larner."

For a full minute she said nothing, and he thought she might get up and walk away. But finally she stubbed out her cigarette and said, "You're a cop. I'd figured you were too polite for a cop."

"I'm not exactly a cop, but I'm looking for Larner. I understand you're his girl."

"Off and on." She lit another cigarette. "He always had a thing for dancers. Even has one tattooed on his arm."

"So I understand."

"You understand a lot. But I guess you don't understand Jack Larner. He's – hell, he's like one of those knights that used to ride around back in the Middle Ages. A perfect gentleman, even a sort of champion of womanhood. Sometimes it's a pleasure just being with a man like that."

Piper snorted. "Jack Larner is a killer and bank robber."

"The killing was long ago, in Miami. He told me all about it. He punched a man in a tavern who was swearing at his girl. The man hit his head and died, and Jack went to prison for manslaughter. See, even then he was something of a knight."

"And I suppose these banks he robs are dragons."

"Maybe to him they are. They're part of the Establishment, the oppression of the minorities. Like what's happened in Greece the last few years. He opposes the Establishment just like the hippies do."

"You've painted him in glowing colors, but I just don't buy a forty-seven-year-old hippie who robs banks."

"Buy it or not, that's the truth. Jack Larner is a fine man!"

"Have you seen him or talked to him since his escape?"

"No. You should know that. The cops have been watching me day and night."

"Does he have any other friends around town? Male or female?"

She shook her head. "He's strictly a loner."

"He escaped with five other people," Piper reminded her.

"He's still a loner. If you find him, he'll be alone."

"Thanks," he told her. He got to his feet and was starting to leave when one more question occurred to him. "Fiona, do you have an agent?"

"A what?"

"A booking agent, a manager. Most show people have one."

"Oh, sure. Marc Litzen handles my bookings, when I have any. Mostly, though, I perform here at The Lifted Veil."

"Litzen." David Piper thanked her again and left. The evening air was crisp and cool, with a bright moon overhead. He walked to where he'd parked the car, thinking about it. Marc Litzen was now connected with three of the escaped prisoners. He was the agent for Joe Reilly's wife and Jack Larner's girl. And he'd been swindled out of some money by Charlie Hall.

Perhaps a coincidence. Perhaps more than that.

In the morning Susan buzzed him on the intercom. "I have Tommy on the phone. He says it's important."

"Put him on."

"Tommy's familiar voice came through, talking fast. "You still want to see Sammy Sargent?"

"I sure do."

"He'll be at the track this afternoon. Box R-11."

"Thanks."

Tommy hung up, and Piper sat tapping the desk for a moment. Then he picked up the phone and dialed the number of Marc Litzen's office. The agent answered at once, his voice gruff and preoccupied.

"This is David Piper."

"Oh, yes."

"We're still investigating the escape from the prison van, and your name has come up again. The third time."

"How's that? I don't know any of the others."

"One of your clients is a dancer named Fiona."

"Fiona?" There was a moment's pause. "Oh, you mean the belly dancer at the Greek's place. She's been down there almost a year now, but I guess I've represented her a few times in the past."

"Her boy friend is Jack Larner, another of the escapees."

"Well, hell, how was I supposed to know that? I haven't even seen Fiona in maybe six months. And I certainly never laid eyes on Larner."

"If you say so," Piper said softly. "How's Joe Reilly's wife?"

"She's taking it pretty good, now that he's locked up again. I may have a good part for her off-Broadway. She's considering it."

"Well, I'll be in touch," Piper said. "If Larner should happen to contact you –"

"Why should he contact me? I don't even know the man."

"Oh, yes, that's what you said." Piper hung up and once more found himself pondering Marc Litzen's place in it all. He could only be an innocent bystander, yet . . .

Next Piper phoned Inspector Fleming at Headquarters. "Anything new on the Hall autopsy?"

"Just what we discussed yesterday – the evidence of sleeping pills in his system. The body's still at the morgue, waiting for somebody to claim it. If nobody shows up by tomorrow, the county will have to bury him."

"No sign of the missing four?"

"Nothing – not a lead."

Piper cleared his throat, remembering something. "My wife thinks she knows the girl – Kate Gallery. Did she do some fashion modeling once?"

"I believe so. Bathing suits, I think."

"That's the girl. I'll have to tell Jennie to keep an eye out for her in New York."

On the other end of the line Inspector Fleming chuckled. "What happened to your theory that they were all connected?"

"It's suffering these days," Piper admitted frankly. "By the way, I understand Bruno is back running things."

"I hadn't heard. But I'm not surprised."

"Look, I'll get back to you. I have to go out to the race track this afternoon."

Fleming sounded interested. "Got a tip on a sure thing?"

"Let's call it a long shot."

November racing in upstate New York was not anyone's idea of a comfortable activity. The days were damp and chilly, with more than occasional snow flurries to whiten the turf. And although the grandstand and clubhouse were enclosed and heated, horses and riders and trainers all betrayed a dislike of the weather. This was the final

371

week of it, though, before the winter closing, and the horse bettors had turned out in force.

Piper made his way through the crowd to the section of box seats. There were four seats in R–11, but only two were occupied – by Sammy Sargent and a girl whom Piper had never seen before. Sammy was dressed in a loud checkered sports coat and a loud striped tie, with fashionably long sideburns that were new since the last time Piper had seen him.

"Hello, Sammy. How's your luck today?"

Sargent glanced up, off guard, his lips twisted into a sort of sneer. He was not the friendliest of men under the best of circumstances. "Piper, isn't it? The state cop?"

"I've been called worse."

The girl twisted in her seat. "Sammy, I wanna bet on Number Four."

"All right, all right! I'll place it for you."

Piper stepped aside to let him pass and then followed along. "Got any good tips today, Sammy?"

The little man turned, pausing on the steps. "What is this, anyway? What're you after?"

"Information, Sammy. Information about Nick Bruno. I hear he's back running things."

"Bruno's gone. South America, I think."

"That's not what I hear, Sammy. I hear he's back in charge, hiding out somewhere."

The eyes squinted menacingly. "Quit bothering me, cop. I gotta make a bet."

"I want him, Sammy. I want Bruno and the other three."

"Well, good luck to you!"

Sargent continued down to the booths, with Piper behind him. The area was hectic with prerace activity, and Piper had to push through the crowd to keep up with Sammy. "The state might be willing to make a deal," he said cautiously. "A lighter sentence if Bruno turns himself in, along with the other three."

Sammy bought his tickets and stood for a moment pondering something. "Come over here," he said suddenly. He led the way to an empty alcove off the main betting area. "All right, now. What do you want?"

"Bruno and Courtney and Larner and the girl."

"Hell, you don't want much, do you?"

"Do you know where they are, Sammy?"

Bruno's lieutenant debated another moment and then asked, "If I gave you a tip on one of them, would you leave Bruno alone?"

"Now you're the one wanting to make a deal."

"Sure, if I can."

"You admit Bruno's back running his rackets?"

"I'm not admitting anything." There was a roar from the crowd as the unseen horses broke from the starting gate. "Come on – I have to watch the race."

Piper sighed. "I'm making no promises unless Bruno surrenders. But I'm listening if you want to give me a name."

Sammy Sargent was staring down at the garishly printed tickets in his hand. "Jack Larner," he said quietly, his voice almost lost in the rising roar from the grandstand. "Don't say I told you, but look for him at Mid-State Airport on Friday morning."

"What? The airport?"

But Sammy Sargent slipped quickly away, fading into the sudden influx of bettors. The race was over, and the winners were anxious to collect.

Piper considered going after him but he knew Sammy would not repeat what he'd said in front of the girl. Friday at the airport. It might be nothing, but it was worth checking out.

He drove downtown to Inspector Fleming's office, and found the detective chief relaxing with a stack of Wanted circulars. "Well, Mr. Piper, good to see you again. Any clues on our missing four?"

"Maybe." He took out his pipe and tobacco pouch and dropped into a vacant chair. "I've gotten a tip from somebody that one of the escapees, Jack Larner, will try to leave town Friday morning. If we're at the airport we might be able to grab him."

Fleming frowned at the news. "How good a tipster is this?"

"Why?"

"It just seems odd that Larner would let the word get around two days in advance that he was catching a plane out of here. Hell, what does he even need a plane for? There are cars and trains and buses out of town. There's even the tour boat down the Hudson to New York. He doesn't need a plane, and he sure doesn't need to spread his plans around town days in advance."

Piper had to admit the validity of Fleming's objections. Nevertheless, he said, "It was a good tip, Inspector. I think we ought to be there." The Manhunter took his leave.

Thursday passed like a day apart. A light fog hung over the city, slowing traffic and fraying tempers, and for the first time since the mass escape, news of it was edged off page one of the papers. Nothing happened – nothing but the fog.

Piper stayed close to his office and tried a few phone calls, but no one answered. Tommy was out of sight, Sheriff Barker was on another case, and even his wife Jennie had left her New York apartment. He felt as if the world were deserting him, and by the time Friday morning dawned he would have been thankful for anything at all in the way of action.

The airport was jammed with travelers – some of them held over from the previous day's canceled flights. Piper and Fleming moved through the crowds near the main entrance, studying faces, watching for signs. A pilot in navy-blue uniform went by and smiled.

"He'll be disguised," the Inspector grumbled. "He's a master of it."

Piper merely grunted. "There are certain things he can't disguise, if only we knew where to look for him."

"I've got a couple of men out at the parking lot. Think I need more?"

"It's hard to say. Maybe we're just chasing another of your will-o'-the-wisps."

Piper's eyes were busy, scanning the passing faces. Remembering that Larner had once dressed in women's clothing, it was impossible to see everyone. "How many other entrances are there, Inspector?"

"Two, but this is the main one. The other is down at the other end, by the bank!"

"Bank!"

As if to emphasize the word, an alarm sounded at that moment from the opposite end of the airlines building. Fleming and Piper looked at each other for a split second, then both broke into a run.

By the time they reached the small branch office of the bank, near the other entrance, Fleming had his gun out and they were plowing a path through converging onlookers attracted by the alarm. Piper went into the bank right behind Fleming, took one look at the stunned manager sitting on the floor holding his head, and asked the frightened girl teller, "What did he look like?"

"I –" She was in a state of shock. Finally the words came out, in a panicked rush. "A priest! It was a priest! He had a gun –"

"Damn," Piper muttered, running outside to the terminal mall. A priest's collar and black bib were too easy to dispose of. By now Larner might be any one of a hundred other people.

Other police were arriving now, and Fleming joined him, the gun back in its holster. "There's a regular currency shipment from the Federal Reserve Bank every Friday morning," he explained. "It's kept in the vault here till the armored car picks it up after lunch. Our so-called priest was waiting when they brought it in."

Piper cursed again. "How much?"

"Two suitcase-sized packages, but he could only carry one. He had to leave the other. They think maybe he got around twenty, twenty-five thousand dollars, but it could be much more, depending on the denominations of the bills."

"All right," Piper said, "it's my fault for not understanding the tip I got. I thought he was going to leave town on a plane, not rob the airport bank. But there's no time for second guessing now. Have your outside men seal off the airport. Nobody leaves."

"You think he's still here?"

"Knowing Larner, he wouldn't try to travel far in that priest's garb. If he took time to change in a Men's Room we just might nab him."

But looking around at the crowded terminal, his words seemed empty. There might be nearly a thousand people milling about. Identifying Jack Larner or anyone else could be a hopeless task. He could hardly check every person's arm for a tattooed dancing girl.

Uniformed officers were fanning out through the terminal now, checking the most likely hiding places. One came out of a Men's Room carrying a collar and square of black cloth. "Found it in the wastebasket," he told Fleming.

"I figured as much." He turned to Piper. "What now? Think he's gone?"

"He must be," Piper answered slowly. "He –" Then he paused, his eyes following the long legs and swinging hips of a girl who had just walked by. Something . . . "Come on!"

"Is it him?"

"Next best thing!" Piper said, catching

379

up with the girl. "Miss Fiona, good to see you again!"

The dark-eyed belly dancer turned at the sound of her name and tried to break away, but Piper held her in a tight grip. "What in hell is this?" she asked.

"You have a bag – going somewhere?"

"I –"

"Step this way, please, Miss," Fleming said, using his most authoritative tone. They led her into one of the little airline offices, and Piper took her suitcase.

"What's the meaning of this?" she demanded.

"We'd like your permission to open this," Piper said. "There's been a robbery."

She unlocked the case and flipped it open. "Nothing but my clothes, gentlemen!"

"Which flight are you taking?"

"The 11:55 to Miami."

"Is Jack Larner traveling with you?"

"Of course not! I told you I haven't seen him. I'm going down there about a job."

Fleming motioned Piper to one side. "What do you think? Can we believe her?"

"He'll be on that plane," Piper said with certainty. "The suitcase with the stolen money is probably already checked through to Miami. It was a clever gimmick – robbing an airport bank and then escaping by plane – but he made the mistake of inviting her along."

"What do we do – check for a tattoo?"

"Damn right! Come on. And bring her along!"

Fleming had a thought. "You're sure she's not Larner in disguise?"

"I'm sure. I saw her dance. Besides, Larner changed disguises in the Men's Room. He could hardly have walked out of there dressed as a woman without attracting some attention. Whatever he looks like now, it's male."

"Then if he's on that flight we've got him."

But it was not quite as simple as that. There were 28 passengers booked on the 11:55 to Miami, including 22 men. It was with much grumbling that they finally consented to take off their coats and roll up their shirt sleeves for an inspection of their left arms.

"Stocky, forty-seven, brown hair," Fleming commented. "A half dozen of them fit the description, but not one has a tattoo."

"And none looks like the mug shot." Piper studied the picture in his hand. "Though it's hard to tell much with that beard. I guess they should have shaved him before taking the mug shot."

"When will we be able to leave?" the copilot asked. "Our flight's five minutes late already."

"Relax," the Inspector told him. "We'll get you out as soon as possible." Then he asked Piper, "What do we do? Hold the most likely ones for fingerprinting?"

"And have a flock of lawsuits on our hands?"

"We could check the bags for the stolen cash."

Piper shook his head. "If there's no tattoo, there's no cash. Maybe he's on a different flight, planning to meet her down there. Maybe her presence here was just a diversion to keep us occupied."

"Maybe," Fleming admitted grimly.

Fiona came at them bristling. "When are you going to let us go? You have no right to hold us here!"

Piper glanced at the passengers' faces and saw that they were waiting for his reply. He took a deep breath and slapped her across the face. "Shut up, you stupid tramp!"

Then several things happened at once. Piper's eyes were on the gasping, incredulous faces of the passengers, and he missed the movement to his left. There was a flash and the deafening roar of a gunshot, and he felt the bullet tug at his sleeve as he whirled. Then Fleming moved fast, throwing himself onto the man with the gun. They went down in a heap, and Piper pulled his own gun free, running to help.

Fleming looked up, holding the man's hands stretched apart. "Kick his gun away and get the cuffs on while I hold him. He's got the strength of a tiger!"

They got him to his feet at last, and Piper looked him over. "The copilot, of all people! We never thought to check the plane's crew."

"I think we'll find he's not the real copilot."

Fleming grunted, holding onto the man. "Damn it, Piper, next time you pull a trick like that, tip me off in advance. You almost got yourself killed. How in hell did you know it would work, anyway?"

"Larner is a real gentleman, aren't you, Jack? He once killed a man defending a

383

girl's honor, and I just thought he might do it again. When I hit Fiona and called her a tramp, he didn't stop to think. He just tried to shoot me."

Fleming looked at him. Fiona had come over to stand by his side, sobbing quietly. "Got anything to say, Larner?"

Larner had nothing to say.

He'd jumped the real copilot in the parking lot at the airport and left him bound and gagged on the floor of a car. Wearing the copilot's uniform under a black raincoat, with only a priest's collar and bib showing, he'd robbed the bank and then made his quick change. The priest's garb was abandoned in the Men's Room and the black raincoat left draped forgetfully over a chair. The suitcase with the money had been checked through to Miami with the regular passenger luggage, and he simply told the pilot he was a replacement for the regular man who was ill.

"Of course," Fleming pointed out later, back downtown, "as soon as he got into the cockpit the pilot would have known he was a fake. Larner didn't know the first thing about flying an airliner."

384

"It didn't matter," Piper explained. "As soon as the plane took off he planned to draw his gun and force the pilot to fly him and Fiona to Cuba with the money."

"We'll hang onto him this time," Fleming promised. "Tattoo and all."

"I should have tumbled to a crew member," Piper admitted. "The priest's outfit needed black or navy-blue pants, and since no pants were found in the Men's Room, he must have still been wearing them. The crew's navy-blue uniforms were a natural answer, if only I'd thought of it sooner."

"You can't think of everything," Fleming said. "Your trick of slapping the girl paid off, anyway."

Piper nodded. "Larner was born four hundred years too late. He should have been a knight in shining armor, when chivalry still meant something, and defending a woman's honor didn't get you arrested."

Sheriff Barker came around the corner then and saw them outside Fleming's office. "I've been looking all over for you guys!"

"What's up?" Piper asked. "We were just getting back another prisoner for you."

385

"Yeah?" Barker seemed less than interested. "Well, all hell's broken out over at the morgue."

"The morgue?"

"Someone got in during the night and mutilated Charlie Hall's body."

A cold chill went down Piper's spine. "Mutilated it? How?"

Sheriff Barker looked at them both, with a deeply troubled expression. "Someone cut off the head and stole it."

Chapter Four: The Bishop

Confirmation of Sheriff Barker's words was not long in coming. At the morgue everything was turmoil. A brief look around was all they needed before going to Piper's office.

"No calls, Susan," he told his secretary, settling down to face the two men across the desk. Inspector Fleming wore a puzzled, worried frown, while Barker's expression was more one of anger and outrage.

"Why would anyone steal a dead man's head?" he demanded.

"I can think of three possible reasons," Piper said, ticking them off on his fingers. "One, to prevent identification; two, to prevent chemical tests of some sort on the brain; three, simply because someone wanted a head."

Sheriff Barker grimaced. "But Charlie Hall had already been identified by his fingerprints – and the fingers weren't mutilated."

"And your third reason suggests nothing short of insanity," Fleming joined in. "Do you think we're dealing with a madman?"

"No." Piper reached for his tobacco pouch. "Which leaves us with reason Number Two. Perhaps the thief didn't know we'd already concluded the autopsy. Perhaps he didn't want us to find out about the sleeping pills."

"You're saying that Hall was set up to be murdered by that room clerk?"

"It's a growing possibility. After all, a number of people must have known that Hall had swindled the clerk."

"But why would Hall go there in the first place, if he feared for his life?"

David Piper breathed a long sigh. "That I don't know. But at least we now have three of the six accounted for, and that should ease the pressure on you, Sheriff."

Barker nodded. "Maybe the newspapers will stop blaming me for the escape."

"I hear the big fish, Bruno, is back," Fleming remarked.

"That's the word around town. What do you think, Mr. Piper? Any lead to Bruno's whereabouts?"

Piper shook his head. He wasn't about to admit that the tip of Jack Larner's whereabouts had come from Bruno's lieutenant. He glanced at the photo and description in the file before him. "Bruno's fifty-five years old. Medium build, dark bushy hair streaked with gray, and the beginnings of a potbelly. The face is quite ordinary, and the description could fit half the middle-aged men in town. I'd guess Bruno could grow a beard and walk down Main Street without anybody recognizing him. And I suppose he could run his underworld empire in hiding for years, meeting only with his most trusted aides. After all, Howard Hughes ran a business empire for twenty years in much the same manner."

"But if Bruno is back at his old activities and three of the others are dead or in jail, where does that leave your theory of a big caper, a joint conspiracy of some sort?"

"Nowhere, and I'm the first to admit it. I still can't understand why the gunmen who actually attacked the van were paid so much, though. There's big money involved here somewhere." He had another thought which he tried to put into words. "Perhaps the plot is *against* the six, rather than *by* them. Reilly was a pawn, easy to catch. Hall was murdered, and Larner was betrayed. Maybe someone just wants all six out of the way."

"Then why not just leave them in prison?" Fleming argued reasonably. "Are you trying to say that someone arranged their escape just so he could put them back in prison?"

Piper had to admit it sounded far-fetched. "What about the person who broke into the morgue? Any clues?"

Sheriff Barker scratched his close-cropped head. "Not a thing. There's no heavy security at the morgue, you know. People aren't usually trying to break in."

"Let's worry about the three still at large," Fleming suggested. "What about them?"

"I'm working on it," Piper said. "I'll find them."

Sheriff Barker smiled, but there was no humor in his expression. "Of course you will. You're the Manhunter, aren't you?"

After they had left, David Piper sat alone at his desk, puzzling over the files before him. He had a bit of a headache, and he knew he needed a rest. A few days off, perhaps a drive to New York to see his wife Jennie.

Susan entered and stood at his side while he thought about it, and when he glanced up she said, "Tommy called. He left this number."

"Thanks, Susan."

"You look tired."

"We had a hard morning out at the airport, and now this business at the morgue." He took the number from her and dialed it himself, knowing that Tommy would be waiting for his call, probably in some shabby lunch counter or third-rate bar across town.

The one-eyed man's voice came over the wire almost at once. "I heard you nabbed Larner at the airport."

"News travels fast."

"Do you want another one? Make it two in one day?"

"Who? The girl?" Despite his dulling headache, Piper felt his stomach muscles contract with excitement. It was the scent of the chase, the thing in his blood that always drove him on.

"Not the girl. Courtney, the Englishman. I've got a friend who knows where he's holed up."

"Where?"

"He wants money, Manhunter. He'll only tell you in person."

Piper sighed. He was used to this. "Where do I meet him?"

"I'll have him at the Winking Moon in an hour."

After Tommy hung up, Piper flipped open the file on Hugh Courtney. British, 34, tall, slim, dark hair. A handsome fellow.

"I'm going out," he told Susan.

The man in the booth with Tommy was lean and sick-looking. His lackluster eyes were surrounded by deep circles, and he pulled back his pallid lips to reveal blunt green teeth such as Piper had never seen before.

"This is Fritz Yomen," Tommy said by way of introduction. "Tell him your story, Fritz."

The sick-looking man with the green teeth peered across the table at Piper. "No story till I see the money."

"How much?"

He ran a black-coated tongue over his trembling lips. "Thirty-five."

"The price of a fix?" Piper wondered aloud, though he didn't believe the man was on heroin. "All right. Where's Courtney?"

"I seen him out at the River View Trailer Park. He's holed up with some dame."

"What's her name?"

He hesitated. "Trotter, I think. Like the horse."

Piper nodded. "If this is a wild goose chase I'll be back for my money. And your scalp."

He left the booth and headed for his car, walking fast. River View Trailer Park was ten miles south of the city, set high on a bluff overlooking the muddy Hudson. It took him a half hour to drive there through the afternoon traffic, and when he arrived he parked some distance away. The car had official state markings, which had caused him trouble more than once. He usually preferred his own vehicle, but there had been no time to get it today.

He moved almost silently in the crisp November air, walking between rows of trailers, avoiding an occasional screaming child and detouring around sagging clotheslines. The place seemed to slumber in its own particular silence. The trailer he sought was a long blue one with ruffled window curtains and the name *Trotter* over the bell. It seemed deserted, but he couldn't be sure.

He slipped the gun from his belt holster and stood to one side as he pressed the doorbell. For a full minute nothing happened. He rang again and waited. This time the door opened just a crack. It was far enough. He forced it open all the way and gazed at the startled face of Hugh Courtney.

The Englishman stepped back, raising his hands at the sight of the gun. "You won't need that," he said. "I'm quite tame, really."

"I don't gamble with killers. Back up."

"You're the one the papers call The Manhunter, aren't you? I'm honored." Close up, he was still handsome, but he seemed older than 34. The hair around the temples was graying and there were creases of age about the eyes.

"That's me," Piper admitted. Inside the trailer now, he risked a glance at the modest furnishings. "Where's the girl?"

"Carol's a nurse. She's at the hospital now, working. She should be home in an hour." His speech was almost fully Americanized, with only the slightest trace of British accent.

"All right. I'm taking you in."

The Englishman merely smiled. "Alone? Aren't you going to call for help?"

"I don't think I'll need it."

"I suppose it wouldn't do me any good to tell you I'm innocent of the murder charge."

"No good at all. A jury convicted you, and then you escaped. That's all I need to know."

Courtney stood there, hands raised, helpless. "Could I at least tell you about it, or are you only interested in my scalp? You American lawmen are an odd breed, really. You track down a person with all the persistence of a bloodhound, but rarely spend half as much effort in establishing the true facts of the case. If a chap has a record, he's as good as guilty in your eyes."

"You're quite a talker," Piper

commented. "I suppose you have to be, in your business."

"Will you let me talk? Will you let me tell you how I got into this fix?"

Piper hesitated. Perhaps what Courtney said was true. Perhaps he'd become only a manhunter, without human feelings or compassion. "I'll make a trade with you," he said. "Tell me everything you know about the escape and I'll listen to your story."

"Fair enough," Courtney said, relaxing at once. "May I sit down?"

Piper motioned to a chair and sat down opposite. "No tricks now."

"My word of honor! You can put away the gun."

"The gun stays out. You're still a convicted murderer."

The Englishman sighed. "What do you want to know?"

"Exactly how it happened. Everything."

"I know very little, actually. I was in the county jail after sentencing, awaiting transfer to the penitentiary. With a murder conviction and a ten-to-twenty-year sentence I was rather expecting a car of my own to take me there. But this day they simply herded me out to the prison van

395

with four other men. The girl sat up front, and I never saw her till later."

"What happened when the truck hit you?"

"Well, it was a closed van, so we couldn't tell too much. All we knew was that something rammed us, and then one of the prisoners – I think it was Charlie Hall – grabbed the guard and started choking him. The others joined in, and the guy was probably dead even before the van was opened."

"Had you any prior knowledge of an escape attempt?"

"No, we just saw our chance and took it. The men who opened the van had gas masks and guns, and that was the first any of us realized it had been planned. I thought perhaps Nick Bruno had arranged it, but he seemed as surprised as the rest of us." He paused and glanced at the low coffee table between them. "May I have a cigarette?"

"No tricks. I'll hand it to you." Piper picked up a teak cigarette box with the single word FRY on its lid. It seemed much too good for its surroundings. He passed the Englishman a cigarette and urged him to continue. "Then what happened?"

"Well, they piled us all into a station wagon and drove a few blocks to where other cars were waiting. That's where we split up – two of us in each car, plus the driver. It was all carefully planned."

Piper frowned at the gun in his hand, as if just remembering it, and rested it on the arm of the chair. "Just how did you split up?"

"I went with Joe Reilly, Larner and the girl were together, and Bruno and Hall. I don't know what happened to the other four. We dropped Reilly at a motel across the line in Connecticut, and then the driver brought me back this way. I phoned Carol and came here."

"No reason was given for the escape? You weren't being recruited for any crime?"

"No, nothing like that." He drew on his cigarette. "That's all I know. Now you promised to listen to my story."

Piper nodded. "I'll listen, but I'm neither judge nor jury. Whatever I think in my own mind, you'll still have to go back to jail."

"Just listen, that's all I ask," Courtney begged. "I've been to the States before, and even served time in your prisons, but this current trip started about a year ago. I made a swing through a number of southern and midwestern states posing as an Anglican bishop collecting funds for the starving natives of East Africa and India."

"Aren't you a bit young for that role?"

The Englishman grinned. In that instant he certainly didn't look like a murderer. "A bit more gray about the temples and some extra lines on the face. They used to tell me back home that I had the look of a bishop. Angelic, you know. In any event, I was quite successful, as I usually am. In fact, I was probably more successful in my fund-raising than a real bishop would have been."

"What about the man you killed?"

"I didn't kill him, old chap," he explained, his accent suddenly thickening. "About six months back, while I was in Columbus, Ohio, some reporter started checking into my background. He became suspicious and cabled England. I had to leave town in a hurry. This other chap, Billings, had been nosing around, too. He was a disbarred lawyer who needed cash, and I suppose I looked like a meal ticket to him. Anyway, he started tracking me down. I was flying to New York, but there was fog that night and my plane was diverted to the Raker County Airport. It seemed as good a place as any to hide out till things cooled down."

"What about this girl you're living with?"

"Carol Trotter is a nurse. She divorced her husband about a year ago, and stayed on living here. I met her at a bar and moved in about a month before Billings was killed. She's a nice girl."

"Nice enough to take in a killer?"

"Look, I didn't murder Billings, I tell you. He was following my trail from Columbus, checking the papers for speaking engagements by visiting bishops. After I'd been here with Carol for about a month, I began to feel restless and decided to raise some funds at the Episcopalian church here. It was a foolish thing to do, because I still had plenty of money left. Anyway, the day before my talk they had a tea for me at the rectory. Billings showed up, and threatened to expose me unless I paid him ten thousand dollars."

Piper whistled. "That's a lot of money."

"He said he figured I'd conned people out of a hundred thousand all together, and he wanted ten percent to keep quiet. He had written out all the charges against me in a letter, and threatened to send it to the police. I told him I'd think about it, and arranged to meet him the following evening at the church where I was speaking. I suppose you know the rest. He was shot and killed in an alleyway behind the church.

"The letter incriminating me was found in his hotel room, and I was arrested for the killing. There was no physical evidence against me, and the gun was never found, but my whole con game came out during the trial. They established motive and opportunity and that was all they needed. I had no alibi for the exact time of the killing, because I'd stepped outside the church to have a cigarette."

"You say you never met Billings that night?"

Courtney glanced away. "No, I didn't."

"If you weren't the one who shot him, who did?"

"Probably a stickup man."

"Was he robbed?"

"Well, his wallet was still there, but the robber might have taken some loose cash."

There was a noise at the door and Piper half turned, raising the gun as he did so. A girl in an open raincoat and nurse's uniform was letting herself in. She stopped, startled, at the sight of him. "Who are you?"

"It's all right, Carol," Courtney reassured her. "I knew they'd find me sooner or later."

She was a pretty girl, though there was a hardness about her eyes that seemed more than she might have expected to acquire in hospital work. When she spoke her voice reflected this hardness, cutting through all pretense of cordiality. "He's innocent! Why in hell aren't you out finding the real killer?"

"The jury said he was the killer, Miss Trotter." Piper stood up. "And he is a self-admitted confidence man."

"I don't care what the jury said! He's not a murderer!"

"Even if the Billings murder is open to question, he could still be tried as an accessory in the killing of those prison-van guards."

The Englishman nodded and stood up, his face suddenly ashen. "You're well named, really – The Manhunter! All the emotions of a robot, or a bloodhound. Track them down and lock them up!"

"Come on," Piper said. "We've done enough talking."

The following morning Piper walked into Inspector Fleming's office unannounced, flopped into a chair, and waited while Fleming completed a phone call. "Tell me about Hugh Courtney," Piper asked finally.

"What's there to tell? He's back behind bars and we only have Bruno and the girl to go."

"I want to know about this killing he was convicted of. Did you investigate it?"

"Billings? Sure, it was my case. He was a disbarred lawyer who'd known Courtney in Ohio. He tried to shake him down for part of the loot and Courtney killed him. Simple as that."

"He told me the story, but he claims he's innocent of the murder."

"Don't they all?"

"I sort of believed him, Inspector."

Fleming snorted and shifted in his chair. "He's a confidence man, Mr. Piper, and one of the best around. If he could convince the congregations in all those cities that he was an Anglican bishop, I guess he could convince you he wasn't a murderer."

Piper had to admit some truth in that, and yet he was aware of a lingering doubt.

402

Was Courtney right about Piper after all? Had he ever in his job paused to give a thought to the human condition? "All right," he told Fleming. "But could I look over the files on the case anyway? Something about the guy bothers me."

Fleming slid out of his chair and opened a file drawer. "Look, he had the only known motive, he was at the scene, and he had no alibi for the exact few minutes of the killing. Billings didn't know anyone else in town, and his wallet was still intact when we found him. That was enough to convince a jury, though I'll admit it might have gone either way. Another jury might have acquitted him for lack of any direct physical evidence."

"Yet you're convinced he was guilty. Why? Simply because there was no one else?"

"Partly that. Partly because you get a feeling about these things. An arresting officer can often tell by the suspect's attitude at the moment of arrest whether or not he's really guilty, but of course that's not the sort of thing you can mention in a courtroom."

David Piper took the file and glanced through the testimony. "Bishop" Courtney had arrived at the church around seven o'clock, a full hour before his scheduled fund-raising speech. He'd chatted with the minister and a few parishioners, and then disappeared for about fifteen or twenty minutes. He claimed he'd merely gone to the men's room, but it was during this period that Billings had been shot dead in the alley next to the church. The weapon had never been found, and no one seemed to have heard the shot. The weapon had been pressed against Billings' coat, muffling the sound.

That was all. Short and simple. Courtney admitted that Billings was trying to shake him down, admitted even that he'd arranged the meeting with Billings. He denied killing the man or even seeing him.

"There's just nobody else," Fleming said, reading over his shoulder. "So it had to be Courtney."

Piper laid the file on the desk. He should have been satisfied, should have let it drop right there. His job was to find the last two – Nick Bruno and Kate Gallery – not to chase the will-o'-the-wisp of Courtney's crime. And yet there was something about the Englishman that invited belief – or at the very least a suspension of disbelief. Con

404

man or not, maybe he deserved a few hours of Piper's time.

"Thanks," he told Fleming. "I'll be getting back to you."

The trailer park was full of morning activity when he arrived, in contrast to the quiet of the previous afternoon. It was a Saturday with the children now very much in evidence, and Piper was gambling that it was also Carol Trotter's day off from the hospital. He was in luck. She answered his ring and was wearing dungarees and a faded sweatshirt.

"Didn't you do enough yesterday?" she asked, trying to close the door on him.

"This time I'm here to help."

"I'll bet!"

"Give me a chance, at least."

She paused, but made no effort to let him in. "Make it fast. I'm cleaning."

"You could be in a lot of trouble, harboring an escaped murderer."

"I've been in trouble all my life, mister."

She sounded as if she meant it. "I'm trying to help Courtney, or at least check out his story. Is there anyone else who knew about him, knew about his meeting with Billings?"

"No, no one."

"You knew, didn't you?"

She looked away. "Yes, I knew. Do you think he had me do his killing for him?"

He ignored that and asked, "What about when he came back here this week? Who knew he was hiding out here?"

"No one. He's never set foot out of the trailer. He figured this was a safe place because I was never mentioned during the trial."

Piper thought about this. Something was wrong, but he couldn't put his finger on it. "Do you know a one-eyed man named Tommy or a drug addict named Fritz?"

"No."

He remember something else. "How about an agent named Marc Litzen?" The theatrical agent had been associated with three of the other escapees, and perhaps he knew Courtney, too.

She shook her head. "I never heard the name."

"Did *you* ever see Billings?"

"Of course not! Hugh just told me about him, and about how he wanted money."

"Did Courtney say he was going to kill him?"

"No. He didn't kill him."

"All right," Piper sighed. "I guess that's all."

As he walked away from the trailer he knew she was still standing in the doorway, watching him.

Sheriff Barker personally led him to the visitors' room of the county jail. "Courtney should be down in a minute," Barker told him. "What's up? You got a line on the other two?"

Piper felt that he should say something to hide the real purpose of his visit. "Courtney talked a lot. One thing he told me was that the six split up after the escape. Bruno and Hall were in a car together. If Hall's murder was set up by someone who fed him sleeping pills, maybe it was done to silence him as to Bruno's whereabouts."

Barker nodded. "Could be."

The door at the far end of the drab room swung open and Courtney entered with a uniformed guard. Wearing a faded, ill-fitting prison uniform, the slim confidence man would hardly have passed for a bishop. He glanced at Piper and the Sheriff uncertainly as he sat down. "I'll want to talk to him alone," Piper said.

"He's already escaped once," Barker grumbled. "If you talk to him alone, you

407

take full responsibility."

"All right."

Barker motioned the guard to wait outside and then followed him out. When they were alone, Piper said, "I'm trying to help you, Courtney, but it's difficult when you don't level with me. You lied about the night of the murder."

The Englishman's expression tightened into a frown. "What do you mean? I didn't kill him!"

"Perhaps not, but I think you met him in that alleyway. Look, Billings wanted money. You agreed to meet him. Either you were going to give him the money or you weren't. But if you weren't paying him off – if you were either planning to kill him or simply tell him to go to the devil – would you have agreed to meet him *at the church,* at the very place where he could denounce you and ruin your scheme? I think not.

"I'll admit to the slight possibility that you refused him the money and then had to kill him without premeditation when he threatened to enter the church and expose you – but the very presence of the gun shows there was a degree of premeditation. Certainly it's not a normal part of even a bogus bishop's gear. Sure, the gun might

408

have been Billings' own, and you could have taken it away from him – but even this theory doesn't justify your setting up the meeting at the church if you had no intention of paying him the ten thousand. With so many safer places to meet, I can't believe you would have risked exposure.

"So it comes down to this: you would only have agreed to meet Billings at the church if you felt it was safe – and it would be perfectly safe only if you did plan to pay him off."

"Pretty smart thinking," Courtney conceded.

"So you did meet Billings in that alley, and you did pay him the money he demanded. That's what you were doing during those missing fifteen or twenty minutes. I said you wouldn't have killed Billings that close to the church and I stick with it. So when you left Billings he was still alive, with your money. Otherwise you never would have gone back in to give your speech and be arrested later by the police. You would have run, as you did in Ohio."

"All right. So it's true. What does that get me?"

"Don't you see, Courtney? The police didn't believe that robbery was the motive,

409

but now we have Billings in that alley with ten thousand dollars – money which was *not* found on his body. So robbery *was* the motive after all." Piper shook his head in exasperation. "Why didn't you tell this at your trial?"

"Would they have believed me any more? It would only have placed me *in* the alleyway, actually *with* Billings, instead of in the church. My way, I figured I had a fifty-fifty chance with the jury. After all, I still couldn't produce anyone who knew I gave him the money."

"How about Carol Trotter?"

"Yes," he admitted. "She knew."

"Could she have killed him?"

Courtney shook his head. "Impossible. She'd wanted to see me as a bishop, and she was in the audience at the church that night. I saw her already in her seat when I came back from the alley, and she stayed there."

Piper's heart sank. It seemed like another dead end. "One more question. Who knew you were back at the trailer, hiding out? Who besides Carol?"

"No one. I stayed inside."

"Know any guys named Tommy or Fritz?"

"No."

It didn't make sense. But then, things rarely did in murder cases.

When Piper got back to the office, Susan glanced up from her typewriter. "Your wife's been calling from New York."

"No time for that now. I'll talk to her later." He sat down at his desk and brooded. Maybe this whole thing was a waste of time. Maybe Courtney had killed the guy after all. He sighed and picked up the phone and called the administrator of the hospital where Carol Trotter worked.

After the usual preliminaries he asked, "I need some information about one of your nurses – Miss Carol Trotter."

The administrator thought for a moment. "I don't know them all personally, of course . . . But Trotter – yes, that's right. She went back to her maiden name after the divorce."

"That's the one. What can you tell me about her? Any recent or sudden show of wealth?"

"No, nothing like that." She paused, a bit uncertainly. "How frank should I be, Mr. Piper?"

411

"As frank as you can. This is a murder investigation."

"Well, we have the lady under investigation at present. A large quantity of coca shrub was stolen from our research lab. That's what cocaine is made from." She paused. "We're pretty certain she took it."

David Piper allowed himself to smile. There was only one more question he needed to ask.

It took him a few hours to get the address, and then another hour to assemble Inspector Fleming and a pair of uniformed officers. At just after eight o'clock that evening they broke down the door of Fritz Yomen's shabby little apartment. The unshaven man was curled on a daybed in one corner of the cluttered room, chewing on something that brought a blackish foam to the corners of his mouth. He reached futilely for a gun, but they pulled it away.

"What do you want?" he mumbled to Piper. "I told you everything."

"Not quite, Fritz. You didn't tell me you were Carol Trotter's ex-husband. And you didn't tell me you murdered a man named Billings."

He seemed to wither then, as Fleming warned him of his rights and snapped on the handcuffs. "Did Carol talk?" Yomen asked.

"She didn't need to. The hospital says she's been stealing raw coca shrub from the lab. Coca is a powerful narcotic, and chewing it turns the teeth green, just like yours. I should have known the first time I went to her trailer. There was a cigarette box with FRY engraved on its lid. It could have been a last name, but it was a lot more likely to be initials – her ex-husband's initials, since Trotter was her maiden name. I didn't know about the R for a middle initial, but I doubt like hell if anyone else connected with the case has F and Y for their first and last initials.

"When the hospital told me she was suspected of stealing drugs it all fitted together. It gave you a reason for still seeing her even after the divorce. I asked the hospital what her married name had been, and when they said Yomen I was sure you were the killer."

"Why's that?" Yomen managed to ask.

"There were two things nobody knew except Courtney and Carol – one, that he was going to pay off Billings in the alley by

413

the church, and two, that he was hiding out at the trailer after his escape. Both Courtney and Carol denied telling anyone, and he certainly had no reason to lie to me. On the other hand, I knew she lied because she denied knowing a drug addict named Fritz and refused to admit you were her ex-husband.

"Since you knew about Courtney hiding out at the trailer, only Carol could have told you. If she told you that and denied it, it was a good possibility that she told you about the payment of the money in the alley, too. In fact, since Carol couldn't have killed Billings, it could only have been someone she told about the money."

"You think any jury will believe all that?" he asked.

Piper shook his head. "Not without some physical evidence, but I'm willing to bet that's the missing gun – the one Billings was shot with. Even with ten grand in his pocket a drug addict isn't likely to throw away a valuable gun."

"We'll check it out," Fleming said. "If you're right I guess Courtney owes you some thanks."

"He can thank me when he gets out of

414

prison," Piper said. "I think that'll still be a good many years."

Piper reached the office before Susan the following morning, and found a stack of telephone messages on his desk. Several of them were from Jennie, his wife, in New York. That wasn't like her. Career-minded fashion designers didn't suddenly start worrying about middle-aged husbands they hardly ever saw.

He direct-dialed the number of her apartment on Central Park West, hoping she'd still be there. "Jennie? I've been very busy. This is the first chance I've had to return your calls."

Her voice was urgent and far away. "David, I must see you! My friend is here!"

"Your friend?" For a moment he didn't understand.

"The one I called about the other day. The girl who escaped from that prison van – Kate Gallery. She's here with me now and she has to see you. She knows something about the escape – and she's afraid, David. She's terribly afraid!"

Chapter Five: The Queen

It had been more than a month since David Piper last saw his wife, but such absences were far from unusual. Jennie lived in a fashionable duplex overlooking the East River, and her annual income from designing was just about three times the salary he received as head of the state's Department of Apprehension. This fact had never really come between them, but it helped explain the reason why they lived and worked apart so much of the time. They were, as a friend had once remarked, simply two very stubborn people. Too stubborn even to get a divorce.

Jennie Piper was tall and slim, with the body of a fashion model and a face that would have easily passed for thirty. She and David had been married, off and on, for twelve years, living their own lives for most of that time. He usually tried to get down to New York at least once a month, but he'd been too busy the past few weeks. Now, standing before her door on business, he felt like a stranger.

"You made good time," she said as she opened the door. "Traffic must have been light." There was no need for the usual hellos between them, and Jennie had never been one to waste words.

"How've you been?"

"Busy! The spring buyers are in town."

"It's not even winter yet."

"You know how it is," she said with a shrug. It was her favorite expression, but in truth he'd never known how it was.

"Where's Kate Gallery?"

"In the bedroom."

"Harboring an escaped murderess is a criminal offense, Jennie."

"I called you, didn't I?" She gave him a mocking smile that showed off her glistening white teeth. "You're the Manhunter – you're in charge of the case."

"All right. Let's go talk to her."

"This way, David."

"I remember where the bedroom is."

She glanced sideways at him from beneath long lashes. "I wasn't sure you did."

Kate Gallery was sitting on the edge of the unmade bed, fully dressed, wearing a

417

Paris original he knew must have come from Jennie's closet. The women were about the same size, though where Jennie's youth was a calculated, manufactured thing, Kate's was fresh and natural. She looked no more than 20, though he knew from her files that she was five years older. In any event, she looked too young to be a murderess.

"I'm David Piper," he said.

She stood, facing him directly, and for a moment he thought she might offer her wrists for his handcuffs. "Your wife has been very kind to me."

"Too kind, I'm afraid. I'll have to take you back, of course."

"I can't believe she killed anyone," Jennie said.

"There's not much doubt. You did kill your hsuband, didn't you, Mrs. Gallery?"

"Yes. I've never denied it."

"The two of you were separated. He came to the house one night and you refused to let him in. As he turned and walked away, you fired both barrels of a shotgun at his back, killing him."

"Those are the facts," she said. "I said at my trial that he'd threatened me. I pleaded self-defense."

"It's hard to believe it was self-defense when he had his back to you and was walking away. The jury didn't buy it, and I'm afraid I don't, either." He motioned her toward a chair and took her former position on the edge of the bed. "But right now I'm not so interested in your crime as I am in what Jennie told me on the phone. She said that you knew something about the prison-van escape – and that you were afraid."

Kate Gallery nodded her blonde head. "It all ties in together. My husband – Bill – was involved with some shady people."

"What sort of people? What did he do for a living?"

"He was vice-president of a firm called Landmark International. They buy up land in foreign countries for American firms planning expansion overseas."

"Sounds like an important position for a young man."

"Bill was ten years older than Kate," Jennie interrupted to explain. "Would you like something to drink, David?"

"Too early in the day for me, but you go ahead." He turned his attention back to Kate Gallery, noticing for the first time the high cheekbones that he had observed in

419

her photograph. They seemed to show only when she didn't smile, and robbed her of the youthful freshness he had so admired. This, he decided was what she had looked like the moment she squeezed the twin triggers of the shotgun.

"It was all tied in with Landmark International," she went on. "After Bill's – death, they came to me and offered to pay my trial expenses if I kept quiet about his work."

"What was so strange about his work?"

"I don't know," she said, looking away. She didn't make a good liar. "But they thought I knew something, so I let them pay the expenses. They wanted to get me off, I think, because they were afraid if I went to prison I might start talking. Well, when the jury found me guilty they had to do something else. So they arranged the escape."

Piper sat forward on the bed. Was it possible? "You mean the whole escape was arranged just to free you?"

"I think so, I really do. These are powerful people, with lots of money behind them. Why else would that sheriff decide at the last minute that I should ride in the prison van rather than in a separate car?"

"You think Sheriff Barker was involved in your escape?"

"He must have been. He's the one who decided who went in the van, and his choice was quite arbitrary. I'd been held in the county jail for two weeks before he decided to send me to the penitentiary."

"That's true," Piper had to admit. "But once they'd helped you escape, did they reveal any of this to you?"

"I didn't wait to find out. They transferred me to a car with one of the male prisoners – a man named Larner. I don't know what they had planned for me, because when the car stopped for a traffic light I opened the door and jumped out."

"You ran away?"

"I sure did! Across an empty lot, thinking at any minute they might start shooting. But of course they didn't. There were too many other cars around."

"You feared they rescued you to kill you? But couldn't they have done that in prison?"

"A male convict can be knifed in the prison yard or mess hall quite easily. It's much more difficult to kill a woman in prison, since usually she's only in the company of other women."

David Piper frowned. "You seem to know a lot about prisons."

"I did some off-Broadway acting during my modeling days. One part was in a prison drama. I never thought then that I'd be living it."

"Jennie said you were terribly afraid. Of what?"

"That they'll find me and kill me! Isn't that reason enough to be afraid?"

"Frankly, Mrs. Gallery, I can't believe that the escape was engineered for the purpose you think. It was much more likely an attempt to free Nick Bruno and return him to his rackets. It was a highly professional job, with a great deal of money behind it. Bruno is the only one who would be worth it, unless some major crime was being planned."

"Then you feel my fears are groundless?"

"Groundless or not, the best place for you is back in the Raker County Jail."

"And if Sheriff Barker is involved?"

"I have every faith in Sheriff Barker."

"Do you?" She stood up, nervously lighting a cigarette. "The Sheriff in Raker County has always been politically active, tied to the party in power. Sheriff Barker is no different. He can be bought, like any politician."

Piper sighed and glanced at his wife. He knew she wanted him to give this woman some sort of help. "Where is the Landmark International office located?"

"Here in Manhattan, on Lexington Avenue."

"I'll talk to them, try to determine if they've any connection with the escape. Meanwhile, you stay here, Mrs. Gallery, Jennie, I'm holding you responsible if she runs away."

Kate Gallery shook her blonde head. "If I wanted to run, I wouldn't have waited here for you. I just want to get out of this alive. I'm trying for a new trial on the murder trial, and I want to live long enough to get it."

Piper rose. "I'll be back but don't expect much. I'm just going down to their office and nose around."

They left Kate Gallery in the bedroom and Jennie walked him to the door. "Thank you for trying to help her, David. I appreciate it."

"You always had a poor choice of friends, Jennie."

"David –"

He saw her anger building and let himself out of the door. "Keep an eye on her."

The day had turned suddenly cold, and he could detect a few snow flurries drifting from the slate-gray sky as he hurried along Lexington Avenue. November snow was commonplace in Raker County, but it was rarer in New York. It brought only grumbles from a few of the pedestrians who bothered to notice it at all.

He reached the offices of Landmark International just after the lunch hour, when the secretaries were still congregated about the reception desk, chatting and giggling. It seemed to be a large operation, with glimpses of corridors that led off to long rows of cubicled offices. He asked the receptionist for someone who knew about Bill Gallery's business activities, and after a ten-minute wait he was ushered into one of the plush executive offices.

The man who rose to greet him was flabby and balding. He looked the way a bank president used to look, and talked like one. "I'm Waldo Forester," he said, extending a chubby hand. "Perhaps I can be of help. As you probably know, Bill

424

Gallery has been dead for almost a year now."

"That's what I came about," Piper showed his credentials.

"You're a detective?"

"Not exactly. I apprehend escaped prisoners and help find missing persons. As you may know, we had an escape up in Raker County recently. Two of the prisoners are still at large, and one is Kate Gallery, the widow of Bill Gallery."

"Widow!" Waldo Forester snorted. "She killed him!"

"That still makes her a widow. I understand from my investigation so far that she killed him in self-defense, because she was afraid of him."

"She shot him in the back, and a jury convicted her."

"What was her husband working on for your firm?"

Forester seemed to grow short of breath. He rose to his feet and began a series of simple calisthenics. It was a full minute before he answered. "He had several accounts. We purchase overseas land for American investors, as you probably know. I couldn't discuss any individual account of his. Frankly, I doubt if I even remember just what he was working on."

"I see."

The flabby man was bending, trying to touch his toes in an impossible maneuver. Finally he straightened up, breathing harder than ever. "Just what did you want to know?" he asked, almost surprised that Piper was still there.

"Why is Kate Gallery afraid of you? Why was she afraid of her husband?"

"I have no idea. Any fear of Landmark International as an organization could only be some sort of neurosis, of course."

"Perhaps. In any event, I wonder if I might speak to some of Gallery's friends here."

"Friends? He had no close friends here."

"But there must have been someone –"

Waldo Forester raised a hand to signal his dismissal. "I've given you quite enough time, Mr. Piper. Landmark International is in no way involved with this affair."

"What about Kate Gallery's escape? Are you involved with that?" The man's attitude was rapidly forcing Piper to believe the wildest parts of the girl's story.

"Certainly not! I think it's time you left." He pushed a desk buzzer and a secretary appeared almost at once.

Following her out, down the long corridor of glassed-in cubicles, Piper asked, "Are any of Bill Gallery's friends still with the company?"

The girl thought about it before replying. Finally she said, "Not really. I knew him, of course, but not well. I suppose Eddie Gibbons was his closest friend."

"Gibbons? Where's he now?"

"Funny thing. He was killed just two weeks before Bill."

"Killed?" Piper came alert.

"Oh, it was nothing like Bill Gallery. No family trouble. He was found dead in a hotel room right here in Manhattan. The police never solved it."

"I see." They had reached the main reception room, but Piper had to try for one more answer. "They worked together, I suppose?"

"Oh, yes," she said. "In fact, they'd just gotten back from Mexico City the day before Eddie was killed."

Piper smiled. "Thank you. You've been a great help." He left the office and went down into Lexington Avenue.

David Piper had a number of old friends in the New York Police Department, and

427

this day he sought out a detective named Blake who was assigned to the precinct where Eddie Gibbons had died. He told Blake what he wanted, and the younger man scratched his head.

"A murder in a hotel room a year ago! My memory's not that good, David."

"Could you check it? The New York Times Index at the library gave me the basic information. The date was Tuesday, November 11th, and the hotel was the Harding, on Seventh Avenue. That's in your area, isn't it?"

A flicker of memory came into the detective's eyes. "I think I do remember it now. Eddie Gibbons, you say?"

"That's right."

"Let me get the file." He was back in five minutes with a fat manila envelope, nodding his head as he glanced through the typewritten reports. "Sure, I've pegged it now. I wasn't in on the beginning, but I did some of the legwork on it."

"Tell me what you've got."

"Eddie Gibbons and another man checked into the hotel together shortly before noon. A chambermaid bringing extra towels found his body about two hours later. The other man, who registered as George Sand, had disappeared."

"Gibbons registered under his own name?"

"Yes. He was a bachelor. He had no reason to hide anything, apparently."

Piper nodded. He was beginning to see a light. "You think it was a homosexual killing?"

"Could be."

"How was he killed?"

"Stabbed with a Mexican dagger. He'd just bought it on a trip a few days earlier."

"You never found any trace of this Sand fellow?"

"None. We were concentrating on people he worked with at Landmark International, but nothing turned up. The room clerk's description was vague."

Piper glanced through the reports. "What about a fellow named Bill Gallery? Did you question him?"

"Gallery? Sure, I talked to him myself. We wanted to know about this trip the two of them took to Mexico City. It was company business, though. No sign of anything irregular. They had separate rooms at the hotel in Mexico."

"Anything in Gibbons' background to indicate he was a homosexual?"

"No, but why else check into a hotel room at high noon with another man, in the city where you live?"

"Just where did he live?"

"With his sister, down in Greenwich Village."

Piper made a note of the address. He didn't know if the sister would still be living there, but it was worth a try. Landmark International had lost two employees in as many weeks, and there just might be a connection with the firm's somewhat secretive activities. If Kate Gallery didn't want to talk about those activities, perhaps the sister of Eddie Gibbons would.

When Piper reached the Greenwich Village apartment, a little before five, there was no answer to his ring. He decided that Stella Gibbons must be at work somewhere, and he found a nearby coffeehouse where he could kill an hour before trying again.

On the second attempt he was more successful. The door was opened by a pale girl with long brown hair that reached past her shoulders. "Yes? What do you want?"

"Are you Stella Gibbons?"

"That's me."

430

He showed his credentials. "I want to ask you about your brother's murder last year."

"Don't you guys ever quit? Eddie's dead and buried."

But she stepped aside to let him enter, and as the overhead light struck her face he saw that she was older than he'd supposed. He guessed her to be close to 30. "Your brother worked for Landmark International, didn't he?"

"That's right."

"Could I ask where you work?"

"I'm the afternoon cashier at a movie theatre. What does that have to do with Eddie?"

"Nothing. What did he do for the Landmark people?"

She shrugged. "Traveled a lot. Scouted for land in foreign countries."

"What sort of land? For what purpose?"

"How should I know?"

"Miss Gibbons, wasn't it a bit odd for your brother to be living here with you?"

"Odd? No. Actually, I was living with him. I'd just come to New York and I hadn't found a place of my own yet. He had this apartment and offered to share it for

431

a few months. After he was killed I just kept it."

"Did he ever mention a coworker named Bill Gallery?"

"Sure, they went to Mexico just before Eddie was killed."

"What about Gallery's wife, Kate?"

"Eddie told me they were separated. Two weeks after Eddie died, Gallery's wife shot him, somewhere upstate."

"Did you ever meet Bill Gallery?"

"At the funeral parlor. He came when Eddie was – laid out." Her composure was beginning to crack at the memory.

"Just one more question, Miss Gibbons, and then I'll go. I'm sorry to ask it, but I have to. Was there ever any reason to believe your brother was a homosexual?"

"The police already asked it. No, there wasn't. He was always popular with girls."

"No hint of anything between him and Gallery?"

"No."

"Thank you, Miss Gibbons. I'm sorry I had to bother you."

He was starting down the stairs when she said, perhaps as an afterthought. "If you're looking for homosexuals, go talk to Eddie's old boss, Waldo Forester. That guy's as queer as they come."

"You know Forester?"

"He came down here a few times, with work for Eddie. I hated the sight of him."

Piper thanked her again and left. There was too much to think about, and the hell of it was that he didn't know if any of it was leading him toward a solution of the prison break. But he did know that a man named Eddie Gibbons had died in a hotel room, just as one of the escaped convicts, Charlie Hall, had died in a hotel room. There might, just might, be a connection.

Jennie opened the door and stepped aside to let him enter. She was wearing bright-red lounging pajamas and a silk scarf gathered about her neck, and he decided that this must be for his benefit. He appreciated it, though he was careful not to acknowledge it. "How's Kate Gallery?" he asked.

"Fine. She didn't run away, if that's what you're thinking."

Kate herself appeared at the kitchen door, a dish towel in her hand. "You missed dinner."

"I grabbed a sandwich."

"You were gone all day," Jennie observed. "Did you find out anything?"

"I talked to a few people, and I found out a few things. Right now I have some questions to ask you, Mrs. Gallery."

"Go ahead." She left the towel on the kitchen counter and came in to join them.

"Tell me about Eddie Gibbons."

Her face went pale for a moment and she had to sit down. "It's been a long time since I've heard that name."

"He was a friend of your husband's, wasn't he?"

"Yes. They worked together at Landmark International."

"You knew him?"

"Bill and I visited his apartment in the Village a few times."

"Why didn't you tell me he was murdered just two weeks before Bill?"

"I didn't think there was any connection."

"Maybe there wasn't," Piper said. "But I've known cases where news of one killing caused a whole chain of reaction. It's catching sometimes, like a virus."

"David!" Jennie was upset, and showed it. "Let's not make things any worse than they are."

434

"You asked me to help. I'm trying to, but it's difficult without all the facts. What was Landmark International involved in, Mrs. Gallery? Why was Gibbons killed, and why did you fear your husband enough to shoot him?"

"All right!" she exclaimed angrily. "I'll tell you everything I know! Then you can take me back up to that jail of yours and be done with it!" She let a moment pass while she steadied herself and then she began to talk. "Bill and I separated in October of last year, about a month before he – died. There was plenty of reasons for it, I suppose. His job kept him away a lot – sometimes I wouldn't see him for weeks on end. Even when he was in New York he often stayed over at Eddie Gibbons' apartment rather than take the long train ride to Raker County every night."

"Wasn't Gibbons' sister living with him?"

"Not steady. She came and went, I understand. Bill never met her till after Gibbons was killed."

"Go on."

"Anyway, we separated. I kept the house upstate and he stayed in New York. He called every few days, and we kept in touch, but that was it. I remember he told me Landmark was sending him to Mexico City on business and that Eddie was going along. This must have been in early November. He was gone about a week, and then he called one night – a Monday, it was – to say they were back.

"Well, now comes the strange part. I had to come into New York the following day to do some banking. I'd kept an account here since my modeling days, and I wanted to make certain Bill couldn't somehow draw the money out. I took care of my business, and I was just coming out of the bank when I ran into Bill himself."

"About what time of day was this?"

"I'd say about two o'clock. He was quite nervous and seemed to be in a hurry. I asked him how Mexico was, but he didn't really tell me. All he did was warn me never to talk about Landmark International, or the kind of work he did. Then he just left me."

"Strange," Piper agreed. "But now perhaps it's time you did tell me about the kind of work he did."

"One other thing first. The next morning I read in the papers about Eddie Gibbons. One article said that a man's tie clasp with an amethyst birthstone was found in the room with the body. I'd given Bill a tie clasp like that for our first anniversary."

"Did you tell this to the police?"

"Of course not. It didn't really prove anything. There are probably a million of them around. I did phone Bill, though, and asked him about Eddie's murder. Just asked him. He said it was a terrible thing, and he didn't know what had happened."

"I see. Now to get back. What about Landmark?"

"Well, it's all tied in together. Because over the next two weeks Bill started phoning me day and night. He seemed afraid that I had some knowledge that might harm him. Perhaps he guessed I'd read about the tie clasp. In any event, he kept warning me that he worked for dangerous men, that if I talked to anybody my life might be in danger. And then that night, the night it happened –"

The door buzzer sounded and Jennie glanced up. "It's probably the newsboy, making his collection. I'll get it."

"– the night it happened," Kate Gallery hurried on, "I was alone at home. The shotgun was his. He'd left a lot of stuff when he moved out. Since I'd been alone,

I kept it loaded, in the front closet, just in case of prowlers. Anyway, he came over that night, and I think he'd been drinking or something. He stood there in the doorway and told me that if I ever said anything about the fields he'd kill me."

"The fields?"

"Yes. The –"

Piper heard Jennie gasp and he whirled around in his chair. Two bulky men had pushed past her into the room. One was a stranger. The other was Waldo Forester.

David Piper rose slowly to his feet. He didn't know if either man was armed, but he wasn't taking any chances. "Well, Mr. Forester, I didn't expect to see you again so soon."

"You're seeing me," the flabby man said.

"How did you find us here?" Piper was keeping his voice deliberately calm.

"I had Steve here follow you when you left the office, after I saw you questioning my secretary."

Steve was a hulking strong-arm man of a type Piper knew only too well. The prisons were full of them. He leaned against the wall with a smirk on his face, and Piper silently cursed himself for allowing such

438

an obvious hood to follow him without spotting him.

"What do you want?" Piper asked.

"Just to talk. To find out what in hell you're after, Piper." The mask of friendliness had dropped completely away, and he was just a cheap tough guy like all the rest Piper had known in his time.

"I'm after some escaped prisoners. One of them, Kate Gallery, is right here, but she's raised some very interesting questions about your company. She seems to think that her life has been in danger because of something she knows."

"Nuts!"

"Did you offer to pay her court costs?"

"Sure. Her husband was our employee. We look after any employee's family."

"Even in a case like this? I doubt it very much."

"We don't have cases like this often."

"What about Eddie Gibbons? He was murdered too."

"Gibbons was murdered by some queen in a hotel room. It has nothing to do with Landmark International."

"A queen? You mean a homosexual?"

"Sure. That's what Gibbons was."

Piper glanced from Forester to the

smirking Steve. Behind him he heard Kate Gallery starting to sob. He turned to her. "Mrs. Gallery, suppose you finish telling me about the fields."

Steve moved from the wall, coming in fast, but Piper was faster. His foot shot out and caught the big man at the ankles. As Steve crashed to the floor, the flabby Waldo Forester moved too, but Piper twisted to one side and brought out his gun.

Behind him, close to him, Kate Gallery was talking at last. "The fields are in Mexico. They're fields for growing marijuana. Landmark International has been buying them up for the big tobacco companies, in case the government should some day legalize it."

Later, when Forester and Steve were gone, Piper allowed himself a moment's relaxation. Jennie came and sat next to him on the sofa. "You were good, David. Very good."

"Thanks. It's my job."

"But you should have had them arrested."

"They had no weapons. They just came here to scare us. Only we scared them instead. When I get back home I'll have a detective friend of mine check up on them. It would appear, though, that they're within the law so far. Buying up land in Mexico is no crime, and apparently they wouldn't use it for marijuana unless the law in this country changed."

"What they feared was bad public relations for their clients," Kate Gallery explained. "They were willing to pay my trial expenses just to keep the facts from getting out. The tobacco companies would have been most embarrassed by the disclosure at this time, when the debate about marijuana is still raging."

"But what about this Eddie Gibbons?" Jennie asked. "Was he killed because of it, or was his murderer a homosexual as Forester said?"

Piper turned to Kate. "I think Mrs. Gallery can answer that question for us, because the murder of Eddie Gibbons was the direct cause of her killing her husband."

Jennie snapped her fingers. "The tie clasp! She killed him because he murdered Eddie Gibbons!"

Piper shook his head and took a step toward Kate Gallery. "No, you've got it backward. She killed him because he knew

441

she murdered Eddie Gibbons."

Driving back, his headlights cutting through the night with its scattering of snow flurries, David Piper told her, "I'm sorry about the handcuffs, Mrs. Gallery, but I can't take any chances on you."

She shifted in her seat and spoke for the first time since they had left Manhattan. "That's all right. One murder or two – what's the difference? I just thought I could beat the rap on Bill's killing, but I knew I didn't have a chance with Eddie's."

"You and Eddie were having an affair?"

"Sure. That's why Bill left me in the first place. Then when they were in Mexico together, I think Bill talked him into dropping me. At least when he came back he told me we were finished, that day in the hotel room. I picked up the Mexican dagger he'd brought to show me and stabbed him with it." She looked sideways at him. "But how did you know, after all this time? Why didn't you believe the homosexual story?"

"Eddie Gibbons registered under his own name, and his companion registered as George Sand. The name Eddie Gibbons is close to Edward Gibbon, the Eighteenth

Century author and historian. It seemed more than a coincidence that his companion was George Sand, a Nineteenth Century woman writer famed for dressing in men's clothes. Rather than a homosexual queen, I started thinking about a female-type 'queen.' One who dressed in men's clothes when she kept her assignations with Eddie Gibbons."

"Maybe that makes it a woman, but it doesn't make it me."

"A tie clasp like your husband's was found in the room. But I never believed your husband was the mysterious Sand. Why go to a hotel with Gibbons after spending a week in Mexico with him? No, Sand was someone else, and most probably a woman. If the tie clasp really was Bill's, it occurred to me that you could have been wearing it, along with other articles of clothing he'd left behind. That would also explain the deception. Gibbons had nothing to hide, especially if he was breaking off with you, but you still did. You couldn't afford to be seen at a hotel with him and thereby give your husband evidence for a divorce."

"You think I could pass as a man?"

"Why not, for the few seconds the desk

443

clerk saw you? After all, you said yourself that you'd been an actress off-Broadway. Maybe you even played a man's role in that prison drama you mentioned."

"You didn't trust me from the beginning, did you?"

"I half trusted you until you lied to me." He turned the car off the expressway at the Raker County exit.

"Lied to you?"

"You said you were in New York doing some banking the day Gibbons was killed. You even said you ran into your husband as you were leaving the bank. But Gibbons was killed last November 11th. That's Veterans Day, and the banks in New York and most other states are closed that day."

She told him then, as they drove downtown, about how Bill had come to her and accused her of killing Gibbons. He asked for his tie clasp, and when she couldn't produce it he said he was going to the police with what he knew. That was when she'd shot him, as he was walking away down the front walk, and made up the story about his threatening her. She thought the jury might buy it, but they hadn't. She even tried to drag Landmark

444

International into it, but in the end even that had been unsuccessful.

Piper listened with only half a mind, because something else was troubling him now. It was a thought she'd planted in his mind, about Sheriff Barker.

Barker.

He saw the lights of the jail ahead, saw the light in Barker's office, and felt that he was nearly to the end of something.

She had said that Sheriff Barker must be involved, and now of course he saw the truth of that. The truth that should have been obvious all along, but a truth he'd discounted because the papers were already on Barker's neck.

But of course it had to be Barker. Whether one or two or all six convicts were the goal, only one man knew when they'd leave the jail. Only one man knew which ones would be in that prison van, which ones would be chosen after weeks of waiting for the drive to the pen. Kate Gallery had been picked only at the last minute, again by Barker. It would have been the same with the others. No time for anyone to get word outside. No time for the smoke bombs and the guns and the getaway cars. No time unless Sheriff Barker was in on the

445

whole damned thing. This time it was no will-o'-the-wisp. This time he was certain.

Piper left the girl with the deputies downstairs and took the elevator to Barker's office. The halls were dark here, because it was almost midnight, but he could see the lighted office at the end, beckoning him.

Barker, you crook.

He felt that the end was very close now. Only Nick Bruno, the King, remained at large, and he had the feeling Sheriff Barker would be able to tell him just where the King's castle was.

Piper pushed open the door and faced the man behind the desk. "Barker, I've come –"

He moved closer and saw that Barker wasn't listening. Something – an icepick – had gone in under his ribs and probably hit his heart. Sheriff Barker was dead . . .

Chapter Six: The King

The morning was gloomy with clouds and depression. A slushy snowfall had brought traffic almost to a halt and Piper watched the cars creeping along from the

446

window of Inspector Fleming's office. It was too early for snow, too early for winter.

"You're certain Barker was involved?" Fleming asked irritably. He'd been asking the same question all night, but he still wasn't satisfied with the answer.

"He's dead, isn't he? To me, that's proof enough. Six people escaped from that prison van. Barker picked them. Barker put them there, and only Barker knew who would be in that van. The newspapers were right in attacking him, but they had the wrong reason. He wasn't incompetent, he was crooked."

Fleming scratched at the bristles of his beard. There had been no time for either of them to shave. "I still can't believe it of Barker. I've known the man for years. What could he hope to gain?"

"Money. It's the oldest motive in the world. Someone paid him and then killed him, possibly because he was getting cold feet."

"Who?"

Piper shrugged. "Nick Bruno is the only one left."

Inspector Fleming nodded. "The only one left, like in that Agatha Christie novel. So where do we find him?"

447

"That's my job," Piper said. "I've gotten the others and I'll get him. First I want you to tell me everything you know about Bruno."

Fleming slipped a folder from his desk and dumped the photos of the six escapees on top, along with their record sheets.

"Is that him?" Piper asked, indicating a half-hidden picture.

Fleming uncovered the top of the head. "No, that's Charlie Hall, our dead man. This is Bruno, with the hair. Nasty-looking character, isn't he?"

Piper studied the face, remembering it now from the newspaper photos. "You said earlier that he'd never been convicted here before."

"That's right. In fact, his arrest record was clean in Raker County until this arson charge – hiring those two guys to burn down one of his own restaurants for the insurance. Of course everyone knew of his Mafia connections. He's their top man in this area, even though his non-Sicilian parentage keeps him from actually heading a Mafia 'family.' He's an odd sort of man – fairly ordinary features, except for that nasty look in his eyes. They say he's worth more than ten million dollars, much more, and he doesn't even have a family to inherit it."

"Never been married?"

"His wife and daughter were killed in an auto accident about twenty years ago. He never remarried, just devoted all his time to building his underworld kingdom. There's a brother somewhere out west, but they never see each other. I understand the brother's quite respectable – an insurance executive."

"I've got his age down as fifty-five," Piper said, checking his own notes. "And you say he came here about twenty years ago?"

Inspector Fleming nodded. "From the midwest, right after the car accident. He'd had a few minor arrests out there, but there's been nothing since he came east. We know, however, that he controls most of the traffic in hard drugs in this state, and a good deal of gambling as well. His only real drug competition comes from the Cuban crowd in New York. Believe me, we were happy to nail him on an arson charge."

"According to my informants, he's running things from a secret headquarters now. Visitors are taken there blindfolded. Any idea where it might be ?"

"It might be anywhere. He bought up a lot of land in the county over the years, for possible future restaurants. Probably the only one who knows is his right-hand man, Sargent, and of course he's not talking."

Piper nodded. "I've met Sammy. He put me on to Larner, the bank robber, apparently to buy time for Bruno. You're right. Sammy's a tough customer, not the talking kind. You think it was Sammy who arranged the prison-van escape?"

"It almost had to be, though I think he was pressured into it by the New York Mafia families. Sammy was doing all right running things in Bruno's absence, and I don't think it was his idea to put the king back on the throne. Still, Sammy's got to be your link if you're going after Bruno. All you have to do now then is find Sammy."

"He's missing too?"

"If you're right about Barker's involvement he might very well go under cover. Sammy was always Bruno's triggerman, according to the rumors."

"Triggerman and icepick man?"

Fleming nodded. "Watch your step. These guys are playing for keeps now."

"So am I," Piper said.

Susan was busy at her typewriter when he walked into the office. She glanced up. "You look like you had a hard night."

"I did. Any calls?"

"Nothing that can't wait. I heard on the radio about Sheriff Barker."

"Yeah."

"You should get some rest."

He glanced at the morning mail. "No time now."

He was heading for the door again when she called out, "Be careful!"

"That's what everybody keeps telling me."

He drove down to the Winking Moon, the bar at which he usually met Tommy, the one-eyed informer who was his best underworld contact. The slush had melted by now, and the sun was making a feeble effort to break through the clouds. Perhaps it would be a good day after all.

He'd been sitting in the back booth for nearly an hour before Tommy finally ambled in, joking with the bartender as he picked up a beer and moved toward the back. "Too bad about the Sheriff," he said, sliding in opposite Piper.

"Damned bad. The lid's blown off this thing now."

"You think it's linked to the escape?"

"I'm sure of it. I think Barker set up the whole thing, tipped off the gang, and made sure the right prisoners were in that van."

"So what do you do now that he's dead?"

"I want Sammy Sargent."

The one-eyed man shook his head. "No can do. He's dropped out of sight."

"I was afraid of that."

"The word is he's holed up with Bruno at their secret headquarters."

"Which is where?"

"If I knew it would be no secret."

"There must be some word out. You know his boys."

Tommy frowned at his beer. "Not any more. Bruno's been getting rid of the old crowd, shipping them off to other cities. He's bringing in a whole new crew, except for Sammy."

"Why would he do that?"

"The restaurant fire was bungled, and he almost went to the pen for it. He probably doesn't want any more slipups like that."

Piper sighed. "I need him, Tommy. I need Bruno, and the only way to get him is through Sargent. I have to find out where they are. You said some people had been taken up there blindfolded. Who are they?"

Tommy thought about it. "Well, one of them was that theatrical agent, Marc Litzen."

David Piper cursed softly. "Litzen again! He keeps turning up in this case like a bad penny! What's his connection with Nick Bruno?"

"The way I hear it, Litzen was picked up outside his office one night last week and taken there for no reason. He got the full treatment – blindfold and all. Bruno talked to him for a while about his theatrical activities and then let him go."

"Strange," Piper agreed. "But it's worth checking on." He slipped a folded bill across the table. "Anything else?"

"I'll keep my ears open."

"Good. Do that. I think we're getting close to the end now. Close to Bruno."

David Piper drove across town and parked his car in the lot next to Marc Litzen's building. He hadn't really liked the agent from the first time he'd met him, and he was ready to believe almost anything about him. Obviously Litzen wasn't about to admit the real reason he'd been summoned to the king's presence.

He entered the glass-sided building and rode up in the elevator to Litzen's floor. The beefy man was alone in his office, studying a contract through his thick eyeglasses. "Hello, Litzen," he said, not bothering to sound friendly.

"Well! It's David Piper again, isn't it? Still looking for your convicts?"

"Just one convict now. Just Nick Bruno."

"Sorry I can't help you." He went back to reading the contract.

"But I think you can. I understand you visited him recently."

Litzen's face went white. "That's not true!"

"I think it is. You were taken there blindfolded and you had a long meeting with Bruno about his narcotics interests."

"Narcotics! I don't know anything about that! He didn't even mention narcotics!"

David Piper smiled. "Then you admit you saw him."

"Damn you, Piper!"

"Just answer my questions and you'll stay out of trouble."

The beefy man removed his glasses and

wiped his forehead. "I don't know a thing. I really don't."

"Where did they take you?"

"I don't know. Two men stopped me outside this building last week and said Bruno wanted to see me. They said to come along and I wouldn't be hurt. Well, I had no choice, so I went with them. In the car they removed my glasses and blindfolded me. We drove for a long time – it seemed like an hour – and then they took me out of the car and led me into a building of some sort."

"Where?"

"I told you I don't know!"

"You must know if it was the city or the country."

"The country. It was very quiet. And there was snow on the ground."

"Snow?"

"Hard-packed. I had to walk on it, and my feet got damp."

"Hard-packed snow at this time of the year? All we've had is wet slush in the city."

"That's why I'm telling you it was in the country."

"All right," Piper sighed. "What about the building?"

"I don't know. They took me up some

stairs and into a room. When they removed the blindfold I was in a large office. The windows were covered with heavy drapes and the lights were dim. They didn't give me back my glasses and I couldn't see very well."

"Who was there?"

"Nick Bruno and another man. Sammy something."

"Sammy Sargent. Go on."

"Bruno was sitting behind his desk, wearing dark glasses. He didn't say much, just asked me about some of my clients."

"Joe Reilly's wife?"

"Yes, and others. I asked questions, but he didn't really want to know anything. I don't know what he wanted. At one point he got up from his desk and came over close to me. I could smell his breath. He said to keep my nose clean if I wanted to stay alive. Then he told the men to take me back to town."

"They blindfolded you again?"

"Yes. And that's all I know."

"Think! There must be something else."

He thought. "Not really," he said at last. "Just one little thing. I said it was in the country, and I'm sure it was. But as I was leaving I could hear voices off in the distance, and what sounded like machinery."

"Machinery? A factory?"

"No, just a noise. Steady, but not too loud. A machine of some sort."

"And nothing else was said on the way back?"

"No. Nothing."

"You have no idea why they brought you to Bruno?"

"None."

"Were you supposed to be somewhere else at the time? Were they keeping you from something, an appointment of some sort?"

"No." He shook his head, honestly puzzled.

"And you told people about this?"

"Just a few close friends."

But the word had got to Tommy, and on to Piper. "All right," he said at last. "I believe you." And, strangely enough, he did.

Piper telephoned the weather bureau from his office and talked to the chief meteorologist. "David Piper," he identified himself. "From the Department of Apprehension."

457

"The Manhunter. I've been reading about you."

"I hope you can help me. I want to know where within an hour's drive from here there was snow on the ground last week. Late last week."

The man on the phone grunted. "That's easy. Nowhere. The temperatures were below freezing, but there was nothing more than a few snow flurries till the last couple of days. Even today it's pretty well melted already. This early in the season –"

"The snow was described as hard-packed."

"No, nothing. The nearest snow like that would be somewhere up in Canada, a good four hours away."

Piper thanked him and hung up. It looked like another dead end. Marc Litzen had lied about the snow, or else he had mistaken something else for snow. But what does one mistake for snow?

"Susan, bring me all the records on this case, will you? I want to go over everything."

She pulled out file folders and the raft of notes he'd dictated to her, and brought them to him. He spent the next two hours poring over everything that had happened, from the beginning. Looking at their faces in the photographs and reading the reports, it all came back to him. Pawn Joe Reilly, married to an actress but leading a double life as an art forger. Rook Charlie Hall, the swindler who'd been murdered in a hotel room and then had his head stolen from the morgue. Knight Jack Larner, the bank robber who was a master of disguise. Bishop Hugh Courtney, the con-man who'd turned out not to be a killer after all. Queen Kate Gallery, the sometime actress and model who'd killed two men.

These, along with King Nick Bruno, had made up the six. Five men and one woman who had played against the odds, and with Sheriff Barker's help had almost got away with it. He studied their faces, and especially the face of the man he still sought, Nick Bruno.

The king.

Like a chess game.

The king.

Could it be . . . ?

Could it be that the game was not chess? That it was checkers?

"Mr. Piper, your wife is here."

He glanced up, distracted, and saw Jennie already entering the office, stepping

459

around the uncertain Susan. Jennie was not one to wait on formalities.

"What brings you up from New York?" he asked, trying to sort out the thoughts racing through his mind.

"Some early-season skiing. I couldn't pass through Raker County without saying hello to my husband."

"Thanks for the sarcasm." She was wearing the powder-blue ski pants and jacket he had given her last Christmas. It was the only one of his gifts she had really seemed to like. Most clothes she designed herself.

"I'm sorry to be bitchy, David, but that was a mean trick yesterday. I called you down to help poor Kate and you ended up involving her in a second murder."

"I'm sorry too. But she killed them both. You don't let people like that just walk around loose."

"I know, but –"

"Skiing, did you say? You're going skiing?"

"Yes. What's wrong with that?"

"What little snow we've got is just about melted."

"Snowflake Mountain makes its own. They've been open since last week."

He sat very still. "Makes its own snow? You mean, a snow-making machine?"

"Of course. What's so strange about that?"

"How long a drive is it up there?"

"Oh, close to an hour, I suppose. It's at the northern end of the county. If you'd ever gone skiing with me you'd know."

"Darling, I'm going with you now! Come on!"

He'd never been up to Snowflake Mountain before, and he was surprised at the spacious grandeur of the place. The ski slope itself, lighted for night use, stretched up toward the sky. It was high enough to frighten even a veteran, Piper thought. But his main interest was not the slope but the large circular lodge at its base. One part housed a ski rental shop, while another held a cafeteria. Upstairs there were a dining room and cocktail lounge. He hadn't bothered to check, but he would have bet the restaurant was owned by one of Nick Bruno's dummy corporations.

"Find what you expected?" Jennie asked him, unlocking her skis from the car's rear deck.

Piper didn't answer at once. A pie-shaped segment of the ski lodge remained in darkness, its windows covered. Offices, he supposed, and yet the space covered both floors – fully a third of the building. Maybe too much for just offices. More the size of a headquarters. It was on the side away from the approach to the slopes, where no skiers were likely to notice a blindfolded man being led in or out.

But the man-made snow extended this far, he noticed, apparently as protection for skiers who overshot the base of the slope. And it was hard-packed snow, as Litzen had said, tramped down by feet and skis. Standing here, off to one side, Piper closed his eyes and listened. Young people talking in the distance, and – what else? Machinery, surely. He opened his eyes and saw that it was the ski lift, making a steady, machinelike hum as its endless cable snaked around the bottom and started back up the slope.

Yes, this was the place. Marc Litzen had not lied.

"Jennie, I don't trust the phone here. Take the car and drive back to that last gas station we passed. Call Inspector Fleming at this number and tell him I think I've found Nick Bruno. Tell him I may need help."

"All right. But where are you going?"

"Inside, to look around."

She paused for just a minute. "Be careful, David. Don't do anything foolish."

He grinned reassuringly. "Only my job."

Then she was gone, and he pushed by some giggling girls in ski pants to enter the lodge. The inside was modernistic in the extreme, with a décor of vibrant colors and wall posters designed to appeal to the younger patrons. Piper took it all in as he moved through the sprinkling of skiers in their heavy boots and made his way upstairs. Here, in the cocktail lounge, the talk was more subdued. The hour was still early, and no one had done much drinking. Most of the customers sat with their half-empty glasses before them, watching the tiny black figures as they streaked and weaved down the slope. Occasionally, when someone took a fall, there would be a little gasp or a checkle.

"Where's the office?" Piper asked the bartender.

"Around back, through that door."

Piper nodded and followed directions. He found himself in a narrow corridor that led toward the darkened third of the lodge that he had observed from outside. His fingers strayed to the gun beneath his coat, and he wondered if he was right.

Not chess. Checkers.

The king . . .

"Freeze, Piper!"

He felt the chill barrel of a gun press against his neck as a hand darted around to pull his own weapon free. It was Sammy Sargent, ready and waiting for him.

"You expected me, Sammy?"

"We got closed-circuit TV at every entrance. Bruno leaves nothing to chance." He pushed the gun barrel a bit harder into Piper's neck. "Straight ahead, and no tricks."

David Piper went through the door at the end of the hall, a thick padded entrance that led into a large, obviously soundproofed, room. The windows were hung with drapes, and no hint of the outside could be seen or heard. It was decorated a bit like a living room, complete with fireplace, and only the large businesslike desk at one end shattered the illusion.

Behind the desk, Nick Bruno turned and smiled, his dark glasses catching the flash of light from above. "Welcome to the spider's web, Mr. Piper."

"So we meet at last."

Bruno ran a hand through his thick graying hair. "It's all my pleasure. I've been reading about the fabulous Manhunter. Tracked down all five of them, didn't you?"

"Six," Piper corrected, "counting yourself."

Sammy had stepped away, but he still kept the gun trained at Piper's middle. "Well, you'll never get a chance to collect on Number Six, Manhunter. You're going out of here in a box."

"How did you find this place?" Bruno asked. "Did one of your pigeons know about it?"

"No, but you had Marc Litzen up here. That was a mistake, even though I realize why you had to do it."

Jennie had been gone ten minutes, and they didn't know about her. If he could only keep them talking long enough, he had a chance.

"Litzen?" Nick Bruno frowned. "Where does he fit in?"

"Cut the clowning, Nick. I know the whole setup. I know the reason for the mass escape. I know all about the big caper."

"What big caper?"

"The biggest one of all, Nick. You really think you can live the rest of your life in hiding like this? You think you can rule a good portion of the Mafia's upstate empire without ever leaving this building?"

"Men like Howard Hughes rule business empires," Sammy Sargent pointed out. "Some South American dictators never leave their palaces. He's doing it too. He's been doing it ever since the escape. He lives downstairs and he runs thing from up here. Our men are all new, trusted, loyal. There's no chance of a slipup."

"There was a slipup with Sheriff Barker," Piper reminded them.

Sammy moved uneasily. "Barker got greedy."

"You killed him?"

"Sure, I killed him. Protecting Nick's interests."

Piper turned back to Nick Bruno. "And now you'll kill me."

Bruno was frowning at him. "What big caper, I asked you! How much do you know?"

"He knows nothing!" Sammy spat.

"I know everything."

"Then talk."

Piper's mind was racing. If Fleming came with his siren on he could be here in another half hour. If he could only keep them talking . . .

"It was the biggest caper of all, bigger than any bank robbery. There were millions of dollars involved, and you pulled it off without anybody even knowing. That was the clever part. A master crime that nobody even knew happened."

Bruno leaned forward, his knuckles white against the desk top. "What crime are you talking about, Piper?"

"The murder of a Mafia leader and his replacement with an impostor. The real Nick Bruno died in that hotel room. You are Charlie Hall."

"Let me kill him now," Sammy Sargent said. "He knows too much!"

"No!" the man behind the desk barked. "Let him tell us just what he knows, and how he knows it!"

"Gladly," Piper said. Talking – he had to keep talking. "There were Six Points – or Six Clues, if you prefer. Point Number One: the escape from the prison van. Sheriff Barker was obviously involved, since only he would have known who would be in that van. Only he could have ordered the girl sent along, forcing one guard to ride inside with the prisoners. But more than that – in describing what happened inside the van, Hugh Courtney told me that Charlie Hall jumped the guard as soon as the van was hit. This was a closed prison van, remember. Charlie Hall could have had no way of knowing, in those first few seconds, that it was anything more than a minor traffic accident. He was not a killer, and he was in for a relatively light sentence.

"And yet in that first instant Hall sprang at the guard and started choking him. Courtney said they had no prior knowledge of the escape, and yet Charlie Hall must have had that prior knowledge. So both he and Sheriff Barker must have known what to expect."

"Very clever. Keep talking."

"Point Number Two: the supposed murder of Charlie Hall. Were we really supposed to believe that Hall would voluntarily seek a hiding place in a hotel where the room clerk was a man he had swindled? Even if the man didn't kill him, he might easily have betrayed Hall to the police. That, plus the evidence of sleeping

468

pills found in the body, convinced me that the killing had been arranged. Hall went there *knowing* the room clerk would probably try to kill him. Why? Did it make any sense at all?

"Yes, it made sense if added to the fact that Hall was part of the original escape plot. The clerk entered a darkened room and fired at a man in a bed who looked like Charlie Hall. There was a back entrance to the hotel, remember, and it was easy to bring the drugged victim up while Hall escaped the same way. And there was no reason for the room clerk to suspect anything. After all, he'd talked to the real Charlie Hall. He knew Hall was in that room, in that bed."

"Hall and Bruno look nothing alike," Sammy Sargent said, but his voice was cracking.

"That's where you're wrong, as you well know. Point Three: the substitution. I suppose it was Sheriff Barker who first noticed the resemblance between his two prisoners and mentioned it to you, Sammy. You had a grip on Bruno's Mafia rackets, and you wanted it to stay that way. You didn't want to give everything up when Bruno got out of prison. So you and Barker worked the thing out together.

"You approached Charlie Hall, and he was all for it. Why not, huh, Charlie? They get you out of prison and set you up as head of the multimillion-dollar business. When you got tired of it you could always skip out and start a new life, loaded, with Charlie Hall dead and buried. So the three of you were in it together – Hall and Sargent and Barker. The other gunmen were hired for the escape and then paid off big and shipped to South America."

"And how did we kill the real Bruno?" the man behind the desk asked.

"When the six convicts split up, two to a car, Bruno and Hall were together. A couple of people told me that. Sammy met the car and slipped some sleeping pills to the real Bruno. You kept him drugged till it was time for Hall to register at the hotel. Of course you couldn't be certain the room clerk would murder the man who had swindled him, but it was a chance worth taking. If it hadn't worked, you'd have killed Bruno yourselves.

"I noticed this morning in Inspector Fleming's office that Bruno and Hall looked something alike. In fact, when he had the top of Hall's head covered in a photo, I mistook it for Bruno. Both in their fifties, both with ordinary-looking faces. The big difference between them was Bruno's hair and Hall's baldness. That and Bruno's nasty eyes. The eyes didn't matter with a dead man, so you simply shaved off all of Nick Bruno's hair after you'd drugged him. The room clerk saw a bald, sleeping man, and killed him. The first police on the scene weren't all that certain of the identification – until the fingerprints checked out. The corpse seemed to have Charlie Hall's fingerprints."

"How'd we get around that, smart guy? Fingerprints don't lie."

"But in this case they did. It was the key to the whole scheme, really, and Sheriff Barker's major contribution to the plan. I was visiting him one day and he told me he sometimes had to refingerprint prisoners when the prints smudged. Now, Bruno had never before been arrested in his county, so there were no prints of his on file. I think Barker simply destroyed the first fingerprint cards and called both Hall and Bruno down from their cells to be printed again.

"Then, as he was fingerprinting them, he simply *switched cards* – putting Bruno's name on Hall's card and Hall's name on Bruno's card. It would have been a cinch to do. Hall was in on the substitution, of course, and Bruno would hardly be expected to notice it. Of course the fingerprint cards sent off to Washington had to be correct, because Washington had earlier prints on file. Only the ones needed here had to be switched – to positively identify the corpse as Charlie Hall."

"You can prove this, Piper?"

"The prints on file in Washington will prove it. Which brings me to Point Number Four: could Hall live the life of Bruno? He certainly could, with Sammy Sargent here to guide him through every move. Bruno's wife and child were dead. He had no other relatives except a brother he never saw. The first thing you did was to get rid of all the old gang members and hire new ones. and that alone made me suspicious.

"The only persons who saw Bruno were brought here blindfolded. None of them knew him well. You had a perfect excuse for this new way of life – you were in hiding from the police. Even your Mafia bosses wouldn't question that. In a year or so, when you were more used to the role,

Charlie, you might even venture down to New York.

"The big test was having Marc Litzen up here. He didn't know Bruno too well, but he sure knew Charlie Hall. You had to see if he'd recognize you. Of course his glasses were off and you wore dark ones to hide the different-colored eyes, but you still had to test your voice. You didn't talk much but if Litzen had tumbled to the truth he never would have left his room alive. He didn't tumble, so you figured you were safe."

"You've built quite a case, Manhunter." The glasses came off now, and also the shaggy gray wig. He was Charlie Hall, bald, middle-aged swindler. The rook, pulling his greatest swindle. "Too bad you'll never leave here to tell anyone."

How long had he been talking? A half hour? Piper went on. "Point Number Five: the nature of the six escapees. Of course Barker had to supply other prisoners for the escape in addition to you and Nick Bruno, just to divert attention from you two. Any law officer, looking at just two photographs, might notice the similar features. Six provided four red herrings.

"I've already explained why the girl was

473

necessary to the mechanics of the escape, but something else occurred to me, as it must have occurred to Sheriff Barker. He needed four red herrings, so whom did he pick? He wanted to mask the substitution, to divert attention from the impersonation, but the four he picked did just the opposite.

"You don't see it? Well, look at it this way. Joe Reilly and Jack Larner and Hugh Courtney and Kate Gallery – all were impersonators themselves! Reilly was married to an actress and led a double life as an art-gallery manager. Larner was a master of disguises that he used in robbing banks. Courtney was a con man who pretended to be a bishop. And Kate Gallery was an off-Broadway actress who, unknown to Barker, had dressed as a man to kill someone.

"Barker hoped these four would muddy the waters if we ever began to suspect an impersonation of some sort. But all they really did was draw attention to the other two – the two non-impersonators, Bruno and Hall."

Charlie Hall nodded and reached into the desk drawer and brought out another gun. "You've talked so much that you must have laryngitis, Piper. Now say your prayers."

Time. He needed time.

"Sammy couldn't just kill Bruno, because then the Mafia bosses would have sent someone else up to take over, or divided the rackets among other bosses. No, the king had to live on. At first I thought of it as a chess game, but it was really checkers. The other five weren't protecting the king, as in chess. Instead it was like checkers, where the man who crosses the board to the opposite side actually becomes a king! That's what you did, Charlie. You were crowned king, just like in checkers. I was chasing will-o'-the-wisps all along, and I forgot that Will-o'-the-Wisp is the name for a traditional opening move in checkers.

"Point Number Six: the stolen head. Why did –"

Then the lights went out.

Piper didn't wait to ask why. Guided by the flickering glow from the fireplace, he threw himself sideways into Sammy Sargent just as Hall fired. He went down on top of Sargent, clawing for the gun, as Hall fired a second time. Then Piper had the gun in his hand, felt the sweaty metal, and rolled free. Charlie Hall fired again and Sargent screamed in agony.

"You shot the wrong one, Charlie. Drop the gun!"

There was a crash against the padded door and it started to give way. Hall ran forward, silhouetted against the firelight, and Piper shot him in the leg.

Then the door burst open and Inspector Fleming was there with a half-dozen state police. "You all right?"

Piper kicked the gun from Hall's fingers and pinned the wounded man to the floor. "I'm all right, but I think Sargent's dead."

The lights came back on again. "I saw the closed-circuit TV," Inspector Fleming explained. "This was the only quick way I knew to get past it. We turned off the power out at the highway." He looked down at the wounded man. "I'll be damned! That can't be Charlie Hall!"

"It can and is. I'll tell you about it on the way back. Where's Jennie?"

"Out in the car."

He went down to her then, feeling good. "You darned fool," she said. "Almost got yourself killed, didn't you?"

"Almost. Move over, I'll drive."

Sometime later, after he'd listened to all

476

the explanations, Fleming asked, "Why did they steal Bruno's head from the morgue, after the body had already been identified as Charlie Hall's?"

"Because they forgot that the body would remain there unclaimed for several days," Piper said. "Most morticians will say it's not true, but there remains a strong belief that in some individuals the hair continues to grow for a few days after death. True or not, Sammy and Hall couldn't take a chance on any hair beginning to sprout on that supposedly bald head. Hair would have told us at once that the corpse wasn't really Charlie Hall, and then we might have figured out the switch in the fingerprint cards. So Sammy went down and stole the head, just to be safe."

After that there was no more to say, and David Piper went home to his apartment. He was tired, but he hoped that Jennie would decide to stay over.

LAWRENCE BLOCK

Gentlemen's Agreement

We welcome Lawrence Block to the ever-growing family of EQMM contributors. Mr. Block has a style and humor all his own, and this story is a "chip off the old Block" – of a burglar and a businessman and what came of their unexpected meeting . . .

The burglar, a slender and clean-cut chap just past 30, was rifling a drawer in the bedside table when Archer Trebizond slipped into the bedroom. Trebizond's approach was as catfooted as if he himself were the burglar, a situation which was manifestly not the case. The burglar never did hear Trebizond, absorbed as he was in his perusal of the drawer's contents, and at length he sensed the other man's presence as a jungle beast senses the presence of a predator.

The analogy, let it be said, is scarcely accidental.

When the burglar turned his eyes on Archer Trebizond his heart fluttered and fluttered again, first at the mere fact of discovery, then at his own discovery of the gleaming revolver in Trebizond's hand. The revolver was pointed in his direction, and this the burglar found upsetting.

"Darn it all," said the burglar, approximately, "I could have sworn there was nobody home. I phoned, I rang the bell – "

"I just got here," Trebizond said.

"Just my luck. The whole week's been like that. I dented a fender on Tuesday afternoon, overturned my fish tank the night before last. An unbelievable mess all over the carpet, and I lost a mated pair of African mouthbreeders so rare they don't have a Latin name yet. I'd hate to tell you what I paid for them."

"Hard luck," Trebizond said.

"And just yesterday I was putting away a plate of fettucine and I bit the inside of my mouth. You ever done that? It's murder, and the worst part is you feel so stupid about it. And then you keep biting it over and over again because it sticks out while it's healing. At least I do." The burglar gulped a breath and ran a moist hand over a moister forehead. "And now this," he said.

"This could turn out to be worse than

479

fenders and fish tanks," Trebizond said.

"Don't I know it. You know what I should have done? I should have spent the entire week in bed. I happen to know a safecracker who consults an astrologer before each and every job he pulls. If Jupiter's in the wrong place or Mars is squared with Uranus or something he won't go in. It sounds ridiculous, doesn't it? And yet it's eight years now since anybody put a handcuff on that man. Now who do you know who's gone eight years without getting arrested?'

"I've never been arrested," Trebizond said.

"Well, you're not a crook."

"I'm a businessman."

The burglar thought of something but let it pass. "I'm going to get the name of his astrologer," he said. "That's just what I'm going to do. Just as soon as I get out of here."

"If you get out of here," Trebizond said. "Alive," Trebizond said.

The burglar's jaw trembled just the slightest bit. Trebizond smiled, and from the burglar's point of view Trebizond's smile seemed to enlarge the black hole in the muzzle of the revolver.

"I wish you'd point that thing somewhere else," he said nervously.

"There's nothing else I want to shoot."

"You don't want to shoot me."

"Oh?"

"You don't even want to call the cops," the burglar went on. "It's really not necessary. I'm sure we can work things out between us, two civilized men coming to a civilized agreement. I've some money on me. I'm an openhanded sort and would be pleased to make a small contribution to your favourite charity, whatever it might be. We don't need policemen to intrude into the private affairs of gentlemen."

The burglar studied Trebizond carefully. This little speech had always gone over rather well in the past, especially with men of substance. It was hard to tell how it was going over now, or if it was going over at all. "In any event," he ended somewhat lamely, "you certainly don't want to shoot me."

"Why not?"

"Oh, blood on the carpet, for a starter. Messy, wouldn't you say? Your wife would be upset. Just ask her and she'll tell you shooting me would be a ghastly idea."

"She's not at home. She'll be out for the next hour or so."

481

"All the same, you might consider her point of view. And shooting me would be illegal, you know. Not to mention immoral."

"Not illegal," Trebizond remarked.

"I beg your pardon?"

"You're a burglar," Trebizond reminded him. "An unlawful intruder on my property. You have broken and entered. You have invaded the sanctity of my home. I can shoot you where you stand and not get so much as a parking ticket for my trouble."

"Of course you can shoot me in self-defense – "

"Are we on *Candid Camera*?"

"No, but – "

"Is Allen Funt lurking in the shadows?"

"No, but I – "

"In your back pocket. That metal thing. What is it?"

"Just a pry bar."

"Take it out," Trebizond said. "Hand it over. Indeed. A weapon if I ever saw one. I'd state that you attacked me with it and I fired in self-defense. It would be my word against yours, and yours would remain unvoiced since you would be dead. Whom do you suppose the police would believe?"

The burglar said nothing. Trebizond

482

smiled a satisfied smile and put the pry bar in his own pocket. It was a piece of nicely shaped steel and it had a nice heft to it. Trebizond rather liked it.

"Why would you want to kill me?"

"Perhaps I've never killed anyone. Perhaps I'd like to satisfy my curiosity. Or perhaps I got to enjoy killing in the war and have been yearning for another crack at it. There are endless possibilities."

"But – "

"The point is," said Trebizond, "you might be useful to me in that manner. As it is, you're not useful to me at all. And stop hinting about my favorite charity or other euphemisms. I don't want your money. Look about you. I've ample money of my own – that should be obvious. If I were a poor man you wouldn't have breached my threshold. How much money are you talking about, anyway? A couple of hundred dollars?"

"Five hundred," the burglar said.

"A pittance."

"I suppose. There's more at home but you'd just call that a pittance too, wouldn't you?"

"Undoubtedly." Trebizond shifted the gun to his other hand. "I told you I was a

483

businessman," he said. "Now if there were any way in which you could be more useful to me alive than dead – "

"You're a businessman and I'm a burglar," the burglar said, brightening.

"Indeed."

"So I could steal something for you. A painting? A competitor's trade secrets? I'm really very good at what I do, as a matter of fact, although you wouldn't guess it by my performance tonight. I'm not saying I could whisk the Mona Lisa out of the Louvre, but I'm pretty good at your basic hole-and-corner job of everyday burglary. Just give me an assignment and let me show my stuff."

"Hmmmm," said Archer Trebizond.

"Name it and I'll swipe it."

"Hmmmm."

"A car, a mink coat, a diamond bracelet, a Persian carpet, a first edition, bearer bonds, incriminating evidence, eighteen and a half minutes of tape – "

"What was that last?"

"Just my little joke," said the burglar. "A coin collection, a stamp collection, psychiatric records, phonograph records, police records – "

"I get the point."

"I tend to prattle when I'm nervous."

"I've noticed."

"If you could point that thing else-where – "

Trebizond looked down at the gun in his hand. The gun continued to point at the burglar.

"No," Trebizond said, with evident sadness. "No, I'm afraid it won't work."

"Why not?"

"In the first place, there's nothing I really need or want. Could you steal me a woman's heart? Hardly. And more to the point, how could I trust you?"

"You could trust me," the burglar said. "You have my word on that."

"My point exactly. I'd have to take your word that your word is good, and where does that lead us? Up the proverbial garden path, I'm afraid. No, once I let you out from under my roof I've lost my advantage. Even if I have a gun trained on you, once you're in the open I can't shoot you with impunity. So I'm afraid – "

"No!"

Trebizond shrugged. "Well, really," he said. "What use are you? What are you good for besides being killed? Can you do anything besides steal, sir?"

"I can make license plates."

"Hardly a valuable talent."

"I know," said the burglar sadly. "I've often wondered why the state bothered to teach me such a pointless trade. There's not even much call for counterfeit license plates, and they've got a monopoly on making the legitimate ones. What else can I do? I must be able to do something. I could shine your shoes, I could polish your car – "

"What do you do when you're not stealing?"

"Hang around," said the burglar. "Go out with ladies. Feed my fish, when they're not all over my rug. Drive my car when I'm not mangling its fenders. Play a few games of chess, drink a can or two of beer, make myself a sandwich – "

"Are you any good?"

"At making sandwiches?"

"At chess."

"I'm not bad."

"I'm serious about this."

"I believe you are," the burglar said. "I'm not your average woodpusher, if that's what you want to know. I know the openings and I have a good sense of space. I don't have the patience for tournament play, but at the chess club downtown I win more games than

486

I lose."

"You play at the club downtown?"

"Of course. I can't burgle seven nights a week, you know. Who could stand the pressure?"

"Then you *can* be of use to me," Trebizond said.

"You want to learn the game?"

"I know the game. I want you to play chess with me for an hour until my wife gets home. I'm bored, there's nothing in the house to read, I've never cared much for television, and it's hard for me to find an interesting opponent at the chess table."

"So you'll spare my life in order to play chess with me."

"That's right."

"Let me get this straight," the burglar said. "There's no catch to this, is there? I don't get shot if I lose the game or anything tricky like that, I hope."

"Certainly not. Chess is a game that ought to be above gimmickry."

"I couldn't agree more," said the burglar. He sighed a long sigh. "If I didn't play chess," he said, "you wouldn't have shot me, would you?"

"It's a question that occupies the mind, isn't it?"

487

"It is," said the burglar.

They played in the front room. The burglar drew the white pieces in the first game, opened king's pawn, and played what turned out to be a reasonably imaginative version of the Ruy Lopez. At the sixteenth move Trebizond forced the exchange of knight for rook, and not too long afterward the burglar resigned.

In the second game the burglar played the black pieces and offered the Sicilian Defense. He played a variation that Trebizond wasn't familiar with. The game stayed remarkably even until in the end game the burglar succeeded in developing a passed pawn. When it was clear that he would be able to queen it, Trebizond tipped over his king, resigning.

"Nice game," the burglar offered.

"You play well."

"Thank you."

"Seem's a pity that – "

His voice trailed off. The burglar shot him an inquiring look. "That I'm wasting myself as a common criminal? Is that what you were going to say?"

"Let it go," Trebizond said. "It doesn't matter."

They began setting up the pieces for the third game whan a key slipped into a lock. The lock turned, the door opened, and Melissa Trebizond stepped into the foyer and through it to the living room.

Both men got to their feet. Mrs. Trebizond advanced, a vacant smile on her pretty face. "You found a new friend to play chess with. I'm happy for you."

Trebizond set his jaw. From his back pocket he drew the burglar's pry bar. It had an even nicer heft than he had thought. "Melissa," he said. "I've no need to waste time with a recital of your sins. No doubt you know precisely why you deserve this."

She stared at him, obviously not having understood a word he had said to her, whereupon Archer Trebizond brought the pry bar down on the top of her skull. The first blow sent her to her knees. Quickly he struck her three more times, wielding the metal bar with all his strength, then turned to look into the wide eyes of the burglar.

"You've killed her," the burglar said.

"Nonsense," said Trebizond, taking the bright revolver from his pocket once again.

"Isn't she dead?"

"I hope and pray she is," Trebizond said, "but I haven't killed her. *You've* killed her."

"I don't understand."

"The police will understand," Trebizond said, and shot the burglar in the shoulder. Then he fired again, more satisfactorily this time, and the burglar sank to the floor with a hole in his heart.

Trebizond scooped the chess pieces into their box, swept up the board, and set about the business of arranging things. He suppressed an urge to whistle. He was, he decided, quite pleased with himself. Nothing was ever entirely useless, not to a man of resources. If fate sent you a lemon you made lemonade.

The publishers hope that this book has given you enjoyable reading. Large Print Books are specially designed to be as easy to see and hold as possible. If you wish a complete list of our books, please ask at your local library or write directly to: John Curley & Associates, Inc. P.O. Box 37, South Yarmouth Massachusetts, 02664